Blackgentlemen.com

Zane
J.D. Mason
Shonda Cheekes
Eileen M. Johnson

A
S**B**I
PUBLICATION
A STREBOR BOOKS INTERNATIONAL LLC PUBLICATION
DISTRIBUTED BY SIMON & SCHUSTER, INC.

Published by

Strebor Books International LLC
P.O. Box 10127
Silver Spring, MD 20914
http://www.streborbooks.com

ISBN 0-9711953-8-2
LCCN 2002106953

Distributed by Simon & Schuster, Inc.
1230 Avenue of the Americas
New York, NY 10020
1-800-223-2336

Cover Illustration: André Harris
Typesetting and Interior Design: Big Dog Studios

Manufactured and Printed in the United States
10 9 8 7 6 5 4 3

Table of Contents

Acknowledgements

Zane

I would like to thank J.D. Mason, Shonda Cheekes, and Eileen M. Johnson for embarking on this journey with me. It has been an honor working with you ladies and I look forward to other endeavors in the near future. As always, I would like to thank my parents (J & L), my kids (A & E), my sisters (C & C), my agent (Sara Camilli), my lawyer (Pamela Crockett, Esq.), and the rest of my extended family.

J.D. Mason

To Zane, Shonda Cheekes and Eileen M. Johnson, my sistah authors for Blackgentlemen.com. Thank you all for allowing me the privilege to contribute to this project. Your talents are all extraordinary and it's a privilege to have been included. I'm anxiously anticipating even more fantastic works from you all.
--Peace

Shonda Cheekes

I would like to thank God for blessing me with a great family and great friends. For bestowing me with the gift of gab and the ability to use it creatively.

To the people who have personally had a hand in this project from its inception; my mother, Dorothy, who has always believed in me;

Calina & Ramzey, my greatest creations. Mommy loves you with every fiber in my body. My Sisterfriend, Michelle V. - thank you for being my breath, eyes and memory. For lending your extensive vocabulary skills when mine went on hiatus. For being my sixth sense. You are a blessing in my life. I don't know how I lived those other twenty + years without you. Zane - thank your for giving me the opportunity to be a part of something huge. For constantly reminding me that I could do this. For being a great role model and an even better friend. Here's to future endeavors!! To Lynette, Lance, Brian and Mario - I know we don't get to pick our families, but if given the opportunity, I would choose each of you. To every single writer and book club who proved that there is a HUGE market for books for us, by us. I can't forget the ladies at the Broward County Main Library in Ft. Lauderdale, Sharon Morris and the crew, who in a minutes notice accommodated anything I put together. Now it's my turn to be the featured author. And last but definitely not least, Warren - this is what all the clicking at night was about. Thank you for challenging me along the way, helping me to see that I can accomplish anything, no matter what obstacles people try to put in my way.

If I were to mention each and every person who in some way or another has touched my life or played a role in me getting to this point, my acknowledgements would be longer than my story…lol So, to each and every one of you, (you know who you are) thank you for all your support.

Much love,

Shonda Cheekes

Dedicated to my mother, my biggest supporter, Lolita for opening doors that I may have never found, and to anyone who's ever been fortunate enough to find a lost love and make it work.

Eileen M. Johnson

To my family, who never grew weary after years of me creeping around with a notebook and pen, to Nadya the brutal muse, my friends (you know who you are), and Saadiq Fadil, the center of my universe.

Duplicity

By Zane

Chapter One

"Nia, I thought I asked you to get my clothes from the cleaners?"

Nia glanced up from her computer monitor and leered at her twin sister, Neena, who'd just walked into the front door of their single-story brick house at the end of a country dirt road.

"Well, hello to you, too," Nia said sarcastically, after sizing her sister up.

"Sorry, I didn't mean to come off foul," Neena stated apologetically. "I've just had a messed-up day and I only have about two hours to get to the airport."

Nia got up from her computer workstation, strategically positioned by a picture window so she could look out at the trees while she did her medical-billing, telecommuting job. She walked over to the front door that Neena had left ajar and closed it before one of the gigantic bumblebees that descended on their home every summer snuck its way in.

"What time does your plane leave?"

"Seven," Neena replied, kicking off her burgundy, three-inch heels and collapsing gracefully into a comfy upholstered armchair. "I still can't believe they're making me go on a business trip at Christmas time."

"That's messed up."

"I know. When I get back, I'm going to start some serious job-hunting. I can't take this anymore."

Nia attempted to mentally tally the amount of times she'd heard Neena announce she was starting a hunt for a new job. Nia knew there was a greater chance of Dennis Rodman giving up his women's clothing fetish than of Neena quitting her job as a district sales manager for a pharmaceutical company. A six-figure income, company car, extremely thick monthly expense account, corporate credit cards, and the ability to travel across country, sometimes internationally, was right up Neena's alley. Having grown up on the outskirts of Charlotte, N.C., Nia was content to hang out in small clubs/juke joints while Neena always craved the city life. They were both still in small town Kannapolis, sharing a rental home less than three miles from the house where they grew up, a house still occupied by their widowed mother.

"Where are you going to find another job with that type of salary and those kind of benefits?" Nia asked Neena, knowing Neena was way too materialistic to settle for anything less. "This is North Carolina. Not New York City."

"What good are the fringe benefits if I can't even spend the holidays with my family?" Neena retorted, rubbing her left foot and cracking her toes.

Nia's face scrunched up when she heard Neena's toes cracking. That noise was right up there with long fingernails scratching a blackboard on her disgusting sounds meter.

"Momma's going to be so disappointed, Neena. Have you told her yet?"

"No, I thought maybe you'd do it for me."

"Oh, no, that's definitely on you. Momma's not going off on me behind this while you're somewhere flying over the friendly skies."

"Okay; all right," Neena conceded. "I'll call her from my cell phone when we're less than five minutes from the airport. That way she can't fuss at me but so long."

Nia flicked on the television to the evening news and sat down on the sofa, propping her legs up on a leopard-print toss pillow. "Good idea."

"You and Bryant still spending Christmas Eve together, kissing under the mistletoe?"

Nia smacked her lips and held the palm of her hand up in Neena's direction. "Please, don't even mention his name!"

"That bad, huh?"

"Bad enough. Bryant is really acting strange lately. I feel like I need to move on."

"Maybe not move on, but you need to explore other options. You're too young to settle down with one man."

"Since we're three minutes apart, I guess we'd fall into the same category," Nia chided.

"Silly heifer."

Nia picked up the matching toss pillow from the floor and threw it at Neena. "Trifling hoe."

"I love you, too, Sissypoo!"

Nia rolled her eyes at her sister and used the remote to switch to FOX so she could catch the end of Judge Judy. "Your clothes from the cleaners are on your bed."

"I knew you wouldn't let me down." Neena jumped up and headed toward the back of the house. "Thanks."

"Don't mention it. You need help packing?" Nia yelled out after her, attempting to be nice since she knew Neena was a slow poke when it came to packing and often had to find a mall as soon as she reached her location because she'd forgotten this thing or that thing.

"No, but can you get my toothbrush and toiletry bag out the bathroom for me?"

"Okay."

Nia walked past Neena's bedroom door and paused long enough to see her toss a silver-plated vibrator into her flight bag. She held back a giggle, but couldn't help but imagine the embarrassment Neena would feel if the damn thing set off a metal detector causing her bags to be searched.

Neena glanced up and spotted Nia in her doorway. She didn't care if Nia had seen the vibrator or not. She knew for a fact that Bryant wasn't dishing out any multiples. Shit, Nia's bed would squeak for a measly five minutes, sometimes less, whenever Bryant stayed over.

"Don't forget to throw in those trial bottles of shampoo. I hate that crap they leave on the sink counter in hotels."

Nia giggled. "That's because it's not made for sistas. At least not for sistas with thick ass hair like us."

"I know that's right!"

Chapter Two

Neena clicked off her cell phone and took a deep breath. "Momma was pissed, huh?" Nia asked, fully aware that she was. "I could hear her clear as a bell."

Neena shifted in the passenger's seat of Nia's Mazda. Their mother definitely had a way of working her nerves at will. "She says I need to quit immediately. She doesn't realize I have bills to pay and responsibilities. I can't just up and quit; not until I find a new job."

Nia laughed and turned the radio back up. Kevon Edmonds was belting out No Love. "With your tastes, absolutely not."

Neena rolled her eyes at her twin, looking at the clock on the dash. If she didn't get to the airport within the next five minutes, she was in serious jeopardy of missing her flight. It was one of the busiest travel days of the year, which meant long ass lines everywhere you looked.

"Very funny, Ms. Potted Meat."

"Hey, you can't knock the hustle. That Hormel Chicken Spread is kicking."

"Oh, damn!" Neena exclaimed, slapping herself on the forehead.

"What? Did you forget something?"

"Not something. Someone."

"Come again."

"I was supposed to be hooking up with Jacob tomorrow."

7

"Who's Jacob?" Nia asked, having never heard the name before.

"Promise you can keep a secret?"

"We're twins, Neena. I've known all of your business since we were born and I've never spilled the beans. Why would I start now?"

"Well, you don't know about these beans." Neena giggled.

"So tell me," Nia prodded, wanting her sister to give up the info quickly because they were getting off on the exit for the airport.

"Look at you, foaming at the mouth and stuff."

"You know I'm nosy."

Neena smacked her lips. "Promise you won't tell?"

"That's the second time you've asked me that, Neena! Now tell me!"

Neena debated about coming clean. She was afraid that Nia would hit the roof once she found out what she'd been up to. While Nia wasn't prone to telling her business, she would if she felt Neena was doing something unhealthy or potentially dangerous.

"What about the Della incident?" Neena asked sarcastically, bringing up the time that Neena had experimented with speed with an older neighbor.

"Neena, now you know your ass had no business doing drugs! I tried to talk some sense into you, but when you wouldn't listen to me, I had to tell Momma."

"You better not tell Momma this!"

"We're older now. Besides, I know you're not foolish enough to mess with drugs."

"True." Neena unzipped her purse and pulled out her plane ticket. "Okay, here goes."

Nia turned the radio not only down, but completely off. She didn't want to miss a word relating to this Jacob person.

"I met Jacob on the Internet."

"The Internet!" Nia said excitedly. "Have you completely lost it?"

"Calm down. It's not what you think."

"You don't know what I'm thinking right now, Neena."

"Of course I know what you're thinking. I'm your twin."

Nia just had to hear this. "So what am I thinking?"

"You're thinking that Jacob is some playa that uses the Internet as his pussy hunting ground, that he's met a ton of women already, used them for sex, and now he's setting me up to hit it and split. Am I right?"

Nia laughed. "Close. You left out the part about him being a midget."

Neena joined her sister in laughter, recalling the mess Nia had found herself in after frequenting a particular chat room for African-Americans on the Sistergirls.com web site. Nia had practically fallen in love with a brotha from the Bronx, solely on the basis of his New Yorker accent. They'd spent hours and hours cybering each other in chat rooms, burning up the telephone lines having phone sex, and making plans for a long and prosperous future. It wasn't until Doug, the loverboy in question, mailed Nia two pictures of himself that she realized he was six inches shorter than she was. Since Nia and Neena were both hovering somewhere around five feet two inches, that made Doug a shoe-in for the role of Mini-me if they ever made a ghettoized version of an Austin Powers flick.

"Nia, Jacob's definitely not a midget."

"And you know this how?" Nia asked snidely. "You've seen his picture?"

"Lawd, have I!" Neena licked her lips. "That's what first attracted me to him."

"He emailed it to you? What chat room did you meet him in? What does the brotha look like? He is a brotha, isn't he? Is he local? Have you already met? Did you fuck him?"

"Nia, shut up! Damn!" Neena stated angrily, trying to get her sister to stop rolling questions off her tongue long enough for her to answer one of them. "Let me respond, will you?"

Nia clamped her lips shut reluctantly.

"I found his picture on a web site and we've never been in a chat room together. Jacob's tall, dark, and fine as shit. You know how I flow. If a man ain't fine, he's not worth my time. Since he's dark, he's obviously a brotha and..."

"Not necessarily," Nia interrupted. "He could be Indian, Pakistani, Egyptian, Por..."

Neena slapped Nia on the arm. "Quit!"

Nia giggled and shut up.

"Jacob lives in Durham and neither one of us has yet to make the two-hour trek to pay a visit because we decided to take it slow so, no, I haven't fucked him."

"Hmm, how long have you been talking to him?"

"A few months. And, to be honest, I was planning on rocking his world on Christmas Eve, but my screwy job has once again interfered."

"Ooooh, maybe somebody's trying to tell you something. Maybe it wasn't meant to be."

"It is meant to be," Neena said, licking her lips. "When I get back, it's on."

"You're not going to invite him to our house, are you?" Nia asked. "Then again, that might be better. That way, I can be there to protect you."

"Nia, Jacob's cool. He owns a real estate company and his house is paid for."

"What about his personality? Demons can own homes," Nia said sarcastically. All Neena was ever worried about were the materialistic offerings of a man.

"Look, just do me a favor." Neena took a grocery receipt out of her coat pocket along with a pen and started scribbling on it. "Here is my password for my Internet account and Jacob's email address. I would call him, but I don't think I'll have time."

"So what do you want me to do?" Nia really wasn't trying to get mixed up in Neena's nonsense.

"Email him and tell him I had to leave town for a few days and that I'll call him when I get back."

"Why can't I just call him?" Nia asked, wondering why people felt it was easier to use email as a means of communication than the telephone.

"Because you might say something nasty to him." Neena shoved the paper at Nia. "Just do it, please."

"Okay, dang!"

Nia pulled up at the terminal in the passenger drop-off section and put the car in park. She popped her trunk, got out, and met Neena at the rear so she could help her with her bag, which probably weighed more than the two of them put together.

"Have a safe trip, Sis." Nia hugged Neena and kissed her on the cheek after a red cap relieved them from the bag. "I'll eat double for you at Momma's house so she won't feel like she overcooked."

Neena giggled. "How kind of you. Love you, Sissypoo!"

"Love you, too!"

Nia watched Neena walk away and almost broke out in tears. The reason neither one of them moved away was partially because of their mother, but mostly because they couldn't stand to be apart for long lengths of time. Sure, they argued and went through much drama at times, but their bond was undeniably strong.

Neena was almost in the terminal when the curiosity bug bit Nia. "Neena, what web site did you meet him on anyway?"

Neena turned and grinned at her before yelling, "BlackGentlemen.com!"

Chapter Three

"BlackGentlemen.com," Nia whispered to herself no less than fifty times on the drive home. She wasn't one for meeting men over the Internet, not since her Lilliputian episode, but this might be something worth checking out.

Bryant was her on again, off again lover, but nothing to lose her mind over if he should ever walk out of her life for good. In the small town where they lived, pickings were slim and Bryant was about the best thing going. He worked as a counselor at a detention home for boys. At least, that meant he was compassionate. He was kind of short and on the pudgy side but at least he had to look down at her, as opposed to the other way around. The best thing about Bryant was his foot massages. He doled out some hellified foot action. In bed, his action was brief and often seemed staged, like he'd thought about the entire thing, move by move, on his way over.

They'd met in the automotive section of the local Wal-Mart, which had managed to put the majority of the Mom and Pop stores out of business upon its inception. Nia was looking for the windshield wiper fluid while Bryant was getting some new sub woofers for his pick-up truck. It was far from love at first sight, but Nia could appreciate a brother with a friendly smile and Bryant definitely possessed one.

Two years later, they were still an item, meaning they went out to eat pizza, Chinese, or took advantage of the all-you-can-eat buffet at the Golden Corral once a week. They also took in whatever movie was being featured at the Gem, an old-fashioned theater where you could still get a "real" cherry cola, buy freshly-popped popcorn instead of stuff that was delivered in thirty-two gallon clear bags from some outside source, and sit in a balcony. That was about the extent of their activities outside of the home. Bryant was boring at best. At his worse, he could be downright depressing.

Nia returned home to find three messages from her mother on her answering machine. Her mother was complaining about Neena's departure, as if Nia could will her to come back. Nia and Neena had separate phone lines and answering machines. Nia figured their mother had left a slew of nastier messages on Neena's machine she'd have to endure after her business trip.

Her stomach was rather queasy so she got some saltine crackers and ginger ale from the kitchen and sat down at her computer workstation. Her computer was barely booted up good before she was signing onto Neena's America Online account. She couldn't believe that Neena was using the screenname CumInNeena and the password dicklover.

Instead of sending an email to Jacob right away, she decided to be nosy and read Neena's email first. There was a ton of junk emails and some from mutual friends of theirs that Nia recognized from their screennames. She also corresponded with them and assumed those same emails were probably blind carbon-copied to her mail box under PatientOne, her screenname.

Then she spotted something interesting. It was an email from the screenname Neena had given her for Jacob, DMan4U2NV, and the subject line was "I Can't Wait To Work That Body Over." Nia wasted no time opening the email so she could read it.

Neena,

I can't wait to see you Christmas Eve. I have some wonderful surprises for you. I am going to cater to your every sexual desire, show you the kind of love and affection you deserve, take you to heights of satisfaction only a real man can achieve, and make you yearn for my loving from now until the end of time.

Blackgentlemen.com

Below is a poem I wrote for you, Neena. While it cannot begin to justify the deep feelings I have within my heart for you, I think it is a beginning. The rest I will just have to show to you.

I Can't Wait To Work That Body Over

I can't wait to work that body over
Take my tongue and lick you from head to toe
Take you to places you never thought you could go
Just relax, baby girl, and go with the flow

I can't wait to work that body over
Insert myself gently and explore you inside
Let you climb on top of me and take a little ride
Make love to you slowly, rock you from side-to-side

I can't wait to work that body over
Feast on you while we share a bottle of wine
Spread your legs, go down there, and spend a little time
Damn, damn, Neena, you are so damn fine

And I can't wait to work that body over.

I hope you enjoyed my little poem, baby. While not a poet, I wanted to at least try to express my feelings. And what I said is nothing but the truth. I can't wait to work that fine body of yours over.

I was sitting here this morning, looking at your picture, and licking my lips. There are so many things I want to do to you and I am making the preparations. All you have to do is bring your little fine self on.

Are we still meeting at Club Oviedo tomorrow night at nine? I hope you won't get scared and back out of our plans. I know it is strange to make plans to become intimate with a stranger, but I feel like we have moved beyond that. I haven't been this excited about anything since my brother and I placed the sign for our real estate agency on a stake and pushed it into the ground.

"Mmmm, he has a brother," Nia said out loud to herself, sitting there about to cream in her pants after reading Jacob's poem. "I wonder what's up with the brother? Probably married."

She went back to reading the email:

Neena, I took a special photograph just for you. The kind we talked about on the phone the other night. Remember? I didn't attach it to the email because I didn't want to risk offending you. But, if you want it, all you have to do is email me back and ask for it. It is yours. I am yours. I only hope and pray that you will be mine for always, starting with tomorrow night.

Until then, sweetie. Are you still wearing that sexy red dress you described in your last email? If so, I might not be able to keep my hands off of you or protect you from the onslaught of men that will undoubtedly try to pick you up.

Love and Kisses,
Jacob

"Mmm, it appears Neena might have lucked up and found herself a winner. He sounds so sexy."

Nia hit the reply button and then hesitated. She knew perfectly well that she should type Jacob a response, letting him know that Neena had been called away on business. Yet and still, she was faced with a dilemma. This man had managed to stir something in her in the span of one email that Bryant had been unable to awaken the entire time they'd been seeing each other. Was he for real?

Nia was tempted to email him back and ask for the picture he mentioned, but knew it had to be something majorly freaky because of the way he delayed sending it. She craved to know what he looked like so she decided to do the next best thing.

She launched her Internet Explorer and quickly typed in www.blackgentlemen.com. When she saw this portrait of three fine ass black men downloading onto her computer from the main entrance, she let out a sigh. "Dang, look at them!"

Nia couldn't believe that she'd never heard of BlackGentlemen.com before. It was the bomb diggity! She navigated through the site and decided to search by state. She was looking for Jacob's picture. She was disappointed when she discovered that some men were using names like Black Stallion and Stud Muffin instead of their real first names. She clicked on a few of the men listed from the Durham area and, although attractive, none of them fit the description that Neena had given her of Jacob.

She was just about to give up her search, go back to the America Online screen, and email Jacob when she spotted The Man For You To Envy from Durham, N.C. on the listings page. She took a deep breath and clicked on the hyperlink. She collapsed back in her chair when she saw his picture downloading.

He was tall, at least six feet four, judging from the way he was towering over the hood of the hunter green BMW he was posing next to. He had the smoothest skin, a dark caramel, and closely-set, hazelnut eyes. He had a perfect and inviting smile and was undoubtedly the type of man that took pride in his appearance. His clothing was neatly pressed, his hair was freshly-cut, and he had muscles rippling all over his body.

"Damn, Neena! You go, Girl!"

Nia stared at the photo for a few moments and ran a series of what-ifs through her mind. What if she emailed him back and asked to see the other photo? What if she flirted with him in the email? What if she showed up at Club Oviedo instead of Neena? What if she found out firsthand what he meant in his poem? What if she let him "work her body over?"

"Nia, keep a hold of yourself," she said aloud, trying to stop her heart from beating so fast in her chest.

If she took Neena's place and Neena found out, she'd never forgive her. But what if she didn't find out? Nonsense; she'd have to find out. Then again, Neena had never actually met him, so it wasn't like she was sleeping with Neena's bonafide man. He was a brother from the Internet, for goodness sake.

Nia had never done something so scandalous before, although Neena had often tried to convince her to play the switching game when they were teenagers. When Nia always refused, Neena called her boring and said she was no fun as a twin.

She gazed into Jacob's eyes and knew he was what she needed in her life, if only for one night.

She clicked off the BlackGentlemen.com web site and hit reply on Jacob's email.

Jacob,

I will be there tomorrow at nine. I can't wait to see you and I definitely can't wait to see how you intend to work my body over. I loved your poem. It made me wet. The good, sticky kind of wet. Did you really write that just for me? I am so flattered.

As for the photo, of course I want you to send it. I bet it's HOT!

Well, let me run so I can get prepared for our big night tomorrow. It has been a long time coming and I want it to be perfect.

I will check back a little later and see if you've sent the new photo. If you don't get a chance to, I will understand and just see you tomorrow.

Love and Kisses,
Neena

Nia signed off and returned the phone call from her mother, listening to her whine and complain about Neena's sudden departure. She kept waiting for her mother to take a break so she could remind her that she had nothing to do with it. After about fifteen minutes, she told her mother she had to go because someone was at the door.

As soon as she hung up, Bryant called. He tried to smooth talk Nia into letting him make a booty call. She thought about the fifty pumps he usually put in before he collapsed on top of her and declined his offer, telling him she was planning to wash her hair. It was a lame ass line but it always worked in movies.

Nia fixed herself a grilled cheese sandwich for dinner and washed it down with a glass of orange juice. She never bothered to cook big meals because Neena was always on the go and she didn't believe in slaving over a hot stove all day for the likes of Bryant, although there was nothing he would have liked more.

She sat down on the sofa to watch Less Than Zero on HBO Plus; one of her favorite movies of all time. Talk about scaring somebody straight. She couldn't imagine a person turning to a life of drugs after watching the movie. Ironically, one of the featured actors did just that.

Halfway through the film, her thoughts turned to Jacob. She had no business sending him that email. She got up and signed back on to Neena's account, determined to email him an apology and explain what was really going on. That is, until...

...Nia spotted a new email from him with an attachment.

"Should I or shouldn't I?" Nia asked herself, halfway expecting someone to yell out an answer.

She bit her bottom lip and hit the download button.

"Oh myyyyyyy!" she cooed.

There before her was Jacob, wrapped in a red satin bow and nothing else. The thick part of the bow was covering his privates and Nia was extremely disappointed. A glimpse of his manhood would have made her night. The view he gave her wasn't half-bad though. He was cut every which way and looked as soft as silk.

"Fuck it! I'm going to do this! I'm sorry, Neena!"

The body of Jacob's email was simple: I hope you like it.

Nia hit the reply button.

Jacob,

I like your picture a lot. In fact, I love it and I can't wait to see you.
We have less than twenty-four hours. I'll be counting the minutes.
Your Baby,
Neena

Nia fell asleep dreaming about Jacob. She was looking forward to one hell of a Christmas Eve.

Chapter Four

The next morning Nia set about the task of transforming herself into her twin. While identical by nature, they did have different styles. She wasn't sure how much Jacob knew about Neena so she decided to play it safe and let her hair down *literally*. Nia always wore her shoulder length auburn hair up in a bun while Neena always let hers hang freely. Therefore, she washed her hair, blow-dried it, and teased it with mousse and a spiral hair brush.

Next was the outfit. She searched Neena's overcrowded walk-in closet for the infamous red dress she'd promised Jacob she would wear to their rendezvous. Nia felt like a fool when she finally noticed a garment bag hanging over the back of the love seat in Neena's bedroom.

She unzipped the bag and pulled out a skimpy red sheath.

"Damn, it's too cold outside for this!" Nia exclaimed.

She took the dress to her own bedroom and went through her closet to match it up with one of her blazers. She decided on a little black wool number and a pair of black leather pumps.

Then she played the waiting game. She had six hours left before she even needed to start getting dressed and it was the longest six hours of her life. She reorganized all of the lights and ornaments on the Christmas tree in their living room, put the greeting cards they'd received in alphabetical order according to sender, and wrapped the rest of the presents she had crammed behind the vacuum cleaner and mop bucket in the utility closet.

No less than twenty times did she change her mind about going to meet Jacob. The bottom line was that she was infatuated with the man and needed to see if he was the real thing or a fantasy. She pinned her hair up long enough to take a long hot bath, got dressed, and started out on the two-hour drive to Durham via Interstate 85.

Club Oviedo was packed and Nia was shocked. She expected it to be practically empty and never realized that so many people hung out on Christmas Eve. Probably because she was always home every year doing absolutely nothing or over at her mother's helping to prepare dinner.

Nia had to wait almost half an hour to get in. Luckily, she was forty minutes early when she first arrived. The bouncers seemed to be picky about who they were willing to let in. Once she let her blazer fall off of her shoulders, exposing much cleavage, they moved her to the front of the line and she was inside in a flash.

Nia despised shallow-acting men like that, but was relieved that her clothing, or lack thereof, helped her out in that instance. She couldn't really talk. She was there solely based on the way Jacob looked all wrapped up in a satin bow. If that wasn't considered shallow, she had no idea what would qualify.

She found a seat at the closest bar to the door and ordered a Seagrams Seven and 7Up. By the time ten minutes after nine rolled around, Nia was a nervous wreck. Where was he?

"My, my, my, you look delicious," a deep male voice whispered into her ear.

Nia swung around on her stool and looked up at Jacob, who'd stood back up after leaning down to seduce her with one sentence.

"Hello, Jacob." Nia cleared her throat. It had never occurred to her that Jacob might notice the difference between her voice and Neena's. She came up with a cover story just in case he did. "You'll have to excuse me, I'm battling a slight cold."

"You look mighty healthy to me." He sat down beside her at the bar. "So, we finally meet."

"Yes, finally," Nia said nervously. She hadn't even touched the man and she was already guilt-tripping in advance.

"I'm sorry that I'm a little late. I had to take care of one last surprise for you."

That made her blush, even though his surprise wasn't really meant for her. "What surprise?"

"I'm not telling. That wouldn't make it a surprise." Jacob waved over the bartender. "You need a refill or would you like something else?"

Nia's glass was still half-full. "No thanks, I'm fine."

While Jacob ordered a sniffer of brandy, Nia checked out his outfit. He was wearing a fly ass, double-breasted, Hugo Boss suit and a red silk tie. Nia couldn't help but ponder why a man so fine would be searching for a woman on the Internet, but wasn't about to ask him. She figured that ground had long since been covered during his conversations with Neena.

They sat at the bar and engaged in inconsequential chit-chat for about twenty minutes before hitting the dance floor. Nia wasn't into dancing and freaked out when Jacob said, "Show me some of those erotic moves you told me you had."

"Erotic moves?"

"Yes, didn't you say that you love to shake your ass?"

Nia let out an uncomfortable laugh. "Yes, yes I did."

Jacob grinned at her and kissed her on the forehead. "Cool."

As if things couldn't get worse, Shake Your Ass by Mystikal started blasting through the sound system and every sister in the place set out to prove that they could do just that better than anyone else.

Nia surveyed her competition on the dance floor, trying to pick up on something. She took off her jacket and let it all hang out. Jacob's eyes practically popped out of his head so she knew he was impressed.

"Ooh, Neena, that dress is sizzling, just like you said!"

"I'm glad you like it."

"I do, but I can't wait to get you out of it."

"And work my body over?" Nia asked jokingly.

"You know it."

Nia decided she wouldn't be outdone by the other hoochified women on the dance floor and started gyrating her hips to the music. She immediately noticed several men, who were dancing with other women, turn their attention toward her. It was attention she wasn't used to getting, but it was flattering. She decided she might need to raid Neena's closet more often.

Before the song had ended, Nia had turned around and was bouncing her ass up and down the front of Jacob's thighs. He had his hands around her waist and was rubbing his fingers up and down her ribcage, making her pussy throb.

He pulled her off the dance floor without uttering a word, took her by the hand, and led her outside. She eagerly followed him. She knew she was ready for whatever came next.

He stopped in front of the hunter green BMW from the photo on BlackGentlemen.com and took her face into his hands, bending down to give her a gentle kiss on her full lips.

"I'd like to take you home with me now to give you all of the surprises I prepared for you."

Nia pulled his face closer and darted her tongue in and out of Jacob's mouth, letting him savor it briefly. "Give them to me."

Chapter Five

After driving for about fifteen minutes, they pulled up in front of a three-story brownstone. Nia was impressed before she even got out of the car. Then she remembered that Jacob was into real estate and wondered why she'd expected him to live in anything less than a slamming ass house.

They got out of his car and Jacob took her by the hand, leading her up the front walk. He unlocked the door and she was about to go inside, but he stopped her.

"No, that's not the proper way for you to come into my home," he said before chuckling. Nia was dumfounded when he swept her up into his arms and carried her over the threshold. He took her over to the sofa and placed her gently down. "That's how you enter my home."

"Umm, I like entering your home that way," Nia responded.

Jacob sat down beside of her. He caressed her cheek. "Neena, you are so fine. I've waited so very long to get you here in my house. I've wanted to taste, pamper, and cater to you for months. Do you mind if I do that tonight?"

A wave of guilt rushed up Nia's spine. This man wanted to do all of those things to her sister, not to her. But she was there now and didn't see any way of backing out. Then again, she didn't want to back out.

"Sure, Jacob. You can do all those things for me."

He kissed her hand and then took each one of her fingers into his mouth and dampened them with his saliva. "Damn, even your fingers taste good."

He got up and walked over to the gas fireplace, picking up the remote and clicking it on. Nia took a good look around his house. He had expensive tastes. Concordian Chesterfield fine leather furniture, Italian marble tables, and fine artwork from famous African-American artists like Poncho, Wak, and Andrè Harris.

Jacob cut off the lamp on the end table that had been on when they first walked in, instantly making the mood more romantic. There was an artificial Christmas tree in the living room with a few presents scattered beneath it. An unusual stocking, a black fishnet one, hung on a hook on the corner of the mantle. Nia couldn't help but giggle. She assumed that was one of his surprises.

Jacob noticed Nia eyeing the stocking. "I bet you think that's for you."

"Isn't it?"

He grinned at her. "Yes, it is."

He took the stocking off the hook and sat back down beside Nia on the sofa. He laid the stocking across Nia's lap. It contained five professionally wrapped presents.

"Can I open them?" Nia asked, dying to know what was inside of them.

"Go for it," Jacob chuckled, watching her pull the first one out.

Nia ripped the paper off, uncovering a Victoria's Secret gift box. "Aw, I wonder what this is," she said jokingly. "I bet this is more for you than for me."

Jacob threw his head back in laughter. "Well, I figured we would both get enjoyment out of it."

Nia took the lid off the box. Inside was a red silk teddy that Nia deduced must have cost a pretty penny. "You want me to put this on?" Nia asked eagerly.

Jacob patted her thigh. "In a few moments. Open up the rest of your gifts first."

Nia pulled out the next gift and yanked the wrap off. A clear plastic case with a ten-inch black dildo was inside. "Oh, my goodness!"

Jacob leaned over, flicked his tongue in and out of her ear, and whispered, "Remember when you told me that you wanted one of those?"

"Yes," Nia lied. She had no doubt that Neena had told him that. She had a flashback to Neena packing a vibrator for her trip and thought, *Neena should have had this. Then she wouldn't have to worry about the metal detector going off.*

She shared a private laugh about it.

Jacob took the dildo from her hands and stared at it. "There's nothing like a real man though. This is only for when we can't be together. When I'm around, I'm going to handle my business."

Nia blushed. "Are you going to handle your business tonight?"

"I'm going to handle it and then some." Jacob pulled out the next gift and handed it to her. "Open this one."

Nia did as he suggested and whipped out a box of candy canes, a bottle of peppermint-flavored massage oil, and a box of chocolate-covered cherries. "Candy canes?"

"Yes, those are the most special gifts of all. Wait until you see what I am going to do with them. Rather, what I am going to do to you."

Nia could feel her panties getting wet. That was a definite good sign. She grabbed the next package anxiously. Inside were two Nina Simone CDs.

"Your favorite, right?" Jacob asked. "I thought we'd play them tonight to get us in the mood."

"Yes," Nia lied again, giving the response her twin would have given. Nia hated Nina Simone. The music depressed her, but if he wanted to fuck her off KC and the Sunshine Band, she wasn't about to object. She gazed into his eyes. "By the way, I'm already in the mood."

He looked down at his crotch. Nia's eyes followed his and saw that he was hard. He looked hard and *healthy*. "Does it look like I'm in the mood?"

"I don't know. It appears that way, but you might have to actually remove your clothing before I can give a final answer."

They both snickered. Nia pulled out the final gift.

While she undid the wrapper, Jacob said, "Now that's the practical one. I wanted to get you at least one gift that would last longer than tonight. Something you would see daily and immediately bring me to mind."

"A palm pilot!" Nia squealed. She'd always wanted one. "Thank you so much!"

She kissed Jacob on the cheek.

"No, thank you for gracing me with your presence tonight. I was afraid that you would back out on me, Neena."

Nia wished he would stop saying Neena's name and prayed he didn't call her that while they were getting busy. She dreaded that he would though.

Jacob stood up and pulled Nia up with him. "Come here."

He led her into the dining room and sat her down at the table. She'd been so preoccupied with him that she didn't notice the delicious smell coming from his kitchen when they'd first entered. She could smell it now though and her stomach started churning.

"You cooked me dinner?"

"Yes, I hope you don't object to a late meal? I meant to tell you in my email earlier not to eat before you came."

"Actually, I'm starved."

"Good, be right back."

Jacob disappeared into the kitchen, returning a moment later with a large platter full of lobster tails and melted butter. He placed it down in front of her.

"I can't eat all of that."

"It's for both of us." Jacob sat down in a chair beside of her. "I thought we'd feed each other."

He pulled a couple of plastic seafood bibs out of his pocket and placed one around his neck and then Nia's. They fed each other the lobster, seductively dipping it into butter before placing it into each other's mouths. Whenever a drop of butter escaped, they licked it off each other's chin before it ever made it to the bibs. Jacob also had a bottle of chilled champagne, which they drank as well.

Things then went into high gear. All inhibitions flew out the window and it was on. Jacob ate Nia off a platter when they were done with the lobster, keeping his bib on. Afterwards, they went upstairs where Jacob had his bedroom prepared. There were red satin sheets on his bed, multicolored Christmas lights swirling around his bed posts, and a unity candle on his dresser.

He lit the two smaller candles and handed one to Nia. "That candle represents everything that you are and this candle represents everything that I am. Once we light the big candle together, you and I will be united as one."

"Damn," was all Nia could manage to say. She'd seen unity candles used dozens of times at weddings but never before sex.

They lit the larger candle together and then blew out the smaller ones.

Jacob gave Nia a bath with peppermint-scented bath gel, told her she didn't need to dry off with a towel afterwards, and licked her dry instead. He gave her a full body massage with the oil and then systematically licked her from head to toe. She was in heaven and hell at the same time. She had no business there, but couldn't stop.

She put on the teddy and then danced seductively for him off of Nina Simone, taking the lingerie right back off within five minutes. They ended up ripping into each other all night long. Jacob did make good use of the candy canes and chocolate-covered cherries as well, dipping them into her juices and then sucking her essence off of them.

After they'd done the deed in his bed, in his shower, and on his balcony under the stars, they returned to his bed where Jacob fell fast asleep. Nia laid there staring at him for a while, before dozing off herself. She was sore all over. She was satisfied with a lover for the first time in her life. She was a traitor to the one person she loved more than life itself: Neena.

Chapter Six

Nia awoke the next morning in Jacob's arms. He was sleeping soundly and had a gigantic grin on his face.

"What have I done?" Nia whispered to herself, guilt-tripping over spending the night with him behind Neena's back.

Jacob stirred in his sleep before opening his eyes one at a time. "Good morning, Baby."

Nia blurted it out before she lost her nerve. "I have to tell you something, Jacob."

"Mmm, I had my heart set on another round." Jacob lowered the sheet off of Nia's breasts and started rubbing one of her nipples between his fingers. "Maybe you can tell me afterwards."

Nia pushed his hand away and sat up, propping her back on a pillow. "No, I need to tell you this now."

Jacob sighed disappointedly. "Okay, so tell me."

Nia took a deep breath before she began. "When I saw that poem you wrote, it stirred something inside of me. And then, after I saw your pictures, I just couldn't help myself. I had to come here."

Jacob chuckled and slid his hand underneath the covers, searching for Nia's pussy so he could finger her. She didn't stop him.

"I already knew you were coming," he said as Nia gave into the pleasure and started moaning, grinding herself onto his fingers. "We'd made plans. I didn't write that poem as some sort of tactic to lure you in. I wrote it because it expressed the way I was feeling and still feel about you."

Nia got lost in Jacob's eyes and the magic of his hand. "That's so sweet. Last night was so wonderful, but..."

"Yes, it was." Jacob leaned over and started sucking on one of Nia's breasts.

That brought her back to reality. She pushed him off. "Jacob, please. Just stop it."

"What's wrong with you?" Jacob asked defiantly. "After everything that happened between us last night, now you don't want me to touch you?"

"Last night, you made love to Neena."

Jacob laughed. "And Neena made love to me."

"No, she didn't."

Jacob was totally confused. "Come again."

"I'm not Neena. I'm Nia."

"Excuse me?"

"Neena's twin."

"Oh, shit!" Jacob exclaimed, hopping up out of the bed. He stood there and stared down at her.

"Neena never mentioned me?" Nia asked with tears in her eyes.

"No, I mean yes. Of course, she mentioned you. Several times. I'm just in shock right now. Give me a moment."

He went into the bathroom and shut the door. Nia could hear him urinating, followed by the toilet flushing and water running in the sink. By the time he returned, Nia was completely dressed.

"Jacob, I'm leaving now," she announced when he came back out into the bedroom wearing a terrycloth robe.

"You don't have to leave, Neena. I mean, Nia."

"Yes, I do need to leave because I had no business here in the first place." Nia knew he was just trying to be polite, despite the fact that he probably despised her. "What am I going to tell my sister?"

Jacob sat on the edge of the bed. "Why do you have to tell her anything?"

"Are you kidding?" Nia asked incredulously, not believing her ears. "I have to tell Neena I slept with you. We haven't discussed you much, but I do know that she has high expectations of a future relationship with you."

"Well, obviously, there can't be a relationship between Neena and me. I'll just tell her that I'm no longer interested."

"And what about me?"

"What about you?" Jacob asked snidely, taking on an entirely different demeanor. "You came here under false pretenses and played me for a sucker. Why don't you just get out?"

Nia couldn't figure him out. There were only two things she was sure of: she'd fucked up and her sister was going to be hurt because of it. "A minute ago you said I could stay. Now, you're kicking me out?"

Jacob laid down on the bed and turned away from her. "I'm not kicking anything, but I would like you to leave."

Nia grabbed her purse and stormed out, yelling behind her, "Fine! I'm going!"

"Good riddance!" she heard Jacob yell out after her.

Nia walked three blocks to a major intersection and flagged down a cab. On her way back to the club to retrieve her car, she buried her face in her hands and cried.

Chapter Seven

As usual during the holidays, Nia and Neena's mother's house was full of relatives and two tables spread with food. Nia couldn't stand all of the joy and laughter so she sought refuge in the wooden swing on the chilly front porch.

Her mother leered at her through the screen door before coming outside and placing her hands on her hips. "Nia, don't tell me that you're going to insult me in my own home."

Nia didn't look at her. She looked through her. "What do you mean, Momma?"

"You're the only one not eating. It's Christmas and you know how much pride I take in preparing Christmas dinner for the family."

"I'm sorry, Momma. I'll go fix a plate right this second."

"It's bad enough that your sister went off to God knows where."

Nia rolled her eyes and got up off the swing, going inside while her mother held the door open for her. "Momma, Neena had to go away on business. It's not like her absence is intentional."

"Nia, telephone!"

Nia had been laying down in her old bedroom battling a migraine when her mother yelled up the stairwell. She sat up and asked, "Who is it?"

Her mother replied, "Neena!"

Nia got up and walked out into the hallway where there was a wooden telephone stand with a small, tapestry-covered bench attached to it. She hesitated for a few seconds and took a deep breath before picking up the extension.

"Hey, Neena!"

"Hey, Sissypoo!" Neena blared cheerfully into Nia's ear. "Merry Christmas!"

"Same to you."

Neena's happy mood made Nia's stomach hurt. She was overwhelmed with guilt.

"I'm just calling to check in. You know I had to try to earn some brownie points with Momma."

That made Nia laugh. She knew all about earning brownie points when it came to their mother. "How's Houston?"

"Boring as hell, but they have some fine ass men down here. Speaking of fine ass men, did you email Jacob and explain why I couldn't keep our date?"

Nia sat down on the bench and shielded her forehead with her hand. Her brain felt like it was pulsating.

"Yeah, yeah, I took care of that," she lied.

"Thanks, I know I can always count on you."

Actually, you can't count on me worth a damn, Nia thought to herself. She tried to rush off the phone before Neena asked any further questions about Jacob.

"Did you want to talk back to Momma?" she asked. "I was taking a nap because my head hurts."

"Are you okay?"

"Yeah, I'm fine. I just probably ate too much," Nia said, telling yet another lie. She'd piled up food on a plate, but picked over it before getting rid of the evidence in the garbage disposal. She knew there would be hell to pay if her mother had discovered a plate of food tossed in the trash.

"Sure, I'll talk back with Momma. I just wanted to holler at you. Is Uncle Earl over there getting tore up?"

Nia laughed. Their Uncle Earl was an alcoholic, but a smooth one. He almost made being a wino an art form.

"He's been tore up. He's already talking about how he was the captain of the basketball team in high school."

"Yeah, right, about thirty years ago." Neena guffawed. "Just try to stay out of his way before he gets to patting asses."

"I know that's right!" Nia exclaimed, remembering the numerous occasions when he tried to feel the two of them up, along with all the other female relatives, when he was in the middle of one of his drunken stupors.

"Take care, Sissypoo. I'll see you in a few days."

"Take care." Nia pressed the handset into her shoulder blade and yelled, "Momma, telephone!"

Nia went back into her bedroom, collapsed on the bed, buried her head in a pillow, and cried. She had created a mess and had no idea how she was going to fix it.

Chapter Eight

Jacob was going through the pile of mail that had piled up on his desk over the last week. His brother, Jaleb, startled him as he walked in. "You're home!"

Jacob got up to give Jaleb a hug. "Hey, baby brother! Merry Belated Christmas!"

"I wish you would cut out that baby brother mess. Eight measly minutes doesn't make you a big brother."

"No, but my balls that outweigh yours two to one do."

"Keep dreaming!"

Jacob sat back down while Jaleb took the seat on the opposite side of the desk. "So what did you do when I was away?"

Jaleb shrugged. "The usual. Just hung out."

"Where did you hang out?"

"I hit a few clubs with Rodney and Keith."

"Picked up some honies?"

"No, not really."

Jacob surveyed his twin and knew he looked upset about something. He could always tell. He assumed it was because he'd been called away on business unexpectedly during the holidays. "Well, I'm sorry I missed Christmas dinner. I felt so guilty since we spend it together every year."

Jaleb smirked and waved off the apology. "Jacob, we're grown men. No need to apologize. I actually went over to Keith's crib for dinner. His wife hooked up a serious meal."

"Cool. I still owe you a present though." Jacob got up and headed outside of the real estate firm they co-owned to his hunter green BMW. He and Jaleb shared the same tastes, right down to their choice in automobiles. "Be right back."

He returned with a set of brand-new Harvey Penick golf clubs.

"Wow, those are fly as shit!" Jaleb said appreciatively when Jacob sat them down.

"Yes, and they cost me a pretty penny too," Jacob added. He wanted Jaleb to know that his gift didn't come cheap. Both being avid golfers, he was sure Jaleb recognized that already but decided to rub it in anyway.

"Your gift is at home. I'll give it to you tonight."

"Great! I can't wait to see it."

"I think you'll like it." Jaleb held in a laugh. He'd purchased Jacob the exact same set of golf clubs. He couldn't wait to see the expression on his face later that night. "I love the clubs, bro. Thank you."

"Welcome." Jacob returned to opening his mail. He asked matter-of-factly, "So, did you get a chance to email Neena for me?"

"Who?" Jaleb replied, acting confused.

Jacob looked up and glared at him, tossing the envelope he'd just opened back on his desk. "Neena. The sister I told you to email about my sudden trip. Please tell me you did it, Jaleb."

"Of course I did, but..."

"But what?"

Jaleb shifted in his seat. "I've been meaning to talk to you about Neena."

"What about her?"

"Doesn't she live down near Charlotte?"

"Yes, she lives in Kannapolis. Why?"

"Because I've heard some things," Jaleb said solemnly, diverting his eyes to the floor. He didn't want Jacob to be able to see his eyes. His eyes always gave away his lies.

"What kind of things?"

"Bad things."

Jacob raised his voice. "Come off it, Jaleb. What did you hear?"

"Rodney said he hit it, man."

"You're lying!"

"No, I'm not. Call him and ask him if you don't believe me." Jaleb got up and picked up the handset, holding it out to Jacob. He was hoping Jacob wouldn't really call Rodney because Rodney didn't know a damn thing about Neena. "He's not the only one, either. I hear she gives it up to just about any man that asks."

Jacob slumped back in his leather desk chair. "Neena lives two hours away. How the hell did Rodney meet her in the first place?"

Jaleb placed the receiver back on the cradle, relieved that Jacob trusted him enough not to call. "Hell if I know. I think he mentioned something about meeting her at a house party in Greensboro."

"It's probably someone else."

"Another Neena? Another Neena with a twin sister named Nia? Your Neena does have a twin, right?"

"Yes."

"See, I rest my case. You never told me that she has a twin so how would I know?"

Jacob was dumbfounded. There was no conceivable way that Jaleb could know that Neena had a twin. As for Neena, he'd never told her that Jaleb was his twin. He planned to take her by surprise when they finally met and he took her to his house. Their house.

"Even if she slept with Rodney, that was a long time ago. It's not like I don't have a past."

"You call last month a long time ago?" Jaleb asked sarcastically.

"Last month?"

"Yes, last month."

"But she was talking to me last month."

"My point exactly. And get this, Rodney said he slammed her less than two hours after they met. Right there on the hood of his car. Nasty hoe!"

Jacob slammed his clenched fist down on his desk in fury. "I can't believe this shit!"

"Believe it! I'm sorry, bro, but maybe it's better that your Christmas Eve plans didn't work out. You were pretty serious about the sister and everyone knows that you can't turn a hoe into a housewife."

Jacob was heartbroken. He'd held Neena in such high regards and had often imagined building a stable future with her. She was beautiful, had her head on straight, and always brightened his mood whenever they talked. "I thought she was special, Jaleb. It really felt like she was the one."

"They'll be others." Jaleb's stomach started hurting. He was having an anxiety attack, not to mention being overwhelmed by guilt. He decided to change the subject. "I'll tell you what. Let's celebrate Christmas late. We can go clubbing tonight."

"I don't feel like it."

"Oh, so now you're going to hole up in the house and sulk over some woman you never actually met?"

Jacob stared at Jaleb. He did have a point. If Neena wanted to spread her legs for every Trent, Dante, and Hakim, let her. He was cutting all ties and moving on.

"You're right! Let's hang out. As for Neena, that skank hoe better not ever call or email me again."

Chapter Nine

Nia came into the house loaded down with plastic bags from Food Lion. Neena's car was outside and she figured she must be laying down since the living room was completely dark. Nia wondered if Neena was suffering from yet another work-related migraine. She was startled when a lamp on one of their end tables suddenly came to life. Neena was sitting on the sofa boring a hole through her with her eyes.

Nia dropped the bags on the floor. "Why are you sitting up here in the dark?"

"Because I'm pissed off."

"About what?" Nia asked, praying it didn't have anything to do with her dirt. However, she knew that everyone's actions always catch up to them sooner or later.

"Do you know that Jacob refuses to take my phone calls and he won't respond to any of my emails?" Neena snarled at her sarcastically.

Here comes the drama, Nia thought to herself before sitting down across from Neena in an armchair. "No, I didn't know that."

"No explanation. No nothing. He just did a complete turnaround." Neena looked at Nia accusingly. "I wonder why."

Nia was a nervous wreck and searched for something to say. "Why look at me? I have no idea. I don't even know the man."

"Strange that you should use that choice of wording."

"Why is that strange?"

"Because after Jacob started dissing me, I got to thinking about the email I asked you to send him. The one you told me you sent."

"I, I...." Nia stuttered.

"So I decided to check my sent mail box and what do I find. Emails telling Jacob that I can't wait to see him at the club and emails talking about how much I love the picture of him that he sent. By the way, I went to my box with old mail received and saw the picture."

Damn, Nia thought. *I forgot to clean out the incriminating emails.* "I can explain, Neena."

"What was wrapped up in the red bow belonged to me, Nia. That poem was written for me."

"I know that. Will you please just listen?"

Neena's voice went up about three octaves. "Just tell me one thing. Did you pretend to be me and meet Jacob at the club, Nia? Did you?"

"Yes, I did," Nia answered, realizing that honesty was the best policy at that point.

"I can't fuckin' believe you!" Neena screamed at her, getting up and walking over to stand in front of any possible escape route Nia had from the armchair.

Nia couldn't even look up at her. She was so ashamed. "Neena, I was confused. I saw his picture and read that poem and something came over me."

"Did you fuck him? Yes or no."

"Yes, I fucked him." Nia heard the slap before she saw it. Her cheek felt like it was on fire. "Neena, you hit me!"

"Damn right! You're lucky I don't beat the shit out of you!" Neena moved away. One slap was enough, even if it was the only retribution she would ever likely get. "How could you? I'm your sister!"

"Neena, I promise that no matter how long it takes, I will make this up to you."

"Make it up? The damage is done, Nia. Does Jacob know it was you?" Neena asked. Nia finally looked at her, her eyes pleading for a reprieve. "He does, doesn't he?"

"I told him the next morning."

Neena placed her hands on her hips. "So now he's playing silly games with me to get me to leave him alone so he can get with you."

"No, he's not trying to get with me. He kicked me out of his place after I told him."

"Serves you right."

"He's just too ashamed about what happened to meet you now."

"This is all your fault. I really care about him, Nia! I was trying to build something with him!"

Nia started weeping. The inevitability of being caught was too much to bear now that it had actually happened. "I'll fix it. I'll go to him and beg him to give your relationship another chance."

"After he was all up inside you, and doing Lawd knows what else to you? I don't even think so," Neena let out a phony laugh before storming out of the room. "I'm through with both of you."

Nia heard Neena's bedroom door slam. Through tear-drenched eyes, she managed to put away the groceries before retiring to her own room and to her own state of depression.

Chapter Ten

Two Days Later

Nia pulled up to the front of a very stylish, upper-class home. An "Open House" sign was on a stake in the front yard. There was a hunter-green BMW parked in the drive. She was relieved that Jacob was there because her hands were trembling so much on her drive to Durham that she didn't think she could deal with it two days in a row.

She got out of her car, hesitated for a moment, and then strutted inside before she lost her nerve. There was no one in sight. She was about to yell out Jacob's name when he emerged from a room in the rear. His eyes were glued to an open manila folder and he didn't see her until he practically bumped into her.

Jacob saw a pair of strikingly beautiful legs and inched his eyes upward until he was staring into Nia's face.

"Jacob, I need to talk to you."

Jacob didn't know what to say. She was even more beautiful than her pictures. "Neena, what are you doing here? How'd you find me?"

"Your secretary told me you were conducting an open house today. I'm not Neena, Jacob, and you damn well know it. At least, you should."

"What?" Jacob asked, having no idea what she was talking about.

"Look, I didn't come here to rehash what happened between us on Christmas Eve. The sex was spectacular, but it wasn't real because you thought you were being intimate with Neena and not me."

"What are you talking about? On Christmas Eve, I wasn't even in..."

Nia cut him off. "Jacob, you don't have to play dumb. No one else is here."

It finally dawned on Jacob. Jaleb had committed a major fuck up and tried to cover his ass. "Okay, I won't play dumb," he said, leaning against the staircase. He decided to hear Nia out. That way he'd have more ammunition when he confronted Jaleb.

"I know that we'd decided that you would just cut Neena off, but it backfired. She found the emails."

"The emails?" Jacob asked, prodding her on.

"The emails. The poem you wrote me, I mean her, and the nude picture."

"The nude picture." Jacob shook his head. Jaleb was just too damn much. He played it off and smirked. "Oh, yeah, the nude picture."

"This is all my fault, Jacob. Neena shouldn't have to suffer behind my actions. I won't lie. She's pissed at both of us and has serious apprehensions about having anything further to do with you. But we live in the same home and she's not even speaking to me. It's driving me insane."

"And what exactly do you expect me to do about it?"

"Talk to Neena. Come by the house. If you don't have the address, I'll give it to you. I'll give you the directions. Just come and try to work things out."

"I have the address, but do you really think things can be worked out?" Jacob asked, his feelings for Neena resurfacing at the speed of light now that he realized she really wasn't the hoe Jaleb had proclaimed her to be.

"I don't know. I really don't know," Nia replied sullenly. "What I do know is that there can never be an us, and I understand that. For what it's worth, I want you to know that Christmas Eve meant a lot to me, even though the affection and intimacy shown wasn't meant for me. I wish things could be different."

Nia started crying and Jacob was tempted to stop her before she stormed out of the house. But, he didn't know what to say. Whatever happened between Jaleb and Neena's twin sister was something they needed to resolve. He glanced at his watch. He had two more hours before the open house officially ended. Two hours too long because he couldn't wait to get his hands on his brother. *Literally.*

Chapter Eleven

Jaleb came into their townhouse a little after seven that evening with a paper bag of Chinese food in one hand and a twelve-pack of Miller Lite in the other. He heard Jacob in the kitchen and went to join him.

"Jacob, the Szechuan Inn was out of white meat chicken so I couldn't get your chicken with cashew nuts. I got you shrimp lo mein instead. Is that cool?" Jaleb asked, wondering why Jacob was washing dishes and then slamming them into the drainer like he was attempting to cause serious damage.

Jacob slammed a saucer and it actually broke. Jaleb was just about to ask him what was wrong when Jacob swung around and punched him in the gut.

Jaleb bowled over in pain. "Owww, what are you doing man? Are you crazy?"

"No, I'm not crazy! You are!" Jacob yelled at him vehemently.

"What the hell are you talking about?" Jaleb was a lot of things, but he was no dummy. He knew what was going on, but tried to play dumb regardless.

"What did you do Christmas Eve, Jaleb? Huh? What did you do?"

"I told you that I hung out with Rodney and Keith during the holidays. Why?"

"Lying ass!" Jacob screamed at him, punching him in the face.

Jaleb didn't have the heart or the desire to hit Jacob back. He knew he deserved it. "Jacob, I don't know what the hell you've been smoking, but you need to stay off it."

"I'm talking about Nia. You know Nia, don't you? Neena's twin that you thought was Neena when you fucked her on Christmas Eve."

Jaleb went to the freezer, took out a cube of ice, sat down at the dinette table, and leered at Jacob. Fuck it, he thought to himself. *I'll just tell him everything and get it over with.* "Okay, Jacob, I'll confess."

Jacob let out a wicked snicker. "You have no choice but to confess."

"It was all a huge misunderstanding," Jaleb said nonchalantly, rubbing the ice on his eye before it could bruise.

Jacob couldn't believe his nerve. He'd rushed home from the open house and scanned through his email until he'd located all the emails Nia had alluded to. "A misunderstanding. I Can't Wait To Work Your Body Over? What a lame ass poem!"

"I thought it was rather poetic myself."

"And the punk ass picture of you in a ribbon?"

"There is nothing punkish about that picture," Jaleb lashed out offensively.

"Why? Why would you do something so stupid?"

"I was bored. I realize I should have just emailed Neena and told her that you were out of town."

Jacob balled his hand into a fist, ready to strike again. He didn't because he knew Jaleb wouldn't hit him back so it wasn't an even playing field. "Yes, you're damn right! You should have!"

"It's just that the pic you have of her as your screensaver at the office is super hot and I just couldn't resist the urge to take a dip in the pool."

Jacob had to agree that the picture in question was hot as hell. He sat down at the table facing Jaleb. "I can tell that poem took all of two seconds to make up, but where the hell did the picture come from?"

Jaleb chuckled. "Denae took that one last year when we were still seeing each other. Remember, you told me that you'd talked about sending her a freaky picture?"

Jacob couldn't help but be somewhat impressed at Jaleb's resourcefulness. "So you dug that one out and sent it, pretending that it was me?"

"Exactly!"

Jacob grew angry all over again. "Jaleb, you have done some low down dirty shit over the years but this is unforgivable."

Jaleb's temper was raising its ugly head also. "Get off your high horse. This isn't the first time we've played this game."

They had, in the past, played tricks on a couple of sisters. Nothing of that magnitude though and it happened when they were much younger.

"This is the first time we've played the fuckin' game when I wasn't in on it!" Jacob reminded Jaleb. "The really messed up part is that Nia was really feeling me, rather you, that night."

Jaleb realized that something wasn't adding up. "How do you know? For that matter, how'd you find out about all of this in the first place? I thought you were kicking Neena to the curb?"

"That's the most fucked-up part of all! You knew you didn't fuck Neena and you led me to believe that she was a hoe just so you could save your own ass."

"Who told you all of this? Neena?"

"No, Nia. She showed up at my open house today, thinking I was the man she spent Christmas Eve with, and confronted me about the situation." Jacob felt like getting up and throwing the chair he was sitting in against the wall, but managed to stay in place. "She said that Neena does know about it, though."

"This is a big mess!"

"Yes, it is a big mess, and it's all your fault!"

Jaleb wasn't about to be the fall guy. "Hold up, now! This is just as much Nia's fault as mine. She was creeping behind her sister's back just like I was creeping behind yours."

"That's makes the two of you the perfect match."

Jaleb grinned, reminiscing about the glorious night he'd spent with Nia. "We were damn near perfect that night."

"You like her, don't you?"

Jaleb took his time before replying, "As much as I'd like to swear up and down that it was only sex, I have to admit that it was special."

"From the way she was acting today, it was special for her, too." Jacob got up, ripped open the case of beer, and yanked one open. "You ruined a good thing for me, Jaleb, and I'm not sure I can ever forgive you."

"Why does it have to be ruined?"

"Excuse me?"

"Neena's mad because she thinks you slept with her sister and then started ignoring her because of it. But you didn't sleep with Nia. I did."

"Like tell me something I don't already know."

"I don't see why your thing with Neena can't be salvaged." Jaleb was trying to make amends with his twin. His dirty deeds had been uncovered so there was no logical reason for Jacob not to be happy if Neena was the woman that could do it. "Why can't it be salvaged?"

Jacob took a swig of his beer. "Good question."

Chapter Twelve

Nia sat at the dining room table, rubbing her stomach, and yelled into the kitchen. "Momma, this country fried steak and cornbread is delicious!" She glanced across the table at Neena, who had refused to say more than two words to her in weeks. "Isn't it, Neena?"

Neena rolled her eyes at Nia. "Don't talk to me."

"Neena, we can't not talk to each other forever. We're twins. We live in the same house. This is ridiculous." Nia realized she was talking too loudly and adjusted her tone. "Besides, do you really want Momma to jump into the middle of this and get all into our business? She's going to know something is wrong if you don't stop this nonsense. It was bad enough that you left me at home and drove over here separately."

"It would serve your ass right if Momma found out. Remember, I'm not the one that did anything wrong here."

"I know that, but I've already apologized a dozen times. What else do you want me to do? Kiss your feet? I'm not thrilled at the prospect but, if it will get you to drop this, I'll kiss your damn feet." Nia could tell she was getting to Neena because she was trying to suppress a smile. "Your crusty, ashy, look like you've been driving a car in Bedrock feet."

Neena threw a dinner roll at Nia. "Oh no, now don't go dogging my feet."

Nia giggled. "You know it's true. You can use an entire bottle of lotion on them and they're still ashy. You need to look into a podiatrist or something because those fly-by-night commercial nail salons you keep going to aren't helping. Don't they make you soak your feet in the same water as their other customers? That's just straight up nasty. Some eighty-year-old woman's fungus is probably causing your feet to dry up like that."

"Get off my feet already," Neena said snidely. "Don't make me turn into Ms. Thang and start on your flat ass."

"My ass is not even flat." Nia got up from the table and turned around, modeling her rear end. "Your butt might stick out an inch or two more than mine, but that's it and it's only because you lost your virginity before me."

Neena couldn't prevent her laughter any longer. She chuckled and Nia joined her. "That is the silliest thing I've ever heard. I lost my virginity like two months before you did."

"What are you girls talking about?" their mother asked, returning from the kitchen with a piping hot apple pie. She loved cooking Sunday dinner for her daughters and looked forward to it every weekend.

"Nothing, Momma," Nia answered, retaking her seat. "Just talking period."

"Good. I was about to get concerned. You two seemed uncomfortable earlier. Is something wrong?"

Neena decided to respond since she was the one that showed up with a funky attitude. "No, Momma. Everything's fine. I was feeling kind of down because of my job."

Their mother shook her head. "Again? Neena, no matter how much they're paying you, get out of there if you're not happy."

"I second that," Nia agreed.

Neena looked from one of them to the other and came to a long overdue conclusion. "You're both right. I might have to take a pay cut, but it would be nice to be stress free for a change."

Chapter Thirteen

One Month Later

"Guess what?" Neena said anxiously, coming into the house and tossing her briefcase on the chair.

The only problem was that Nia said, "Guess what?" at the same exact time, jumping up from the sofa, grinning from ear-to-ear.

Nia was disappointed and anxious at the same time but conceded to her twin. "You can go first."

"No, you first."

"No, you, because I'm sure my 'guess what' is more exciting than your 'guess what'."

Neena shrugged her shoulders. "I doubt it but, anyway, listen up. You might want to sit down because this is going to shock you."

Nia plopped back down on the sofa. "Okay, I'm sitting. Hit me with it."

"I finally did it. I quit my job."

Nia was stunned. "You're kidding!"

"No, I really did."

"You go, gurl!" Nia exclaimed. Neena sat down beside of Nia and slapped her a high five. "So, what are you going to do now?"

"You'll never guess."

"I'm not even about to try."

"You remember Tai from high school?"

Nia's eyes narrowed like she was deep in thought. "Yeah, didn't she move to Charlotte or something?"

"Yes. I ran into her a couple of weeks ago in the airport and, since both of our planes were delayed, we decided to grab some coffee at Starbucks and catch up."

"That's cool, but what does that have to do with what you're planning to do?"

"Patience, Sissypoo." Nia rolled her eyes, hoping Neena would get to the point quickly so she could reveal her own news. Neena continued, "Tai is in public relations now and owns her own firm. Business is booming and she's taking on too many clients, but refuses to turn anyone worth the effort away."

"Who are her clients?" Nia asked, unimpressed. "Charlotte's not exactly Hollywood."

"You're so silly. Movie stars and writers are not the only people that use public relations specialists. Charlotte is growing by leaps and bounds in big businesses and then there are the various athletic franchises."

"So her clients are big business people and athletes?"

"Yes, mostly athletes."

"Fine athletes?"

Neena giggled. "Yes, Sissypoo."

"Does she represent Phillip Keller?"

"From the Panthers? I'm not sure, but she might."

"Gurlllllllllllll, if she could hook me up with him, I'll kiss her feet. Not your feet, but her feet because hopefully hers aren't jacked up like yours."

Neena slapped Nia gently on the arm. "Can I finish?"

"Go ahead."

"I'm going to become her partner. Her *full* partner. I have some money saved up and Tai said if I buy out a certain percentage of the firm, then it's on."

"You doing public relations? Your background is in sales."

"Sales. Public relations. It's all about making people comfortable enough around you to do some business."

"True and you are the master of that." Nia did admire Neena's sales skills. Girlfriend had it going on and could sell sunglasses to a blind man.

"So what do you think?" Neena asked, uncomfortable with the silence that ensued.

"I think it's a wonderful idea, but..."

"But what?"

"Sounds stressful. Isn't the whole point of this exercise to get the stress out of your life?"

"This is different. I'll basically be setting my own hours, I'll get to go to a lot of sporting events and hang out in the skyboxes rubbing elbows with bigwigs, and I won't have to be flying across country half the damn year."

"But didn't you run into Tai at the airport?"

"Yes, but she was taking a rare trip and it wasn't business-related. She's seeing a brother in Houston and was flying down to surprise him for his birthday."

Nia, satisfied with Neena's answers, threw her arms around her sister's shoulders and gave her a bear hug and kiss on the cheek. "Neena, I'm so proud of you. I never thought you'd actually do it. I wish you the best."

"Thanks, Sissypoo!"

"Now, I do get to hang out in some of those skyboxes with you, right?" Nia asked jokingly. "If you come falling in here all the time excited about meeting this person or that person, I might get a tad bit jealous."

"Don't worry. I'll hook you up, even if I only have one ticket. We'll wear the same outfit and take turns going in and out if we have to."

That caused memories of Christmas Eve and the depressing aftermath to come flooding into Nia's head. She still felt extremely guilty about what she had done. "Neena, once again, I'm sorry for pulling that switch on Jacob."

Neena waved off her comment. "Forget about it. He's history. Nothing and no one comes between you and me. I'm sorry I even treated you badly. Everyone makes mistakes. Even me from time-to-time."

"Dang, and all this time I thought your ass could walk on water."

They both laughed.

"Now, what's your 'guess what' all about?" Neena inquired.

"I almost completely forgot. I was so caught up in the moment."

"Get uncaught and spill the beans."

"You'll never guess who called here today!"

"Hmm, Publisher's Clearing House to let me know I won ten million dollars?"

"No, they always come knocking at the door with balloons and television cameras. Besides, you'll never win that shit. I don't know why you bother entering."

"Okay, since it wasn't them, could it have been Prince calling to tell me that he's finally come to his senses and wants to become my sex slave."

Nia smacked her lips at Neena. "You got jokes!"

Neena shrugged. "It could happen."

"Neena, you met Prince in passing *one time* after a concert when we were fifteen. You have a better chance of winning that damn Publisher's Clearing House than him calling here."

Neena realized that Nia did have a point. "I give up then. Those are the only two things that could happen that would rock my world right about now."

Nia started giggling and almost catapulted off the sofa. "How about the *Anissa Brand* Show calling and asking us both to be on the show?"

Neena threw her hands over her mouth. "Us? On a talk show? You can't be serious. Stop kidding."

"I'm dead serious. They want us on the show next Monday. They're willing to pay our plane fare to Chicago, put us up in a hotel, and cover all expenses if we'll do it."

"But why the hell would they want us on a talk show?" Neena wasn't buying it. It didn't make any sense for a talk show, especially the number one show in the country, to call them up. "Our lives aren't exciting enough to be on a talk show."

"Hmph, tell me about it. I was wondering the same thing until they told me the topic of the show."

"What is the topic?"

"Identical Twins, what else?"

"So we're twins. That doesn't mean we have something to sit on stage and talk about for an hour."

"Our segment will be more like ten minutes because we won't be the only twins on the show."

"But what on earth will we talk about, even for ten minutes?"

"What it's like being a twin, do we have ESP when it comes to each other, silly shit like that. And ummm..."

Neena didn't like Nia's hesitation. "And ummm what?"

"I wasn't going to tell you this part because I know it'll make you nervous. You'll have to find out sooner or later though."

"Find out?"

"The exact title of the show is 'America's Sexiest Twins.' They're having a contest."

Neena thought she was hearing things. "A contest? Oh, hell naw! You mean we have to wear bathing suits and do a talent portion and all of that?"

"Yeah, all of that." Nia held her breath, hoping Neena would at least consider it. She didn't have to wait long for an answer.

"No way, Nia," Neena said defiantly.

It's time to go into whine mode, Nia thought to herself. "Neena, don't do this to me. You know I've always dreamed about my ten minutes of fame and, now that the time has finally arrived, you're not messing this up for me."

Neena shook her head in dismay. "But a contest is so demeaning. It's like saying, 'Look at our asses and vote for us.' That's so shallow."

"Well, according to you, your ass is all of that anyway so that shouldn't be an issue," Nia said sarcastically. The whining wasn't working so now it was time for bitch mode. "Neena, don't make me get nasty. I can't do this without you. All I'm asking for is one day. More like two or three actually, but just one favor."

"The *Anissa Brand Show*, huh?" Neena asked, smiling a little.

That was her favorite talk show. "That's my girl. Remember when she was on that show *Ghetto Blues* when she was a kid."

Nia looked at her like she had completely lost it. "Of course, I remember. *Ghetto Blues* was better than *Good Times, What's Happening,* and *The Jeffersons* all rolled into one. I wonder what happened to the other cast members."

"Who knows? I heard Gary Lindsey, the brother that played Tyrone, got locked up for dealing drugs."

Neena got up and headed into the kitchen to get a Mystic out of the fridge. Nia followed her saying, "Damn shame so many child stars grow up and lose their minds."

"Yeah, well, Anissa didn't. She's got her shit together big time. She's big-boned, but the sister can dress her ass off."

"I just love it when bigger sisters tell the world, 'Fuck you! I'm big, but I'm the shit so kiss my ass to the red.'"

"I don't know if they say all of that, but I'm feeling you. Society places too much emphasis on body weight instead of what's inside."

"Amen to that." They high-fived each other. "I also like the way Sanaa Lathan was willing to put on twenty or thirty pounds to play Zora in *Disappearing Acts.* It was mad cool to see a sister with a realistic body frame in a love story."

"Yeah, more and more books are featuring healthy sisters, too," Neena commented.

"Cool, but back to the task at hand. Are you going to do the show or not?"

Nia put her hands on her hips and blocked the exit from the kitchen. She was determined to pull a Regis and get a final answer.

"I'll do it on one condition," Neena finally responded after downing half her bottle of grape juice.

"What's that?" Nia asked, hoping that it was a reasonable request.

Neena looked down at her navy pumps. "You help me do something about my feet before we go. I don't want the camera picking up chalk shots on close-ups."

Nia fell out laughing. "You're so silly! I'll scrub and buff those babies from now until Monday, if I have to, in order to go on the show."

They both guffawed and walked back out to the living room. Neena grabbed Nia by the back of her shirt to keep her in place. "Hold up! How did the *Anissa Brand Show* even find out about us anyway?"

Nia turned to face her. "Hell of a question and one of the first ones I asked. They said a friend of the family called in when they advertised the segment on a previous show."

"A friend of the family?"

"Are you thinking what I'm thinking? Who do we know that watches the Anissa Brand Show every single day?"

"Momma," Neena blurted out. Their mother was the number one Anissa fan.

"Yes, Momma. She probably demanded that they didn't reveal that it was her. She knew we'd be embarrassed."

Neena shook her head. This was just too much to be hit with in one day. "Let's just hope that Momma's not the only one who thinks we're sexy."

Nia spun around, bent her knees, and stuck her behind up in the air doing the dance called the Booty Bounce. "Sis, as good as we look, they better hire some extra security guards that day to keep the audience members from attacking."

Neena slapped her on the ass and giggled. "You're wild!"

Nia stopped dancing and started pulling Neena by the hand. "Let's go back here and decide on what to wear."

Neena pulled her backwards, toward the front door. "We're not wearing shit that's already in our closets. This calls for a trip to the mall. Are you driving or what?"

Chapter Fourteen

Neena glanced over at Nia, who'd been gnawing idly on her nails since they'd entered the Green Room. "Nervous?"

Nia sighed. "Can you spell Prozac?"

Neena took her hand and started rubbing it gently. She was shaking like a leaf. "Calm down, Nia. You were the one demanding that we go through with this. Now look at you, acting like you're ready to run for the nearest exit."

Nia glanced around the room, full of nine other sets of twins that were all beautiful, big-boobed, and banging in general. "Look at all these other sets of twins. They're gorgeous."

Neena let go of Nia's hand, resisting an urge to give her a beatdown. After all, they were in a beauty contest. "What did you expect? That they would have an America's Sexiest Twins Contest and we'd be the only ones here that didn't look like frogs?"

"Of course not, but the competition is fierce. Look at those blondes over there. They'll probably win. You know how men feel about blonde-haired, blue-eyed women."

Neena eyed the twins in question up and down and sucked on her teeth. "Yeah, well, I doubt that is their real hair color and I know their breasts aren't real. I'm surprised they're not leaking. Not to mention their flat asses."

"Oooh, Neena," Nia chided. "I think I see your fangs showing."

"Now that we're here, I'm determined to win this billy. You know me. If I can't win, I..."

"Don't want to play," Nia said, completing her sentence. One she'd heard Neena wear out since childhood.

Neena pointed her index finger at Nia. "Exactly."

Nia sat up straight in her chair. She had quite the competitive spirit herself. They'd come a long way and she wasn't content with leaving empty-handed. "Okay, I'm with you. Let's do this. Let's go out there and take that grand prize trip to Cancun and the cash prize."

Neena slapped her a high-five. "It's on now, Sissypoo!"

Anissa Brand, decked out in a ruby-red Eddie Bauer double-breasted pantsuit and a pair of sexy, high-heeled tan slingbacks took center stage to the monstrous applause of her studio audience. "Welcome! Welcome! Welcome to the *Anissa Brand Show*!"

"That sister is just too damn cool! Starr Jones doesn't have a damn thing on her!" Nia exclaimed as they all crowded around the monitor in the Green Room trying to see.

"Shhh, I'm trying to hear this!" Neena stated angrily.

They watched Anissa step down off the stage just long enough to shake the hands of some of the audience members in the first row.

"Have we got an extra special treat in store for you today," Anissa said, returning to the stage. "The first thing you'll probably notice is that today's audience is all male. We wanted to ensure that as many men as possible were given the opportunity to witness today's contest firsthand. That's right! I said contest. The men in the audience will get to vote on America's Sexiest Twins. Female, that is."

Neena shook her head in disgust as the studio cameras scanned over the men looking anxious like they were about to enjoy a peep show or porn flick. She elbowed Nia in the ribs. "I told you this was going to come down to an ass competition. Look at them, acting like animals and shit before anyone even walks out on the stage."

"Didn't you just tell me to be quiet?" Nia asked sarcastically, now all into what Anissa was saying.

"We searched the country for the cream of the crop and let me tell you, I've had a sneak peek at the photos sent in by friends and

family members that did the nominations and the women are all
extremely beautiful. Are you men ready?"

"Yeah!" one older white man yelled from the rear. He
appeared unshaven and looked like he could chew soda cans with his
razor-sharp teeth.

"Bring them on!" a young brother shouted out from the third
row.

Anissa grinned and threw her unbeweavable head back in
laughter. "The men look ready to me. Let the contest begin."

Nia and Neena made it through the first rounds of
competition to the finals. They'd endured the bathing suit round,
where they sported gold thong-back bikinis. They'd endured the
talent round, where they did a one-act play entitled *Lawd, why can't I
find a good man!* They figured the men in the audience would be
putty in their hands after that and they were. Men always like to feel
like the world revolves around them. They'd even endured the
degrading round, where the twins had to smear their choice of
chocolate sauce, whipped cream, or honey all over each other. Nia
could have sworn that one man had actually creamed in his pants
because he had that cum face.

It had all come down to the evening gown competition with
three sets of finalists: Nia and Neena, the blonde bimbos, and a pair
of redheads that seemed to turn men on because they looked studious.
The redheaded twins went first, while the other two pairs were placed
into soundproof booths so they wouldn't be privy to the question and
have time to make up a better answer.

They were followed by the blondes and then it was Nia and
Neena's turn.

"Neena and Nia, congratulations on making the finals,"
Anissa said, sashaying toward them as they came onto the stage.

"Thank you," Nia and Neena replied in unison.

"I am going to ask one question and give you both the
opportunity to answer individually."

"Okay," they replied in unison again, nervous to the nth
degree.

"What do you feel was the most significant event of this past millennium year?"

Neena was about to answer but Nia beat her to the punch, grabbing the microphone out of Anissa's hand, even though they were both wearing mikes attached to their black, skintight, back-out, Vera Wang evening gowns. Neena knew Nia was just trying to show off.

Nia rolled out her answer in one long, swooping breath. "Without question, I feel it was the 2000 Presidential Election. It was disheartening to find out that America is not the true democracy that our forefathers fought so hard to achieve. While every vote may count, electoral votes count more and that is unfortunate. Since the candidate that received most of the popular vote is not the one residing at 1600 Pennsylvania Avenue, I feel it is time to rethink the electoral college altogether and for Congress to take desperate measures to make sure that this never happens again."

"Excellent answer!" Anissa exclaimed. The audience rose to their feet in applause. Anissa took that opportunity to whisper in Nia's ear, "Preach on, my sister."

Nia blushed hard while Anissa turned her attention to Neena. "Neena, your response."

Neena leaned over and snarled into Nia's ear. "You took mine, heifer."

With that, she grabbed the microphone from Anissa that she'd retrieved from Nia and went for it. "The Elian Gonzalez fiasco. Don't get me wrong. I felt sorry for him and all of that, but the situation went on for far too long. Too much drama ensued, too much taxpayer money was wasted, and his father had the right to exercise his parental rights from jump street. While I sympathize with his Miami relatives, they had no legal rights to the boy and should have just turned him over peacefully instead of forcing the Attorney General to do what had to be done. There are far too many homeless, starving, and otherwise needy individuals in this country to spend millions of dollars and thousands of man-hours on one child."

Once again, the male audience members rose to their feet, putting their fingers in the corners of their mouths to whistle and yelling out chauvinistic remarks.

"Dang, you sisters ever considered going into politics?" Anissa said jokingly. She turned to look directly into a camera for a close-up. "We'll be right back to announce the winners after these messages."

During the commercial break, all of the twins, even the ones that didn't make it to the finals, came onto the stage awaiting the big moment. Some looked disappointed and a couple were even fighting back tears.

Neena asked Nia, "So what do you think our chances are?"

"Who knows? I bet we answered the questions the best though. Either that or Anissa is just pumping us up because we're the only Nubian sisters left in the contest."

Neena was about to comment on the statement when the blinding, bright lights came back up and Anissa struck her *I'm-the-shit* pose.

"We're back. Time to announce the winners of the America's Sexiest Twins Contest 2001."

A brother in a g-string that looked like he was hung like a bear sauntered onto the stage and handed Anissa an envelope. The men in the audience booed him away, trying to make sure people at home would realize that they weren't gay.

Anissa ripped the envelope open and pulled out an oblong card. "In third place, Mary Lou and Mary Ann from Nashville, Tennessee."

Nia looked at Neena and smirked. "I told you they wouldn't win. Blonde or not, those countrified accents did them in."

"Shhh!" Neena replied, hoping their mikes weren't still on. Nia was right though. The moment they'd opened their mouths, they were doomed and the horrid banjo talent act didn't help matters any.

It was the moment of truth. Nia and Neena clasped hands, already thinking about spending the money and catching bomb ass tans on the sandy beaches of Cancun.

"In second place, TJ and BJ from Dover, Delaware," Anissa announced. "That means that Neena and Nia from Kannapolis, North Carolina are our grand prize winners!"

"Oh, my goodness! We won! We won!" Nia started acting a

fool, hugging Neena so hard that she almost knocked her to the floor. She turned to Anissa and grabbed her elbows, jumping up and down.

Neena pulled her off Anissa, who was holding onto her head to make sure all the jiggling didn't make her weave fall off. "Calm down, Nia," Neena said. "Remember that we're still on TV."

Nia and Neena were given cheap tiaras, bouquets of roses, and had to strut down the makeshift walkway in front of the men. One man reached out and grabbed Nia's ankle. She glared down at him and he mouthed the words, "I want you, baby."

She yanked free from him and kept on going, catching up to Neena, who was a few steps in front of her.

"You know, normally I don't play favorites in situations such as these but, now that you've been declared the winners, I must admit that I was rooting for you," Anissa said after everyone had calmed down and the rest of the twins had been escorted off the stage and sent home with nothing but the memories of a free trip to Chicago. Nia and Neena looked at each other, finding it hard to believe that Anissa would come right out and admit her biased opinion. She continued, "That makes what is about to happen next even more rewarding."

Nia was lost and asked, "Happens next?" She looked at Neena and she shrugged, just as confused.

"Even if Nia and Neena didn't win the contest, they were still going to walk away with something more impressive than a trip to Cancun and money. Something that lasts a lifetime."

"What is she talking about?" Neena asked Nia. Not waiting for an answer, she asked Anissa directly, "What are you talking about?"

Anissa started giggling like a schoolgirl. "Ladies, during your pre-show interview you were asked if you've ever played that old switcheroo trick on unsuspecting victims." She stared at Nia. "Well, we should have administered a lie detector test on you, Nia, because we know all about what you did this past Christmas Eve."

Nia glared at her sister. "Neena!"

Neena went on the defensive. "I didn't have anything to do with this. I swear. You were the one that told me about the show."

"Ladies, don't bicker amongst yourselves. You'll ruin the

moment. Anyway, we know all about it and so does the studio audience. They've been in on this the entire time."

Nia was pissed off by that point. Her business was all over the airwaves—at least, the fact that she'd engaged in less than flattering behavior was. "Been in on what?"

"This is killing me and I can't hold it in one moment longer." Anissa chuckled.

"So don't!" Nia hissed at her.

"Nia, you weren't the only one playing games that night." Anissa decided to drag it out for a few seconds and let the possibilities of her last statement sink into the twins' heads. "Welcome Jacob and Jaleb from Durham, North Carolina to the stage."

Jacob and Jaleb came walking onto the stage, decked out in matching Aurelio Mattucci tuxedos. You couldn't tell one from the other.

Nia almost lost her balance. "Holy shit!"

Anissa leered at her. Kodak moment or not, she liked to keep the language on her show clean. She didn't like for those annoying bleeps to be placed over the chat. "Watch the mouth, sister!"

Nia rolled her eyes at Anissa and pushed Neena on the shoulder. "He has a twin?"

"I knew he had a brother but I didn't know they were twins!" Neena exclaimed, just as surprised about the turn of events.

When Jacob and Jaleb made it over to them, Anissa started squeezing their arm muscles. "This question goes out to all the ladies watching us at home. Are these two fine specimens of manhood or what?"

Some of the men in the audience looked annoyed, but most were elated about it.

"Hello, Neena," Jacob said, taking Neena's hand and kissing it.

"Hello, Nia," Jaleb said, repeating the same exact movements as his twin.

Nia yanked her hand away from Jaleb. "Are you trying to tell us that you...?"

Jaleb grinned uncomfortably. "Nia, I was the one you were with that night. Not Jacob."

"You bastard!" Neena shouted out, slapping Jaleb across the face and then turning to Jacob to slap him, too.

While Jacob was rubbing his cheek, Jaleb pleaded with her. "Neena, don't blame Jacob because he didn't know anything about it. He was kept out of the loop just like you were. This is all my doing." He looked Nia up and down. "Well, mine and Nia's. I'm just sorry you two got hurt in the process."

Jacob, determined not to leave Chicago without the woman he was meant to be with, recovered and pulled a slim, black velvet jewelry case from his inside tuxedo pocket. He handed it to Neena. "These are for you."

Neena opened the case. Inside was a string of expensive white pearls. "Thank you," she cooed, realizing that she would be attached to Jacob like sticky glue from that moment on. She'd never recovered from her feelings for him, no matter how much she'd tried to fool herself.

Jaleb figured since Neena was so receptive, Nia would be also. He took a similar case out of his pocket and held it out to Nia. "These are for..."

Nia knocked the case out of his hand and pushed him in the chest. "I hate you! Leave me alone!"

She stormed off the stage leaving everyone dumbfounded.

Chapter Fifteen

Two Months Later

Nia sat in front of her computer monitor, trying to concentrate on some work but feeling pitiful just the same. "Seeing Jacob again tonight?" she asked Neena, who'd just strolled into the living room from her bedroom decked out in a revealing black jumper.

"Yes, I am," she responded excitedly.

"That's good."

Neena was sick of watching Nia look pathetic. Every day when she came home, Nia would be sitting there with a deadpan expression on her face. She'd often sit in the dark for hours without the television or stereo on and didn't even leave the house at all except for basic needs. She was ready for Nia to cut the bullshit and deal with the facts. It was obvious that she was pining over Jaleb despite her professed hatred of him.

"You know Jaleb is still sulking around because you dissed him on national television," she said matter-of-factly.

"Let his ass sulk," Nia snarled back at her. "What he did was wrong."

"As opposed to what you did?"

Nia smacked her lips and got up from her desk chair to face her twin. "Okay, I admit I was wrong too but the next morning when I confessed, he should've done the same thing."

"True, but that doesn't mean he doesn't care about you." Nia took off down the hallway and into her bedroom. Neena was right on her tail and continued, "I don't know what happened between you that night, but it damn sure must have been magical. He's sweating you big time."

"I like Jaleb. I like him a lot." Nia collapsed on her bed and hugged a pillow. "I just can't see being with him now. Our relationship, if you can even call it that, started out based on a pack of lies. How can anything real come out of that?"

"Maybe it can. Maybe it can't. Only one way to find out."

Nia was quiet for a few seconds before asking, "He's really sweating me, huh?"

"Like you're a naked woman in a towel and he's a sauna." They both laughed. Neena sat down on the bed and started stroking Nia's arm. "Come on, Sissypoo. Take a chance. Go to Durham with me tonight to see him."

Nia pondered the invitation. Jaleb was wonderful. At least, he was at first. "That night, Christmas Eve, was the most romantic night of my entire life. I've never had a man do those things for me or to me."

Neena nudged her. "Then don't let him get away. You hate all the men you meet around here. Why keep dealing with them just to have a warm body in the bed next to you when you can have Jaleb?"

"Yes. Why indeed?"

Nia knocked on the door of a house she'd only spent one night inside of but yet still felt quite familiar. Jaleb answered the door without really looking at her. He just opened it and walked toward the kitchen.

"Neena, come on in. Jacob will be down in a second. He's upstairs on the phone."

She stood in the doorway and responded, "I'm not Neena."

He turned around and grinned. "Nia?"

Nia walked in and met him halfway in the center of the living room floor. "The one and the same. I asked Neena to let me come in first, hoping you would answer the door, so we could have a moment together."

Jaleb put his hands around her waist, leaned down, and whispered in her ear, "How about a lifetime together?"

Nia blushed and giggled, happy as hell that she'd allowed Neena to talk her into coming with her. "That might be able to be arranged."

By the time Jacob came downstairs and Neena came inside, Jaleb and Nia were making out heavily on the sofa.

"Let me grab my jacket," Jacob said to Neena, tiptoeing to the hall closet. "I think we should go out to dinner. Those two could use some privacy."

Once Jacob got his coat, Neena looped her arm through his. "I think we could use some privacy, too. Did I ever tell you that I have a discount card for the Holiday Inn?"

They shared a laugh as they walked out the door, leaving Jaleb and Nia to get reacquainted with one another.

Lessons Learned

By Shonda Cheekes

Chapter One

Clarissa looked over at the lifeless form that lay in the bed. The sight of him made her sick to her stomach. Her feelings for Clark had been through dramatic changes over the past few years. She tried to remember a time when the thought of him would bring out flutters in the pit of her stomach. Now the only feelings she could muster up for him made her nauseated.

Her nights had gotten longer within the past year, as she stayed clear of the bed long enough for him to fall into a deep, deep sleep. If she climbed in any sooner, she took the chance of him being all over her, and tonight was no different than any other. She was definitely in no mood to be prodded, poked, or pulled at. On those rare occasions when he was able to catch her off guard, she'd lie there almost as stiff as a board. The whole process felt as if she were being raped. And even though some would disagree that such a foul act could be committed by one's very own husband, no one's disagreement could invalidate Clarissa's feelings. She knew how and what she felt–and what she didn't.

She slowly crept out the bedroom pulling the door in ever so softly behind her, making her getaway downstairs to her office. Burying herself in a little work seemed like just the thing to occupy her long enough for the coast to be clear. She even thought of pulling out the sofa bed and just sleeping downstairs.

As she walked in and switched on the light, she searched

through the stack of papers for the new manuscript that had been overnighted to her. She needed to have it read and edited before week's end and today was already Wednesday.

She looked over at the computer and remembered that she'd forgotten to email her girlfriend about her upcoming visit. *Damn! I know she's probably overloaded my mailbox with a thousand emails,* she thought to herself as she switched on the monitor, simultaneously placing the manuscript to the side. The light from the humming machine began to fill the room and Clarissa's eyes were drawn to the illumination.

Sure enough, there were three emails awaiting her. "I'm waiting" was typed in the subject area. Clarissa smiled at the thought of her best friend. Sometimes she didn't know what she'd do without her.

Jeanette had been her roommate in college the entire four years. They'd been through both good and bad times with one another. Once college ended, Jeanette returned home to New York to make her mark in the fashion industry while Clarissa married Clark and followed him to Atlanta. They used their frequent flyer miles every chance they got to get together for something they called "Girlfriends Day"–a ritual they'd thought up their senior year, which consisted of a full day of pampering and fun. And it was time for another one of those spectacular get-togethers.

This time they were meeting on Jeanette's stomping grounds. She'd already made plans for a special spa day, knowing that Clarissa would surely need some rejuvenation after dealing with Clark on a day-to-day basis.

Clarissa opened the email and smiled at the idle threats from Jeanette. After reading the second one, she hit the reply button to send a quick note confirming her plans.

Hey girl, sorry I'm just getting back to you, but you know when duty calls I have to answer. And why are you asking me if I'm coming? Have I ever canceled out on you before? Well, other than the last time that is. N-E-way, count me in. I've already made my flight arrangements and my ticket will be waiting for me at the counter. So pick me up at JFK at our usual spot around 9:30 am. I can't wait to get there for a reprieve from my mundane existence around here. We'll talk more when I get there. Oh, make sure that the spa day is a full one. I *really* need it. Love ya…

Clarissa hit the send button and sat back in her black leather swivel chair as she waited for the confirmation telling her that the email had indeed been received. Suddenly a box popped up in the corner of her screen. "Another late night?" the familiar screen name asked.

"I'm always up this time of night. The question is what are you doing up this late?" She hit the send button.

"Checking to see if you'd gotten any of my messages. Is that rat still chasing your cat?" Jeanette typed in LOL, letting Clarissa know that she was laughing.

"You know it. Maybe in another hour or so, it'll be safe. Now, why are you really on here this late? You could've checked for my email tomorrow if anything. Don't you have an early morning?"

"I'm checking out this new web site."

"What new site?"

"BlackGentlemen.com. A friend from work sent me a link."

"BlackGentlemen.com? What, is it some kind of escort service or something?" This time Clarissa typed in LOL.

"Check it out and judge for yourself."

Blue highlighted and underlined writing appeared in the box flashing like a neon-lit entryway. Clarissa sat and stared at it for a second before deciding to take a peek.

After a few prompts she entered a site with pictures upon pictures of gorgeous black men.

"Are you there?" Jeanette asked.

"I'm here," she typed back.

"So…what do you think? Like what you see?"

Clarissa imagined the naughty grin that Jeanette probably had on her face as she asked that question. "I'm still looking."

She scanned the pages and pages of pictures until she came across one that was extremely familiar. "Oh, my God…" Her mouth hung open as she stared at the picture on her screen. "It can't be," she whispered as she clicked on the thumbnail to enlarge the image for a better look.

Before her was a picture of the man who had been a major part of her not too distant past. Her mind began to flood with memories as she continued to stare without blinking.

"JEANETTE!" Clarissa typed in so she'd get the effect of her screaming.

"I'm here. What's wrong? Did Clark come in?"

"You will not believe whose picture I'm looking at."

"Whose?"

"See for yourself." She sent Jeanette a direct link to the page.

"Oh, my God. Good ol' Julian Tulley. Or as I was calling him after your infamous incident—'Foolian' Tulley. I can't believe it."

"Me either."

"When's the last time you've seen him?"

"Not since that night."

"Damn. That's a long ass time. Ol' boy is still good-looking, too. Hey, his email address is on here. You should email him and see how he's doing."

"What?!! Are you crazy?"

"What's the harm in that?"

"Let's see… I'm married now." Before Clarissa could type the rest of her response Jeanette had beat her to the punch.

"Now didn't we just have a conversation the other day about your sorry ass marriage? Or am I just imagining that?"

"I know things aren't that great, but this is Julian."

"So? That's what so sweet about it."

Clarissa knew exactly what Jeanette meant by that comment. Clark had been extremely jealous of Julian. He was always throwing up in Clarissa's face how Julian had broken her heart. Never missing an opportunity to remind her that he had been her knight-in-shining-armor during those times.

"I don't know about this, Nette. I mean, you do remember that I was the dumpee in that relationship? Have you forgotten how long it took me to get over that?"

"Of course, I remember, but I also remember how Julian called nonstop trying to talk to you and how hard Clark blocked that from happening."

"I still don't know about this though. I mean…"

"Did you ever think of giving Julian a chance to explain why? Ya know, tell his side of the story?" Jeanette knew the answer to the question before she'd asked it.

Clarissa thought about the point Jeanette was making. She'd never given Julian a chance to explain himself. She'd simply never talked to him since.

"I really think you should email him. Even if it's anonymously at first. Feel him out and see if he has any ill feelings toward you. I'd say six years has been enough time for both of you to get over it by now."

"I'll think about it."

Reading over Julian's bio, she noticed that he'd never been married, didn't have any kids, and when she looked at his current place of residency, a smile slowly spread across her face.

"Did you get a chance to read his bio yet?" Clarissa asked Jeanette.

"I'm going through it now. Why?"

"Look at where it asks where you live." There was a pregnant pause before the screen became active with a virtual scream.

"GIIIIIRRRLLL… You've got to email him now! You'll be here in a few days and you can hook up with him while you're here!"

"Now why would I want to do that? You just keep forgetting that I'm married."

"And if you know like I know, you'll forget about it too. Look, all I'm saying is that you need some closure and I can bet he does also. And please don't mention anything else about that sorry relationship you keep calling a marriage. If your marriage is such a good thing, why is it that you're on the computer talking to me at this hour of the morning? Correct me if I'm wrong, but I thought married people *liked* to sleep with each other."

Clarissa had never really gone into all of the details of what was really ailing her marriage when talking with Jeanette. All she'd told her was that she wasn't physically attractive to him anymore, but she never gave her any specific reasons why. She never told her of the gradual changes that had begun to take place. But Jeanette's "best friend" intuition made her privy to information that didn't have to be communicated with words. She knew Clarissa would give her the details in time.

"I'm not going to push the issue anymore. Just think about it. Okay?"

"Okay."

"Well, I'm off to bed. Unlike you, I need a full five to seven hours of sleep if I want to function the next day…lol"

"All right then. I guess it's safe for me to crawl into bed now. I'll talk with you tomorrow. And I can't wait to see you!"

"Ditto for me. I'll give you a call tomorrow while I'm at work."

"All right, Girl. Love ya."

"Back at you."

Clarissa sat for a minute staring at the picture of Julian. Nothing about him had changed since the last time she'd laid eyes on him. Satin-smooth, caramel-colored skin; the set of identical dimples, twinkling light-brown eyes, and the smile that had once melted her heart stared back at her. Feeling a sudden urge to click the heart at the top of the page to add this page to her file of favorites, she simply placed his email address into her address book. "Maybe," she stated aloud to the empty room, as she signed off.

Chapter Two

Clark sat at the table with his head buried deep into the paper. Within reach was his daily cup of morning coffee. "Well, it's about time. I thought you'd never get up. Didn't you ever hear the expression 'The early bird catches the worm'?" was the greeting she received as she made her way into the kitchen.

"And good morning to you, too," Clarissa mumbled as she walked over to the fridge and pulled out the package of bacon, three eggs, and a box of opened grits.

"How long is it going to take you? I've got to be somewhere in less than an hour," Clark questioned.

Becoming agitated with his smugness, Clarissa silently searched through the cabinets.

"Well?" he poked.

She slowly turned around to look at Clark with all the disgust she felt for him at that moment blazing in her eyes. "Well what?! If you're in that much of a rush, then I suggest you pick something up on your way out. My breakfast will be finished once it's done." She bent down to pull out the pans she needed from the cabinets, making extra efforts to slam the pans around to let him know that she was on the verge of being pissed.

Clark laid the paper down on the table and looked at Clarissa as she turned her back on him to turn on the stove. "If your ass would get up like regular people, we wouldn't be having this conversation."

"Last time I checked, I remember being in charge of my own schedule. So getting up like regular people doesn't apply to me. That's one of the main reasons I elected to work from home. And come to think of it, you've been up long enough that you could've had breakfast waiting on me for a fucking change. But that would be too much like right." She cracked the eggs on the side of the glass bowl.

"That's why you work from home, Clarissa? Oh, so that's what you call it? Well, I hardly call what you do around here all day work," Clark snapped.

"You know, you can go to hell, Clark."

"So it's another one of those mornings, I see." He picked the paper up again and rolled his eyes toward the ceiling.

"And what type of morning would that be, Clark Keller?" She grabbed the whisk to blend the eggs and half-and-half, then poured the mixture into the pan awaiting on the stove.

"The type where you're a bitch. Keep getting smart with me and…"

Before he could finish his sentence, Clarissa had slapped the paper from his hands and was up in his face. "And what, Clark? Huh? What the fuck are you going to do? Because like I've told you before, you put your hands on me and it'll be the last time you ever touch anyone. So if that's what you're thinking, you better get that thought outta your head. Oh, maybe you're gonna say your favorite quote–what is it, Clark–oh, yeah, that you'll go somewhere else… a place where you're appreciated? Well, do us both a favor and stop making idle threats. Why don't you make like Nike and 'just do it'!" She stood directly in front of Clark, waiting for him to make a wrong move so she could spring on him like a cat.

"I think you need to check your food. Smells like your eggs are burning," Clark said coldly, trying to quickly change the subject and not lose face. He'd overstepped the boundaries and was in no mood to suffer the consequences. She glared at him as she slowly turned back around to check the food that was now sizzling on the stove.

After breakfast was finished and Clark was long gone, Clarissa went into her office to start on the manuscript again. Trying her best to get into the right frame of mind so that she could finish, she laid it down and stared at the computer. It seemed to beckon to her. No longer able to fight the urge, she gave in and booted it up.

"You've got mail" greeted her. Since Jeanette was the only person other than her boss who emailed her, she wondered what she wanted. The first email at the top of the page was from Jeanette, asking her the same question that she'd ended their conversation with the night before. "Are you going to email him?" Clarissa smiled to herself as she clicked open the message. Jeanette had to be admired for her persistence.

Hey, Girl, it's me. Like you don't know that already. I just wanted to know if you'd gotten around to emailing Julian? I know you haven't, but I really thought you should so…

Clarissa's heart began to pound against the wall of her chest as if it were trying to escape at the sight of that 'So.' She knew from past experiences that meant Jeanette had done something.

I did it for you. Yes, I know you'll think I'm overstepping my boundaries, but I was overcome by a spirit and it made me do it…lol (that's supposed to make you laugh) So, this is just a quick note giving you a heads-up so you won't delete any unfamiliar emails. Please don't be mad. You'll thank me later. Believe me. Love ya, Nette.

"How could she?" Clarissa blinked her eyes a few times in hopes that the message would somehow go away. But she knew no matter how many times she blinked, it would be the same. After a moment of reflecting on what was the worst thing that could happen, a feeling of hope replaced the ones of anger and fear. Then it dawned on her that she hadn't paid attention to any other messages in her box.

Closing the note from Jeanette, she began to quickly scroll through the rest of her emails. She received so much junk mail that she'd gotten into the habit of deleting them without even opening them. But not today. She rolled past them until she came across something that was from an actual person. After opening and closing five different emails, she saw it. There, at the very bottom, was an email from ThBesMn4u. Typed in the subject area was "A Blast From The Past" and immediately, she knew it was from him. Shocked at how quickly he'd responded, she was a little hesitant about opening it. Her hand began to shake slightly as she positioned the pointer to open it. The nasty way things had ended between them rushed back to her and she began to hope that he'd had a chance to put it behind him as she'd done…

Six years before, Clarissa was a senior at Hampton University and deeply in love with her high school sweetheart. For three years, they'd managed to sustain a long distance relationship and had plans to marry as soon as they were finished with school.

It was a few days until Christmas break. Midterms were done and everyone was packing up for the long awaited break. Clarissa and Julian had made plans to spend some time in the Bahamas during the first part of their break and enjoy the last few days at home in Orlando with their families.

Ever since he'd laid eyes on her coming out of freshman orientation, Clark had done everything possible to get with Clarissa. No matter how many times she'd told him that she was involved, he'd never given up. There'd even been occasions when he'd seen her with Julian during his monthly visit down from Georgetown.

This would torment Clark to no end–especially since he'd bragged to his frat brothers, three years earlier, that Clarissa was going to belong to him.

But over the years, despite his arrogant and sometimes obnoxious ways, Clarissa saw a soft side beneath Clark's overly confident exterior. Thus, she befriended him and grew to trust him. Believing that their friendship was harmless, the two began doing things friends did, along with a host of other friends, of course. But in Clark's mind, this mirage of a platonic relationship was merely part of his plan to get Clarissa to be his. He figured he'd just wait it out and when the time was right, go in for the kill. After all, he had the upper hand over Julian. He was there every day.

Clark had just returned from a weekend visit to his family in

D.C. Needless to say, he couldn't wait to get back to tell Clarissa of his findings while there.

"What's up, Jeanette? Where's your girl?" he asked as he approached Jeanette coming out of Magrew Towers.

"Oh, it's you. She's in the room packing. I thought you were gone already." Jeanette looked at him, wrinkling up her nose. She never liked Clark, nor did she trust him. Being from a big city, she was much more skeptical of people than Clarissa and although she could never pinpoint it, there was something about Clark that just didn't sit right with her.

"Naw. I just went for the weekend. I'll be here during break." He zipped his coat up higher and shoved his hands deep in the pockets.

"Oh," she dryly responded, not wanting to waste any more time than necessary talking to him.

"Do me a favor and get Clarissa for me? I need to talk with her 'bout something."

Jeanette looked down at the boxes in her arms and then back at Clark. "Homey, I don't think so. You seem to know how to barge in any other time so, as Martin says, 'Get-to-steppin'." She turned and walked off in the direction of her car in the parking spaces across from the building.

"All right then. Be that way. I hope she's dressed," he yelled behind her.

"Yeah, I bet you do," Jeanette called back over her shoulder.

"You've got that right," he mumbled under his breath.

Clark sauntered into the building and glanced at the empty desk where visitors were expected to sign in. Room 102, which was just around the corner, had been Clarissa and Jeanette's for the past two years. Lightly tapping on the door, he stood back and waited to hear her sweet voice invite him in.

"Who is it?" she yelled through the door.

"It's your favorite man. Open up."

"Who?" she yelled back.

"It's Clark."

"Clark?" she said to herself as she walked over to the door.

Flinging it open, she stood with her hands on her hips.

Decked out in Georgetown sweats, her golden skin was glowing from the light layer of sweat that she'd worked up while packing.

"Hey, Beautiful. You busy?" He leaned against the door frame.

Does he always have to ask stupid questions, she thought. "Yeah. I guess you could say that. What do you need?"

He straightened up and brushed past her as he walked in. Knowing that the words "Come in" never passed her lips, she suppressed the urge to tell him off. She thought she'd be nice today. Maybe he'd be of some use and help her get the rest of her things packed up.

"I came on campus to pick up something from Darryl and thought I'd check on you before you left."

"Well, you've seen me. Now, I'm hoping you'll help me finish packing. You can talk and pack, can't you? Julian will be here tomorrow to pick me up and I'm only halfway finished." She proceeded to put her things in the neatly-aligned duffel bags on the floor.

Clark walked around checking out the pictures that were posted on the walls and the corkboards. The majority of them were of her, Julian, and Jeanette while others were of the various friends she'd made over the years at Hampton. He was surprised to actually find one of him and her. They were hanging out at the student union after a concert at the Convocation Center.

"You know I went up to D.C. over the weekend?" With his finger, he traced the flowery design on the top of the porcelain jewelry box that sat on her dresser.

"I think I remember you saying something about going up there. Did you have a good time?" she asked as she stood in her closet, pulling out the last few items.

"Oh, no doubt. I love hanging with my peeps." He picked up the box and handed it to her so it would seem that he was helping. She gestured for him to put it in one of the bags.

"I wish I would've been able to go, but Julian was tied up with finishing his exams." She closed the closet door and made her way over to the dresser.

"Oh, really?" He grabbed a few of the things she had on the bed and placed them in her trunk.

"Yeah. We barely talked this weekend. But, we'll make up for it in a few days." She smiled as she started to place the pictures in one of the photo albums that sat on Jeanette's bed waiting to be packed.

Clark knew this was an opportune time to hit her with the news he'd ultimately come to give her. From the moment he'd left D.C., he couldn't wait to see her. The information he had was so hot, it was burning a hole in his tongue.

"Is that so?"

"Yep."

Clark grabbed her arm to make her stop and look at him. "Clarissa... I have something to tell you."

"What? I can do more than one thing at a time." She removed his hand from her arm and went back to packing.

"I think it's best if you sit for this." He sat on her bed and patted a spot next to him. Clarissa opted to sit across from him on Jeanette's bed instead.

"Okay, Clark, what is it?" She gave him her undivided attention.

"I don't know how to tell you this but..."

"But what?" Clarissa hated when people dragged things out.

"I saw Julian this weekend. And he didn't look like he was testing to me."

"What are you talking about, Clark?"

"I guess it's best to just tell you."

Clarissa felt her stomach churn. She didn't like where this was going. "I guess so."

"My cousin and I saw Julian at the movies with another girl. And they looked a little more than friendly to me."

Clarissa immediately jumped up to resume her packing. "You are so full of shit."

Clark walked over and grabbed her by the shoulders. "Look, I'm telling you the truth. If you don't believe me, we can call my cousin. He has no reason to lie to you."

Clarissa tried her best not to think about what Clark had just told her. She snatched the remaining clothes off the bed and stuffed them into her suitcase.

"Ya know, Clark–I knew this day would come. You've been trying to get with me for years, but I thought you'd gotten over that. I knew this day would come! Julian told me this day would come!" she irately spewed.

Clark threw up his hands. "Hey, game recognizes game, Clarissa–and your boy, Julian–oh, he's got more game than Dave & Buster's. Look, I'm just trying to be a friend. I'd hate to see you get hurt."

"Well, thanks for telling me, Clark. If you don't mind, you've gotta go. I've got things to do." She walked over and opened the door for him.

He slowly rose from the bed and strolled to the door. Just before he was fully out, he looked back at her. "If you need someone to talk to, just call, okay? I'm here for you, Boo. Remember that. Okay?"

She focused on the socks on her feet. "Thanks, but no thanks."

As soon as he was gone, she ran over to the phone. "I know Clark is lying." She nervously punched in Julian's number.

"Speak to me," his roommate piped into the phone as he picked up on the second ring.

"Hey, Manny, it's Clarissa. Is Julian there?"

"What up, Rissa? Naw, he ain't here." He yawned.

"Well, could you tell him to call me as soon as he gets in? Tell him it's very important that he does. Okay?"

"Aiight. I'll do that. Yo, tell that fine ass roommate of yours that I'm still waiting on her call."

"I will. Thanks, Manny."

"No problem."

"Bye." Clarissa slowly placed the phone on her dresser. Still reeling from the shock of the news that Clark had delivered, Clarissa lost her desire to pack. She walked over to the window and watched as people packed up their cars and said their good-byes. Some hugged while others kissed, all trying to seal the short separation that lay ahead. Trying her best to keep her emotions under control, she blinked her eyes to fight back the fountain of tears as they built up in the corners of her eyes. She shook her head. "He's lying."

"Well, that's almost everything. You're not finished yet?"

Clarissa hadn't noticed that Jeanette had come back in the room. She tried to dry her face of the evidence that something was wrong. "I was just taking a quick break." She lifted her sweatshirt to wipe a little more effectively.

"A break? Girl, please. You have more junk than anyone else in the dorm. If you don't get up and finish, you'll still be here packing when everyone comes back. I keep telling you to give away some of these clothes and shoes." Realizing that she was engaged in a one-sided conversation, she walked over to the window where Clarissa was standing.

"You okay?"

"Okay," Clarissa answered halfheartedly as she walked over to her empty closet.

Jeanette followed her as Clarissa stood staring into the empty closet. As soon as she placed her hand on Clarissa's shoulder, a flood of tears gushed out. Her shoulders began to heave and quake from the heavy sobs that escaped her throat.

"What's wrong? Did Clark do something to you?" Jeanette rubbed Clarissa's back as she guided her to the bed to sit.

"No. He didn't do anything," she managed to gulp out in between sobs.

"Then what is it?" Jeanette grabbed a few tissues out of the box on Clarissa's dresser and began to mop the tears from her face.

"It's not what he did... it's more of what he said." Clarissa began to cry at full blast again.

Jeanette was doing her best to calm Clarissa down. She wanted to get to the bottom of what had just happened in the short time she'd been outside.

Clarissa spilled out the story of what had unfolded to Jeanette. After listening intently to everything Clarissa was telling her, Jeanette knew her question would sound cruel. "And you believe him? Girl, Clark's been trying to get with you since day one. Don't you know he'd do anything to break you and Julian up?"

Clarissa shrugged her shoulders and flopped back on the bed. "I don't know, Nette. It's just that..." she sniffled, "when I tried to call

Julian this weekend, I either got no answer or Manny on the other end telling me that Julian wasn't there. And when I called a few minutes ago to find out what's going on, Manny said he wasn't there again." She grabbed her pillow and hugged it tightly to her body.

"Well, first things first. Let's call Julian again. Give him a chance to deny it or admit it, ya know? 'Cause it's pretty hard for me to believe anything that Clark tells you about Julian. You know damn well that he has nothing but animosity toward him. And as long as he's been after you, that makes it even harder to believe." Jeanette grabbed the phone up from its resting place.

"Who are you calling?" Clarissa asked.

"Who do you think?"

"I just called there a few minutes before you came into the room and he wasn't there."

Jeanette continued to dial the number anyway. "Well, he may have walked in since then."

Clarissa sat up in the bed, leaning her back against the wall. "I don't know... I mean, I don't think I want to talk to Julian right now."

Jeanette looked at her with disbelief. "What?! Girl, get yourself together. We're going to get the bottom of this To-day! Even if it means we have to drive our asses up to D.C. tonight. "

"Hello?"

"Who is this?!" she barked into the phone.

"Who you wanna speak to?" the male voice barked back.

"Julian, if that's not a problem!" Jeanette sat down in the chair.

"Yo... who this callin' here actin' like they ain't got no manners?"

Jeanette instantly knew it was Manny. Only he could murder the English language so horribly.

"It's Jeanette. I need to speak to Julian. Now."

"He ain't here now. What I wanna know is, why you callin' him and not me? He's already spoken for—while on the other hand, I'm 100% A-VAIL-A-BLE."

"Because I need to talk to him and not you... Okay?" He could really work her nerves. If he weren't so damn cute, she wouldn't even waste her time going back and forth with him. He would've heard the dial tone right after he said he wasn't there.

"Why y'all lookin' for him? Rissa just called here not too long ago and now you. What's up?"

"Look, can you get in touch with your boy? It's ex-treeem-ly important that he call us. And soon. Okay?"

"I'll see what I can do."

"Thanks, Manny. When this is all straightened out, I'll give you a call. Okay?" Jeanette said, sounding as sexy and convincing as she could in an attempt to make him locate Julian sooner.

"Aiight. Let me hurry up and find dude so you can do that. Later right?"

"Yeah, later." Jeanette hung up the phone before he was able to pull her into anything else that she didn't want to be a part of. But, at the moment, she was willing to give him a call if he could get Julian to call them back.

"What did he say?" Clarissa looked at her through partially swollen eyes, her nose almost as red as Rudolph's.

"He's going to try and find him. Don't worry. I know this is just a hoax. But if it isn't, Julian's going to regret this day forever."

After not hearing anything for hours, Jeanette decided it was time to make that drive. Clarissa was skeptical at first, but Jeanette convinced her that it was the best thing to do.

True to his word, Clark volunteered to drive them up in his car. While Jeanette wasn't too enthused with him being in the mix of things, she went along with it because of Clarissa. And the fact that Clark's '91 BMW was a lot more comfortable than her old clunker made his offer even more enticing.

By the time they reached the campus, the sun had long said its good-byes. The campus buzzed with life as students celebrated the end of the term.

Clarissa gave Clark instructions on how to get to Julian's place. Once there, she asked him to wait in the car while she and Jeanette went inside. He tried to talk her into letting him come just in case, but she convinced him to stay behind.

The walk to the front door was the longest Clarissa had ever taken in her life. Her heart pounded violently against her ribcage and filled her ears with the unsteady rhythm of its echo.

Jeanette looked over at her as they reached the door. Clarissa's face was blank as her skin began to lose its color.

"You want me to do it?" Jeanette asked as she hovered her finger in front of the doorbell.

Clarissa slowly shook her head "no." If it had to be done, she'd be the one to do it.

As soon as she'd pressed the small white button, the door opened and an unfamiliar face greeted her. As Clarissa tried to find her voice, the impatient girl on the other side spoke up.

"Can I help you?" she asked.

Clarissa slowly blinked her eyes and she was about to give her answer when she heard a voice call out, "Who is it, Brie?"

"I'm trying to find out. I guess they're here for Manny." She looked back at Clarissa and Jeanette with a wicked grin that curled up the corners of her mouth.

"If you don't mind waiting a few minutes, he'll be right back. He just made a quick beer run."

"Brie!" Julian called out.

"Coming, J," she crooned in a sexy voice. "Why don't you guys come in? I have to take Julian a towel."

Clarissa was speechless as Jeanette shoved her into the apartment to confront her biggest fear. She looked around at the familiar place. She'd been there numerous times, but this was the first time she'd ever felt uncomfortable. This was the first time that she actually felt like a guest–and an unwelcome one at that.

The almond-colored girl with a short, light-brown bob, who Julian had endearingly referred to as "Brie," left them standing in the living room as she disappeared into Julian's room. Clarissa could hear the bathroom door open and him thanking her for the towel.

"Girl, get your ass in there," Jeanette stated to Clarissa between clenched teeth.

Her feet felt like ten-pound weights as she trudged her way toward Julian's room. The door was closed and panic began to set in.

What was going on in there? She placed her ear to the door so she could eavesdrop.

"So, who was at the door?" Julian asked.

"Two chicks for Manny."

Clarissa couldn't believe that she'd made no mention that they were still waiting in the living room. She placed her hand on the knob and slowly turned it. When she finally opened the door, what she found would take years to remove from her memory.

Julian stood in the doorway of the bathroom with only a towel draped around his waist. Brie was sprawled out across his bed in nothing but her Vicki secrets.

"What the..."

"Rissa?! Wha-whaa-t are you doing here?" Julian glanced over at Brie, who was trying her best to cover up.

"How could you?" Clarissa screamed.

Jeanette jumped to her feet and ran to the door as Clarissa came storming out. She glanced in the room and shook her head.

Julian tried desperately to grab something quick to put on.

"Let's go, Nette. Now!" Clarissa screamed as she fumbled with the door.

Jeanette came up behind her and opened the door just as Manny appeared on the other side.

"Hey! What's up?!" he excitedly questioned when Clarissa nearly knocked him down as she made her escape. In his stumble, he caught Jeanette by the arm and asked, "What's going on? What happened?"

Jeanette shrugged her shoulders and shook her head in disgust before replying, "Go ask your boy." She squirmed free of his grip and ran to catch up with Clarissa, who was racing down the narrow steps of the building.

"Rissa! Rissa, wait!" she yelled to her friend's back.

But Clarissa refused to stop until she reached Clark's car. "Let's go! Now! Get me out of here!" Her face was streaked with a constant flow of tears.

Clark started the car and waited for Jeanette to scramble into the back. "What the hell happened?"

"Rissa?" Jeanette sighed, reaching over and touching her friend gently on the shoulder.

Because Clarissa began to bawl uncontrollably, Jeanette talked her into sitting in the back with her. As Jeanette made her way to the rear seat, she heard someone calling her name. She knew it was Julian. Too shaken to confront him and too enraged to reply, she hurriedly climbed in and demanded Clark drive off.

"Clarissa, Baby, wait! It's not what you think!" Barefoot and running, he was trying to pull his shirt over his head in an attempt to cover up from the cold air.

Jeanette rolled down the window. "You're right, Julian! It's what she saw that has her upset!" she screamed as Clark nearly hit him while backing up.

Beating on the window of the car, he begged, "Please, Rissa! Don't leave! Let me explain!"

Clark rolled down his window this time. "My man, I don't think she wants to hear it. Now, if you don't mind, get your fucking hands off my car and move before I hit you this time." Clark smiled at Julian as he sped off. He felt victorious as he left Julian cursing him and begging his soon-to-be ex-flame.

The ride back was eerily quiet. The only sounds to be heard were those of the traffic outside and the engine of Clark's beemer. Jeanette sat with Clarissa's head in her lap while she tried to console her and stop her crying.

As Clark pulled up in front of the dormitory, he couldn't help feeling just a wee bit guilty. After all, he had been the bearer of the news. However, he simply justified to himself that all was fair in love and war and that he was the best man standing. And although he had only been the messenger, Clarissa was upset with him too, not even saying good-bye as she exited the rear door of the vehicle.

Upon arrival back to the room, the girls couldn't help but immediately notice the answering machine's red light swiftly flashing, indicating that someone had been trying to reach them. Knowing that it was none other than a barrage of calls from Julian, Clarissa quickly erased the messages without so much as taking a listen.

"I don't ever want to hear his voice again," she sternly stated.

"What are you going to do now? I mean, your plans for the break? I would tell you to come with me, but it's too late to make other arrangements. Buying you a ticket now would cost a grip," Jeanette explained.

"Don't worry about me. You go and have a good time. I'll be okay," Clarissa responded through clogged nostrils.

"Well, you can't stay here. Are you going to call your parents and have them come pick you up?" Jeanette asked.

"I'll manage." Clarissa walked around the now empty room, pulling her luggage to the door when the phone rang. The two young women simultaneously made eye contact and after the fourth ring, Jeanette walked over and picked it up.

"Yeah?" she asked into the receiver.

"Oh thank God, you're there. Nette, please let me speak to Rissa. I'm on my way there," Julian pleaded with Jeanette.

"Look, I don't think you should come here. She doesn't want to talk to you now. So do us all a favor and just stay away," she replied.

"Nette, please. It's not what she thinks. I just need to talk to her for a moment. Please, Nette," he whined.

Jeanette began to feel sorry for him, but her loyalty belonged to Clarissa. She placed her hand over the mouthpiece of the phone. "What do you want me to tell him? I think he's crying, Rissa."

Clarissa paused for a moment, then shook her head violently and began to grab her bags. "Tell him I'm not here. Tell him I don't want to see him. Tell him I don't want to talk to him. Tell him that he's dead to me!" She frantically ran around the room shoving the last of her things into a knapsack.

"Look, Julian, I know you want to talk to her, but I think you should give her some time now. She's not going to talk to you and, by the time you get here, she'll be gone," Jeanette explained.

"Gone? Where? How?" he asked.

"Just turn around, Julian. Turn around." With that, Jeanette hung up the phone on him and looked at her best friend.

"Is he still coming?" Clarissa asked.

"I guess he's on the freeway now. So, what are you gonna do?

If you don't want to talk to him, you're gonna have to leave tonight," Jeanette told her.

Clarissa picked up the phone and punched in Clark's cell phone number. After talking for a few seconds, she turned to Jeanette. "Help me get my bags."

"Please don't tell me you're going to Clark's?"

"Where else am I going to go? Everyone else is gone and Julian doesn't know where he lives."

Jeanette was uncomfortable with the arrangement, but she knew there was no other way. She reluctantly helped Clarissa pull her bags out to the circular drive and stood with her as they waited for Clark to pull up. She prayed Julian wouldn't get there before Clark got back to pick Clarissa up. Hopefully, he wouldn't come before she was able to get out of there herself. There was no way she was going to talk with him either.

"You know if you need me, just call and leave a message. I'll check my voicemail every chance I get, okay?" Jeanette assured her.

"No. I don't want to ruin your cruise. Why should you be miserable because my life is pathetic? You have a good time and call me when you get back." She tried to smile as they hugged.

Clark came around the corner almost at full speed. He stopped in front of them, popped his trunk, and quickly jumped out to load her bags.

"You be careful with that snake, Rissa," Jeanette whispered into her ear.

She smiled for the first time since Clark had dropped the bomb on her. "He's harmless, Girl. I'll be okay." They shared their final embrace for the year of 1992 right before Clarissa and Clark pulled off.

When school resumed, Clarissa surprised Jeanette with a key to their new off- campus apartment, along with the news that she'd spent the break with Clark, and that they were now a couple. For the remaining four months of school, she'd refused to make any contact with Julian. And as soon as they'd graduated, she and Clark were married and moved to Atlanta. How her life had changed in the blink of an eye.

Clarissa sat immobile in front of her computer, thinking she'd buried the memory of that horrible night in an unreachable place years ago. But how easily it had come back at just the thought of seeing him again. She felt it was time for her to hear him out. But was she ready for what he had to say?

Chapter Three

Checking one last time to make sure she wasn't forgetting anything, Clarissa placed her bags at the foot of the stairs. "You ready yet?" Clark yelled up to her.

"In a sec. Could you put my bags in the car for me?" She closed the junk drawer in the bathroom and turned out the light.

"Damn. You'd think you were going forever with all the shit you've got here." He picked up the larger bag and headed to the car.

"I wish I was," she mumbled to herself.

She straightened the waist of her jeans and adjusted the collar of her black leather, three-quarter-length coat. Making one last glance at her room, she turned out the light and headed down the stairs. She picked up the last two bags at the bottom and walked out to load them in Clark's convertible BMW.

"Why didn't you just drive my truck?" She motioned toward the black Lexus RX300 that was parked next to him. "It would have more room for my bags." She dropped the bags at his feet.

"I don't want to drive that shit. What's the big deal? It's just the two of us riding, so what I can't get in the trunk can go in the back." He threw the other bags in the trunk.

"Well, I hope you're not planning to put the top down. I don't want my hair to be a mess when I get there." She placed her carryon bag in the back seat along with her laptop.

"Actually I was, but since I don't feel like hearing your mouth, I'll keep it up until I drop you off."

"I appreciate it," she said to him. Glancing at him from the corner of her eye, she couldn't wait until she stepped foot out of his car at Hartsfield. She would do her best not to make much conversation with him on their short drive to the airport. She was still angry with him for asking her if he could drop her off at MARTA to catch the train to the airport.

Asshole, she thought. It would be so nice to be away from him for a week.

He pulled into Delta's terminal and jumped out to unload her bags. She gathered her things from inside and motioned for a skycap.

She walked around to the back of the car where Clark was close to tossing her bags out. "You don't have to be so eager. I'll be out of your hair... I mean your scalp—in a few minutes." She knew Clark was sensitive about the loss of his hair. After his hairline had begun to recede, she'd talked him into just shaving it all off.

"Not soon enough," he tried to mumble under his breath. Clarissa fought the urge to challenge him on it. She reminded herself that she was almost gone. And she refused to let him put a damper on her trip.

After squaring things up with the skycap, she turned to Clark to bid him farewell. "Don't have too much fun while I'm gone." He made a half-hearted attempt to kiss her.

"I'll try not to," he said dryly.

She turned and walked into the terminal without looking back, not wanting Clark to see the smile that was on her face.

Two hours later, she was standing in the terminal at JFK. She was so excited about seeing Jeanette. They'd had to cancel the last Girlfriends Day. Clarissa was trying to meet a deadline and Jeanette was away on business in Europe.

Spotting Jeanette, Clarissa rushed toward her with outstretched arms.

"Nette!!" she exclaimed as they hugged each other tightly.

"Rissa!!" Jeanette called back as they made a spectacle of themselves.

"Girl, I thought I was going to be late. I just got here." Jeanette grabbed one of the bags from Clarissa's hands.

"I'm surprised to see you here. I thought I'd have to meet you in our usual place. In baggage claim." They both laughed.

"Well, I shocked you, didn't I? Let's get your bags so we can go grab something to eat. I hope you're starving. There's this new place that I want to try out."

"Girl, am I! I was rushing so to get out of the house this morning that I forgot to eat something."

Once they were comfortable in Jeanette's '99 silver Passat, she chimed in about Julian.

"So…"

Clarissa knew where she was going, but decided to string her along. "So what?" She looked out the window at the beautiful New York skyline.

"Don't play with me, Woman. You know what I'm talking about. What's up with the man?" She playfully tapped Clarissa on her shoulder.

"Oh… Clark is his usual self."

"An Asshole," they both chimed in unison.

"Stop playing, Girl. I want to know if you had a chance to talk to Julian." She clicked on the radio to Hot97.

"Oh, that. Yeah. I emailed him back." She turned her attention back to the scenery.

"Well?"

"Well, what?" She smiled.

"Don't make me go ghetto on your ass, okay?"

Clarissa laughed. "Well, now, since you put it that way." She laughed.

"I'm serious. What did he have to say?"

"Nothing much. We talked about how each of us is doing now… He asked me about you… Oh, yeah, we made plans to meet up for dinner tomorrow night."

Jeanette began to scream at the top of her lungs with delight, swerving slightly as she wiggled around in her seat.

"Girl, you better keep your eyes and mind on the road." Clarissa sat up and pulled on her seatbelt.

"I'm so happy, Rissa."

"Why? We're just having dinner. He may not be romantically interested in me any more. And I keep telling you..."

"Please don't say anything about being married again. I don't need to be reminded of the terrible mistake you made years ago."

Clarissa was hurt by the comment, but knew that Jeanette was telling the truth. As much as she loved her friend, she was too in love with the idea of marriage to listen to her warnings.

Clarissa turned her attention back to the passing scenery. She always wondered where she would've ended up if she hadn't married Clark. Jeanette tried to get her to move to New York with her. At one point, she'd seriously considered it, but after getting involved with Clark, the thought never crossed her mind again.

Jeanette glanced over at her. "What are you thinking so hard about?"

"Nothing. Just enjoying the ride." She leaned her head back against the headrest, closed her eyes, and relaxed as the sun made its way into the car to warm her face.

"Yeah, right. You're over there reminiscing about what it used to be like."

"Your mind is forever in the gutter," said Clarissa.

"Well, evidently he's looking for somebody or he wouldn't have his info posted on that site."

Clarissa hadn't given it a second thought that she found him on BlackGentlemen.com, which was clearly a site that was in the business of helping people connect.

Jeanette reached down and turned the radio up. Her favorite morning show was on Hot97.

Feelings from the past were running rampant through Clarissa's brain. I'm married, she told herself. She'd regretted the breakup with Julian and had considered trying to work things out at one point. But she knew she'd never get beyond that fateful night. She thought back to the email...

Hey, lady,
I must admit that I was shocked when I saw the email from Nette. Especially after trying to reach you for years. I'm glad that life is

treating you well. I'm doing okay myself. Can't complain. Heard you're going to be in the Big Apple in a few days. I hope you can find it in your heart to make a little time for me. I'd love to see you. Send me an email and I'll give you all my information. If you don't get back to me, I'll know that you don't want to see me and I won't bother you again. I hope that you do though. I was in Orlando a few months ago and rode by your parents' house. No one was there and I never got around to going back before I left. Can't believe it's been six years since we've seen or talked to each other. I'm still trippin' on you marrying Clark. I guess he got what he wanted. Do me one favor… please email me. Give me a chance to make things right between us. I hope that's not too much to ask. So, I'll be waiting for your response. Thinking of you, Julian.

After she'd emailed him a short and simple response, he sent her his information and made arrangements to take her to dinner. He promised her that he'd set things straight about that night for once and for all.

Wonder what he has to say? she thought to herself. Deciding to hear him out, she'd find out tomorrow night.

Chapter Four

Clarissa and Jeanette spent the morning being pampered at Gazelle's Beauty Spa in Manhattan on 54th Street and Madison. They'd gotten one of the deluxe packages. Jeanette turned Clarissa down when she offered to pay her share of the bill. She insisted that it was her treat.

"Girl, is this nice or what? I love coming here. Sometimes I come during my lunch break. After I get back, I feel refreshed and then I can deal with the assholes on my job."
Clarissa laughed at her. "That's one of the things I love about New York. Everything is so centrally located. You can either walk up the block or round the corner and find whatever you need." Clarissa lay stretched out on her stomach, enjoying her full body massage.

"That's why I'm never leaving. I'm too adapted to New York life. I hate to hear people complain about New York. It's no worse than anywhere else. Besides, most New Yorkers are very successful. That is, if they put their mind to it." A pleasurable moan escaped her lips as the attendant kneaded her shoulders.

"This has got to be what heaven is like. At least, I hope it is." They laughed out loud.

Their lite lunch from the spa had worn off two hours after their departure from the facility. "Let's go to Au Bon Pain and grab a couple of pastries. Can't have you too full tonight," Jeanette suggested as they strolled down the street.

Clarissa had thought about Julian more than a few times

throughout the day. Trying hard to clear her mind of everything, her brain seemed to be preoccupied with thoughts of him. Then she remembered something.

"Oh, shit!" she shouted.

"What's wrong?" Jeanette glanced at her, concerned.

"I just realized something."

"What?"

"I've been here for twenty-four hours and I haven't called Clark." They looked at each other for a moment, then burst into laughter.

"Noticed something else? He hasn't called me either." They started to laugh even harder.

"I guess he's got that syndrome that Eddie Murphy joked about," said Jeanette.

"Which one?" Clarissa laughed.

"Remember that joke about how a man never thinks that his woman would cheat on him while she's away because his mind is too preoccupied with how much pussy he's going to get while she's gone."

"Oh, yeah! I remember that. I bet that's exactly what Clark is doing." Clarissa laughed again—a little too much for Jeanette not to pick   up   on   the   sincerity   of   the   remark.

"So, you think he's cheating on you?" Jeanette looked over at her. The smile that had previously occupied her face was replaced by a very concerned look.

Clarissa had yet to confide in her friend about her discovery six months earlier. Knowing that she'd eventually tell her, she hadn't been in the mood to be nagged by Jeanette about how she should leave him. They'd worked through it. At least, she felt they had. She knew her feelings toward him had changed drastically since then.

"So, are you going to tell me? Or do I have to go into ghetto mode on you?" Jeanette stopped and sat on a bench along 5th Avenue.

Clarissa knew it was time to get it all off of her chest. She pulled her coat tighter around her body to ward off the slight chill that had suddenly passed over her skin.

"Clark had an affair," she quickly spat out.

Jeanette looked at her with bitter disgust blazing in her eyes. "How long ago? Why didn't you tell me?"

Clarissa began to fidget with the belt on her coat. "About six months ago. And I don't know." She threw her hands at her side and sat down next to Jeanette. "Nette, I thought I could handle it by myself. And you know how you feel about Clark. I know how you feel about Clark."

Jeanette had made it known that she didn't care much for Clark on many occasions.

"And now you know why. I never trusted that brotha."

"I've always known why. You've only told me a million or so times."

"And for good reason. He's always been after you, and you and I both know that Clark is nothing but a snake. But, somehow he was able to put blinders on you and make you forget about that."

"We went to counseling and worked through it. But..."

Jeanette cut her off. "But what? Everything is back to normal? I mean, how long has it been since you've actually enjoyed having sex with the man? When's the last time that you've had a decent conversation with him? You just said, a minute ago, that he's so meaningless in your life now that you haven't even thought to call him and tell him that you got here safely. If that's working through something, then I'd hate to have seen what would've happened if you hadn't." She looked over and noticed the onset of tears sitting in the corners of Clarissa's eyes.

She grabbed Clarissa's gloved hand in hers. "Look, Rissa, I'm sorry. I know it seems like I'm hard on you when it comes to him. It's just..." She struggled to gather the right words.

"I know. I know." Clarissa swiped at the tears on her cheeks.

"I've never been comfortable with the way things went down that night with Julian. Especially since Clark had a hand in it. But I love you and I try to support anything you do. Hell, I postponed my graduation trip to stand witness for you when you decided to marry him at the last minute. Even though I thought you were making the biggest mistake of your life, my love for you made me stand there and endure it."

"I should've listened to you. Ya know, I beat myself up about that almost every day. I wonder what my life would be like if I hadn't made that dreadful decision."

"Don't waste time beating yourself up about it. You're too young to be going through, 'If I, could've, would've, should've.' Hell, do something about it. It's not too late." Jeanette squeezed Clarissa's hand.

Clarissa shook her head. "But I don't know, Nette. I always thought marriage was for life. Like my parents."

"Girl, I don't want to hear that shit. Our mothers were completely different women than we are today. Lived in a totally different time than we do. There are plenty of women who are single and happy."

"If you say so."

"I know so. If your definition of happy is being in an unloving, unfeeling relationship with a dickhead that you can't stand to look at… Then your kind of happiness is something I never want to experience."

Jeanette's words, lined with the truth, cut Clarissa to the core. She knew that Jeanette loved her and she could always count on Jeanette to be there for her. Clarissa had been thinking about the possibility of leaving Clark for a few months. But she had to make sure that she was doing the right thing. She'd grown quite accustomed to the lifestyle that he had to offer her and questioned her own ability to maintain such.

"Look, Sistah-girl, you've got to preserve whatever dignity you have. If you don't, he's going to put you through hell and then some. This I know." Jeanette grabbed Clarissa and hugged her.

They sat on the bench for another half-hour, without any words being passed. Jeanette wanted her words to sink into Clarissa's thoughts.

"If we don't get a move-on, we're going to turn into human Popsicles. Besides, I have to get you ready for your date tonight. You've got to look extra special." Jeanette stood and pulled Clarissa up by the hand.

"Did I tell you that he wants to talk about that night?"

"I'm glad. Hell, I want to know what was going on in his mind to mess up like that. If I hadn't seen it with my own eyes, I never would've believed it. He was so in love with you."

"I'm going to hear him out. I think six years has been long enough. I'm not mad anymore." They both laughed as they headed to Park Avenue and a few blocks over to Jeanette's rent-controlled apartment.

Chapter Five

As soon as they hit the door, Jeanette ordered Clarissa to the shower. She gave her the expensive stock of perfume that was sure to have Julian drooling at the mouth by the end of the evening.

Two hours later, Clarissa was ready and waiting. Her beautiful hair, compliments of Joseph's on 60th and Lexington, rested softly on her shoulders. Her eyebrows had been formed into two identical arches. Flawless makeup made her golden skin look as if it were glowing.

She donned an elegant, just above the knee, patchwork leather skirt that Jeanette had designed along with calf-high, block-heeled, brown leather, Calvin Klein boots. A snug-fitting, chocolate-colored, mock turtleneck sweater accented her perfectly round, full breasts. In a word, she was absolutely stunning.

"Girl, you know you should start your own line instead of busting your hump for someone else," Clarissa told Jeanette as she inspected herself from every angle in the full-length mirror.

"Yeah, I know. But I'm not sure if I'm ready for a step like that." Jeanette turned Clarissa around as she straightened the collar of the jacket.

"Please. I know you're not doubting yourself, Ms. You Can Do Anything You Put Your Mind To," said Clarissa in a small, mocking voice.

"Be still now. Can't believe your grown ass still can't dress yourself." She turned Clarissa back around so she could finish.

"Oww, you don't have to kill me." Clarissa rubbed her shoulder as Jeanette ignored her and continued.

"Now, that's better." She turned Clarissa around to face her. A smile slowly took over her face as she admired her work. They both squealed with delight.

The door buzzed. "Oh, my God, it's him!"

"Look, calm down. We've got to look and act calm when he gets up here." Jeanette ran around quickly putting everything in place.

"You stay in the room so you can make a grand entrance. That way, it'll have more of an effect on him than if you're standing right here when I open the door." Jeanette pushed Clarissa off toward the bedroom.

"But how will I know when to come out?"

"Wait for about two minutes. Then it's show time."

As they stood there looking at each other, the door vibrated with the knock.

"Now go." Clarissa ran off in one direction as Jeanette gathered her composure. She smoothed out her clothing and hair and swiftly opened the door.

"Hey, Stranger!" They grabbed each other in a tight embrace.

"Check you out. Nette, girl, you look like you did the first day I met you." He pecked her on the cheek.

"You better say that." She returned the peck.

He handed a bouquet of yellow roses to her as he held on to the red ones.

"You always did know how to make a girl feel special," Jeanette said with a mock southern accent.

Clarissa pressed her ear near the small crack in the door, waiting for the right moment to appear. She straightened up and made one last glance in the mirror. "Here goes," she said to the reflection staring back at her.

She grabbed her handbag and slowly opened the door. Walking toward the voices engaged in happy chatter, she felt her knees suddenly become weak. Get it together, Girl, she said to herself.

Julian flopped down on the leather sofa. "So, where is she?" No sooner than the question had passed his lips, she appeared. The effect that Jeanette assured her would happen, did. His bottom lip slowly made a descent from the upper one. It was definitely about to be on...

Chapter Six

Clarissa stopped almost directly in front of him. She glanced over at Jeanette, who was smiling so hard that her face felt as if was about to crack.

Clarissa cleared her throat, praying that her words wouldn't come out sounding like a croaking toad. "Well, hello, Mr. Tulley." She gave him the quick female once-over. His six-foot, three-inch frame was picture perfect. Needless to say, he was still as fine as he was the day she'd met him.

"Rissa…" He couldn't get his brain and mouth to work together. He handed her the roses. She took a quick whiff of them and cradled them close to her chest.

"Well, you kids get going. Wouldn't want you to miss your reservations." Jeanette pushed them toward the front door as she handed out coats.

"I guess we should get going," Julian said, still in awe of his date.

"Do you think we have a choice?" Clarissa smiled as they all laughed.

"Let me put these in some water for you." Jeanette grabbed the roses from Clarissa. "Now have a good time–and don't do anything I wouldn't do–which of course leaves the door open for plenty!" Jeanette called behind them.

They made their way down the corridor, to the elevator, and ultimately through the lobby and out to a waiting car. The driver got out and opened the door. Julian stood back as Clarissa climbed in.

"So lady… how's everything?" Julian sat in one corner and she was pushed up in the other.

"I guess it's pretty much okay. Could be better, but what couldn't?" She laughed dryly.

"Yeah, you have a point. But, there are some things that are so perfect that there's nothing you can do to make them better." Julian turned so that he could look into her eyes.

Feeling a bit uncomfortable, Clarissa began to blush and turned her attention to the window. She couldn't get over how much of a gentleman he still was—how much of a charmer. It had been so long since anyone had given her a compliment. She couldn't believe that she was actually blushing like some sort of silly teenager.

"So, is this your first visit to the city?" Julian asked.

"No. I've been here a few times. You know I've always been a city dweller at heart." She smiled at the memory of how they would hang out in downtown Orlando as teenagers.

"I haven't forgotten. In fact, there are lots of things that I remember about you."

The driver pulled up to the curb and got out to open the door for them. Julian grabbed Clarissa's hand to help her out of the car. He placed his hand on the small of her back as he guided her into the restaurant. Windows on the World was one of the most upscale establishments in the city of New York, attracting tourists from near and far. Sitting one-hundred-seven stories high in the sky overlooking the world's most popular metropolis, its incomparable view of the Big Apple made it a once-in-a-lifetime American attraction and a must-see for any visitor. Needless to say, it was the perfect setting for their reunion.

"Wow… this is nice."

"And wait until you taste the food. It's delicious." Julian walked over to the hostess, who instantly recognized him and gave him a quick hug.

Jeanette began to wonder how many other women he had brought there to enjoy the food and awesome view. "Am I jealous?" she questioned herself as she smiled and tried to push the thought out of her head. She couldn't imagine how she could be jealous of something that had absolutely nothing to do with her.

Julian introduced Clarissa to the woman as she led them to their table. "Janel, this is an old friend of mine, Clarissa."

"Nice to meet you, Clarissa. Is this your first time here at Windows?"

"I have to say it is. I'm here visiting from Atlanta."

"Then we have to make sure that you really enjoy yourself so that you'll return soon." Her radiant smile assured Clarissa that she was sincere.

"You don't have to worry; I know I will just be looking around," Clarissa replied.

"We reserved your usual table and there's a chilled bottle of Crystal waiting for you." Her heels clicked on the tiled floor before she stopped at a dimly-lit table near the rear of the restaurant.

Julian winked at her. "Thanks for looking out." He slipped a little something in her palm and gave her a quick peck on the cheek.

Julian quickly pulled out Clarissa's chair before he slid into the elegantly set table from the opposite side. Clarissa couldn't believe how nervous she was. It reminded her of their very first date.

"You comfortable?" Julian asked as he set his coat to the side of him.

"I'm okay." She glanced around the room, taking in everything—the décor, the other sophisticated and well-dressed patrons, and especially the spectacular view of the New York City skyline.

"Just okay? You look great." He gave her a sexy, dimpled grin.

"See you haven't lost your sense of humor." She smiled.

"I'm still Julian. Nothing new here." He motioned for her to pick up the menu.

"So, what do you suggest since this is your spot?" She hoped she didn't sound sarcastic.

"You're taking suggestions? Well then, why don't I order for both of us? Let me test my skills and see if I still remember what you like." He looked over the menu as she steadily kept her eyes on him.

When the stocky waiter approached them, he greeted Julian. "Julian, my man. How's it going?"

"What's up, George? I'm cool."

He directed his attention to Clarissa. "Oh, where are my manners? How could I speak to him and not acknowledge such a beautiful lady? The name's George and I'll be your server tonight."

Clarissa found his compliment amusing. "Nice to meet you, George. I'm Clarissa Keller." She instantly felt terrible about saying her last name. She felt as if she'd just slapped Julian in the face. She looked over to see if it had registered, but his face gave nothing away.

"Damn, Julian, how did you get this gorgeous woman to go out with you? Tell me your secret, Man," George joked with him.

"Guess somebody upstairs likes me. But not that much 'cause this woman was supposed to be my wife," he replied jokingly, but seriously as he noticed Clarissa shifting around in her seat.

"Well, I heard the word 'supposed,' so how'd you mess that up?" George realized too late that he'd stepped into uncharted water.

"Long story, Man. One I hope I'll have a chance to talk about." Julian looked at Clarissa. She stared back defiantly.

"Ooo-kay. I think that's my cue. So, what will it be tonight?" George began to recite the specials of the evening. After deciding that they needed a little more time to look over the menu, he ran off to get their drinks.

Julian hid his face behind the menu. "Let's see... I think I'll have the honey-glazed beef short ribs and for you, Madam, how about the stuffed shrimp?" He peeked over the top of the menu, trying to see if he'd remembered.

Clarissa smiled at him. "I'm impressed."

George came back with their drinks and quickly took their orders, leaving them alone once again.

The entire evening was spent savoring good food, drinks, and each other's company. Clarissa couldn't remember the last time she'd enjoyed herself so much.

After the fantastic meal and spectacular service, they made

their way out to the car. The drive was filled with laughter and chatter about old times and new. It didn't take long for Clarissa to realize that memory lane was a place she really enjoyed revisiting.

"Well, Mrs. Keller, did you enjoy yourself tonight?" He placed his hand over hers as she rested it on the seat near his leg.

"I wondered if you'd caught that. You have to realize that it's out of habit. Not pride." She turned her hand over to grip his.

"So there's trouble in paradise?" he boldly questioned.

"What makes you think a thing like that?" Clarissa asked, on the defensive.

"Well, let's see, Rissa...I may call you Rissa, right?"

Clarissa gave a short frown as she cocked her head to the side, wondering where he was going with this conversation.

"All evening, we've discussed nothing but all the good times we used to have in the past. You've mentioned nothing about your present, nothing about your life in Atlanta, and nothing about Clark. And don't think I haven't paid attention to the fact that you and Clark have been married six years and there are no children. I would have thought good 'ol 'Clark the Shark' would have had you knocked up, oh, at least four or five times by now...He always has had something to prove." He chuckled.

"I'm working on a career, Julian..." Clarissa sagaciously replied.

"Okay, if you say so. But if I know my Rissa, which I think I do, I'd say that I hit the nail right on the head."

Clarissa took her eyes away from her date and began to concentrate on the atmosphere beyond their Lincoln Town Car. She was in no mood to go there with Julian. After all, he was the one who had some explaining to do. Not her. Hell, if it hadn't been for that fateful day six years ago, Clark wouldn't have even been an issue. The way she saw it, it was all Julian's fault that she was miserable right now.

Noticing her sudden solemn expression, Julian asked, "Wanna talk about it?"

"I'm on vacation and I'm trying to have a good time, Julian, so let's just drop the subject." She took a short pause before continuing, now in a perkier disposition. "Where to next? A late night show?"

Following her lead, Julian decided to drop the issue and replied, "I thought you'd like to take a horse-drawn carriage ride through Central Park. It's turned out to be a beautiful October night and if you get cold, I'll warm you up." He smiled as he pulled her close.

She stared into his beautiful brown eyes. "I'd like that."

Julian informed the driver of the change in plans upon which he let them out alongside Central Park South as they spotted an available carriage. After flagging down the tuxedo-clad driver, Julian helped Clarissa climb into the carriage. A slight breeze blew around them and she instinctively snuggled close to him. He pulled her in closer and she pressed her head against his chest.

"Told you I'd keep you warm," Julian whispered in her ear.

Clarissa felt as if she was in the most secure place in the world as Julian held her in his arms. He began to run his fingers through the soft tendrils of curls that draped the nape of her neck. As she basked in the enjoyment of their contact, it felt as though they had never broken up–like the years had been mere hours. She could not deny that this was where she belonged.

"Umm." A soft moan escaped Clarissa's throat.

"So it still works." Clarissa opened her eyes and looked up at Julian. An evil grin was pasted on his handsome face.

Clarissa sat up. "You sure have memorized lots of things about me."

Julian turned so that he could look directly in her eyes. "It's hard to forget about someone when you loved them as deeply as I have loved you."

Clarissa's heart fluttered. She sank back into his embrace, relishing the feel of being held in his arms. She couldn't help but focus on the rhythm of Julian's heartbeat as he gently massaged different spots on her back. Something in Clarissa came alive with each stroke and she was overcome with a desperate urge to have him love her.

A guilty voice reminded her that she should've been thinking about Clark and their marriage vows, but Julian's presence made it absolutely impossible.

She looked up to find her ex-beau staring lovingly down at her as he stroked the side of her face gently with his finger.

As if connected to a forceful magnet, their heads began to slowly gravitate toward each other. Before she could protest, Julian began to place soft kisses on her lips. Seeing that she was receptive, his tongue longed to reunite with hers. Unable to fight the feelings any further, Clarissa reached up and wrapped her arms around his neck.

Finally coming up for air, Clarissa asked, "How far do you live from here?"

He glanced around at their surroundings. "No more than ten minutes in a cab."

"Pay the man."

"Are you sure?"

"I asked, didn't I?"

"I mean, I don't want you to have any regrets in the morning."

"No regrets here," she said as she leaned up to kiss him.

Julian tapped the driver, signaling that the ride was over. Just as he'd said, ten minutes later they were walking up the steps to the front door of his brownstone. He unlocked the glass front door and then the solid wood one that led into the living room. He clicked on the lights and helped Clarissa out of her coat. Within a moment's time, he had removed his coat and she was aggressively pulling at his shirt.

Clarissa undressed Julian with an urgency she couldn't contain. Before long, Julian stood before her in all his glory, his clothes piled at his feet. He scooped Clarissa up in his arms and carried her to the bedroom.

He gently placed her in the middle of the king-size bed as he slowly removed her clothing. Bare of everything except her bra, panties and her seductive boots, he draped her right leg over his shoulder to free her from them. Methodically, he slowly zipped her boot down and exposed her beautifully-pedicured toes. Stopping long enough to shower each one with attention, he went on to the other leg and repeated the steps.

Clarissa moaned with delight as she felt her middle become slippery wet.

Julian stood at the side of the bed and pulled Clarissa up to him. She immediately wrapped her arms and legs around him and hungrily searched his mouth. He relieved her of her satin chocolate bra—one of her many Victoria's Secret purchases. Like a skilled scientist working on a special brew, he pulled away from her kiss so he could explore her breasts. He traced his tongue along the areola before taking the entire nipple into his mouth. He then pressed them both together in an attempt to pleasure both simultaneously. His manhood slapped up against her stomach as it throbbed for what was to come.

"Oh, Julian. I want you so bad, Baby. Please love me. Love me now," Clarissa begged.

"I will, Baby, but slowly. I'm going to make love to all of you." He went back to suckling on her breast.

He laid her back on the bed and slowly began a downward trail of kisses until he reached her inner thigh. He propped her legs up on the bed so that he could have a full view of her dripping wet center. Pausing long enough to register the look of pure satisfaction on her face, he knelt down and lapped his tongue across her, flattening out his tongue so that he would leave no spot untouched. Massaging her bottom as he lifted her up closer to him, Julian worked his tongue skillfully up and down until he tasted the rich cream that burst from her center.

Clarissa thought she was going to explode, as he took her to heights she hadn't reached in a very long time. She gripped the back of his head and ran her fingers through the soft, loose curls on top of his head.

"Oh, Julian, damn, Baby, ooh shit!" she cried out.

Julian was pleased with her satisfaction and after making sure that he'd lapped up every drop, he slowly climbed up to join her on the bed.

He stopped momentarily to give a quick kiss to her perfect C cup breast before continuing his climb upward to her mouth. He proceeded to kiss her neck, her eyelids, ultimately finding his way to her swollen lips.

Julian had done such a wonderful job down low that she thought it was only appropriate that she return the favor. She pushed him up so that she had enough room to free herself from under him and forced him on his back, repeating the steps he'd just performed on her.

Julian was blown away when Clarissa ran her tongue over the head of his penis. She grabbed hold of it with both hands as she hovered above it, slowly taking in inch by inch, until his entire shaft was lodged inside her warm moist mouth. She began to work her cheek muscles to intensify the sucking motion. As she drew him deeper into her mouth, she reached between his legs and softly massaged his sack.

In all the years they'd dated, he'd never been able to get Clarissa to quench his oral desires. The thought of being in her mouth sent a sudden urge to release himself, but before he reached the point of no return, Clarissa released her mouth-hug on his piece.

"Damn, Baby," he moaned.

She gave his rock-hard part one last lick and became upwardly mobile. She paused. "Where's your shield?"

He motioned to the nightstand near the bed. She reached over and grabbed a blue-wrapped condom from the top drawer, tore it open, and began to roll the contents over his shaft. She stood over him again and gently eased down on top of it.

Clarissa moved up and down in a slow and sensuous rhythm. Julian enjoyed her taking control. She slowly leaned forward until they were eye to eye.

"Feel good?" she huskily breathed into his face.

"Yeah, Baby. Feel good to you?" He grabbed hold of her hips.

"Yesss. So good," she hissed. Kissing him, she continued her up-and-down rhythm enjoying the ride.

The sexy sounds she made intensified Julian's need to fill her. He began to thrust his hips in an upward motion, matching her every move. But now it was his turn to be in charge. Overcome with an urge to push all he had deep inside of her, he quickly flipped her over and held her legs straight up in the air. He thrust deeper and deeper in her. The sound of skin slapping against skin filled the room as the scent of lovemaking filled the air.

"Oh, Julian! I'm coming, Baby. I'm coming!" she yelled out.

"Come, Baby," he demanded as he worked at getting her to that point for the second time in less than ten minutes.

"I'm coming! Come with me!" she cried out.

"Yes, Baby. I'm coming." The dialogue intensified as they informed each other that the edge was near. Reaching their climax together, they collapsed.

"Oh, God! Yes! Yes!" Clarissa cried out as she locked her legs over his shoulders.

"Baby, baby, oh, baby," Julian grunted out as he tried to control the involuntary spasms that his body was experiencing. He clung to Clarissa as if his next breath depended on it.

Drenched in after-sex sweat and breathing as if they'd just run a twenty-mile marathon, they clung to each other tightly. Unable to control her emotions, Clarissa began to cry.

Feeling the warm moisture against him, Julian looked down at her. "What's wrong, Baby?"

Clarissa shook her head. "Nothing. I'm just..." She tried to collect her thoughts.

Julian rolled over, sat up, and pulled her into his chest. He gently began to brush the hair away from her face.

At that moment, Julian wished he could place her inside his chest and keep her there forever. His hand explored her soft skin. Looking down at her, he knew it was time to set the record straight about the night that took away his greatest love.

"Why wouldn't you take my calls?" he began.

"I-I, I was so devastated. I mean, all I could see was her... lying there, and you... standing there. Why? I thought you loved me and only me." She sat up, searching his face.

Julian stroked the side of her face. "I did. I mean, I do. Rissa, I haven't been able to get you out of my system and I don't think I ever will. Brie was to me what Clark was to you."

Clarissa cringed at the mention of their names. "What are you talking about?"

"She wanted me, but knew my heart belonged to you. When I began to piece it all together, I realized I had been set up. Brie knew who you were when she saw you at the door that night. You don't remember meeting her before?"

Clarissa tried to think back. After all these years, the only thing that she'd recalled was the scene in the bedroom. But now that she gave it another thought, she remembered the evil grin she had on her face when they were at the door.

"You'd met her before," Julian continued.

Clarissa gave him a confused look.

"After the homecoming game. Remember? The party we went to at the Marriott?"

Just then, a light began to shine in her eyes. The memory of that day had come back to her like she'd pressed the rewind button on a VCR.

"Yeah. She was with Kevin's girl. What was her name?" She snapped her fingers.

"Sharon."

"So why the hell was she at your house that night? And what in the hell was she doing in your room while you were in the shower!?" Her emotions began to flare. She tried to pull away from him, but he held her tight.

"Listen to me. I called out for Manny to bring me a towel and she told me that he'd just stepped out. So, she offered to bring it to me. Before she could get back with it, you and Nette got there. When you walked into the room, I'd just walked out of the bathroom and I was just as shocked as you to find her damn near naked lying in my bed," he explained.

Clarissa stiffened up and with a raised eyebrow asked, "After all these years, how do I know you're telling the truth?"

"What reason would I have to lie to you now? I've already lost you. You married him. He won."

He turned to her so he could look into her eyes. Her face was illuminated by the moonlight glare that peeked through the open curtain. "Did you know that I'd planned to ask you to marry me while we were in the Bahamas?" He rolled over and reached inside the top drawer of the nightstand. He retrieved a small square shaped box and handed it to her.

She sat and stared at it for a moment.

"Open it. I've kept it all this time," he continued.

Clarissa slowly opened the box to reveal its contents. Perched in the center was a one-carat, princess-cut diamond ring set in platinum.

Mouth gaped slightly opened, she looked up at him. A fresh set of tears glistened in the bottom of her eyes. "Oh, Julian, I, I…" She struggled to find the words.

Placing his finger over her mouth, he silenced her. "I've been trying to figure out what went wrong since that night. So when I got that email from Nette, I knew God was giving me a chance to make things right." He kissed the tears as they fell from her eyes.

"A second chance? I wish it were that easy," she whimpered.

He smiled at her. "Are you talking about Clark? Well, there's more to the story. Look, after everything went down, I blamed Brie for ruining my life and refused to talk to her ever again. I couldn't understand why she did it. I'd never given her any reason to think that she had a chance with me. But about a month after graduation, I ran into Sharon. She told me that I really needed to call Brie so that I could get the real scoop on what had happened that night. Needless to say, my curiosity made me give her a call."

Clarissa hung on his every word.

"Come to find out, Clark and Brie went to high school together. She told him that she was at Georgetown and he asked her if she knew of me. She went into how she felt about me and I guess he knew, at that moment, he'd found a way to get you. Brie told me that she'd met him at Tyson's Corner the day before and he told her his plan and said he'd make sure that you were there," Julian explained as he adjusted the bed sheet.

Clarissa's eyes reddened with anger as she remembered how he'd been so anxious to come to her with his findings, how he'd told her that he was there for her, and how quickly he'd offered to drive her up there. Ashamed and embarrassed, she buried her face in her hands. "Nette tried to warn me. She's always believed that he'd played a bigger role than messenger in the whole thing. How could I have been so blind?! Oh, Julian, I'm really sorry."

"Shh... don't cry. Everything is going to be okay." He cradled her in his arms.

"I've spent many nights thinking about what our lives would've been like if it hadn't been for that night," he continued. "For the longest time, all I could think about was righting the wrong we'd been dealt.

"Rissa, I love you more at this very moment than I did then." He kissed her. Right then, his mind was on taking advantage of the second chance he'd been given. Thus, they made love well into the wee hours of the morning.

Chapter Seven

The sun persistently pried its way into the room through the window, slowly making a path across the two bodies that lay intertwined between the tangled sheets.

Clarissa peacefully slept as Julian watched her. He felt blessed to have been given another opportunity to love her. This time, he'd never lose her again.

He slid out of bed carefully, trying his best not to wake her. He stood at the edge of the bed, admiring her toned, size six frame. Covering her nakedness up with the comforter, he walked into the bathroom to freshen up.

Hearing the electric razor, Clarissa stirred in bed. She had a feeling of completeness as she lay there staring at the ceiling. Making love to Julian again had been everything she'd dreamed of and more.

Slowly sitting up in bed, she looked over at the clock on the nightstand. "Eight o'clock. Damn, I need to call Nette." She scrambled for the phone that lay next to the clock.

"Well, good morning," Jeanette beamed into the phone.

"At least I know you didn't put out a missing person's report." They both laughed.

"Did your toes curl?"

"Girl, and some."

Jeanette squealed with delight. "So, are you coming this way today? If you decide not to, believe me, I'll understand."

"Did you have any plans for us today?"

"Nothing that can't be broken. Girl, get your freak on. Shit, it's about time you got some good dick." They giggled.

"Well, since you have no use for me, I'm about to go into the bathroom and jump in the shower with this fine ass man. Ya know, get me some mo' good dick. Bye."

"Get some for me. See ya later."

Clarissa hung up the phone and tossed it on the bed. She jumped up and ran off toward the sound of the running water.

She slowly opened the door and focused on the outline of Julian's bare body in the glass shower stall. She walked over slowly and tapped on the door.

"I thought I was going to have to come and get you," he said as he opened the door and yanked her in. He pulled her under the running water, wetting her hair as he placed a trail of kisses up and down her neck. This was one time she didn't complain about her ruined hairdo. The experience was erotic.

As he bent down to kiss her full on the mouth, she realized that she hadn't had a chance to brush her teeth. "Wait, Baby. I need to do something." She jumped from the shower.

"What's wrong?"

"I need a toothbrush. Do you have a spare?"

He laughed. "Look in the medicine cabinet."

She quickly finished up and hopped back in. "I didn't want to repulse you."

"I doubt seriously if anything about you could be repulsive to me. Good morning, Sunshine," he whispered in her ear as he pulled her to him so she could feel his erection.

She smiled with delight. "This is definitely a good morning."

After making love in the shower and then in the bed again, it was time to quench their hunger for food. Julian handed her the top to his pajamas as he pulled his long legs through the bottoms. "So, what will it be for breakfast?"

"What do you have?" she asked.

"Anything your heart desires, Madam." He hoisted her up on his back and carried her downstairs to the kitchen.

The bleached wood floors glistened under his feet. "Was your place this nice when you first got it?" she asked.

"Not quite as nice. I spent a pretty penny on renovations. But it was well worth it."

They entered the kitchen, which was done up in bleached wood cabinets, stainless steel appliances, and black granite countertops. She was really impressed at his taste.

He continued to impress her with his culinary abilities as he prepared a breakfast fit for a queen. There was nothing that he'd forgotten, fresh fruit, scrambled eggs, French toast, the works.

"So, what time do you want me to take you back to Nette's?" he asked as they stood side by side at the sink, washing up the dishes.

"You trying to get rid of me? I'm yours today if you want me. I just need to go and get something clean to put on. That is, if you want me today."

He kissed her on the neck. "I want you every day."

She smiled at him and pecked him on the lips. "Then we have to work on that."

"I know. Once we finish up in here, I want to go to Nette's so we can sit down and strategize about what we have to do. I can't let Clark have you any longer." Julian wrapped his damp hands around her hips. She placed her head on his chest, enjoying that sense of security he gave her.

She couldn't wait to tell Jeanette that her assumptions about Clark had been correct all these years. If only she'd listened to Jeanette years ago. "Well, let's get a move on." She slapped him on his tight rear and ran up the stairs with him in tow.

Maneuvering through traffic with ease, they pulled up in front of Jeanette's building. He parked his Legend out front and walked around to open the door for Clarissa. Once inside, they filled Jeanette in on the real scoop regarding that dreadful night.

"I told you he was a fucking snake!" Jeanette exclaimed. She was livid.

"I know, and like you told me the other day, it's never too late to make changes." Clarissa smiled.

Jeanette looked at her and smiled an evil grin. "So what are we doing?"

They spent the rest of the afternoon huddled together like three skilled private eyes, mapping out their master plan to make Clark pay, only taking time out to enjoy their newly-rekindled passion. Saying goodbye was going to be hard, even if it was only for a short time. Clarissa realized that she'd never stopped loving him. Julian was the man she was meant to be with. Now she had to get rid of the man who had deprived her of that. And pay he would.

Chapter Eight

Clarissa hated to cut her stay short, but the sooner she got back, the better. Saying goodbye to Julian was even harder than she'd expected. However, knowing that it wouldn't be long before they were together again made it easier.

She had opted to surprise Clark and snatched a cab to get home. During the ride, she looked out the window at the scenery that had been home to her for the past six years. How had she let him dupe her so badly?

The cab pulled up in front of their stately home. The driver brought her bags to the door and thanked her for the hefty tip she'd given him.

Clarissa searched her leather Biasai bag for her keys and unlocked the door. After dragging her luggage upstairs and placing them in her closet, she jumped in the shower. She had to get herself ready for the performance of a lifetime.

Wrapped in her favorite, ice-green chenille robe, she emerged from the clouds of steam toweling her hair dry. She went to her walk-in closet and clicked on the light in search of something comfortable. As she combed through the endless supply of clothing, she could hear the sound of the front door closing. Finding something suitable, she rushed from the closet to get dressed before Clark came upstairs.

As she stood at the top landing of the stairs, she could hear Clark on the phone in the kitchen. Wanting to surprise him, she quietly crept in. Rounding the corner, she caught a glimpse of her husband standing in a loving embrace with another woman.

"What the fuck is going on?!" she yelled.

Clark nearly broke his neck as he spun toward the sound of Clarissa's voice. He stumbled toward the other end of the kitchen. "Clarissa. What are you doing here? You weren't supposed to be home until…"

She cut him off. "No, Clark–the question is what the hell are you doing here? I decided to come home early to surprise you. I guess the surprise is on me." She inched closer to Clark and the cowering woman behind him.

"Clarissa, wait now. Don't do anything stupid," he said with raised palms.

"Stupid?! You're not worth it. I'm through with being stupid. Sweetie, you can have him." Clarissa turned on her heels and headed up the stairs two at a time.

She slammed the door for effect. As soon as she heard his car pull out of the garage, she leaped into the middle of the bed and began to squeal with delight. Clutching the pillow to her chest and kicking her feet in the air, she felt total vindication.

As much as Julian had wanted to be in charge of the plan, she knew that returning home early would do the trick. Just as she and Jeanette had guessed, Clark was only thinking about the freedom he would have while she was gone.

She jumped up, snatched the phone from the base and punched in Jeanette's number. "Hello?"

"Just as we thought!" she screamed in the receiver.

"What happened?"

"Nette, he's been playing house the whole time. When he saw me, he damn near pissed in his pants." They both laughed.

"Were they there when you got there?"

"They came about half an hour after I arrived. It all just happened less than ten minutes ago."

"What?! Where is his ass now?"

"He burned rubber getting away from here."

"Are you going to call Julian?"

"Not yet. I have lots of packing to do."

"You want me to fly down so I can help?"

"Girl, I'm going to arrange for the movers to be here tomorrow morning. All I have to do is get my stuff packed."

"Well, get busy. Call me back once you have everything arranged."

"Okay. Talk to you tomorrow." She clicked off the phone and tossed it on the bed.

She walked out to the garage to retrieve the rest of her luggage. She felt as though a fifty-pound weight had been lifted from her chest. Suddenly, as Toni Braxton said, she could finally breathe again.

She stood in the middle of her closet evaluating how she would be able to get all of her clothing in the few bags she had. As she looked at each suit she pulled from the closet, she realized that they all represented her life with Clark. She suddenly walked back to the kitchen and grabbed the box of heavy-duty garbage bags from under the sink. She snatched everything from her closet and stuffed them in bag after bag. Two hours later, her closet was bare and fifteen thirty-gallon bags lined the foot of her bed.

She dragged each one down the stairs and loaded them up in her truck. Without a second thought, she pulled up at the Goodwill drop off station and unloaded them.

The slender attendant stood with her mouth gaped open. Clarissa turned to her before jumping back in her truck. "I don't know if you're allowed to go through the merchandise, but there are lots of designer suits in there that would fit you perfectly."

"Wow, really?!"

Clarissa winked at her. The attendant thanked her as she drove away.

Clarissa didn't expect to see Clark any more that day. It was his way to stay clear of her until he believed the smoke had cleared. Using his own behavior against him, Clarissa knew that his absence would give her an opportunity to pack in peace, take all that she wanted, and then get the hell outta Dodge. Taking advantage of her good fortune, she cleaned the house from top to bottom–throwing out unwanted things and packing up everything that was going with her.

As she cleaned and packed everything up in the guest bedroom, she came across a briefcase. Thinking nothing of it, she pried it open. Inside were documents of several bank accounts, investment portfolios, and deeds to a number of real estate properties. All of them in Clark's name. Upon closer inspection of the dates, she realized that he'd purchased all of them during the marriage. She'd seen enough episodes of Divorce Court to know that whatever was acquired during the course of the marriage was in fact property of the marriage. Oh, she was going to take Clark to the cleaners for years to come...

"That slimy, no-good asshole. He thinks he is so smart," she said as she walked to her office to make copies of each and every one. It was quite clear to her that she'd just secured her financial position.

At seven o'clock the next morning, the movers arrived. Clarissa had packed and labeled everything that was leaving with her. Everything else, she'd either left for him or promised to the consignment shop down the road.

Clarissa loaded her truck up with the few pieces of luggage she'd packed before the driver arrived to pick it up. She showered for the last time in the bathroom she'd shared with Clark for the past four years. Bare of her things, she closed the door forever. Approaching the bed, she eyed her parting gear—dark denim Guess jeans with a matching jacket and a black pullover. As she zipped her boots up, she could feel a set of eyes watching her. She looked up to find Clark standing in the doorway.

Ignoring him, she finished stuffing the last of her things in her bag and zipped it closed. Clark flinched at the sounds of her leaving. "What are you doing?" he asked.

"What I should have done ages ago..." she snapped.

"Looks like you're going somewhere," he said softly.

"Uh huh..."

"Where you going?" he asked weakly.

"Where I should've gone six years ago, Clark."

"And where's that?"

"Why don't you call your friend Brie and ask her. You do remember her, don't you?" she shot at him.

Guilt registered on his face as he realized that the secret he'd been able to keep away from her all these years had finally come to light.

She grabbed her purse from the dresser and picked up her carryon bag from the floor. With her head held high, she walked up to Clark and placed the keys to everything they'd shared in the palm of his hand. "Now you don't have to sneak around. I could say that I hate you, but I don't. I only hope that you're able to look back on this day and realize that my leaving was for the best." She brushed past him as she headed down the stairs.

Leaving behind a half-empty house, Clarissa felt a sense of triumph as she sat in the back of the cab.

Defeated, Clark stood in the bedroom window and watched her ride out of his life forever.

Chapter Nine

Standing in their usual spot at JFK, Jeanette paced back and forth as she awaited the arrival of Delta flight 554. As soon as Clarissa disembarked from the plane, Jeanette ran and flung her arms around her best friend's neck.

"Would you believe that I've been here for an hour?!" Jeanette exclaimed.

Clarissa smiled at the one person who had been a constant force of strength in her life. "Thank you, Nette."

"For what?"

"You said I would thank you later and I am."

It dawned on Jeanette that she was talking about the fateful email that she'd sent to Julian. "You're more than welcome. I just want you to be happy, Girl. You deserve that."

They stood at the gate embracing as if it had been years since they'd last seen each other.

"Now let's get my luggage so I can go see my man." Clarissa smiled at her reference to Julian. Something she'd never felt when she thought about Clark.

Twenty minutes later, they were turning on East 118th toward the new beginnings that lay ahead for her. She dug through her purse in search of her cell phone and punched in Julian's number.

"Hello?" he answered on the first ring.

"Hey, Baby. Guess who?" she cooed in a seductive voice.

"Where are you? I waited for you to call me last night. I was worried about you." His voice was full of concern.

"Aww, were you really? I'm sorry, but things happened and things needed to get done and I guess I just lost track of time."

He began to go on about not being able to sleep at all because he didn't know if Clark had hurt her or what. She listened until she couldn't take any more.

"Could you just calm down and hush for one minute? I called for a reason."

He quickly shut up.

"Are you dressed?"

"What?" he asked, caught totally off guard.

"I just wanted to make sure that you were decent before Jeanette came in."

Confused by her statement, he asked her, "Where is Jeanette coming into?"

No sooner than he'd asked the question, the door chimed, indicating it had been opened.

Using the key he'd given her, Clarissa let herself and Jeanette into the brownstone. With the phone still clutched in his hand, Julian raced down the stairs and scooped her up in his arms. Overwhelmed by feelings of love and joy, he cupped her face in his hands and kissed her lightly on the lips. "I hope you're here for good. I love you too much to let you leave again."

"Do these bags look like she's leaving anytime soon? Come and give me a hand." Jeanette stood in the doorway with Clarissa's bags at her feet and a big smile on her face.

Julian's brown eyes misted over as the reality of the moment set in. She was his again. This time it would be forever.

After putting her things away, Julian felt it was an appropriate time to give her the surprise he had for her. He reached into his pocket and retrieved a tiny square blue velvet box. He walked over to Clarissa and grabbed her hands. Jeanette stood frozen in front of the fireplace as she watched the scene unfold.

"Six years ago, I bought a ring with the expectations of asking you to be my wife. I've held on to that ring all these years in hope of one day giving it to you. But I realized that was the ring of a boy. So, I set out to find the perfect ring for this man to give to the woman he loves." He flipped the box open to reveal a three carat, princess-cut, center diamond surrounded with four princess-cut, side diamonds set in a platinum band.

Taking her hand in his, he slowly lowered himself to the floor and kneeled at Clarissa's feet. "I know that it may be a little too soon to ask this, but I don't want to miss the chance again. Clarissa, I love you more than the air I fill my lungs with and if you'll have me, I want to spend the rest of my life breathing in scents of you. Will you marry me, Baby?"

Choked up with emotions, Clarissa looked into the face of the only man who'd ever really loved her. "Oh, Julian... Yes. Yes. Yes." Tears of joy escaped her eyes as she pulled him to his feet. He showered her face and neck with kiss after kiss.

Epilogue

"Hurry up or I'm going to be late!" Jeanette hissed at the cab driver. He dipped in and out of traffic trying to get her to her destination and out of his cab.

As the cab pulled into the circular drive, Jeanette spotted Clarissa climbing out of the Black Onyx LX470. "Don't forget to grab my bag." Clarissa called to the other side of the truck.

Jeanette threw the fare at the cabby and hopped out the back seat. "Thanks."

"I'm here!" she yelled to get Clarissa's attention.

"Nette, you're here. Thought we were going to have to start without you."

"How many times do I have to tell you that I wouldn't miss this for the world?" She grabbed Clarissa's hand and guided her over to the wheelchair that sat at the curb waiting.

Julian handed Jeanette Clarissa's overnight bag. "Here. I'm going to go park."

"Hurry up, Honey. I don't want you to miss anything," Clarissa said as she squeezed his hand to fight off another contraction.

"Look, give me the keys and I'll park the truck. That way, if anything unexpected should happen, you won't miss it." Jeanette held her hand out.

"Thanks, Nette," Julian said as he dropped the keys in her hand and pecked her on the cheek.

The nurse escorted the proud parents-to-be toward the bank of elevators that would take them to their reserved birthing suite on the 11th floor of St. Luke's hospital.

"Ohhh…" Clarissa moaned out, clutching the arms of the wheelchair.

"Another one, Baby?"

Concentrating on her breathing, Clarissa shook her head to confirm that another contraction had rippled across her swollen abdomen.

"How far apart are the contractions?" the heavyset nurse questioned.

"Less than five minutes now."

"Well, once we get you in the room, we'll check to see how things have progressed. If you've started to dilate, it won't be long then."

Clarissa's mouth formed a perfect O-shape as she continued to breathe through each contraction like she'd learned in Lamaze class. The elevator came to a stop and the doors slid open. The nurse rolled Clarissa into the second door on the right and helped her into the full-sized bed of a room that looked like a page out of Better Homes and Gardens.

Julian dropped her bag in the rocking chair sitting directly in front of the bed. There was a bassinet for the baby and a hydrotherapy tub used for relaxation to ease the pain of labor. The hardwood floors reminded Clarissa of the beautiful brownstone that had become home to her over the past year and a half.

Her divorce from Clark was finalized within a month after she filed. He was advised by his lawyer not to contest it. He would stand to lose much more than she'd asked for if he did.

Even though Julian didn't want her to get anything from Clark, she wasn't about to let him get away with the hurt he'd caused her scot-free. She was only collecting on a debt that he owed her.

Two months later, she and Julian wed before five hundred of their closest relatives and friends at the lavish New York Palace Hotel on Madison Avenue in Manhattan. With Jeanette standing by her side, she finally said "I do" to her Mr. Right.

"Here... comes... another one." Trying her best to keep breathing, she gritted her teeth as the severe pain ripped through her body.

Julian stood behind her, rubbing her back as he helped her into the hospital gown. "That's right, Baby, breathe."

Jeanette walked into the room. "Did I miss anything?"

"Not yet. But I don't think it'll be long," the nurse replied.

She popped the latex glove on her hand. "Now let's see." She checked to see how far Clarissa had dilated.

Awaiting the verdict, Julian and Jeanette watched closely as Clarissa twisted and turned against the pain.

The nurse snatched the glove from her hand and walked out the room.

"What's wrong?" Clarissa asked.

"Let me go find out," Julian replied. Before he was able to take one step out, a team of nurses rushed in the room. Clarissa's doctor was on their heels.

"Hello, Mrs. Tulley. I have good news," Dr. Trehearn said as he put on his mask.

"Really?" she asked, as another contraction ripped through her.

"You're ten centimeters. The baby's head is already crowning."

After that, everything began to move quickly. There were nurses everywhere—rolling in equipment, pulling things from the ceiling, breaking down the bed for delivery. "You ready, Baby?" Julian kissed her on her damp forehead.

"I don't think I have a choice at this point," she panted.

After a few grunts and a short round of "Push, Baby, push," little Madison Marie made her debut. All seven pounds and twelve ounces of her. Jeanette leaned over the bed after the doctor finished stitching Clarissa up.

"You know this was God's plan for you? That's why he wouldn't allow you to bear any children until now. Rissa, she's beautiful." Jeanette held on tightly to her friend's hand.

"Thank you, Nette, for sharing this with us."

"Girl, please. Thank you for allowing me to."

Julian walked over with their precious bundle covered in a pink blanket and placed her on Clarissa's bare chest. After two attempts, she latched on and began the bonding process with her mother.

Jeanette thought it was a good time to slip out to the family room next door.

Julian sat on the bed admiring the two most important things in his life. He pushed a strand of hair from Clarissa's face.

"So, Daddy, you got your shotgun ready?" Clarissa teased in a raspy voice.

"I guess so, Mommy."

"She's so beautiful," Clarissa said as she stroked the baby's pudgy little jaw with her finger.

"Just like her mother," he replied, kissing her gently on the lips.

Jeanette walked back in to catch the scene of the new family cuddling. Jeanette's heart swelled with pure happiness, as she knew things were finally the way they were meant to be. Clarissa had learned a hard lesson in love, but she'd emerged triumphant.

Your Message Has Been Sent

By J.D. Mason

Chapter One

"Thank you so much, Mr. Davies, for agreeing to teach this class for us at the last minute. I was afraid we'd have to cancel it completely, which would have been terrible since so many kids have signed up for it."

"Well, Tony was looking forward to being here, but when an assignment calls..."

Mo smiled. "I understand."

He's handsome, she thought to herself. It had been years since she'd noticed good-looking on a man, but on Kevin Davies it was kind of hard to miss, being that it was his best feature.

"Classes are held on Tuesdays at six. Will that be a problem for you?"

"Not at all. I'm an independent and I make my own schedule. Six is fine."

Pretty black women, soft and round in all the right places, had a way of making his mouth water and Kevin fought the urge to smack his lips. Yeah, this Mrs. Beckman was fine. A little on the conservative side, but probably full of surprises. Most of the conservative ones usually were. Too bad she was afflicted with that "Mrs." ailment or he'd have made it his goal in life to walk away with those digits. Over the years, he'd learned that life had a way of playing some mean tricks on a man. When he was set on being single, every woman that crossed his path wanted to get him walking down the aisle with her. But the minute a brotha made up his mind to find the right woman, do the right thing–wedding, honeymoon, little house

139

on the prairie with the white picket fence, fate slapped him upside the head with females not even trying to commit. Or women like Mrs. Beckman here, who were already spoken for.

Actually, it was nice getting back over to this side of town. He'd grown up here and had wreaked his share of havoc in this neighborhood, which hadn't changed much at all. The rest of Denver might've been going through a metamorphosis, but not East Denver. The same solid brick houses had been there when he was a kid, only now they looked smaller. This was one of the few neighborhoods left in the city that looked as if it had been held captive in a time warp. It had yet to be invaded by big shopping centers, or fancy new developments. This part of the city had been considered the "bad part of town" ever since the first black family moved into the neighborhood and all the white folks moved out. A few blocks over, larger East Denver homes loomed majestic and expensive. The white folks stood their ground over there, refusing to budge despite the appearance of an occasional black face in the neighborhood. Like most people living here, he could never quite understand what was so terrible about it. Sure, it was full of black people, but did that make it bad? Not to him because he was a black people. He guessed it just depended on your point of view.

She felt him watching her. Mo celebrated a twinge of pride in knowing men still found her attractive. Different time, different place, different planet, just different—period, and maybe she'd have batted her eyes a little more, switched her hips hard enough to put the man's eye out, even asked him if he'd had any plans for the weekend. But the smoke had only recently seemed to clear. It had been three years since her husband's death. She'd spent those years in a fog, numb to everything and everyone around her with the exception of her son, Ty. Life had been about going through the motions and not much more than that. Lately, however, her senses had started to pick up on the little things she'd taken for granted like sunsets, lyrics to love songs, an appreciation of tall, dark-skinned men with velvety smooth voices, goatees and pretty smiles. At first she figured it had to be spring fever, seeing as how it was spring and all. But eventually she concluded that the man was fine and it didn't matter what season it was.

Kevin walked a half-step behind her as she escorted him to the door. She had it going on all right. It was a damn shame about that "Mrs." thing, though. "Thank you again, Mr. Davies."

"Please. Call me Kevin." He smiled.

His smile was contagious and Mo responded in kind. "All right. Kevin. I usually leave for the day at five. I have a little one I have to get home to, so...I won't see you on Tuesday. But I'm sure everything will go just fine."

A little one to get home to. What about a big one? he wondered. There had to be a "Mr." looming around out there somewhere. She was holding on pretty tight to that wedding ring, so ol' boy was definitely still in the mix. Damn, the bad luck!

Chapter Two

When did masturbating get to be as routine as brushing teeth? Maureen sighed a dispassionate orgasm, then lay staring up at the ceiling. It was late and the house was quiet. Too quiet, and she wished she could sleep. Mo and quiet didn't get along at all because it insisted on throwing revelation up in her face, reminding her lately of how lonely she was. In the past, she'd been pretty good at keeping it at bay, filling space, time, and quiet with busy work. Keeping busy had been imperative after Jonathan's death. By surrounding herself with activity...work, their son Ty, more work, aerobics, yard work, housework, more work, she'd been able to block out the fact that her husband wasn't working late at the office again, or that he wouldn't be walking through the door at any minute. Keeping busy blanketed the truth that she'd become a single parent and the task of raising their son now fell solely on her. But he'd been dead for more than three years now and keeping busy had become a way of life for Mo. It had stopped being the crutch she needed to get through losing him and had turned into her routine.

Too much quiet pissed her off, forcing her to listen to the whispers of her needs both emotional and physical. Especially physical, which is why she'd sexed herself to boredom. Even after his death she'd depended on him, imagining it was him making love to her, nibbling on her neck, licking her nipples. It was him moaning, "Oh, Baby" over and over again in her ear, slowly easing himself in and out of her until she climaxed all over him and her. In Mo's mind, Jonathan kissed her tenderly, nuzzled his face in the crook of her neck, until he'd eventually fall asleep on top of her, inside her, and she'd fall asleep beneath him. But time had a way of dulling her senses and resurrecting him wasn't so easy anymore. She closed her eyes, trying desperately to recapture the smell of him, the warmth of his body, the rhythm of his breathing, the essence of him. Lately, she'd been losing that battle to sleep, passing out before a clear image of him had completed forming in her mind.

When the cancer began to take its toll on him, Mo had to step up to the responsibility of being everything to both Jonathan and their son, Ty, who was just a toddler at the time. To everybody on the outside looking in, she was Jonathan's angel, tirelessly taking care of her husband, devoting herself to him, with all the love and compassion a good wife could muster. But Jonathan had known the truth despite her best efforts to hide it from him. For Maureen, love or compassion had nothing to do with her dedication to him. Cancer made her angry. And sometimes, the only way to get away from it was to give in to it. Mo spent many late nights curled up on the bathroom floor, crying into a towel she'd balled up in her lap. She was angry that her man had to be the one to get that nasty disease and that they'd only been married five years when he found out. She was angry that the strong man who'd ridden into her life like a knight on some big ass horse, swept her off her feet, promising her him for all eternity, had been reduced to one hundred forty pounds from puking up chemotherapy poisons that were supposed to keep him alive. She was mad as hell that he'd been the one to convince her it was time to start a family, only to end up leaving her alone to have to take care of that little chocolate family all by herself. But more than anything, she was angry that the other half of her soul had been ripped from her, leaving her to live her life feeling incomplete.

"You need to learn to be whole all by yourself, Mo," her sister Naomi preached. "You were born alone and you're going to die alone. You ain't never supposed to make a man your whole world, 'cause he ain't nothing but human like you human and there's no guarantee he's always going to be there."

Of course Naomi knew how to be whole all by herself. The woman hadn't sustained a meaningful relationship for more than three months in almost ten years. Her sister's words certainly held a ray of truth in them, but for Mo, being bonded to Jonathan hadn't been a burden. It wasn't something she loathed. Before he came along, no man had ever touched her heart the way he'd touched it. He knew her even better than she knew herself, and right or wrong, he'd become her security blanket. That other half that instinctively took care of those things she'd neglected. And she liked to think, maybe, she'd done the same for him.

The thing is, after he died, life seemed to melt into itself. Clocks didn't stop ticking. The sun and moon continued rising and setting like they'd done since God hung them in the sky. Summer turned into fall, into winter, into spring, and back into itself again. All without missing a beat. The only thing that had stopped was her passion for life because everything she'd lived for died with Jonathan. Yeah, quiet usually ended up kicking her in the behind and Mo tried to avoid it at all costs. But lately, she found herself losing that battle too and one message seemed to be revealing itself more and more. Mo was lonesome. Finally, after three years, the idea of meeting someone new excited her, but more than that, it scared the mess out of her.

Jonathan had the easy part. After all, he was dead. Couldn't get much easier than that. But for Mo...living was a trip. Because with all that had happened over the years, she wasn't sure she remembered how.

Chapter Three

Becoming director of a neighborhood community center hadn't actually been part of Mo's plan for her career path, but that's where she ended up. She'd graduated with a masters in education degree and landed smack dab in the middle of hell. The public school system. Like most young teachers, she left college determined to take on and even beat a system that held little regard for the people it was designed to help–the children. Minority children were especially at risk and Mo was going to make a difference. Between breaking up fights every other day in the school cafeteria and having to endure the mindless chatter of teachers in the teacher's lounge complaining about this "little bitch" or that "little bastard," Mo saw what her future looked like and decided it wasn't the place for her. So, she quit after her first semester and got a job in Corporate America teaching adults who had bosses paying them to be there. A willing audience. At times, she hated herself for giving up her "change the world" mentality so easily, but when that little girl from that last fight that Mo'd broken up took a swing at her, she finally said–enough.

When the opportunity presented itself to run the East Denver Mile High Community Center, she jumped at the chance. Maybe she still could make a difference in a young person's life. The center was the hub of the predominantly black neighborhood and it gave the kids a place to hang out and use their time working toward a goal, even If it was as immediate as winning a basketball or football game. The center was volunteer-driven so whatever a volunteer wanted to add to the curriculum was cool with Maureen as long as it was positive. All able bodied, good-hearted individuals willing to give of his/her time were welcomed with open arms and a real nice thank you letter.

The fiscal year was winding down and it was time to go to the board for some money, which meant only one thing–budget. Mo had been wrestling with this budget for over a month now, trying to find more ways to squeeze more money from those tight bastards. Sheila, her receptionist had strict orders...NO INTERRUPTIONS! The thing is, she hadn't laid a hand on that budget all morning. Instead, Mo sat staring out the window at absolutely nothing, trying to remember when that empty feeling inside started to become uncomfortable.   People had accused her of being cold and unemotional, but Mo knew better than that. Maybe that's how she came across on the outside. Inside was a different story altogether. Inside, there were words she longed to say, thoughts she would've loved to share, and desires she desperately needed to set free. Only there never seemed to be an outlet for her to do any of these things. So she left them pent up inside and ended up coming across as a bitch. She wasn't a bitch. Just frustrated.

Mo also knew it was time for her to pick up her own personal pieces and move on. Start another chapter in an otherwise dull book called her life. It was time for her to get out more and do other things besides working all the time. She'd thought about taking a vacation, getting on a plane and letting it drop her off on an island somewhere. The idea of basking in the sun on a warm beach brought a smile to her face. She'd sip on something blue that matched the ocean, dig her toes into warm, soft sand, stroll hand in hand with the most handsome Rasta-man on the planet, smiling while he sang songs in her ear about her and romance. Or maybe it was time to let Naomi drag her off to one of those nightclubs she enjoyed going to so much, and shake her behind all over the dance floor, bumping and grinding some man into a frenzy.

Mo shook her head. She hated clubs. They were all full of people wearing neon signs on their foreheads that said, "Get Your One Night Stand Here!", which is why her sister changed boyfriends like she changed panties. Mo needed so much more than that. Yes, she needed a lover. But she also needed a man who could be her friend. Jonathan had spoiled her, and to think she could ever possibly find anyone to replace him would be so unfair and highly unlikely. But she'd at least like to find someone to rival him. Maybe someone capable of stirring feelings inside her that Jonathan hadn't had time to stir. That's what she wanted. In all this time, no one had even come close to piquing her interest. Meeting men wasn't the problem. But, being interested in them enough to make an attempt at a relationship seemed nearly impossible for Mo. Naomi accused her of being entirely too picky. Like that was a bad thing? Mo didn't agree with that. There were no real physical requirements that had to be met. Even financially—as long as the man had a job—a steady paying job, that was fine with her. It wasn't like he had to drive a Lexus to impress her. His soul just had to mesh with hers. That's all. Was that asking too much?

When the phone rang, Mo thought to herself, "Somebody had better be in need of a blood donor, or else…" She glared at the door where Sheila sat helplessly on the other side.

"Hey. Whatchu doin,' Baaaby?" Troy sang from the other end of the phone line.

Lord, she is not in the mood for this man today. "Working," she said dryly.

"On?"

"What is it, Troy? I'm really busy, Baby."

Like what difference did that make to him anyway? Mo's younger brother was not intimidated by his sister's attitude. Other people might've been scared of the woman, but not him. "You always busy, Mo. If I waited until you weren't busy to call you, I'd never get to talk to you."

"And…your point is?" she asked sarcastically.

"I'm in a good mood today, Maureen, and even you can't steal my joy."

"I'm happy for you."

"See…that's why you don't have any friends, Mo. That bad disposition of yours is gonna get you a good ass whooping one of these days. You need to be careful who you talk to like that. And you need to be glad I even bother calling you. At least somebody out here gives a shit about your mean ass."

Mo smiled. "Thanks, Troy. I love you, too."

"Good. Does that mean you'll go to lunch with me? I'm right downtown and I could be there in a few. Or better yet, I could meet you someplace. How about Ms. Thea's? I'm in the mood for some Picadillo."

Mo sighed. "Troy, I've got a budget to put together and I brought my lunch today."

"C'mon, Maureen," he pleaded. "Pleeeeease? I'm buying."

Pleading usually meant he had something on his mind and wanted to talk. And the fact that he was willing to buy her lunch meant he had a new man in his life he was dying to brag about. Damn! Family could be such a pain in the behind sometimes. And Troy could be especially relentless. If she absolutely insisted on not meeting him for lunch, chances were he'd show up tomorrow morning at six expecting breakfast.

"I'll meet you at Ms. Thea's then. Noon?"

"Yeah...noon's cool."

"You do understand, I really don't have time for this."

"Mo, how many times are you gonna tell me that? Like I care?"

Actually, she was crazy about him and he knew it, which is why he took liberties the way he did. Troy was the only boy in the family sandwiched between two sisters who spoiled him rotten with attention and he took advantage of every minute of it. Five years ago, he'd "come out" so to speak, which for Troy really wasn't necessary because it was obvious to everyone that he'd had a little sugar in his tank. Naturally, the only person who seemed surprised at all had been Daddy. Troy's announcement hurt and embarrassed him, but it never changed his love for his son. In Daddy's eyes, "God made you a man, Troy, and that's what you always gon' be to me. I don't wanna hear 'bout none of that other mess." Out of respect, Troy tamed down the feminine antics around Daddy, but he could put on one hell of a show for Mo and Naomi. Even Momma had caught him in action from time to time.

He was late as usual, but made an entrance like a fresh, cool breeze on a bright, summer's day. Mo halfway expected to see a blue bird land on his shoulder. She rolled her eyes, disgusted that he'd managed to pry her away from her project (that she really wasn't even working on but was about to start working on) only to take his sweet time getting here. Her first diet cola was almost gone and she was just about to order another one before he blew in.

He ignored her chilly demeanor, because Troy felt too good to let Miss "I've Got a Chip on My Shoulder All the Damn Time" get the best of him. "Hi," he said, grinning. "How are you?"

Maureen wasn't the least bit amused. "So...what's on your mind, Troy?"

"Fine, thank you. Oh, this?" he said, referring to his new sweater. "I got this the other day. On sale, Girl. You like this color on me? You know I normally wear earth tones, but I thought I'd spice up my wardrobe a little bit."

The waiter came back over to the table. "Y'all ready to order now?"

"Yes. We're finally ready to order," she said, cutting her eyes at her brother.

He ordered that Picadillo he'd been craving. Mo decided to try something new for a change and settled on the Curried Coconut Shrimp and Sweet Potato Fries.

Troy could barely contain his excitement. "Guess what?"

"What?"

"Guess."

"Troy!" Mo could barely contain her annoyance.

"You're being pissy, Mo. You know I can't stand it when you're pissy."

"Will you just tell me?"

"Hmph! Not if you've got to ask me like that." He rolled his eyes this time. "You know...you really need to learn how to talk to people, Maureen. Now I know we're family and all, but..."

Mo put her hand on his arm. "Troy," she said sweetly, stopping him before he decided to leap into a long-winded, useless tangent about nothing. "What is it you want to tell me? I'm listening, Honey."

Troy grinned. "Oh, all right. Since you insist. I met a man."

"You always meet men, which is more than I can say for some of us."

"Well, Mo, acting pissy all the time doesn't help."

"I'm not pissy all the..."

"Anyway," Troy interrupted, "his name is Gregory and he is absolutely divine."

Divine? What a dumb word, she thought to herself. Only gay men and rich old white women used words like "divine."

"He's about six feet two inches, weighs maybe one hundred ninety pounds, which is a tad bit leaner than I like but...oh Mo, the brotha's got it going on. He's an engineer, single, well...divorced. Got two kids, both grown. Let's see...he's forty-five, got big, brown eyes you just wanna drown yourself in."

She couldn't help but smile. Troy talked about this man like he was describing a gourmet meal, smacking and licking his lips. "Dang, Troy. He does sound...divine. Where'd you meet him?"

Troy hesitated, then leaned in close and whispered, "On the Internet."

She chuckled. "On the Internet? You met him on the Internet?"

"Yes, I did. What's so funny about that?"

"What...was he running an ad or something?"

"As a matter of fact..." he said smugly.

When she realized he wasn't joking, Mo tried to compose herself. "You can't be serious, Troy. He had an ad on the Internet?"

"Lots of people do it, Maureen. This is the new millennium, or haven't you been paying attention?"

"But Troy...on the Internet. Do you know how many freaks hang out on the Internet?"

"Freaks aren't particular, Mo. They'll hang out any damn where they please, including restaurants. Look around you," he said, waving his hand in the air. "I'd be willing to bet that you got plenty of freaks right here." The lady at the table next to them looked at Troy like he'd lost his mind.

"Troy. You're a bright man. Why would you trust meeting

some stranger over the Internet? And don't give me that crap about it being the new millennium. I know what year it is. But do you know how dangerous something like that can be?"

"Maureen. It's not like I just answered his ad, we met, fucked and that's it," he snapped. Now who was being pissy? "We've been taking it slow, which is why the Internet is cool. We emailed each other for awhile, then exchanged phone numbers, then after we both felt comfortable, we hooked up in person. Where's the pressure?"

"Well, you sound like you know what you're doing."

"I know what I'm doing."

"And you really like this guy?"

Troy smiled. "Yes. I really do and you'll like him, too. I want you to meet him."

"I'm looking forward to it. I really am."

Troy went on and on about Gregory all during lunch.

"So he was married?"

"Yes. Greg is like a lot of gay brothas. He'd been in denial when he got married; then, they had the kids, so he felt obligated to stay. You know...did what society says he's supposed to do, never mind the fact that the man was miserable, which made his wife miserable, which made the dog miserable. Why do you think people are so quick to deny themselves, Mo? I mean...you know when you're doing something that just isn't you, but you do it anyway because you're afraid of what everybody else is going to say. I don't know. Life's too short for all that in my opinion. You're born. You die. The in-between is what it's all about. You ever thought about that?"

"Not really." She shrugged.

"Oh. I guess you ain't got time to dwell on shit like that, huh? Too busy to waste all that time thinking about philosophy and stuff," he said sarcastically, which Mo chose to ignore.

"If you must know... I don't think about it 'cause I'm one of those people too busy denying myself." She smiled.

"Praise God! Chile, at least you can admit it."

"Yeah...I've been admitting a lot of things to myself lately."

"Like?"

"Like...I'm getting tired of denying myself."

Blackgentlemen.com

"It's about time. I was wondering when you were going to wake up and smell the Chai Tea, Girl."

"Well, I'm up and I'm smelling it. But I'm not sure what I'm gonna do about it. I'm tired, Troy. Do you have any idea how hard it is to live in a box?"

"You know better than to ask me that."

"I'm just... I want out."

He shrugged. "So get out."

"I don't know how. I've been living like this so long, I wouldn't even know where to start changing."

"Mo, you're making this way too hard."

"I'm not trying to make it hard. I'm trying to do something about it and the problem is, I have no idea what to do. I used to be so outgoing. Now...I'm this pent up, uptight, ball of..."

"Barbed wire?"

"Thanks, Troy. So how do I undo all that?"

"A little at a time, Baby. Girl, it took you years and lots of hard work to build up those walls. They can come down, but don't be so hard on yourself. It's all about a process. It'll take time, but now that you know what the problem is, that's half the battle."

Mo smiled. Troy had always been so patient with her. Especially after she lost Jonathan. Naomi had taken Ty to her place for awhile, while Maureen fell apart, and Troy would stop by every day on his way home from work, bringing a bottle of Chardonnay or a six pack of Coronas and some of Pierre's fried fish or Kapri chicken. They'd get drunk, eat until they couldn't eat anymore, cry, then pass out from being drunk, full, or just plain exhausted.

Growing up, he'd been the little sister Naomi had gotten there too late to be. Mo and Troy were only two years apart in age and they'd been closer than brother and sister. Troy learned at a very young age that he wasn't like the other little boys and he paid dearly for it. But he was tough and Mo was tougher, ready to give or get an ass whooping for him at a moment's notice.

"I'm a sissy, ain't I Mo?" he cried one day after being called a fag by a group of bullies.

"Boy! You ain't no sissy! You my best friend!" She meant it

then, and it still held true, even now. She worried about him, though. Troy liked living on the edge and did the kind of things Mo knew could get him hurt. But he swore up and down that he knew what he was doing. Whatever the case, Mo was still big sister and she was still willing to whoop up on any son-of-a-bitch stupid enough to try messing with her little brother.

Troy pulled out a pen and piece of paper from his organizer, quickly scribbled something on it, then handed it to Mo.

"BlackGentlemen.com? What is this?"

"It's where I met Gregory."

"So why are you giving it to me? I'm not looking for gay men."

"They're not all gay, Mo. I found Gregory in the MSM section."

"MSM?"

"Man Searching for Man. You need to look in the MSW section. I checked it out, Girl. They got some fine ones in that section."

"No thank you, Troy." She slid the paper back over to him. "I'm not interested."

"How come I had a feeling you were going to say that? You don't have to use it, but will you at least think about it? Just check it out. What can it hurt?"

"This isn't exactly the way I'd planned on having my debut, Troy. I'd like something a little more...normal."

"Child, please. Normal is as normal does."

"What's that supposed to mean?"

"It means...ain't nobody's business what you do up in your house but yours. You're a young, attractive woman. Don't let it go to waste."

"Thank you, little brother."

He slid the paper back over to her. "It's easy, Maureen. If you meet someone and it turns out he's not your type, cut him loose. Hit the 'delete' key and...Boom! Pow! It's over." He snapped his fingers. "Just like that, Baby. But if you do happen to find someone you like, take your time...write each other, build up your confidence again.

Before you know it, you'll be back to your old flirtatious, teasing self."
He smiled.

Mo shook her head, folded up the slip of paper, and put it in
her purse. Of course, she'd never use it, but if it made Troy feel better
to think she'd think about it, then yeah. She'd pacify him. She owed
him that much.

After Jonathan died, Mo vowed to spend the rest of her life
alone. Of course, that was impossible. She missed all those things
women miss when they're in love. Like having her hand held. Having
her lips gently sucked on and kissed. Being told how pretty she was.
Having someone stroke her hair, or her back, or her pussy. She missed
having big, strong shoulders wrapping arms around her. She missed
falling asleep to deep, slow, rhythmic heartbeats buried somewhere
behind a broad chest. No, being alone wasn't cool anymore. Not cool
at all.

Chapter Four

Kevin eased out of bed at 6:27 a.m. He quickly and quietly finished dressing, then stopped to gaze down at the delectable Kiara... What was her last name? Did she even have one? Had she told him what it was? Hell, he couldn't remember. "Damn!" he mouthed. If nothing else, that woman was definitely creative. And flexible. A little too damn flexible. With some serious stamina. Way too much stamina. Made him tired just thinking about it. Like most men, Kevin had done his share of bragging about how long he could keep it up. Truth is, most of the time his claim, like that of most men, was bullshit. In his mind, it wasn't healthy for a man to cum more than four times within a twenty-four-hour period. And Kiara seemed determined to milk a brotha bone-dry. He eventually had to tell the woman—enough! She pouted, rolled off him, then fell right off to sleep. Shit, she knew she'd had enough, too, but for some reason he felt she was out to try to prove something. Like the fact that she could outlast him. Hell, yeah, she could outlast him! It's a known scientific fact...when a man cums, he must have sleep! Period. Just a few minutes is all it takes, but Kiara wasn't even trying to be considerate. A woman like that would fuck a man to death in less than a year.

Leaving before she woke up was both a matter of life or death (his) and probably the most considerate thing he could do. After all, what did they have in common anyway besides fucking? He shuddered at the thought of the two of them struggling to hold a meaningful conversation over coffee and eggs. Things had been different between them the night before. There hadn't been any real conversation. But there had been plenty of innuendoes and signals, typical to the ritualistic habits of mammals mating like those on animal shows. Nothing personal, just sex. He didn't even feel guilty because he knew that's all it had been for her, too. He just hoped she wasn't one of those women who believed that good pussy was powerful enough to justify putting a leash around a man's neck, and dragging him behind her like a dog in heat. Damn! If that's what she thought, then maybe he ought to wake her up and enlighten the sistah. Pussy was pussy and all pussy was good pussy. Sure, some pussy was better than other pussy, but Kevin couldn't remember ever having had bad pussy. So despite what some women might think, devouring a man with some good pussy was not the answer to winning a man's heart.

Maybe a more weak-minded man was cool with good sex, but Kevin was looking for the not-so-obvious. For him, there were other factors at play. He wanted a woman who could look into his eyes and make him feel like there was no other man in the world for her but him. A woman whose smile filled him with more passion than a fuck ever could. He wanted a woman who, by just touching him, could send his heart reeling into outer space. He hadn't seen any of those things in the lovely Kiara. Maybe he could've if he'd looked hard enough. But he hadn't been able to see much from behind all that ass she slung at him on the dance floor and all that cleavage she'd doused him with at the bar. Not that he should put all the blame on her. Shit, all he ever had to do was "just say no." But what the hell? He hadn't had any good pussy in ages and Miss Kiara was all too willing to oblige a brotha. Kevin shook his head, then bent and kissed a shapely calf. Kiara moaned, and he quietly slipped out of her apartment before she woke up.

He'd just turned thirty-six years old. Before that, he didn't even know men had biological clocks. Kevin always thought that was a woman thing. But he was beginning to relish the idea of having one woman in his life, maybe even some kids. And the idea of having them while he was still young enough to enjoy them was even more appealing. All his married friends said they envied him. "Man...you don't know how good you got it. You got all the freedom, all the women..." But these were the same brothas who could only stay at the club long enough to admire a shapely view and have a drink or two before heading home. The same brothas packing up the kids for family vacations, celebrating anniversaries, "Baby this-ing and Baby that-ing" their wives. These were the same brothas who knew who they were going to go to bed with every night and as much as they might've said they envied him, not one of them seemed to be in any hurry to let go of what they had in exchange for his lifestyle.

It wasn't like Kevin hadn't enjoyed being single. He knew for a fact that he'd lived his single life to the utmost. It had been an outta-sight ride and he'd be the last person to claim otherwise. He'd spent his time with some fine, intelligent, creative, funny sistahs, many of whom would've loved to settle him down. Only at the time, he'd been too greedy for his own good, feeling that there was more than enough of him to go around. Any woman worth anything wasn't having it and, consequently, he'd missed out on some wonderful possibilities. Well, now he'd made up his mind not to miss out on any more, and Kevin set his sights on getting married.

Chapter Five

"Ty! C'mon, Baby. Auntie's here," Mo called upstairs. Naomi walked in wearing plenty of attitude and plopped her little behind down on the couch, then folded her arms across her chest.

"What's wrong with you, Miss Lady?"

Naomi's bottom lip was poked out so far, Mo was afraid somebody in the neighborhood might trip over it. "How come you and Troy didn't invite me to lunch?"

It was no secret that Naomi was the fiercely insecure, jealous child in the family. Being the youngest, she felt obligated to make sure her presence was felt and acknowledged by Mo and Troy. Probably because when they were kids, Naomi was always being left behind for being too small and too slow to keep up, locked in closets, left in trees that were too high for her to climb out of, and teased mercilessly by her older brother and sister. Thirty years old and she still hadn't truly forgiven them.

Mo sat down next to her and patted her arm. "Naomi...you work all the way in the Tech Center. Now would you really have driven all the way over to the Points just for some sweet potato fries?"

"That's not the point, Mo. Y'all could've at least invited me."

"I'm sorry, Baby. And you're right. We should've, and next time, we will," she said in her most condescending tone.

Naomi smiled and kissed Mo's cheek. Yeah, she still knew how to push ol' girl's buttons. Naomi had decided to let Ty spend the weekend with her because lately, she'd been hit by some of those irritating maternal instincts. Usually, a few days with her nephew was just the kind of medicine she needed to cure that ailment. Not to mention, she knew Mo needed a break sometimes, and she hoped that maybe this weekend, the woman would cut loose and go out and get herself a life...something outside of work and the boy. "He tell you about Gregory?" Naomi grinned.

Mo rolled her eyes. "Yes. He told me about Gregory."

"He tell you how he met him?"

"You know he did. Which is absolutely ridiculous, if you ask me."

"Not all that ridiculous. I think it's kind of romantic."

"You won't think it's all that romantic if this Gregory turns out to be a serial killer."

"He's not a serial killer, Mo. He's actually very nice."

"You've met him?"

"I went with them on their first date. Troy insisted."

"And you didn't tell me?"

Naomi smiled. "I assumed Troy would tell you. He tells you everything else. Or...at least he used to." Naomi loved it when she was in the loop and Mo wasn't. "Besides, wasn't much to tell. I didn't stay long. Just long enough to have a drink, meet the man...you know. Check him out. And he's nice. Very handsome."

"Yeah, well...Troy needs to be careful anyway. You know how wrapped up he can get in somebody. Remember Walter? Took that boy ages to get over Walter's lying, skinny ass."

Naomi stared at Mo in dismay. "If that isn't the pot calling the kettle black."

"Don't start, Nay. Ty...hurry up, Boy! Your Auntie's gonna leave without you." Mo glared at Naomi.

"I'm just saying..."

Ty came stumbling down the stairs carrying a backpack bigger than he was. "Hi, Auntie Nay Nay. I'm ready," he said, grinning, out of breath, and standing at the door. Obviously, chit chat time was over.

"You sure you got everything this time, Ty? 'Cause we're not coming back." Naomi half-heartedly scolded the boy, knowing good and well, if he asked her to, she'd be back.

"I'm sure." He smiled.

"So," Naomi asked turning to Mo, "What kind of plans do you have for the weekend? As if I don't know."

"Give me a break. Please? Please? I'm begging you, Naomi." Mo fell to her knees, tugging on Naomi's jacket. "Please. Just give me one little break? Please?"

Naturally, Ty found the whole scene so funny, he nearly fell over under the weight of his backpack. "You look silly, Mom."

Naomi rolled her eyes. "She is silly, Ty. Let's go before we end up silly like her." She rushed him out the door and raced him to her car.

Mo waved after them. "Be good, Ty!"

"I will. Love you, Mommy."

Mo slowly got up off her knees to the very disturbing sounds of bones popping. Just before she closed the door, Naomi shouted, "Remember, Mo! This weekend? Get a life!" Then she hurried into the car and sped off.

If Ty hadn't been within earshot, Mo would've definitely shouted back a solid, "fuck you!"

She closed the door behind her and stood there for a moment. Yeah, she needed a break from the little man, but she was sure gonna miss him. Even if it was only for two days. Then it hit her. There it was again, weighing down on her head like a ton of bricks. That damn quiet.

She had to get this budget done this weekend. The board was meeting on Tuesday and Mo had planned on working on it while Ty was gone. Little man didn't understand the importance of things like budgets and the board of directors. He felt that asking Mo permission to hook up the video game was far more pressing an issue. His being gone was going to get rid of all the little excuses she had for why she couldn't get it done. Mo sat at the dining room table, adding up receipts, bills, salaries, setting expectations, goals...hell! Why couldn't she be spending her Friday night doing something else? She threw down her pencil, and rubbed her head. "I need a break. A real break."

Mo got up from the table and looked around her empty, quiet house. First, she stared at the television, thinking that maybe she'd find a good movie on or something. No...Mo hated television. Music. When's the last time she had turned on the stereo? Music would be nice. Mo looked through her very short stack of CDs, trying to find something that wouldn't depress her or remind her of things she didn't want to be reminded of. Then she remembered a birthday present Naomi and Troy had given her last year. Where was it?

"Ah! Here it is." Mo blew the dust off, cracked open the cellophane, and popped the brand-new old CD into her stereo. The Best of Earth, Wind and Fire. Mo loved her some Earth, Wind and Fire. She could listen to Maurice and Philip sing about Septembers and Devotions for the rest of her life and never get tired of it. She'd grown up in the seventies, before the term "house party" became synonymous with the title of a movie. It cost twenty-five cents to get in, and parents usually pulled up in the driveway before midnight to pick up their kids and take them home. She remembered disco balls twinkling from basement ceilings, onion dip and chips, and fruit punch that, by the end of the night, had been spiked with more punch than fruit. Mo remembered how all the boys would line up against one wall together, and how all the girls would gather against the other one. Everybody would secretly pray for a slow jam to be played, and be scared to death when one did come on. And if you were lucky enough to have a boy ask you to slow dance, and if he got a hard-on and you felt it, you knew he liked you. Of course, boys knew the real deal. Getting a hard-on at fourteen didn't take any real effort at all. Most of them could get a hard on if the cat rubbed up against them.

Before she knew what was happening, the music had taken her hips captive and Mo found herself dancing around her living room, shaking this and shimmying that. She laughed at herself and how ridiculously exuberant she felt. Oh, she hadn't felt this good in so long. She pulled out the insert from the CD and caught herself singing along, grabbing a hairbrush and pretending it was her singing. "...that's the way...of the world..." Sadness tried creeping in, reminding her of Jonathan, but Mo wasn't having it. Not tonight. She wasn't going to let him rob her of what she was feeling right now. This second. Mo was happy. She felt good and thoughts of Jonathan couldn't have that.

She'd almost forgotten the other part of her present that she never opened. Naomi had given her the CD, but Troy had given her the joints. She looked in her stereo case behind the CDs and...yep.

There they were. Two perfectly rolled joints all wrapped up nice and neat in a plastic bag. Mo giggled and hurried into the kitchen to find a cigarette lighter. She'd never really cared much for smoking weed. But Troy felt it might do her some good, loosen her up some. Boy did it ever. Mo held the smoke deep in her lungs for as long as she could, then let it escape slowly from her mouth. She twirled around the room, laughing and shaking her body to the point that she literally collapsed on the sofa. Mo laughed harder than she'd laughed in years. She laughed so hard she thought she'd pee on herself, so she ran to the bathroom, plopped down on the toilet, then remembered...she'd forgotten to pull down her pants. "Shit!" she said. Then laughed some more, pulled off her clothes, and jumped in the shower.

She didn't even dry off after she got out. Mo walked around the house completely naked and she hadn't done that since... She lit the last joint, went upstairs to her bedroom, then rummaged through her drawers trying to find that one tee-shirt. Her favorite one. Where was it? Where is... Mo caught a glimpse of herself, naked in the mirror. She stopped and stared back at this woman who she hadn't seen in so long. Tears welled up in her eyes, because this woman was beautiful. Her skin was the color of caramel, her dark brown hair hung loosely, barely touching the tops of her shoulders. She'd never been as tall as she would've liked, but five-three looked perfect on her. Mo pressed the palm of her hand against her stomach. No, it wasn't ironing-board flat and she could still see the stretch marks left behind from carrying Ty, but the slight bulge wasn't nearly as ugly as she'd once thought. Mo turned to the side. She smiled. Yes. She had a nice ass. Still. She'd always thought her breasts were too big, but men loved them. They were firm and shaped like teardrops.

"I missed you," Mo slurred. "Where've you been, Maureen?"

She stared at herself, seeing that yes, she was still a desirable woman. Jonathan used to tell her how lovely she was all the time. And he'd been right. She was lovely. Too damn lovely to be at home alone on a Friday night. A woman like her should be out someplace doing something special with someone incredible.

"There's no excuse for this." Mo wiped her face, then dumped the contents of her purse on the bed, looking for the website address

Troy had given her. Hell! Maybe it was ridiculous, but at least it was something. At least it was a way to get out of this rut. It was a way to come back to the world again. Mo found the website address, then sat down in front of her computer and pulled it up. The man of your dreams is waiting for you flashed at the top of the homepage. What man? What dreams? Since Jonathan's death she hadn't dreamed of any other man, and lately, she hadn't even been dreaming of him.

A long list of options beckoned her to design the man of her dreams. "Pick your flavor, Girl." She grinned. "Like 'em tall? Choose tall. Like 'em in Colorado? Shoot! Click on Denver. Like 'em young? Click...jailbait! No. No jailbait. I've already got a son. How about thirty-five to forty? That's good."

Over two-hundred ads popped up meeting her criteria. Maureen slowly browsed through them, thinking about a time when she could've given some of these brothas hell. Back in the day, she used to drive the fellas wild, strutting around in high-heeled shoes, short skirts, swinging hips that swayed to the sound of African drums. She grinned. "Baby, you so damn fine," Jonathan used to say. Yes, she was. Dang! Why was she sitting here acting like she was about to be late for her own funeral? She was only thirty-seven, which isn't even close to being old. "Hmph. I still got it going on." She smiled.

Would it really be so crazy to answer one of those ads? Other people did it all the time, so it couldn't be all bad. Of course, some of the ads were questionable. Written by confused men in confused times.

Afternoon Delight...
Classy, clean-cut, disease-free, passionate man, seeks uninhibited female for discreet encounters.

I got the beef!
Well-hung brotha looking for a woman to share moonlit walks, candlelit dinners, and meaningful conversations.

Let's do this thang
Culturally aware and active black man, seeking the right woman to share his life-journey with. Race unimportant.

Blackgentlemen.com

It was all she could do not to fall out of her chair laughing. Some men even had the nerve to post mug shots...um, photos of themselves with their ads. She came across a few who looked promising, even handsome, but some of them looked like they'd scanned in their driver's license pictures, which in Mo's opinion was no way to impress a woman. Finally, she came across one ad that did get her attention. "Oh, my goodness!" Mo had to blink a couple of times to make sure she was seeing what she was seeing. Staring back at her with that pretty smile all loaded up and ready to take aim was Mr. Davies. Kevin Davies. The same Kevin Davies who'd been sitting in her office the other day. The very same one who'd be at the center every Tuesday at six o'clock. As gorgeous as that man was, why in the world did he need to put an ad on the Internet?

Black Man...Searching

"I've been out here long enough to have sown any wild oats left in my system and now I'm ready to settle down. Or perhaps, I'm ready to settle up. Being single has its benefits and I've taken advantage of them all, but I don't believe man was intended to spend his life alone. I've tried the clubs, church, the gym, grocery store and I haven't been able to find her. Let me describe her to you: I'm intelligent, but she's brilliant. I'm artistic, but she's my inspiration. I'm ambitious, but she's goal-oriented. I'm a free spirit, but she's...longing to be free. Am I asking for too much? Maybe. But I'm only asking for as much as I'm willing to give. Soulmate...are you feeling me?"

Unlike the others, this one was real. Really real, like reach-out-and-touch-a-woman kind of real. Like reach-out-and-kiss-those-full-soft-lips kind of real. Like feeling the sensation of his tongue between —well, just about anywhere was fine with her kind of real. Damn! She missed sex. Real sex. With a real man.

Mo laughed. "Whoa! He is so fine."

Mo stared at his picture so long she started hallucinating. The on screen Kevin winked at her, then seemed to pucker up and blow a kiss in her direction.

So, what if she took a chance and answered his ad? Mo smiled. He'd never know it was her. Would he? How would he possibly know?

"That's not cool, Maureen," she said to herself.

Why wouldn't she want him to know? Because he had no business placing personal ads. That's why. Who was he trying to fool? Men like Kevin Davies should be banned from placing personal ads. It's not proper. Not to mention, responding to personal ads was not her style. What style? Since when had she had any damn style to speak of? Not in years. And what a waste of time. After all, the man was a volunteer at her center. If she wanted to talk to him, all she ever had to do was be there on a Tuesday evening at six and she could say whatever she wanted to him. Now that made more sense than sending an anonymous email to him. Of course, it did. Mo grinned. It might make more sense, but it definitely wouldn't be as much fun. Mo became excited over the notion of being impetuous. She'd forgotten what it felt like to be spontaneous. It wasn't like giving out her phone number where she'd end up dodging calls if she didn't like him or changed her mind about getting to know him. What did Troy say? "...just hit the 'delete' key." She laughed again, then hit the "Respond to this ad" button beneath Kevin's picture. An email screen popped up.

"Now." She paused. "What should I say?"

Mo typed, "Well, hello there, Mr. Davies." She giggled. "That's stupid, Mo. I mean...talk about...stupid." Maureen backspaced over what she'd just typed to erase it. "This is silly. Just plain silly." Here was an opportunity staring her right in the face. An opportunity to say whatever she wanted to say to this beautiful man without running the risk of suffering any real consequences. "But it's...childish and immature," she said out loud. Well, yeah. It might've been childish and immature, but it definitely held a spark of excitement in her otherwise dull life. And knowing who this man was only added to that excitement.

She braced herself, then started again.

Black Man,
You are absolutely—divine. Anybody ever tell you that? Well, you are. I for one find you breathtaking, beautiful, and —bomb! Why would someone like you feel the need to place an ad to find a woman? You're very handsome, and your ad is charming. So why would a handsome,

Blackgentlemen.com

charming man need to go on the Internet to meet women? Maybe you've got the wrong idea about where to find this "soulmate." Maybe she's right under your nose and you just aren't paying attention. But I'll bet she is. And I'll bet she's just waiting and hoping for you to ask her out to dinner. Flash that smile of yours in her direction, ask her how her day is. I'll bet she's at home right now, this second, trying not to think of you. In my opinion, you're overlooking the obvious.

–So Interested

Before she had a chance to reconsider, Mo hit the send button and cast her response out into the cyber ocean of no return. Marijuana is a mind-altering drug with the power to affect any reasonable woman's sensibilities. Maureen stared at her email, which slowly faded into cyberspace to be replaced by the words "Your message has been sent." What in the world had she just done? Panic tried to set in, but all that weed she'd smoked wouldn't let it.

"Mr. Davies. Got an ad on the net. What is this world coming to when a brotha like that's got to put out an ad to get a woman?" Mo shook her head. Not to mention, what had this world come to when she found herself answering personal ads on the net? Damn! Things sure had changed a lot in three years.

Mo finished off the last of the joint, then crawled into bed. She felt so good. And not because of the weed either, though that definitely had something to do with it. But she felt—like she'd taken a deep breath for the first time. She felt good enough to even be a little horny. Images of Kevin Davies flashing across her mind didn't help. She closed her eyes and recreated him in her mind. "I wonder...if he's a good kisser." She giggled like a schoolgirl. "He had some big, pretty lips. Brotha can probably kiss the hell outta somebody." His hands were nice, too, big and strong. Sleep was beginning to override horny. See. That's why Mo never liked weed. She could never stay awake long enough to enjoy it. She knew one thing. She'd definitely have to do this more often. Wonder if Troy could get some more weed?

Oh, Lord. He answered. Curiosity beckoned her to her PC before the sun even came up and Mo immediately opened her inbox.

manhattan245@email.com...RE: Black Man

Hello So Interested,

Thanks for responding to my ad. I've been called many things in my lifetime, but never "divine." I put up the ad on the advice of a friend. He promised that women would come out of the woodwork to respond and he was right. They have. I'd hoped to find one who I might explore long-term possibilities with, but that hasn't happened. Your response is flattering and very mysterious. The flattery, I like. But the mystery? I'm not sure. Your implications about my soulmate being someone that I might know intrigue me. Have we met? Do I know you? Who are you?

Who are you? Well, last night she'd been a lonely woman, extremely high on an illegal substance, living out a brief, but invigorating, fantasy on the Internet involving flirting and innuendoes with a handsome man she hardly even knew. And today? Today she was Maureen Beckman, who had laundry to do, a house to clean, a car that needed washing, and a budget that still wasn't any closer to being finished than when she committed herself to working on it last night. She was no one very exciting at all. That's who she was. Maureen was a lonely woman looking for something extraordinary with a man she hardly knew. The end. Was that a desperate cry for help welling up inside her? Sure sounded like it. The tiny voice inside her begged, "Please. Please, Mo. Do something before it's too late. Spoon me up something besides this rut you've been force feeding me all these years. Give me something to look forward to. I'll pay you back, Girl." Her tiny voice sounded pitiful and it broke her heart to have to listen to it, which is why she ignored it most of the time. But not this time. This time, her tiny voice warned, "If you keep ignoring me, eventually I'm going to stop talking to you, Maureen." Not cool, she thought to herself.

Mo thought long and hard before responding to Kevin's email. She had to be careful not to reveal too much or too little about herself. She thought about telling him something that resembled the truth:

I'm the director of a community center, lonely, widowed, 37-year-old mother of one, who has no life outside her child and work, which was an answer capable of squashing even the best wet dream. Or she could spice it up a bit. Mo thought carefully, then opted for the spice:

MizMOcha
I'm thirty-something years old, single, adventurous, and uninhibited. But I'm bored with the typical dating scene and have opted to try something new. Something more exciting. I was surprised to see your picture on the Internet, but I'm glad I found it. I'm glad I found you. Yes, we've met before. I like the excitement of mystery and I like having the advantage. You have no idea who I am and I find that exhilarating. Don't you? Rest assured, however, I'm harmless. Not a stalker or crazed lunatic looking to run amok in your world. I'm an admirer. Nothing more. Nothing less. I've been looking for a way to tell you how I feel, but the opportunity hasn't presented itself, until now. You're a delicious man, Kevin. Eventually, I'll reveal myself to you, but for now, I prefer to leave you guessing, wondering. Use your imagination, Kevin. This might be fun. And who knows? Maybe we'll even get the opportunity to fulfill some wild fantasies of lust, love, and living happily ever after. Do you think that's possible? –Mo
      She finished typing, then quickly clicked the "send" button on the screen. Suddenly it hit her. What wild fantasies?

      "Damn!" Ron said, after Kevin finished reading Mo's email to him over the phone.
      "Naw...tell me what you really think, Man?"
      "What do I think? Man...I think you got yourself a damn psycho on your hands. That's what I think. But then, you know that's what I think about all females lurking around on the net looking for men. All of them are psychos, if you ask me."
      "She says she knows me."
      "Which makes her crazier than the rest of them. She knows you, but instead of telling you straight up, ol' girl decides to get Houdini on a brotha. Poof! First you see her, then you don't."
      "I don't know any 'Mo's', Man. I know a Mona, a few Moniques, maybe a Monica..."
      "I'm telling you, Bro'...delete that email and block that ass.

Mo's probably a four-hundred-pound Sumo Wrestler with pimples all over his ass. You don't wanna mess with no shit like that. Your ass comes up dead, don't say I didn't warn you. You need to take your damn picture off the Internet. That's what you need to do."

"Took it down this morning, Man. But she's still got my email address."

"Yeah, well...don't play with no shit like that, Man. Let it go. Hell, if she's all that interested, she'll let you know."

Ron Sanders. The voice of reason. Everything the man said made sense, but the little bit of optimism Kevin had left drowned out all of Ron's reasonable argument. It was only email, and if he did end up finding himself face to face with a four-hundred-pound Sumo Wrestler instead of some beautiful, exotic woman he'd hoped for, he'd just sic medium-built, three-hundred-fifty-pound Jennifer on his ass. He wrote back:

manhattan245

I believe the possibilities are endless and I'm looking forward to exploring with you even more. I can appreciate a good mystery as well as the next man, but I'll be honest. I also like to know what/who I'm dealing with. You might appreciate having the advantage, and for the moment, it's yours. Eventually, I plan on having an advantage of my own. As for fulfilling fantasies, I prefer reality. I prefer satisfying all my senses and hers. I hope you aren't content with just teasing a man, Mo. I'm looking forward to finding out who you are. And I can be relentless.
Kevin

Sometimes a man's got to give it one last chance before letting go. He couldn't explain it, but Kevin had a feeling about this one. That wasn't necessarily a good thing, but he was definitely curious about who was on the other end of that computer. Of course, curiosity had killed that damn cat. Hmmm....

Chapter Six

Normally, she'd have beaten herself up for being late for work, but lately Mo found her usual level of motivation waning and she strolled into the office like she hadn't a care in the world.

"Good morning, Mo," Sheila said, looking unnecessarily concerned. "Everything alright?"

Mo smiled, which was rare before coffee. "Morning, Sheila. Everything's fine. Why?"

Before Sheila could answer, Kevin walked through the door loaded down with boxes. Maureen's mouth fell open at the sight of him. What was he doing here? It wasn't Tuesday evening at six o'clock. That's when he was supposed to be at the center. That was his time. This...Monday mornings...this was her time. He wasn't allowed in her time and suddenly, she resented him for something that was absolutely not his fault.

"Hey, ladies." He smiled.

Mo stood frozen. She hadn't laid eyes on him since the first time they'd met. Of course, his picture was burned onto her computer screen at home and tattooed on her brain from staring at it so much. But somewhere along the line, she'd lost sight of one very important fact. Kevin was real. The man was a walking, talking bag of fine that breathed, ate, and slept like everybody else. And now, here he was standing in the same room as she was, sharing–air.

Mo's speechlessness made Sheila entirely too uneasy and she quickly hurried to his rescue. "Let me help you with some of those, Kevin." She grabbed the smaller box from the top.

"Thanks," he said. "I was afraid I'd lose that one."

The words flowed from her mouth like diarrhea and Mo was sure she sounded just as foul. "What are you doing here?"

Kevin hesitated for a minute and the corners of that beautiful smile fell off his face for a moment. But he quickly gathered them. "Well, I had some extra equipment just gathering dust in my garage and I figured the kids could get some use out of it here."

"That's a great idea," Sheila said with her enthusiastic self. "We never turn down donations. Do we, Mo?"

Mo felt her body sway slightly, as she wallowed in a boat load of uncomfortable and it took every ounce of energy she had to look like she had herself together.

"No," she said trying to feign a smile. "We never do. Thank you, Mr. Davies."

"I thought we agreed you'd call me Kevin?"

"Yes. Well...thank you, Kevin. We certainly appreciate your generosity," Mo said coldly. "Sheila will give you the necessary forms to fill out for tax write-off purposes."

"Oh, that's really not..."

"Nonsense," Mo said quickly. "Sheila, make sure Mr...Kevin understands how to fill out the forms."

"No problem, Mo."

"You'll excuse me. I've got to get to work." Mo went into her office, closed the door behind her, and collapsed in her chair. She wanted to laugh and cuss all at the same time, but first, she had to wait for that knot in her throat to dissipate before it strangled her.

"That was totally uncalled for," she mouthed silently. Why had she been so cold to him? He hadn't done anything. It's just that seeing him face to face like that made her feel–defensive. As long as he was a fantasy, he was cool, but the minute he put on some skin, suddenly he was a threat. The kind of threat that could unfold and make her look like a complete and total fool. Surely, he had to be able to see that on her. Foolishness. Yep, she wore it like a skin tight outfit.

"You're making such a fool out of yourself," she whispered. Lord have mercy. She wondered if Sheila could see it, too. Mo pulled her compact out of her purse and grimaced at what stared back at her.

Lonely, desperate, foolish, and definitely not woman enough to tell the man, "Hey! I think you've got it going on and let's do this!" Now, she felt like crying.

Kevin went to the classroom and quickly started setting up his equipment. *Where in the hell did that come from?* he wondered while he worked. "That" meaning attitude from Mrs. Beckman. He hadn't imagined it. Mrs. Beckman, who'd been so warm and receptive a few weeks ago, had turned into the Ice Queen all of a sudden and he just didn't get it. The expression on her face when he walked in nearly screamed, "Oh my God! It's you!" But he played it off, figuring that maybe she didn't remember him and with all those boxes he was carrying, maybe she thought he was selling something. It didn't take him long to figure out that ol' girl definitely had a problem with him. Only thing was, he had no idea why. As far as he knew, things were going great with the class. He hadn't had any problems with the students and he didn't think they'd had any problems with him. So what was up with that demeanor of hers? Once again, his theory had proven true. Women were a trip. A man just couldn't get comfortable, where women were concerned. One minute everything was cool and the next... Kevin decided to come back later to finish setting up. He'd make sure to show up after-hours from now on. Better to do that than have to face Sybil again anytime soon.

Chapter Seven

He'd written her half a dozen times and still no word from MizMOcha. Kevin had decided that she was indeed lost in Cyberspace when finally, she answered him.

MizMOcha
Kevin, I've been a bad girl, and you have to punish me. I tried saying I'm sorry by meeting you at the door in the sheer, black teddy, garter belt, and silk stockings you bought me for my birthday. Remember how excited you get whenever I wear that? But, you're still so disappointed in me. You order me into the bedroom. "Lay down!" you scold. Obediently, I lay across the bed. "Turn over! I want you on your stomach." I do as I'm told because I know how angry you are with me. I try pouting, but it doesn't work. Where did you get those, Kevin? Handcuffs. You take each of my wrists, and cuff them to the posts on the headboard. I don't like this. I'm powerless and this excites you. Whap! You smack my ass with your open hand. "You've been a bad girl, Mo. A very bad girl and I have to punish you." You go over to the dresser and pull out the gift I gave you last Christmas. Three black, silk scarves. I thought you'd forgotten about those. You spread my legs apart and tie me by my ankles to the posts at the foot of the bed. Then, you use the last scarf to blindfold me. "Are you going to hurt me, Kevin?" I ask. My excitement drips between my legs. I'm totally at your delicious mercy. You're undressing. I can hear you. I lick my lips in anticipation. "You're a freak," you growl. "You're my freak, baby." I feel the cold, hard steel of your belt buckle

against my back, dragging down to my ass, then finally resting between my legs. I squirm against it. "Yes, baby," I whisper. "I'm your freak. I'm all yours, Kevin." "Shut up!" you shout. "I didn't tell you to speak."

You slap the leather against my ass. "Kevin," I whimper. "Please, baby. Please?" I beg, and this time, you're the one who's obedient, Whap!, and you do it again. "It hurts, Kevin." You can't see them because they're hidden behind the blindfold, but there are tears in my eyes. Tears from the pain, and tears anticipating you. You lean down to kiss me where it hurts. "I'm so sorry, baby." I can feel you crawling on the bed, kissing my ass again and again and I raise it up to meet your beautiful, full lips. Lips that eventually find their way between my legs. You lap up the juices like a thirsty man, sending my hips spiraling against your face. "Ohhh!" I moan. I want to hold you, to wrap myself around you, but I can't touch you. That pisses me off. That excites me. I feel the weight of you on top of me, Kevin. You enter me from behind, and with your hand, you massage my clit. I'm wiggling beneath you like a snake. "Be my freak, baby," you whisper in my ear. I throw my ass at you, meeting you thrust for thrust until finally...

That was good for me. Was it good for you, Kevin?

"Damn," he mumbled, reading Mo's email. Kevin looked down and noticed his hard-on bulging against his pants.

manhattan245
Mo—call me. 303-555-4445

Chapter Eight

Naomi couldn't believe it. This time when she said, "Mo, girl, let's go to the club Friday," Mo actually surprised her and said "yes." Naomi wasn't sure what was up, or what had gotten into the woman, but she decided not to push her luck or press the issue, so she answered simply, "Good. I'll pick you up at ten," and left it at that.

Mo came downstairs wearing a black crepe pantsuit and some kind of pink, ruffled, satin blouse thingy underneath. Naomi cringed at the sight of her. "No, no, no...Momma." She took her sister by the hand and dragged her back upstairs to her bedroom. "You are not going out with me looking like a schoolteacher."

"What's wrong with this?" Naturally, Mo was offended. "Don't trip, Nay. I'm too old to be going around letting my ass hang out all over the place like some folks I know. Besides, it's chilly outside." Mo looked at her sister, in her brown leather jeans, and spaghetti-strapped, next-to-nothing blouse and wondered how on earth the woman could stand to dress like that when it was no more than forty degrees outside. At least she had the decency to wear boots or else Mo would've refused to leave the house until the girl put on some decent shoes.

Naomi rummaged through Mo's closet trying to find something that screamed some semblance of sexy. When she didn't find that, she looked for something that might whisper it, or at least, imply it, finally settling on a conservative, but clingy little black knit dress. "Here. Wear this."

"It doesn't fit," Mo said defiantly. "I'm wearing what I have on, Naomi."

"Mo. You look old."

Mo stared back at her sister with big, hurt eyes. "I don't look...old."

"You look old, Sweetie. Trust me on this." Naomi had never been one to mince words and tact was never her strong suit. She'd learned and accepted this about herself a long time ago.

Reluctantly, Maureen changed into the dress that fit tighter than she was comfortable with. When she first bought it, yeah, it clung to some curves, but over the years, those curves had shifted a bit and weren't in the same place they were the last time she'd worn this thing. "Naw...this is too tight, Nay. I look like a fool."

"You look nice, Girl. Here...try these shoes on with it." Naomi handed Mo a pair of black, strappy sandals.

"No. It's too damn cold for sandals, Nay. Give me those black pumps." Naomi sighed. Black pumps? Boring. But black pumps without stiletto heels? Horrifying. She knew better though, and decided again, not to push it. Mo would back out for sure if Naomi wasn't careful.

Maureen tried adjusting the black dress. Like moving it around would hide the fact that she'd ditched the last three months of her aerobic classes. "I need a girdle."

"Girl, you look fine. Remind me to pick you up on my way to the mall next week."

"I thought you said I look fine?"

"You do. But you need to update your wardrobe...just a little bit. 'Kay? Now. Let me fix your hair and..."

"What's wrong with my.... You know what? Forget this. I'm not going." Mo stepped out of her shoes.

"Mo! C'mon." Naomi picked up a brush and some hairpins and started pinning up her sister's shoulder length hair. "Baby, this won't take long. I'll be done in a minute and you'll see, Mo. I'm just updating it a little bit. That's all."

By the time they made it to Mardi Gras, Mo's mood had

mellowed a bit and she figured this might not be so bad. Nothing had changed much since the last time she'd been to a nightclub. Different club, same scene. She'd decided to give it a chance though. Tonight, she was going to have a good time, let it all hang out, cut loose, and get her groove on if it killed her.

"Hey, Baby. You wanna dance?"

Naomi beamed and turned to her sister. "Hey, Mo! Hold my purse!"

Maureen smiled and watched her sister sashay off into the sea of flailing booties. Okay, so she'd hold her purse. This time. But she was not going to spend her night babysitting baby sister's bag. She'd planned on being too busy flailing her own booty. Mo watched the dance floor, relieved that no one was doing anything she couldn't do. Basic finger snapping, hip swinging, two-stepping was still acceptable. Probably because there wasn't much room on the floor to do much else.

"I'll have a...Corona with lime, please," she told the bartender. She couldn't believe how nervous she was about being there. Mo wasn't easily intimidated by anyone, but she definitely felt like a fish out of water. Looking around the room, she saw what Naomi had meant by updating her wardrobe. Hoochies abounded and she knew she wouldn't go there, but maybe she could do better than a closet filled with business suits, sweats, and stretch pants.

A deep, baritone voice penetrated beneath the sound of the music, causing a surprising flutter inside her. "Excuse me," he said. Mo braced herself, smiled, cleared her throat, then turned slowly, quickly preparing herself to accept his invitation to dance, talk, settle down, raise a family. The handsome man smiled back. "I'm trying to get to the bar? Sorry," he said apologetically. She nodded, then stepped aside, giving him room to order his drink.

Mo downed two Coronas standing in that spot and not one man asked her to dance. Don't they do that anymore? she wondered.

"So ask them, Girl!" Nay screamed in her ear, "Don't be shy."

"Ask them? Why can't they ask me? They're asking you."

Naomi shrugged. "They know me. I come here all the time. They know I like to get my groove on."

"I'm not enjoying this, Nay. Not at all."

Naomi rolled her eyes. She'd been trying to get this woman out for months, and Mo wasn't even trying to have a good time. What was worse, she was trying to rain out her party too and Nay wasn't having it. "You're not trying to enjoy it, Mo. Why don't you try getting out of this corner, smile, and walk around or something? At least act approachable."

Approachable? Sure, she was approachable. Hell, she'd been approachable all night standing near the bar, looking like "Please. Somebody ask me to dance." How much more approachable could a woman look? Whatever. Naomi could keep her little snide remarks to herself. She was the one who'd been begging Mo to come to this meat market. All of a sudden, she got attitude?

"Fine." Mo shrugged and handed Nay back her purse. "I'll see you later."

"Good for you."

This was harder than she thought it would be. Mo was supposed to come out here, shake her booty, have a ball, go home, and grin herself to sleep. Promising to do it again next weekend. But her mood had soured and she really didn't feel like smiling and playing nice anymore. Mo was agitated that the evening hadn't lived up to her expectations. Or maybe it was Mo who hadn't lived up to her own expectations. She'd lost something over the years. That spark hidden behind her personality that had drawn people to her was gone. There was a time when she'd have walked into a place like this and brought the party with her. There was a time when she could've shown Miss Naomi a thing or two about "getting her groove on." But Mo felt as old and out of place as her old wardrobe and old hair. No one paid any attention to her, and she might as well have been invisible.

Squeezing through a crowded bar was not his idea of the perfect way to end a long week. When did that happen? Didn't seem like it was that long ago when he couldn't wait to hit the club, down a few drinks, and get his mack on to any and every woman who'd listen. Kevin had spent all week at a video shoot directing young photographers who had the audacity to think they knew more than he did. His throat was still sore from talking all day, explaining every shot and arguing his point of view. What he really wanted to do was go home, turn the phone off, and watch pay-per-view movies until he fell asleep. Damn! That didn't sound like him at all. Ron had called as soon as he'd gotten home and talked his "lazy, punk-ass" into hanging out tonight. Ron was going on forty years old. Kevin figured that his old ass should be tired of "hanging." Hell, he was "hanging" ten years ago when they first met.

"Man, I'm not staying long," Kevin said. "You know I've got that shoot in the morning." Making a stop at Mardi Gras on a Friday night had been a ritual of Ron's since it opened. All the fine ladies hung out there on Fridays.

Ron should've been a preacher. That's how he talked to Kevin, like he was preaching to him. "Kevin, you want to meet attractive women, you need to go where they go, and most of them don't go online. Why do you think you keep ending up with all those rejects from the human race, Man? Online is where the desperate women go, but the real women, the ones who know they got it going on, ain't afraid to meet a man face to face. Know what I'm saying?"

All that damn "I told you so" rhetoric was getting on his nerves, but Kevin was beginning to buy into Ron's point. Since posting his ad on BlackGentlemen.com, he'd met super freaks (namely Kiara) and women in denial, like Jennifer, who was convinced her three hundred fifty pound frame was considered a "medium build." There was Lisa, who talked nonstop about the last man in her life and how wonderful and horrible he'd been all at the same time—she'd kill him if she could get away with it. Her words exactly. And last but not least, Asha. Asha was gorgeous. She was as tall as Kevin in heels, had long, dark brown tresses flowing down her back, full pouty lips, and a voice capable of lulling a man into an erotic moment just by saying "hello" over the phone. Yep. Asha was all that and then some. Short of nothing less than a dream, she'd hypnotized Kevin the first time he'd laid eyes on her at dinner. She was breathtaking and he could hardly take his eyes off the woman long enough to eat. Conversation flowed easily with Asha. It clicked with her right from the start and Kevin fell in love with the chemistry between them.

"Being single is cool, but at some point in his life, a man needs more than booty. Pardon my expression."

Asha smiled. "Believe me, I understand. Women want more than booty, too," she assured him.

"My folks have been together for almost fifty years. And it's real. The love...it's all good. I just wonder if finding that kind of commitment these days is possible. Does that kind of devotion still exist?"

"Sure it does. Most of us just don't want to work at it, that's all. Couples used to appreciate the value of commitment, now..." She shrugged.

"Yeah, well...anything less than that is a waste of time, if you ask me."

Asha laughed. "You're a special man, Kevin. Very special." It was during dinner that he'd walked in and all of a sudden, Asha turned a weird shade of gray, and practically slid under the table.

"What's wrong? Asha?"

"Shhh! My husband," she whispered.

"What?"

"My husband's here." Asha picked up her purse, kissed him quickly on the cheek, and left his ass sitting in her dust, wondering what the hell had just happened. This whole Internet thing had been a bust and Kevin had already turned it off.

Mo could hardly believe her eyes. Was that Kevin standing at the bar? Good Lord, it was him. Her first instinct was to walk over to him and say hello. Then she remembered. She was in a terrible mood and had a bad attitude, wearing old clothes and old hair on her head, and that was no way to try and impress a man. Mo felt like an out of date, out of style, out of touch woman who had no business being in a nightclub trying to push up on anybody. Especially any man who looked that good. Attitude is absolutely everything, and right now, Mo's attitude screamed "Let go and let God, Girl. Time to call it a night." She knew he hadn't seen her, and all she had to do was gather up Naomi and slip out as quietly as she'd slipped in. The problem was Naomi hardly ever left the dance floor. Girlfriend was getting her party on, oblivious to the fact that her sister was right in the middle of having a moment and a miserable time. Of course, Mo could call a cab. As a matter of fact, she could use Nay's cell phone, which was in the purse she'd been babysitting all night, the purse she'd sworn earlier that she wouldn't have time to watch. Mo fumbled through her sister's purse looking for the phone, then remembered, Naomi had left it plugged up in the car.

"Got some fine honies up in here tonight!" Ron exclaimed while watching one of those fine, golden brown, honies switch past him at the speed of light. "Now that's what I'm talkin' 'bout." He grinned. "Real women...not Internet women. See what you're missing out on?"

"How many times are you gonna make your point, Man? I hear you. I've been hearing you," Kevin reiterated.

Ron lifted his glass to toast and Kevin raised his beer in kind. "Fuck the Internet! Here's to meeting the right woman the right way. At Mardi Gras!"

Kevin wasn't all that convinced his "right" woman could be found here, but she definitely hadn't been found on the net. "Here, here, my brotha! Real women!"

Mo watched Kevin from across the room. He had no idea it was her ass he'd smacked in that email. Kevin turned slightly in her direction and Mo backed farther into the corner, until she was confident he couldn't possibly see her. He'd become the cat and she the mouse. She couldn't help but laugh. Two days ago, she'd sexed the man over the Internet. He responded immediately, asking her to call him. Yeah, right. Like that would ever happen.

"Hello, Kevin. It's me. Psycho woman from the center? Yes, well...I just wanted to call and tell you that I'm the one who emailed you the other night. Remember? I'm the one into bondage? Yes, I thought you'd find that quite hilarious. I was just...in a mood, I suppose."

Oh, yes, he was fine. Kevin wore a black turtleneck and some gray slacks. The belt cinched around his waist accentuated the kind of physique women squirmed over. Dark men in dark colors always did excite her. Kevin wrapped his full lips around the opening of the bottle he drank from. Mo's imagination started playing tricks on her. She envisioned walking up to him and touching him slightly on the shoulder. *Hello, Kevin. Remember me? I'm Mo and I think you're divine,"* she imagined herself whispering. Then, Kevin would turn to her, smile one of those pretty smiles of his, pucker up, and kiss her lips, sucking on them like he was sucking on a big, juicy orange.

"Mo! Mo!" Naomi's squealing voice interrupted Mo's fantasy.

"What, Nay?"

"Girl, I'm out of cash. Can you front me a twenty? I'll stop at the ATM tonight on the way home and give it back to you."

Mo reached into her bag and handed her sister a ten dollar bill. "Twenty's all I have."

"That brotha is fine, ain't he?" Naomi had noticed her sister staring at Kevin since he walked in.

"Who?"

"Who? The one you've been staring at all night, Mo. I ain't blind."

"You know who that is?"

"I've seen him before, but no. I don't know him."

"That's one of my volunteers. Kevin Davies. He's a photographer."

"Really? Girl, did you say hello?"

"No. He's...he's with his friend."

"Mo, stop being silly and go over and say 'hi' to the man. So what, he's with his friend!"

"C'mon, Baby." Nay's dance partner tugged on her arm. "They playin' our song."

Naomi thrust her purse back into Mo's arms and followed her date onto the dance floor. Naomi was right. She was being silly. She needed to act like a grown woman, go over, and say hello to the man. Hellos were usually harmless. As soon as she started in his direction, gearing up for her introduction, Kevin was led out onto the dance floor by a beautiful, young, hoochie goddess, who wore next to nothing and shook it all over the man. Mo stopped dead in her tracks. How on earth could she compete with that?

"I haven't heard from you in awhile, Kevin. I thought you said you were going to call me?" Kiara pouted.

Kevin knew better. Kiara wasn't the type to sit by the phone waiting on a brotha to call. "I've been meaning to, but my schedule has been hectic lately."

"Too hectic to hook up with me?" She guided his hands down to her highly agile hips, which had the power to hypnotize a man out of his mind. Bottom line? Kevin was only human and no human man he knew had the power to resist a force as potent as agile, female hips.

Maybe he'd been too hard on the woman. Hell, if nothing else, she knew how to have a good time and he'd been missing out on plenty of those lately. "What in the world could I have been thinking, Baby?" He raised her hand to his mouth and kissed it.

Mo watched in horror as this man put her...his precious lips on that woman's body. That was his idea of a soulmate? Who'd have guessed soulmates wore next to nothing, had big booties, little titties, fake nails, and hopefully, a year's supply of condoms on hand (if the rest of the world was lucky). Kevin's hands were all over that woman's hips and behind. And that behind was all over him. Mo compared her behind with soulmate's behind, then concluded, nope, her behind wasn't even in the same league with soulmate's behind. Tears welled up in her eyes, and she hadn't expected that to happen at all. Disappointment washed all over her body. Sure, he was only a fantasy, but until soulmate popped into the picture, he'd been her fantasy.

Kevin and Kiara made tentative plans to hook up later on that night. Women like that were cool and had their place in a man's life. Just like he was sure he had his place in hers. Kiara wasn't complicated, that's for sure. She let it be known what she wanted and she knew how to get it. No strings attached and hopefully, no drama. Just pure, unadulterated sex. There had been a time in his life when he'd have paid a million bucks for a harem of Kiaras. Pure, unadulterated sex was all he wanted back then. But it lacked one thing. Intimacy. Sex was cool, but it paled in comparison to making love. He could count the number of times on one hand that he'd actually made love to a woman. That's what Kevin had hoped he'd find. But now that he was looking for it, it avoided him like he was the plague. What a damn shame.

He made his way back over to the bar and the bartender brought him a drink he never ordered. Along with it was a note written on a napkin.

Kevin. I'd have said hello, but you look like you're having a wonderful time with your friend and I didn't want to interrupt. By the way, you look good tonight. Enjoy. —Mo.

He looked around the room, hoping to see some woman who looked like she'd sent him anonymous emails and beers and notes written on napkins. But what the hell would a woman like that look like? He was flattered, but this was tripping him out. He didn't like what he was feeling. The fact that Mo had been this close to him, that she knows him, and he's totally in the dark. Yeah, he had an uneasy feeling about it. He wasn't cool with this, not at all. He searched the crowd, seeing faces of some women he knew, some he'd slept with, some he recognized, most he didn't know at all. Which one was she? Was she stalking him? No...it could've just been a coincidence. After all, he had posted his damn mug shot all over the net. Lots of people came to Mardi Gras and maybe Mo was just one of those people. But damn! She definitely had a brotha tripping.

On the drive home, Mo decided to tell Naomi about her encounter with Kevin. "So let me get this straight. You met this brotha at the center?"

"I told you, he's a volunteer."

"You smoked a couple of joints... A couple of joints, Mo? All by yourself? Damn! Girl, two joints would have had my ass in a coma. You need to be careful with that."

"It was stupid. I know."

"And then decided to answer the man's ad from BlackGentlemen.com? And he doesn't know it was you?"

Mo had to admit, it did sound ridiculous and reliving it again by way of her sister's mouth wasn't helping matters any. "At the time, it was cool. It was fun, Nay. Look, I was high. All right? It made sense at the time."

"A whole lotta things make sense after smoking two joints. So, he answered?"

"He did. He's afraid he might know me."

"He does know you."

"But he doesn't know it's me writing him, Nay. Pay attention. He thinks it's someone else."

"Why would he think that?"

"'Cause I implied it."

"Because..."

"I don't know, Nay. I was high. Remember?"

"But if you like this man, Mo..."

"I never said I liked him. I just said I saw his ad on the Internet. I just thought it was kind of weird, that's all."

"You must like him."

"Nay, I'm a grown woman. If I liked the man, why wouldn't I tell him?"

"That's what I'm trying to figure out. I mean, if you want to get to know the brotha, you need to step up and tell him."

"Who said I wanted to get to know him? I'm not interested."

"Which is why you stared at him all night. That makes sense."

"Nay, it was a joke. A prank. It was stupid. That's all. I was..."

"I know. You were high...alright? There's always an excuse with you, Mo. Always."

"What's that supposed to mean?"

"It means you've always got an answer for everything."

"And that's bad?"

"No, but... Ain't you bored? You never do anything or go anywhere. You never step to any brothas and say, *'Hey, I'm diggin' you.'* Ain't you bored just...doing nothing all the time?"

"I'm not bored, Nay. I've got plenty to keep me busy."

"That why you spending your nights at home by yourself, running around the house naked, smoking way too much weed, emailing men you don't even know?"

"It wasn't that bad."

"Sure it was. Time marches on, Maureen. You'd better keep

up, Girl, or life's gonna pass you right on by. Before you know it, someone else will snatch that man right out from under your nose. Then you'll be wondering what happened."

"I'm not interested in him, Nay."

"You said that already."

manhattan245

The drink was a nice touch, Mo. But I wished you'd have introduced yourself. I'm disappointed you didn't. What are you hiding? Call me. Please.

Kevin

Chapter Nine

Troy paced his living room floor, wearing a black do-rag and red silk pajamas, balancing a lighted cigarette between his fingers, fuming over an argument he'd had with Gregory.

"When did you start smoking again, Troy?" Mo asked.

Troy glanced at the burning butt. "I never stopped," he said nonchalantly.

"You told me you had."

"I lied."

"I see." Sometimes Troy was too passionate for his own good. Especially when it came to relationships. When he was in love, he was entirely too in love, but when he was pissed, that temper of his was hell. "So is there trouble in paradise, little brother?"

The phone rang, and Troy glared at it like he was a superhero trying to incinerate it with his X-ray vision.

"Aren't you gonna answer it?" Naomi asked. When she saw that he had no intention of answering it, Naomi took the liberty of picking it up herself. "Hello?" She looked at Troy, who was staring her down with his laser eyes. "Gregory?"

"I ain't here!" Troy yelled out. "Tell his ass I ain't here!"

"Gregory, can Troy call you back later? He's not feeling well. Okay?"

"What's going on, Troy?" Maureen asked.

"I'm p-i-s-s-e-d pissed, Maureen. Or can't you tell?" he snapped. "That mutha fucka had the nerve to try and get abusive on a brotha."

"What?"

"No he didn't," Naomi said, looking at Mo.

"Called his self checking me. Always talking about, *'Where you going? Who you been with? Who's that calling you? How come you didn't answer my page? Who else you fuckin', Troy?'* Like who the fuck does he think he is?"

"Sounds to me like he thinks he's your man, Troy." Naomi snickered.

"Don't start, Nay." Naomi might not have taken this whole thing seriously, but Mo knew when to push Troy's buttons and when to back off. Naomi knew, too. She just didn't care. "What happened, Troy?"

"Got all up in my face, pushed me up against the wall...You know I don't play, Mo! I told his ass, I might act like the woman in this relationship, but don't fuck with me 'cause I'll put my foot so far up your ass you gonna have to tie my shoe for me. Then, I pushed his ass up off me. You know I don't play!" Troy took a long, hard drag on his cigarette.

"I know you don't, Sweetie," Mo said, concerned. "So did he move out?"

"I put him out, Mo. Which I shouldn't have even had to do in the first place since I never told him he could move up in here anyway. But you know how men are. First time they spend the night, they leave a toothbrush. The next time, they leave a pair of drawers, then some suits move up in here, then some shoes. Next thing I know, he's got his hands all over my remote control like he bought the damn TV!"

Finally, Naomi exploded and fell out laughing on the floor.

"Fuck you, Nay!" Troy hissed.

Mo rolled her eyes at her ridiculous sister. "I'm sorry, Troy. I know how much you wanted somebody."

"Somebody, Mo. Not any damn body! His ass been calling here all day, talking 'bout he's sorry. Fuck sorry! Sorry was ever meeting his sorry ass in the first damn place!"

Naomi pulled herself up from the floor, and wiped tears from her eyes. "I'm sorry, Troy." She swallowed. "I really am."

Naturally, he wasn't even trying to hear Naomi anymore. Sometimes, her childish ass got on his last nerves. "You need to get over yourself, Nay. This shit ain't funny."

Naomi looked at Mo. "What?" She shrugged. "I said I was sorry."

Troy rubbed his temples with his middle fingers. A migraine was coming on. He could feel it. He sat down, then looked at Maureen. "Stay away from them fools on the Internet, Baby. Ain't none of them right. They all crazy. Every last one of them, just waiting to get crazy on folks."

Naomi mumbled, "Too late."

Mo glared at the little idiot. "Would you just shut up!"

"Don't tell me to shut up!" Naomi snapped back.

Mo put her hand up in Nay's face. "Your mouth's too big, Nay. Too damn big!"

"What's up?" Troy asked, relieved that the focus was shifting off his issues and on to someone else's. Naomi and Mo were too busy being pissed off and neither of them said a word. "Naw...now somebody's got to tell me something," he said. "Mo? What's up, Baby?"

Mo pressed her lips together, determined not to say a word.

"Tell him!" Naomi urged.

Mo knew that if she didn't tell Troy, Naomi would eventually get around to it and she knew for a fact, she would not like her sister's version of the story. "I met someone on the Internet," she mumbled.

"What?" Troy grinned. "What did you say?"

"She said she met a man on the net," Naomi interjected.

"Actually, I met him at work. He's a volunteer at the center."

"But she found his ad on the Internet, then emailed him, but he doesn't know it's her."

"Can I please tell my own story?"

"Sorry. I was just trying to help."

"If I needed your help, Nay..."

"Wait a minute. Wait a minute. You met this man at your job, then found his picture on BlackGentlemen.com?"

"Yes."

"And you emailed him, but he does or doesn't know it's you?" Troy found himself trying to make sense of what obviously made no sense.

"He doesn't," Naomi answered.

"Yet," Mo interjected, rolling her eyes at her sister.

"You gonna tell him?"

"I don't think she will," said Naomi.

"Troy, it's not that simple."

"It's not?" he asked.

"No."

"You got a thing for this brotha?" Troy's voice dropped a couple of octaves every time he stepped into his serious brother mode.

"She likes him."

"Naomi?"

"You do."

"So why don't you tell him who you are?"

"It's not that simple."

"I'm lost, Mo. How come it isn't?"

"God! I don't know, Troy. I want to, at least, I think I do...but... Hell, I'd probably be just wasting my time anyway. What if he's not interested?"

Naomi stared at her. "What if he is?"

Troy sat back in his seat. "How do you plan on finding out if he is or isn't if you're not planning on telling him how you feel?"

"Well, what if it doesn't work?"

"What's supposed to work, Baby? Everything isn't all or nothing, Mo. How many times I gotta tell you that? It's not about working or not working. Shit, sometimes, it's just about checking it out. Sometimes, you just got to learn to make the best of the in-between."

"Yeah, why can't you just do something for the sake of doing, it, Sis? Some things just aren't all that serious."

"I just don't want to get that close to someone again to..."

"Lose him?" Troy asked. "You and Jon were a phenomenon, Mo. Most people only dream of having what the two of you had, but that's over now."

"But that's what I want, Troy. That's where I fit best. With a man I love, who loves me."

"Pay attention, Baby. Look at what you're doing. You got yourself all shut up, not even trying to attract somebody, simply because you're afraid it won't be like it was with you and Jon. Nothing can be like that, Mo. Because he's gone. But that doesn't mean you can't make something new with someone else. It doesn't mean it can't be just as good with another man, just because it's different. Brotha might be interested, but you'll never know if you don't give him a chance."

"It might not lead to anything." Naomi shrugged. "Then again...you can at least have a good time. It could be one hell of a ride, Mo."

The possibility of starting a new relationship was like being born again. She'd met and lost the love of her life in Jonathan. Nothing can prepare a woman for that kind of joy and that kind of pain. The fear is what kept her shut off from dating again. Fear of never finding what she'd lost. Kevin was a stranger to her. But Mo had been drawn to him since she'd first laid eyes on him. Part of her wanted to write it off as just the desperate needs of a desperate woman. The other part of her knew it was more than that.

manhattan245

You've got my mind reeling trying to figure out who you might be. I'm a patient man about some things, Mo. This isn't one of those things. If there's a chance you might be someone special, then I don't want to waste time on silly games. Let's get together and talk. I'm harmless and we can meet anywhere and anytime you choose. But don't tease a brotha like this. I've been looking for someone to share a life with, not games. At least pick up the phone and call me. Anytime.

"How would I ever explain something like this to him?" she wondered out loud. Mo laid in bed, staring at the sandalwood-scented candle burning by her bed. Even if she ever did come clean, how would she explain her actions so he'd understand? Okay, so maybe expecting him to understand was a huge order. But, maybe if she could just get him to empathize? Maybe that was a large order, too. Mo sighed. If the man had any sense at all, he'd have no choice but to think she's some kind of lunatic. That's what she'd think if she were him. *"You're crazy, lady,"* she imagined him saying. And he'd be right. Mo blew out her candle and decided to go to sleep.

Love was definitely too big a tag to put on what she felt for Kevin. Lust seemed sufficient enough at the moment. Desire was good enough. In-between...well, maybe there was a ray of hope in that, too.

Chapter Ten

The day had dragged on, feeling more like twenty-four hours instead of the eight she'd been in the office. Being preoccupied with Kevin didn't help. He'd been on her mind all day. Troy's advice had held so much truth in it. She had been avoiding life for fear of being disappointed by it. Actually, until Troy had pointed that out, she hadn't really noticed that's what she'd done. There was no guarantee Kevin was the man for her, but how would she ever know, one way or another, if she never stepped out from behind that wall she'd built around herself. Mo wasn't sure how, or even if, she'd ever be able to explain that whole secret admirer thing to him, but for now, all that mattered was taking that first step and letting the man know she was interested in him, to his face. She'd begin by apologizing to him for her behavior the last time they'd seen each other. It was now or never, in her mind. Tony would be back to continue teaching the photography class next week and Kevin would be gone. If she was going to make amends, this was the time to do it.

He'd arrived a little early to pack up some of his things. Kevin would have to remember to thank Tony for asking him to do this. Teaching the class had been an awesome experience he'd not soon forget. The enthusiasm from the kids had been incredible and unexpected, but what surprised him most was his own enthusiasm. He was going to miss these kids. For sure.

"Knock! Knock!" Mo smiled from the doorway of the classroom, looking beautiful and a lot less pissed than the last time he'd seen her. Kevin figured her good mood was probably directly related to his leaving. He never did find out what he'd done to the woman to justify that attitude she threw at him. Didn't matter now, though. Brotha would do this thing one more time, then he was out.

"So...tonight's your last class, huh?"

"Yeah. This is it," he said simply. Somehow he knew the less he said, the more uncomfortable it would make her feel, and he liked that.

Mo's nervousness wasn't easy to hide, but she did her best to try to look at ease. "These kids are really going to miss you, Kevin. Even more than Tony, I think." She put her finger to her lips. "Shhhh...don't tell him, though."

Hell, he couldn't help it. He smiled because she was right. And she was cute. "I wouldn't do that to the man. He did me a favor by asking me to sit in for him."

Mo laughed. Then an awkward silence stood between them, but she was determined to get past that. She'd rehearsed all day the speech she'd prepared for him. The one where she apologized about how she acted toward him the other day. The speech where she told him how attractive she found him and the same one where she asked him out to dinner if he were free some night next week. Oh, and how she'd need his phone number or maybe she should give him hers so that they could stay in touch. That speech.

"Now that your Tuesday nights are free...any big plans?" Not very smooth, but it was a good beginning.

He shrugged. "Not really."

She hesitated, hoping he'd say something funny or elaborate, not his answer that was much too simple for her to really work with. "Well...we've really enjoyed having you here," she said nervously. "Did I say that already?"

"Yeah. Yeah, I think you did." He didn't quite know where she was heading, but Kevin was getting a kick out of this. She was squirming, trying to make a point or something, and he was pretty flattered by the whole thing.

"I never said I was sorry...did I?"

"Sorry? For what?"

"For the other day. I was kind of rude to you and... Well...I really didn't..."

"Hey!" one of the kids yelled out coming into the room. "Mr. D! Whattup?"

Kevin's face lit up and he and the young man exchanged dap. "Hey, Von. You bring that negative with you, Man?"

"Yeah...I got it." The young man looked at Mo. "Whattup, Mrs. B?"

Mo smiled. Sadly, Von was her cue to leave. "Hello, Von. How are you? How's school?"

"School's aiight. You know?"

Mo could hear the other kids coming down the hall. "Well...I'd better get going," she said to Kevin. The kids had planned a surprise going-away party for him. They loved Mr. D. She would've liked to love him. "In case I don't see you again..."

"It was nice working with you, Mrs. B." He smiled.

"I wish you'd call me...Maureen." She'd almost slipped and said Mo. She'd have died on the spot if she'd said Mo. Thank God she didn't say–Mo.

Chapter Eleven

Kevin had pretty much given up on MizMOcha. He hadn't heard from her in weeks, which disappointed him, but he figured it was all for the best. Ron was probably right. More than likely, she was somebody with issues he wasn't in the mood for, and he figured the gods were looking out for a brotha after all. If she was someone he knew, then she needed to piss or get off the pot. Either fess up or leave him alone altogether. Internet dating had proved interesting, but that's about it. He decided it was probably best to take his chances like every other man out there and hope for the best. Miss Right was out there somewhere. That much he knew. And when the time was right, they'd hook up, fall in love, make some babies and chill for the next fifty years. In the meantime, he'd at least enjoy the search.

He hadn't had any contact with the center since he'd left, and seeing an email in his inbox from Sheila bought a smile to his face. She'd been so sweet to him while he worked there. If she'd been a little older... Back in his dawg days, her age wouldn't have mattered to him, but at nineteen, hell, she was young enough to be his daughter and he wasn't cool with that. Not to mention, she was a little skinny to suit his tastes.

"We Miss U!" was typed in the subject line of the email. He clicked to open it, figuring it was one of those e-greeting cards or something. She'd do something like that. Kevin blinked in disbelief when he opened the email. Maybe his eyes were playing tricks on him. He'd spent most of the night in his darkroom and his eyes were tired, but... It just didn't make any sense. Kevin stared at the email Sheila had sent him, his eyes pinned on the email address— MizMOcha. Sheila had courtesy copied MizMOcha and the name beside it read, "Maureen Beckman." There was no way he could excuse that to coincidence. No way in hell.

Kevin called the center and managed to catch Sheila just as she was walking in. "Hello?" she answered, out of breath.

"Sheila. I'm glad I caught you. This is Kevin Davies."

"Hi, Kevin," she said excitedly. "How are you?"

"I'm wonderful, Baby. I called to thank you for the email you sent me."

"Oh...you're very welcome. We all just wanted you to know you haven't been forgotten. The kids keep asking about you."

"Well, tell them I miss them and I'll try dropping in sometime soon."

"I'll tell them."

"By the way, is Mrs. Beckman available?"

"She's in a meeting right now. Do you want me to have her call you?"

"No. No, I just... Maybe you can help me." He'd been under the impression she was married. After all, the last time he'd seen her, she still had a ring on her finger. Asha had tried pulling that shit on him. Creeping on her husband with men she met over the net. Was Mrs. Beckman playing the same game? That's the first question he needed answered. The first of many.

"I met a gentleman the other day by the name of William Beckman," he lied. "He wouldn't by chance be related to Maureen would he...her husband, maybe?"

"Oh...no. Not her husband. Mrs. Beckman's a widow. But he might be an in-law or something. I wouldn't know."

Damn! A widow. "I see. Well...you uh...have a nice day, Sheila, and tell the kids I'll try to make it in to see them next week."

"Okay, Kevin. Thanks for calling."

Maureen Beckman. A widow. He wasn't sure how to feel about that. Or how he should feel about any of it. She just didn't strike him as the type of woman who'd do something like this. Kevin scratched his chin. It just didn't jibe. She'd flattered him. She'd made a fool out of him. She'd played him. Hell! No wonder she'd been moody. She was confused. That's for damn sure.

Now that the weather was starting to warm up for real, Mo decided to take advantage of it, and open up all the windows at the house before leaving for work, hoping the breeze would eliminate the stale aroma of winter. She frowned while searching her closet for something to wear. Naomi was right. It was definitely time for a new wardrobe. Apparently, somewhere along the line, her favorite color had become black. Mo couldn't remember when that had happened. Today was not a black day. It wasn't a business suit day. A cool breeze wrapped itself around her, assuring her that today was going to be a good day. Finally, Mo found something to wear that fit the mood. She hadn't worn this dress in ages. Mo held it up against her, while she stared at herself in the mirror. Yes. This would work. She loved this dress because it looked good on her even when she didn't look good. The dress poured over the top of her head and down her body like water, kissing her hips and feeling heavenly against her skin. Why not take full advantage of this mood? she thought. Mo slid out of her panties, put them in the dirty clothes hamper, grabbed her briefcase, and left.

She'd thought a lot about Kevin after he left. He'd emailed her several times, but Mo decided it was best just to leave that whole charade alone. It wasn't real and the Internet was just another brick in that wall she'd decided to tear down. Mo had learned something about herself, though. She'd learned that she was finally ready to step out on faith and try her hand at love again. Getting to know Kevin, personally, would've been nice. But there were other Kevins out there and she wanted to be ready when they crossed her path. Emotionally ready. She'd thought about getting his number from the office and calling him, but she had no idea what she'd say to him, so she opted to file the whole experience away as a lesson learned. No more hiding. No more games. No more trying to make every man measure up to Jonathan. Jonathan had been his own man and other men may not be him, but that didn't mean they couldn't be just as good as themselves.

It wasn't until she made it into the office that she remembered it was Sheila's day off. The center was closed to the public and she could finally make adjustments to that budget she'd been too preoccupied to work on before she had to present it in two days. Incoming calls were automatically routed to Sheila's phone and Mo could get busy without interruption.

Maureen turned on her PC and opened her inbox. She scrolled down her list of new messages and came across one from Sheila "We Miss U" and opened it. It was addressed to manhattan245 and directly beneath his name was hers, MizMOcha. Dread filled her stomach and tied a big knot in it. "Oh, shit," she mumbled. "I wonder if..."

She never even heard him come in. Kevin stood in the doorway to her office, and Mo knew it was no coincidence. Yep. He knew. "Mrs. Beckman," he said smugly. "Or should I call you...Maureen? I'm sorry. You prefer Mo. Isn't that right?" Mo's mouth fell open, but absolutely nothing would come out of it. Not even breath. "Yeah, I was speechless, too, when I first found out," he said, much too calmly. "Never in a million years would I have guessed it was you. You're good. That's for sure. Damn good."

Showdown at the OK Corral? Maureen's moment of truth was finally here. Only, she wasn't prepared for it. All she wanted to do was sweep the whole thing under the rug as a lesson learned. That's it. Just leave it alone. Obviously, he had other ideas. "I..I...was going to call you."

"Now we both know better than that. Don't we, Mo? When were you going to call? Honestly, I don't think you ever had any intention of calling me." His dark eyes pinned her down in her chair.

"I just...I didn't know how to tell you." Mo's heart pounded in her chest and she swore the damn thing was going to kick its way out and run screaming into the streets.

"You just tell me. It's not hard to say, 'Kevin, I saw your picture on the net. That was me who emailed you. Isn't that funny?' How hard would that be?"

"I was embarrassed, Kevin. I didn't..." She shrugged.

"I'm embarrassed, Mo. I feel like a fool. I'll bet you got a kick out of this whole thing. Didn't you? Probably bragging to all your friends about my clueless ass. Why'd you play me like that?"

"I'm so sorry, Kevin." Mo felt the tears stinging her eyes. "I didn't mean to..." He had no right to feel foolish. That privilege belonged to her. Not him. She felt like a big idiot in a pretty dress, and she'd be damned if she'd feel sorry for him. After all, she's the one who'd written that ridiculous email about being tied up and tortured. Not him. How in the world could she ever live that down?

Kevin stepped inside the office and closed the door behind him. "You liked this game?" He stepped slowly in her direction. "You enjoyed...keeping me in the dark the way you did?"

Mo eased out of her chair and backed up towards the wall. What on earth was he planning on doing? She wanted to run out of the office, but between Mo and the door, there was Kevin, making his way toward her, with a wicked look in his eyes.

Panic set in. "I said...I apologize, Kevin. Now...this whole thing was a misunderstanding, and..."

"No, it wasn't. I understand completely, Mo. And I think you do, too."

Kevin maneuvered her into a corner of the room. Maureen stared back at him, perplexed by the look on his face. He smiled, knowing panic was eating her up inside. "Don't do anything... Kevin, this is all so... You need to leave!" she shouted. He was scaring her, but she'd fight him if she had to. She'd try to kick his ass if it came down to it.

Mo was backed up as far as she could go. Kevin raised his arms up on either side of her, then pressed the weight of his body against hers. "Leaving is not what I need to do, Baby," he whispered. Kevin tilted his head, then kissed her lightly on the lips.

Mo gasped, surprised by what he'd had the audacity to do, here in broad daylight, in her office. Her heart pounded relentlessly in her chest, and Mo decided to try a different approach. Calm voice. Reason with the man. Be kind. Then kick him in the nuts and run like hell. "Kevin, you really need to... It was all a misunderstanding. That's all. Nobody got hurt."

This time, he filled her mouth with his tongue. Mo wanted

to be angry, but she couldn't. He tasted too damn good for all that. "Mmmm," she moaned. Good Lord, how could anybody taste that good? Without realizing it, she put her arms over his shoulders and pulled him closer to her.

Kevin put his arms around her waist, then led her back over to her desk. Mo hungrily sought out his lips, while he pushed every page of her budget onto the floor, along with her stapler, her paper clips, her in-basket, pens, pencils. Then he lifted her up on the desk, laid her down on her back, and lifted her knees. To hell with being embarrassed. Mo's whole body tingled in anticipation of anything and everything he wanted to do to her.

Kevin stared down at her. "I liked the game too, Mo. I liked the game a hell of a lot."

Kevin was pleasantly surprised when he discovered she wasn't wearing panties. Once again, his theory had proven true. Don't ever underestimate a conservative woman. He knelt down in front of her, then raised her hips to meet his mouth. Kevin's tongue explored Mo in ways she'd only imagined possible. She swirled her hips against his face, holding his head against her, praying he'd never stop what he was doing. Mo's eyes rolled up into her head, and the room spun around like a Ferris wheel. The sensation of his tongue welled up screams inside her, but Mo fought the urge, biting down on her lower lip.

Obviously, his ass had it going on. Or rather, his mouth did. This woman was wet enough to drown a man. She moaned and groaned out an orgasm that exploded all over him, and Kevin smiled at his achievement. "Take that!" he wanted to say, but didn't. Mrs. Beckman was too damn delicious for I told you so's. He pulled out a handkerchief from his pocket, and wiped his mouth. He'd think about washing her off him. Later on. Mo lay limp, drained of the best sex she'd had in years.

Kevin stared at Mo, then flashed one of those irresistible smiles at her. "Call me. Please? He kissed her one last time, then left.

Chapter Twelve

Dark Cranberry Cream was her favorite color lipstick. It wasn't red enough to be out of style, but it wasn't so brown that her lips faded into her face. There was just enough color without being brash or tacky. Valerie loved the feel of smoothing the concoction over her full lips. Women took the strangest things for granted. Like applying makeup. It pissed her off seeing a woman half-assed applying makeup at a stoplight in the middle of rush hour. Hell! Get your ass up a half-hour earlier and do it right! For Valerie, painting a face was as important as painting a picture and not something to be rushed. Why on earth would you want to rush through the canvas of your face?

Valerie fingered through her wild, cocoa brown mane, satisfied that she could wear her hair all over her head looking like she didn't even know how to spell comb better than any other woman she knew. She loved bangs. They added a softness and an innocence to her striking features. She didn't use them to hide behind because, as far as she was concerned, she was too beautiful to want to hide anything. But bangs enhanced her smoldering brown eyes. Valerie's eyes were hypnotic, and she could entice a man to do just about anything for her just by getting him to look into her eyes. She stared at her reflection, smiling back at the beauty smiling at her. Valerie was breathtaking and not a soul on earth could convince her otherwise. Men stopped dead in their tracks, damn near tripping over their chins dragging the ground. She loved it. Heterosexual men too overcome by her physical appeal to know better. She loved that even more. A knock at the door interrupted her admiration. "Hey, Sweetie. You're on in five."

"Thanks, Bobby," she said. "I'm ready." Valerie stood up and adjusted the straps on her dress, then smoothed down the sides and back, admiring the flawless shape of her behind. She looked so damn good in red. People told her that all the time. Oooh, Girl! Don't even go there. Valerie blew herself a kiss. "That's better." She smiled. Her public was waiting, dying to see her perform tonight. Adoring fans. She laughed. Of course they adored her ass. Who wouldn't? She was beautiful and talented and Valerie.

Mo and Naomi had been waiting for this night for weeks. Valerie had become one of the hottest tickets in town and they weren't about to miss this, her opening show at Sasha's Supper Club. They had perfect seats, compliments of the diva herself. Right up front, center stage, and the maitre d' had been told to treat these two special ladies like royalty. Mo'd invited Kevin to come along, but he insisted that he had some developing to do that just couldn't wait. She knew the deal, though. He wasn't into drag queen shows. That's all he had to say, but Mo figured he didn't want to risk hurting her feelings since the star attraction happened to be none other than Troy, a.k.a. Valerie.

The show was about to begin and all the lights were dimmed down to a single spotlight on stage. "Ladies and gentlemen," the announcer said simply. "Valerie."

Troy strutted out on stage looking absolutely stunning and the audience went wild.

"Damn! He looks so good!" Naomi squealed. She'd seen her brother in drag before, but not looking like this. She was almost jealous. Troy had been playing dress up for as long as she could remember. In fact, he'd been the one to teach both her and Mo how to properly arch an eyebrow.

Mo gently nudged Naomi with her elbow. "Well, you know what they say? If it looks too good to be true..."

Naomi finished, "It is too good to be true."

Troy lip-synched Tina Turner songs better than Angela Bassett ever could. The crowd roared. Valerie walked over to her two guests, elated that they'd finally come to see her act, and seemed to be having a damn good time, too. She was especially glad that Maureen had come out. Since she'd started dating Kevin, she'd shed that shell she'd been wearing all these years. Mo was looking like her old, beautiful self again. Her spirit had come back to life, and the woman was actually fun to be around. Of course, Valerie knew Kevin had to be "hittin' that thang" on a regular basis. Girlfriend had a glow about her that a woman could only get from regular doses of the miracle protein called "sperm."

Gregory was in the audience. Valerie had looked out earlier and saw him come in. She didn't speak to him for weeks after he tried to get violent on her. Eventually, though...all his begging and pleading paid off. Valerie loved it when men begged for her. He'd sent her flowers and candy. Taken her out to fancy restaurants and plays, just to get back into her good graces.

"I need you, Troy. I've never felt this way about anybody else. Please. Give me one more chance."

"I can't deal with the jealousy, Gregory. What kind of relationship can we have if you don't trust me?"

"I do trust you. I just... This is all new to me, Troy. Being in love...really in love for the first time in my life...I'm not sure what to do with it."

"Don't strangle it. Don't try to hold it down or lock it up. You need to let me be me."

"I don't want to lose you."

"What you don't understand is...I don't want to lose you either, Gregory. I'm in love too, but I will not put up with the bullshit."

"I understand."

Troy adored Gregory and the last thing he'd ever want to do was hurt him. But he wasn't about to let Gregory or any other man put chains on him. Not until he'd made up his mind that he was cool with it. With Gregory, Troy still hadn't decided whether or not he was ready to settle down, but he was willing to consider it.

On the way home, Mo pulled an airline ticket from her purse. Nosiness was faster than a speeding bullet on Naomi and she snatched the ticket from her sister's hand. "Ooooh, Girl! Where you going?"

Mo grinned. "To the Cayman Islands. Kevin's got a shoot there next month."

"And he's taking you?"

"No, Nay," Mo said sarcastically. "He's taking some other woman. He just wanted me to hold on to the ticket for her. Of course, he's taking me. Duh?"

Naomi rolled her eyes. "Nice of you to give your sister some warning. I guess you expect me to watch Ty for you while you're gone?"

"Nope." Mo eased her ticket from Naomi's hand and slipped it back into her purse.

"You taking him with you? What kind of romantic vacation is that?"

"No, I'm not taking him with me. Not this time."

"So...who's going to baby-sit..."

Troy bounced up and down in his seat and raised his hand. "Me! Me!" he squealed excitedly.

Naomi stared at him with hurt feelings all over her little face. "You'd rather leave your son with your gay, drag-queen brother than with me?"

Troy grinned. "Child, lighten up. I ain't contagious. The boy will be with me for a week. It's not like he'll be a flaming six-year-old by the time Mo gets back. It takes years to get like me."

"But I usually keep him, Troy. Me and Ty...we tight like that."

"Well, me and Ty would be tight like that, too, if you weren't monopolizing all his time like..."

"Hey! Hey!" Mo interjected. "Let's just cut the boy in half and both of you can have a piece. I'm going to the Cayman Islands and I don't need the drama before I leave."

Naomi grinned. "You gonna give him some?"

"What makes you think I haven't already?" Mo asked nonchalantly.

"So that's why you've been so nice to me lately," Naomi concluded.

"Yep," said Mo. "That's exactly why."

The Adventures of the Bold and Bourgeois

By Eileen M. Johnson

Chapter One

In the Beginning there was Perfection...

Akinyele was a twenty-five-year-old, educated, beautiful, upper-six-figure- making sistah. And she loved it. Her condo was well on its way to being paid for; the bank had just sent her the title to the Acura that she'd paid off in two years flat; and her closet looked like Kate Spade, Kenneth Cole, and Donna Karan paid her to rent the space.

Akinyele's natural was maintained by the trendiest salon in the city while her toes and feet were coaxed into soft submission by an actual podiatrist. A bi-weekly visit to a masseuse rolled away the stress and strain of her everyday life.

At her job, Akinyele was totally in control. Graduating magna cum laude from Xavier and breezing through an MBA program at the prestigious Tulane, she'd slammed onto the professional scene at the tender age of twenty-two. Three years later, she was Assistant Operations Manager at Jazz City Bank. She'd managed to beat out others with seniority and more education simply by exercising her natural gift of perseverance and constant hunger to be at the top. Not only was Akinyele the youngest person in the bank's history to hold the title, she was also the first woman and the first African-American to boot.

Socially, Akinyele was active in her sorority's graduate chapter. Plus, she was being courted by several well-established social groups.

In the past year, she had been on both the Best Dressed Lists and was listed as one of New Orleans' most eligible bachelorettes in Cachet, the city's magazine of Nouvelle Black Society.

Akinyele was a sistah who also did her share of volunteer work. Whenever she could find a free Saturday, she breezed down Henry Clay Avenue with her bag of books and read funny stories to the patients in Children's Hospital. The catchy phrases and loopy hooks of Dr. Seuss coming from her mouth made little bodies forget about the recent surgeries and chemo treatments as their little bellies vibrated with laughter. It was something Akinyele naturally loved doing. She also sent a healthy amount of checks to several foundations across the city and the state. There wasn't a charity event that she wasn't invited to and she always accepted all invitations. While Akinyele loved doing charity work, she also loved seeing her name in a caption under a flattering picture of herself on *The Times-Picayune's Society* page. Akinyele was a natural ham.

To her family, Akinyele was the golden girl. From birth, she was treated like the princess she believed herself to be. No one could visit her parents without hearing about her latest achievements or being forced to leaf through an album with her latest pictures. The sun definitely shined on her life. The sister was high on the hog. She was young, gifted, fly, and African-American. She loved her lifestyle.

Well, she thought she did anyway. The problem? Akinyele was lonely. She couldn't get a man to come within six feet of her Manalo Blahnik enclosed feet. In the three years after she left Tulane, she had managed to alienate every upwardly mobile, available man that the city of New Orleans had to offer.

This was not Atlanta where the male-to-female ratio was like something out of a horror movie. African-American men were not scarce in New Orleans. In fact, they were everywhere–getting their cellular plans upgraded in the line before her at Mobile One, perusing lambskin jackets in the Canal Place shopping center, buying cloves of garlic and cayenne peppers in the French Market. New Orleans was just full of single, African-American men, but they were all the same in Akinyele's eyes: sweet but as plain as pound cake. She wanted something different. Someone who had been places. Someone who knew that endives went in a Caesar salad.

During a monthly meeting of the New Orleans Black MBA Society a few months prior, she'd sat down after locating a cup of coffee. While waiting for the meeting to begin, Akinyele looked up right into the eyes of this delectable chunk of chocolate. Seated across the table from her, his Cerutti cologne tickled her nostrils and made her want to take a bite out of his milky mocha skin. As they always do, he approached her after the meeting. Five minutes was all it took for him to offer to make her dinner the following Friday night.

Arriving at his Uptown townhouse, Akinyele noted the smooth shades of cream, white, and mocha used to decorate. The brother had definite taste. The latest electronics were stacked on his alabaster entertainment center and his kitchen was restaurant style. He had potential. *This could be the one*, Akinyele thought to herself. Could've been the one, that is. When she sat down to dinner and he served her a Caesar salad chock full of iceberg lettuce, his husband points went down. *Considerably.*

Akinyele didn't ask for much. All she wanted was an educated, cultured, childless African-American man who made more money than she did and didn't slaughter the King's English. She had met many who fit all her criteria, but they just seemed to fall short. People had told Akinyele for years that she was far too high-strung and demanded things from people that she wouldn't even think of entertaining. While it might have very well been true, it was her world and she expected people to remember that.

Akinyele finally hit rock bottom one night after she found herself eating through the ass end of a five-pound box of Godiva truffles. As she wiped some of the chocolate away from her lips and cheeks, a wet hand indicated that she had been crying. It had occurred to her that she had been making love to her Kenmore every night for the past eight months, but she didn't think it had that big an effect on her. Akinyele decided to face facts. She was lonely, but she was not desperate. That's why she knew her best girl Nadya was on drugs when she told her to log on to her neglected personal computer and check out BlackGentlemen.com.

Akinyele had spent many stolen minutes laughing at several of her friends behind their backs. Several of them spent their weekends jetting to the far corners of America to see men that they'd met over the Internet. Akinyele thought this was absolutely ludicrous. Personal ads were bad enough, but what kind of man actually took the time to place a personal on the Internet? Even worse, what kind of woman took the time to read and answer such an ad?

After playing the role of Cleopatra, Queen of Denial for so long, Akinyele admitted to herself and everyone else how lonely she really was. Maybe the Internet dating thing wasn't so bad after all. Akinyele was determined to find out.

Chapter Two

Cyber Cruising

"Welcome....You've got mail," the dumb and monotonous male voice of America Online greeted Akinyele after she finally remembered her password. Her computer was somewhat of a necessary purchase. She paid her bills online, sent cyber-greeting cards when it was too late to send the real thing and, of course, she did some hellified cyber shopping. But never did Akinyele think of it as her dating service. Being the daring diva that she was though, she'd try anything once.

After seeing that her lazy ass had one hundred forty-one pieces of unread mail, Akinyele opened the browser and typed in www.BlackGentlemen.com. She was so reluctant to do so that she'd avoided Nadya and her other girl Iris' phone calls. Being the friends they were, they kept insisting that lonely wasn't healthy. Akinyele finally broke down that night as her stomach rumbled and cramped after all that damned chocolate. Nadya and Iris were just as high-strung as she was, but they both swore that they met a series of quality men on the site. Akinyele continued struggling with the pros and cons as she waited for the page to load.

"Okay, this is too cheesy," Akinyele grumbled to herself as she got up to go to the refrigerator.

Returning back to the screen with lox, cream cheese, and the better half of a bagel crammed into her mouth, Akinyele plopped down and began to browse the selection of men. Most of them weren't half-bad, but she could smell desperation seeping through the screen. Akinyele swore she could see their issues and isms pouring out from every pixel on her monitor.

Browsing through the ads placed by males, Akinyele was surprised to see that most of them were educated and gainfully employed. A few were even in New Orleans. Whoa! Here were handsome pieces of chocolate with jobs and an education just waiting to be chosen like cherry cordials and chocolate-covered nougats from a Godiva box. These men appeared to be too good to be true. If this thing was for real, then Akinyele had definitely been missing out!

Everyone on the Internet lies, Akinyele! her inner voice screamed out to her. On the real, Akinyele wanted her to shut up. It was her inner voice that ruled out perfectly desirable men just because they'd worn the wrong shade of brown shoes with their outfits on a date with her.

Chapter Three

Nakalem

Single in Savannah. Thirty-three-year-old Black male seeking eloquent, articulate woman to share stimulating discussions, my cup of Earl Grey, and the occasional warmth of a thick wool blanket.

Hmm, he stood out from all the other ones. He was dark. Correction. This Negro was Black. With winter white teeth. He smiled at Akinyele while reclining on a jet leather couch. Taking in his Faire Isle sweater and neatly-trimmed noveau Afro, she just knew that he was gay. Gay or married. But to satisfy the two yapping magpies that she called best friends, she decided to answer.

"Okay, you can do this," Akinyele said as she began to type a reply.

From: ABabaloa@JazzCitybank.net
To:SmooveAFROrican@Pries.com
Re: Single in Savannah

Hello...my name is Akinyele and I came across your ad while browsing through BlackGentlemen.com. Now, I want you to know from the beginning that I am not desperate at all. I merely wish to try something different. I am twenty-five, the Assistant Operations manager at a branch of the second largest bank in Louisiana. I was educated at Xavier and Tulane and I put much stock in education. I am single with no kids.

My ideal man could be someone like you. In a man I require brutal honesty, no kids, no excess baggage, no hang-ups, no self-esteem issues, attainable goals, steady and secure employment, financial security to match my own, a zest for life, and a desire to always rise to the top. If you fit this description, please don't hesitate to reply. If you fall short and fit one or more of the categories that I deemed undesirable, please don't waste your time or mine replying.   Peace! A.

Humming as she clicked away on the keyboard, Akinyele attached a picture and clicked send. There. Done.

Being the cynic that she was, Akinyele just couldn't wait to log on in a day or so and see a very nasty email from his wife or, better yet, a different picture from the one staring down at her from the web page.

Clicking the page closed, Akinyele logged off without reading any of the unread mail. That could wait until tomorrow when she logged on to check for a receipt from a recent Ebay order. Satisfied with herself because she had made an attempt to do what others had pushed her to do, she carried her behind to bed.

Entering her office and closing the door, a tune from her computer's sound card sang out, signaling that she had a new email message. This was work, real life, real important. Unlike America Online or the silly personal ad site that she'd visited the night before, emails at work signaled real, real life. Akinyele used her email address at work to stay abreast of the stock market amongst other business matters. She corresponded with other members of management at her branch as well as the other thirty-one branches of Jazz City Bank scattered across Louisiana. After sleeping on the news that had caused two other banks to fold within the past year, Akinyele knew now that when it came to work, she had to stay on top of the information game.

After buzzing Solange, her administrative assistant, and asking her to bring in a fresh carafe of coffee, Akinyele sat down and opened her email icon. Dang! She realized that she was feeling so sorry for herself the night before that she had given the guy from BlackGentlemen.com her work email address in her reply to his ad.

To: ABabaloa@JazzCitybank.net
From:SmooveAFROrican@Pries.com
Subject: Single in Savannah

Hello there. Unlike others, your reply made me laugh and warmed my heart at the same time. The reason? I see much of myself in you. I, too, was once cynical and thought that all women were alike. God opened my heart and let me know that I was wrong. I may not find her today. I may not find her tomorrow. I may not even find her next year. But eventually, I will find her. And when I do, there will be no letting go! Please, email me back and let me know a little more about yourself. Judging from the pictures you included in your reply, I can see that you are a beautiful young woman. Wild hair and meat on her bones...just the way I like them. And judging by what you told me about your occupation, I can tell that you are educated and intelligent...more pluses. But you neglected to tell me so much. Who hurt you? What caused you to put up the cynical cinderblock in front of your heart that I could detect from your words? Your expectations of men are high and that is potentially a good thing but you mentioned that you were nitpicky. Do you require much in a man because you feel you deserve it or is it simply because you feel that you are lacking much inside that it would take a super human to fill the space? Once again, please write me back and let me know these things along with other things you left out...the good stuff....Nakalem.

Oh, hell no! He had his nerve! Akinyele was fuming so badly that it took her several minutes to notice that he had enclosed a zip file with additional pictures of himself. Curiosity was killing her, but she had to calm down. Who the hell did this Negro think he was? What did he mean who hurt her? *Geez!*

Taking a deep breath and clicking the *download later* tag on the zip file, Akinyele clicked reply and started typing. He wanted to know the truth? The real her? Fine, she would tell him.

Chapter Four

A Friendly Game of Tag

*F*rom:*ABabaloa@JazzCitybank.net*

TO:SmooveAFROrican@Pries.com
Subject: You Have Some Kind of Nerve!

Okay, Nakalem. You're a handsome man, without a doubt. And I can also see that you are somewhat of a busybody. You want to get inside my head? You want to ask me questions that you probably don't want to know the answers to? Well, ask me no questions and I'll tell you no lies. You asked who hurt me? Everyone! That's who!

Sit back because there are many people on my shit list! The guys in college who couldn't look past my weight and smell class dripping off me like glaze from a Krispy Kreme donut. The ones who looked past my extra pounds, gave me a few uneventful fucks, and then never called again. The women who spread rumors about me being loose. Those people! Well, lo and behold! The fat girl has graduated and really has her shit together now! My main objective is to never lower my standards and attract or even entertain the kind of man who wouldn't have looked at me then....see, now I realize that it was THEIR loss and MY gain because now I know that I am really something special. There! I told you....and as for the things that I want? I want a man who is capable of loving me (and only me)...a man who paints my toenails, a man who buys me goldfish (I can buy myself anything that I desire. However, I do have a knack for wanting whimsical items), a man who takes my car to get inspected. A man who doesn't judge me on how I look but on how I treat him. A man who can hold his own in a world of craziness. A man who loves his Blackness. A man who cherishes his freedom yet yearns to belong to me. That's what I want. Are you up for the challenge? A.

There, Asshole! Akinyele thought with a self-satisfied smirk as she clicked send. She could already picture him getting up and hauling ass after reading her reply, never to be heard from again. Getting up, she walked over and poured fresh coffee from the carafe that Solange had quietly brought in while she was hunched over the computer typing away like a madwoman.

Before she could take the first sip, her computer sang out again, indicating a message.

Plopping the cup down, Akinyele walked over and hit the refresh button.

From:SmoovAFROrican@Pries.com
To:ABabaloa@JazzCityBank.net
Re:You Have Some Kind of Nerve

Akinyele, I was delighted to see that I struck a nerve! I knew that there was much to discover beneath that hard, shiny exterior. See, I too was once too dark and too chunky to be considered attractive. I know what you have been through because I was there myself. As for the challenge? You're on! By the way, which branch of Jazz City Bank are you at?

Ohhh! A die-hard! Pulling out the keyboard, Akinyele began her latest reply.

From: ABabaloa@JazzCitybank.net
To: SmoovAFROrican@Pries.com
Subject: Oh, yeah???
All right. So you're up for the challenge, huh? Well, one more thing...you seem to be forgetting that you are in Savannah and I am in New

Orleans...Long distance relationships are fine but this sistah has some needs that AT&T doesn't reach out far enough to touch.......A. And by the way, I am located in the St. Charles Street tower.

Akinyele sat sipping her lukewarm coffee until her computer's sound card sang again. This time, her heart skipped a few beats as she hit *refresh.*

From:SmoovAFROrican@Pries.com
To:ABabaloa@JazzCitybank.net
Re: Oh Yeah???
My dear, in case you didn't know...at least ten planes leave both of our cities headed to the other every day. I have nothing but time and frequent flyer miles!

Clicking save, she closed his last email and drew a long breath. His words sounded so serious! Getting up to pour herself another cup of coffee, she tried to weigh out the pros and cons of a long distance relationship. The last one she had been involved in began in her senior year of high school when her boyfriend decided to go to Grambling instead of one of New Orleans' numerous colleges. When the semester started, it was kind of fun hitting the road to see someone that you cared about. But the boring four-hour drive through Louisiana's dull Kisatchie forest soon had her disenchanted. Of course she was older now, but she was basically the same person. If she couldn't handle four hours, how could she potentially handle ten or twelve hours of driving?

The minute that Akinyele's car was visible in the parking tower, she broke into a run. Pressing the unlock button on her keyless remote, she jumped into her car and headed home. Navigating through the awful five o'clock New Orleans traffic, she couldn't wait to get there.

Savannah was on EST, an entire hour ahead of New Orleans. This pretty much meant that by the time she straggled into her Pontchartrain Park condo and kicked off her kidskin pumps, Nakalem was probably already relaxing and sipping on a mint julep, or whatever the hell they drank in Savannah.

Pulling up in her parking space, Akinyele sprang from her car and went inside. As Frankie Beverley and Maze sang, this was the golden time of the day. She began to strip in the doorway and didn't stop until she was down to her underwear. Slipping on a raw silk kimono, she retraced her steps downstairs and retrieved the assorted items of clothing that she had discarded on her way in.

Picking up her the remote for her stereo, Akinyele clicked the power button on. As Sade began to sing about faith, trust, and hope, she turned on her computer and allowed it to warm up. She walked into the kitchen, poured herself a glass of Merlot, and grabbed some Carr crackers, Stilton cheese, and red grapes. Bringing her bounty back to the computer, she signed on and squealed when she saw that Nakalem was logged onto America Online.

Okay, Akinyele...why are you getting excited about another human using the computer at the same time as you? she asked herself. And a human that you have never met! Geez!

"Oh, shut up!" Akinyele said out loud to that damned inner voice. Crunching noisily on a cracker, she typed away in the instant messenger box.

It was delightful, sitting there and type/talking about anything and everything. She was learning more and more about this person who was halfway across the country without either of them even saying a word.

SmooveAFROrican: Hey...my fingers are getting tired...can I call you?
OnlyOneAkinyele: I don't care..that's cool...
SmooveAFROrican: #?????
OnlyOneAkinyele: 504-555-1809
SmooveAFROrican: Ok.. give me five minutes.
OnlyOneAkinyele: Can you give me twenty?? I have to jump in the shower...I signed on as soon as I walked in from work.
SmooveAFROrican: Cool...twenty minutes then.

Clicking on save before closing the instant messenger box, Akinyele shut down the computer and ran upstairs. Drenching her hair with good-smelling shampoo from Carol's Daughter, she stood under the warm spray and scrubbed away at her dense, natural hair. Putting on a pair of bath gloves, she scoured away at her already soft skin and thought about Nakalem.

Nakalem seemed to be everything that she could want in a man yet she had never met him, had never even heard his voice. During the course of their America Online conversation, Nakalem told her that he had *friends*. Geez, she hated that word! That normally meant that he had a serious woman who would wait in the wings while he got his freak on with whomever he chose. Then, after the smoke cleared, she would still be his main thing. Akinyele wasn't settling for anything like that. If she couldn't have her own man, or a man who had the potential to be only her man, then she didn't want any at all. If she wanted some quick and easy satisfaction, she had several losers that she could call to satisfy her. However, that was no longer acceptable in her world. Dicks, although few and far between, had to come with intellectual conversation and class. If they didn't, then fine because she had a dick in the dresser with four brand-new batteries.

Basically, it boiled down to this. Although she felt like she and Nakalem were doing a decent job of getting to know each other online, he was really going to have to tap dance and jump through fiery hoops if he wanted to be with her. She was lonely, but she still felt the need to stick to her guns. In her mind, she was almost sure that he wouldn't be willing to.

She was sitting at her vanity, thinking of ways she could make him prove himself when her phone started ringing. Running over to the nightstand, she checked the Caller ID, saw the area code, and guessed that it was Nakalem.

"Hello?" she said in her sexiest voice.

"We have a very important message for you concerning your water softener," a plastic Caucasian female voice began.

"Oh, shove it where you need it most!" Akinyele screamed into the phone before slamming it down. She felt tricked!

Glancing at the clock on her bedside table, she noted that it had been more than twenty minutes since she'd logged off the computer. In fact, it had been more than thirty. Just when she was about to give up and turn her ringer off for the night, the phone rang.

"No, I don't want to buy anything. Get a real job," she answered. *Geez!* She was even more pitiful than she thought! The only people that she could get to call her were telemarketers.

"Whoa!" the deep voice at the other end of the line chuckled out. "I was not planning on trying to sell you anything, but now I feel the need to warn everyone else in this world of your wrath! How are you? This is Nakalem."

Instantly embarrassed, Akinyele just stood with the phone next to her ear and twirled a lock of hair with her free hand.

"You were quite vocal a few seconds ago and now the cat has your tongue?" Nakalem jeered.

"Oh, no, I am here. Just surprised that you actually called," Akinyele admitted.

"You? The most placid diva herself?" he asked in a serious tone.

"Wait a minute. Have I ever told you that I was a placid diva?"

"You never said it," Nakalem replied with laughter in his voice.

"Great. Well, we shall get along fine if you drop these assumptions from the beginning," Akinyele stated, hoping he would realize how serious she was.

"Akinyele, please allow me to call you right back," Nakalem said and promptly hung up.

"Oh, hell no!" she screamed to the room around her. Getting no response from the walls and ceilings, she decided to scream again. "Who the hell does this Black Negro think he is?"

The shrill ring of the telephone answered her this time.

"Hello?" she said with fire in her voice. If this was a telemarketer, they were going to get it.

"Hello. Might I please confabulate with Akinyele?" Nakalem's voice poured out like liquid fudge.

"This is she. You should know that. You just hung up on me."

"Not I. The person who hung up on you was a person on his way to making a bad first impression on you. The person calling now is he, the same person yet better and more knowledgeable. So how are you tonight?" Nakalem asked.

"I am fine," Akinyele said with a smile. She could tell already that he was an expert at tap dancing.

"That's good to hear. First of all, let me say this. I am not in the habit of calling women that I meet over the Internet," he explained.

"I am sure you say that to all the women on your buddy list," she said, only half-joking.

"Actually, of all of the females that have responded to my ad, you are the only one to be graced with a call from me."

She wanted to believe him. Although Iris and Nadya had told her about the good men available online, they had also hipped her to the Internet players and the online whores.

"Okay. Answer this question. What made you decide to call me?" Akinyele asked.

"I knew from the moment I saw your response to my ad that we would be having this conversation," Nakalem began. "Most of the responses sounded desperate. Needy. Frantic. You were caustic. You made it seem like you didn't care whether or not I responded. Like you weren't in the least bit pressed."

Walking over to her vanity, Akinyele looked into the mirror and observed the prominent grin across her face. Yep, she was hard to get and he knew it. She baited the line and he bit. Now, he was playing on her turf.

"That's probably because I am not pressed," she said with confidence crowding her voice.

"So I guess you would not be too pressed to fly to Savannah next Friday?"

"I...I...,'" she stammered. "I don't even know you!"

"That's the point of this call and those emails and all of the future calls. Getting to know you and you getting to know me," Nakalem explained.

"Okay. But what if I still don't know you by next Friday?" she challenged.

"Then you'll go home Friday afternoon and we'll have a nice

conversation over the phone and continue our getting-to-know-you process," he said logically.

"Okay, you just gave me an offer that I cannot refuse," she admitted.

"Great. So...tell me about Akinyele," Nakalem said.

"OK...I am..." she began.

"No," he interrupted. "I want to know about the real Akinyele. Not the corporate raider who has the world by the balls."

Akinyele was about to object when she decided to just break down and tell him all about her. She never let anyone know the real, real her and he seemed to be up for the challenge. Fine, he wanted to know; she would tell him and watch him run for the hills.

She talked. And he talked. And they both talked. She explained how good it made her feel to go to a mall knowing that she could pretty much buy anything in any store without any regrets because she was the only person that she had to look out for. He told her how people sometimes padded their surroundings with material items to fill voids in their personal lives. He told her how much he loved his job and making money but often had dreadful dreams of growing old alone. She told him that she knew exactly what he was talking about. She told him how rejecting men who she felt weren't up to par made her feel like she was in control. He told her how rejecting perfectly innocent people for no good reason often made us feel better but just added to the scar tissue left by those who had once rejected us. She told him how the Wonder Woman role got tired and how, just once, she wanted Superman to come to her rescue. She also told him how good it felt to pull up next to a car full of African-American men who wouldn't have given her a second look a few years earlier but were now salivating over her new, improved, fly persona knowing that they could never have her. She hated admitting these things to anyone, especially herself. But he asked. And he added. He told her how it felt good to be an African-American man who had made it and was still in the ever-changing process of making it. He told her how it felt to be desired by women because of his capabilities. He told her about being passed up by single women time and time again because they had found the fabled one better. She told him how it felt to be on top of the world in public and then in the pits once you got home, locked the door, and took off the power suit.

Looking at the clock, Akinyele was shocked to see that they had been talking for four hours. True, they'd talked about anything and everything but it felt like minutes instead of hours.

"Geez, can you believe that we've been on the phone for four hours?" she asked.

"Not at all. It feels like we've been talking for minutes but knowing each other for a lifetime," Nakalem said in a serious tone.

"Well...I don't know what to say," Akinyele said. She was truly at a loss for words.

"Say goodnight and I'll talk to you tomorrow," he said.

"Goodnight, Nakalem....I'll talk to you tomorrow."

"Goodnight, Akinyele, and thank you."

"Thank you for what?" she asked.

"Thank you for being you and opening up and allowing me to talk to the real you."

"Okay...I still don't know what to say."

"Goodnight, Akinyele," he said.

"Goodnight."

Chapter Five

It Just Happened...

Akinyele's room looked like Saigon after the fall of Vietnam. Clothes were strewn everywhere. Personal items spilled out of her Kenneth Cole train case. Shoes were stuffed inside of a shoe bag that she had no intention of bringing with her to Savannah. An open Reaction suitcase sat amongst the mess, empty and confused.

Her plane was scheduled to leave Moissant/New Orleans International airport in an hour and a half and she still wasn't packed. Geez! She was the same woman who had wowed the locals in Madagascar and was pursued by every man she came across in Lagos. She had globetrotted in the best and most appropriate rags all over the world yet she didn't know what to bring on a simple trip to Georgia.

She and Nakalem had been getting to know each other over the past two weeks and although the visit seemed slightly rushed, she was excited. Apprehension played no part in her visit. She was ready to meet him. She wanted to see if Nakalem in person matched Nakalem the personality. She wanted to like him and she wanted him to like her. She was never one to want for approval, but Nakalem was different. A little part of her actually wanted him to really like her. Actually, a huge part of her wanted him to like her. Although she really wanted him to be wowed by her, Akinyele knew that the best she could do was to be herself.

Selecting five warm weather outfits, a pair of jeans, a windsuit, and a light sweater from the closet, she folded them neatly into the suitcase. This was what she was taking. She walked to the dresser and selected the matching hosiery and underwear along with a few fiery pieces of lingerie just in case he liked her a whole lot. Teasing was her bag! Closing the latch on the suitcase, she sprinted around the room gathering accessories and toiletries. *Well, Akinyele, she told herself. This is it...sink or swim.*

"Soft drink? Cocktail?" the blonde flight attendant asked Akinyele as she pulled out the folding lap tray and placed a small bag of honey-roasted peanuts in front of her.

"I'll have a ginger ale," Akinyele replied as she went back to reading the *Essence* that she had purchased in the airport newsstand. "On second thought, let me get a Stoli on the rocks," she said as she remembered that first-class passengers were entitled to the drink of their choice.

"Coming right up," the flight attendant replied as she walked to the rear of the first class section.

Getting sauced wasn't going to diminish her anxiety completely, but at least a good strong drink would pacify the butterflies.

"Thank you," Akinyele told her as the flight attendant politely handed her the drink and moved to the passenger behind her.

After downing the Stolli at a record speed, she took out a moistened towelette and wiped off her lipstick. She was starving and the nuts looked appetizing, but the last thing she wanted to greet Nakalem with was protein breath. Instead, she took out a few Altoids and munched away noisily on them. Opening the mirror of the train case that she had stored in the overhead compartment, she went to work on repairing her already perfect makeup. Satisfied, she fluffed out her already fluffy seven-inch natural. When the pilot announced that they were making their descent into Savannah, Akinyele doused herself with Happy and said a quick prayer. She was going to have a good time on this visit regardless of whether he liked her or not. She needed a getaway from New Orleans, even if it was just for one weekend. The worst case scenario was that she would return home on

Sunday night with a new platonic friend and she could definitely deal with that.

Her feet ached as she made her way into the airport through the tunnel leading from the plane. Why had she chosen couture over comfort? The four-inch heels on the Enzo sandals dug into her newly-pedicured feet so hard that she thought they would leave a permanent impression. Akinyele wanted Nakalem to be knocked out by her appearance but now it seemed like a limp would mar everything anyway.

She was so busy concentrating on each painful step and not stumbling over onto her face that she didn't even realize that a very warm, very fragrant body was embracing her.

"It's so good to see you, Girl," a delicious voice said as her cheek rubbed against his chest.

God he's tall! And he smells so good! Those were the first two things on her mind as she returned the embrace.

"How was your flight?" Nakalem asked as he took the heavy case out of Akinyele's hands.

She switched her purse from her right shoulder to her left. "My flight was fine...and you have to be the absolute most gorgeous creature that I have ever laid eyes on," she blurted. *Oh no Sista Gurl! That's not in Akinyele's rules! You NEVER compliment a man before he compliments you!*

"Likewise," Nakalem said.

"What? Your flight was good, too?" she said in a flip voice.

"No. You know what I meant. You're the most gorgeous woman I have ever seen."

"I bet you say that to all of the women that you import into Savannah," Akinyele replied, making sure to add the inflection of a joke in her voice.

"Yep...the girl I fly in next week will be even prettier than you." Nakalem winked as he took her hand and led her toward baggage claim.

Walking through the airport was a high in itself. Akinyele had always been a hog for attention and here, she definitely got it. Her wild auburn hair stood out like a beacon amongst the sea of flat perms and weaves worn by the women milling around. She was definitely turning the heads of the male locals. And as if that wasn't enough, every time she would glance over at Nakalem, she would find him looking down at her. Smiling, she sped up to keep pace with his long strides.

Nakalem looked so different from his pictures. Alike yet different. He was taller, bigger, darker. Much more handsome. Real life added twenty pounds to the frame of the man who had burned up the phone lines to make Akinyele feel welcomed into his city and his home, but she didn't mind. She liked large men. Not fat but extremely large and that was definitely what Nakalem was. Of course, she was no lightweight herself. She was what Louisiana natives call *country thick.* They made an interesting pair as they stood by baggage claim, waiting for her luggage on the turnstile.

"Are you hungry?" Nakalem asked as he slapped away Akinyele's hands when she reached for her suitcase.

"A tad bit," she replied, her stomach grumbling a note of deception. "Are there any good restaurants around here?" she asked with a guilty smile as Nakalem led her out one of the exits.

"You are about to have the best seat in the house at the best restaurant on the Southeastern seaboard," Nakalem replied as he rolled her suitcase with one hand and carried her train case with the other. Nakalem made the weight of Akinyele's bags seem non-existent as compared to odious. "You are about to dine at Chez Nakalem."

"Hmm...I didn't know you cooked."

He stopped in front of a big black Land Rover Discovery. They'd never talked about what he drove but she was impressed. Finally, a man with a vehicle that made hers look like a Gremlin.

"And I didn't know you smelled like love," Nakalem said as he placed Akinyele's bags in the back and then opened the front door for her. Nakalem stopped Akinyele as she was about to step in.

"Can I get a hug now?" he asked, making eye contact with her for the first time.

"You gave me one already," she said. Although she loved Nakalem's smell and the way that he felt, she didn't want to spoil herself. If the weekend was a disaster, she certainly didn't want to go home yearning to feel his arms.

"Think of that one as a *hello-I am-so-happy-to-see-you-hug*," Nakalem said with his arms akimbo.

"And what is this one going to be?" she inquired in a panicky voice.

"This one is the *welcome-to-my-world-embrace*," he said as he gripped her in a hug that felt like Home. Yep...he felt like Home.

"Pretty interesting city," Akinyele complimented as they exited off onto a quiet street. "I can see why Sherman thought it was too pretty to burn!"

Turning slightly in his seat, Nakalem peered at her.

"I knew that you were intelligent and were on the up and up on your cultural history, but I didn't know that you were a Civil War buff."

"Actually, I am simply a history buff in general. Civil War, African history, Vietnam, World War II...the usual," Akinyele said casually. Hell, he needn't know that she often spent her nights making love to the History and Discovery channels.

"I'm excited!" Nakalem exclaimed.

"Huh?" Akinyele asked, turning to get a good look at him. Surely he wasn't going to ruin a nice time by talking about his erection. But, in her own weird way, she was curious about what he was packing. A man that size had to be...

"I mean, you're beautiful, smart, and your perfume is breaking me down. I am looking forward to this weekend," Nakalem explained, interrupting Akinyele's filthy thoughts.

"Oh!" she answered. Her lack of dick was definitely taking a toll on her mind. Of course he wasn't talking about an erection.

Akinyele drew in her breath as they pulled up in front of a pastel-blue wooden house with a snow-white picket fence. It was absolutely gorgeous. Simple, yet so wonderful. The flora and fauna of the yard were amazing. Bright pink hibiscus peeked through dark green shrubs. Tiger lilies were everywhere. It seemed as if a tornado had uprooted a house and yard in Antigua or St. Thomas and had placed it gently on the ground in Savannah.

"Wow," Akinyele said as Nakalem shut off the engine. "Your gardener must make a fortune."

"Nope, not at all," he said, blushing. "I do it all myself."

"You don't look like the type to stand around pouring fertilizer on flowers to make them grow," Akinyele stated earnestly.

"Gardening can keep you grounded. Teach you a whole bunch about life," he said.

"What can playing in dirt teach me about life?" she asked.

"It teaches you, amongst other things, that it requires a whole bunch of shit to make anything beautiful bloom, be it a flower, a plan, or even a relationship."

Speechless, Akinyele's mouth hung in an open smile as he came around to open her door. Looks, a nice house, a nice ride, a good job, and a sense of humor. Did it get any better than this?

"A little harder, Baby."

"I thought you liked the way I was doing it in the beginning."

"I did, but now I need you to go a little bit deeper."

"Okay, if you insist. Let me grab a little more oil," Akinyele said as she got off Nakalem's back and crawled over to the bowl of warm sesame-almond oil. Dipping her hands in the fragrant oil, she resumed her sitting position on his back and began to knead away at knots of tension in Nakalem's neck and upper back.

It was as if she was manipulating warm, chocolate taffy in her hands. The man's body was gorgeous. When she'd suggested an after-dinner massage, he'd reluctantly come out of his shirt.

For dinner, Nakalem had made Oysters Rockefeller, which she'd told him in one of their early conversations was her absolute favorite food. The wine coordinated perfectly with the shellfish and the conversation flowed over the soft sounds of Joe Sample on the sound system. The only way to end such a perfect dinner was by showing Nakalem her appreciation with a sensual massage on his wonderful, but tense, body.

"How can any man let you go?" Nakalem moaned as Akinyele squeezed his left shoulder blade.

"Are you moaning because this feels good or are you moaning

because my weight on your back is killing you?" Akinyele asked in a teasing manner.

"You know the answer for that." Nakalem flipped onto his back, nearly knocking Akinyele to the floor.

"Hey! You could've hurt me," Akinyele uttered with false concern as Nakalem looked up at her straddling his lap. She could feel a definite lump rising up to meet her crotch but chose to ignore it for the sake of tact.

Being so close to a man was a feeling that melted something deep inside the pit of her stomach. It had been ages since she'd had even the simplest affection and here she was, sitting on top of a very large piece of fudge.

"What are you thinking about?" Nakalem asked, leaning up on his elbows.

"Everything and nothing at the same time," Akinyele answered. "I'm thinking about how nice this is...you, your house, your hospitality. It's overwhelming. I'm just thinking it's too good to be true."

"Maybe it is....but then again, maybe it isn't," Nakalem said as he sat up to join her.

The first kiss was like honey. Scratch that. The first kiss was like silk. No....the first kiss was like honeyed, silken heaven. His lips were smooth. His tongue was warm. His embrace was reassuring. Akinyele felt like she was melting in Nakalem's arms. She'd always wondered what it was like to see fireworks when you kissed someone. Now, she was an expert on the subject.

Flipping Akinyele gently onto her back, Nakalem kissed her and ran his strong hands through her thick, kinky hair. Groaning, he lowered himself onto her and explored her mouth with his tongue.

"Akinyele?" he said between kisses.

"Yes, Baby?" she answered.

"Akinyele, Akinyele, Ak-in-ye-le," Nakalem murmured as he crushed his mouth down on hers.

It was pure sugar. She had never been held like this. Never been kissed. An old Alexander O'Neal and Cherelle song chimed in her head. *I've been kissed but I never knew love like this. I've been missed but I never knew love like this.* It wasn't love...yet. But Akinyele did understand what they were singing about.

"Let's go upstairs," Nakalem said as he pulled Akinyele to her feet.

Before dinner, she'd showered and changed into a linen shift that hugged her voluptuous curves, and tied a matching scarf around her head to contain some of her Afro. Now, her hair stood in shocks and her perky dress was limp. Climbing the stairs in front of Nakalem, she could feel his hands cupping her ass and stroking her exposed thighs.

With a flick of Nakalem's wrist, Akinyele's dress was unzipped and falling to the floor.

"Damn, Baby," he murmured as she stepped out of the fallen circle and reclined on his bed. "I knew that you were hiding something inside of those clothes, but I had no idea that you had it like this."

"I have been known to pack the pork," Akinyele said jokingly as she leaned forward, allowing her triple D's to strain against the emerald satin bra that attempted to restrain them.

"It's all them greens and cawn brade and hawg maws ya'll eat down in Loosieana," Nakalem said in a fake country accent as he fingered the skin at the edge of her bra.

Stripping down to his snow-white boxer briefs, Nakalem joined Akinyele on the bed. When he reached over to embrace her, she rolled over to the opposite side.

"Come here," Nakalem said in a low voice, looking at her through half-closed eyes.

"I am here," Akinyele said as she got under the soft down comforter.

"No. I mean come closer."

Moving into Nakalem's arms, she melted away as he kissed her and caressed every inch of exposed skin. After a few minutes, Akinyele drew away.

"Goodnight, Nakalem. I had a wonderful day."

"Akinyele?" Nakalem placed his hands upon her satin-encased hips. "It gets even better."

"I am sure it does. Now goodnight." Akinyele kissed him on the cheek.

With a look of absolute shock on his face, Nakalem gave Akinyele a wry smile and reached over to snap off the lamp.

Akinyele was hot and bothered. She couldn't sleep. It wasn't the balmy Savannah night robbing her of slumber either. It was the man spooned against the backside of her body.

Nakalem's breath against the nape of her neck felt so...so...so ooooh. She could hear him breathing, but he wasn't asleep. He was wide awake. Having the same lascivious thoughts that Akinyele was. Any minute now, Nakalem was going to...

"Akinyele?"

"Yes?"

"Are you asleep?"

"You know better," Akinyele answered as she backed a little bit more into his steely erection.

It just happened. All of her life Akinyele had been hearing that phrase slip from the mouths of those around her. A person pulled over by the police for running a red light. *It just happened.* A brand new white refrigerator decorated with crayon marks. *It just happened.* An overworked and underpaid secretary going off and slapping her boss. It just happened. Buying a winning lottery ticket. *It just happened.*

Akinyele hated the phrase. Her world was black and white. No shades of gray. Things had reason. There was a definite chain of events that set the slightest thing off. There was a logical explanation for everything in the universe. Nothing *just happened* until...

...Nakalem reached down and felt the wet crotch of Akinyele's satin tap pants. Stealthily sliding his fingers within her soft folds, her body responded by throbbing warmly and wetly against his finger. With a moan, Akinyele turned over to face Nakalem as he lifted her finger to his lips and sucked it as she watched in lust. Removing her bra, he massaged Akinyele's breasts and erect nipples with his hands and mouth until she purred like a Persian kitten.

Sliding down under the covers, Akinyele lost sight of Nakalem but definitely felt his presence as he gently licked her inner thighs.

With gentle nibbles, he bit the plumpness of them as she gasped and dug her nails into his shoulders. Opening the folds of her pussy, his tongue traced a hot trail until her brain melted and she was moaning like a widow at a grave. The man was a pro. Not to be outdone, Akinyele maneuvered her body to where his mouth was still in paradise and her mouth was sucking on Candyland. After a few seconds of oral competition, Akinyele couldn't tell who was moaning louder or whose mouth was fuller. By the time Nakalem entered her, Akinyele was well on her way to the fabled earth-shattering orgasm that *Cosmopolitan* always promised her. Nakalem began with slow, deliberate strokes, which gradually increased to hard, slapping pumps that hit places that she forgot existed. When Akinyele began her climax, she could hear Nakalem moaning loudly and calling out her name, signaling his own.

They came. Together. They saw stars; they saw colors; they saw lights. They saw heaven. *It just happened.*

Chapter Six

After the Morning After

Hanging her loofah on a shelf in Nakalem's shower, Akinyele stepped out and began rubbing Happy scented lotion onto her skin. Rubbing some shea butter into her hair, she spritzed herself with more Happy. Being the fashionable person that she was, she'd packed nothing but dressy clothes. When Nakalem said he'd wanted to spend a lazy morning, Akinyele had been forced to borrow a pair of fleece cut-offs and a Morehouse T-shirt. The shorts were warm and hugged her behind while the shirt was soft and oversized. It impressed Akinyele when a man's shirt was large enough for her to get lost in.

Walking into the bedroom, Akinyele grabbed her makeup and then put it down, deciding to let Nakalem see the real her. Walking downstairs, Akinyele sniffed her way into Nakalem's kitchen. The smell of blueberries assaulted her as she took a seat at his table.

"Good morning, Princess," Nakalem said, as he sat a fresh blueberry bagel in front of her.

"Good morning, Shuga," Akinyele replied.

"So what would you like to do today?" he asked as he sipped aromatic black coffee across the table from her.

Flinging away the napkin and pushing the bagel aside, Akinyele walked over and took a seat on his lap.

"Today," she began. "Today, I want to pretend that I am your woman."

"Your wish is my command," Nakalem said as he reached up to kiss her.

The day turned out to be somewhat of an epiphany for Akinyele. That night as she lay in his arms watching him sleep, she'd began to muse on how life was. It's amazing how doubt can almost make you miss your train. Pessimism had almost marred her time with him. She almost didn't swallow her pride and answer his ad. She just knew they wouldn't be able to relate face to face. Boy, was she wrong.

He'd hit places that had never been hit. In that day alone, he'd opened every door, bought her goldfish and flowers, washed her hair, painted her toenails. He'd climbed inside her head, told her that money and status weren't suitably important, made her believe in fate, faith, and destiny. He'd read her Ntozake Shange, told her that he saw himself on top on the world (not to mention her) in five years. He sang her Bill Withers, taught her how to dance really slow, shared a bottle of his best brandy, said, "I think I love you," lifted her head to the clouds and taught her that her feet needed to be on solid ground, and showed her the best use for costly chocolates.

This was her man. She could feel it.

Hallelujah!

Chapter Seven

Fooled Around and Fell in Love

"American Flight 2681 non-stop from Savannah to New Orleans is now boarding," the squeaky Asian voice announced.

"I want you to know, Akinyele, I had a wonderful time," Nakalem said as he wiped a tear from the corner of her right eye.

"I hate saying goodbye," Akinyele choked.

"Don't say goodbye," he answered.

"What do you want me to say?" she cried out.

"I want you to say I'll pick you up at New Orleans International on Friday at 7:15 p.m."

It had been three days and twenty odd hours since she'd felt Nakalem's touch. Sitting in her house surrounded by costly things felt like she was trapped in a mausoleum. Akinyele was so unhappy without Nakalem. She had spent less than three days in his company and now she felt like she couldn't live without him.

Monday morning, Akinyele had been bombarded with flowers, emails, and phone calls. Tuesday, she hadn't heard from Nakalem at all. Nor did she hear from him on Wednesday or Thursday.

Today, she'd sent Nakalem a grand total of seven emails without getting one single reply. She'd called his office all day and got no answer at his extension. She'd dialed the main line for Pries, Inc.

where he was an investment banker and was informed that he was out of town until the following Monday. What was up with that? Did he not have the decency to tell her that he was jetting off to somewhere?

Akinyele missed Nakalem so bad that she'd even gone to BlackGentlemen.com to look at his picture and re-read his ad, but it was gone. She felt like such a fool. A lovesick fool. She'd flown halfway across the country and slept with a man who had disappeared.

Akinyele had left work early in a funk. She missed him. But it was clear that he didn't miss her.

The ringing of her phone was nothing compared to the dull thump of her heart.

"Hello?" she said sullenly into the mouthpiece.

"Miss Akinyele, this is Solange. A call came in for you this afternoon but the gentleman didn't leave his name," Solange said.

"Woohoo!" Akinyele shouted. It had to be him.

"Are you okay?" Solange asked with concern in her voice.

"I'm fine. Now I must go," Akinyele said, hurrying her off the phone.

Pressing flash, she punched in Nakalem's home number. She knew that he wouldn't go long without calling her. Thank God for secretaries. Without Solange, she would never have known that Nakalem called.

"Hello?" a female voice answered with the inflection of lukewarm dishwater.

"Nakalem?"

"Does this sound like Nakalem?" the woman asked in a rude manner.

"No, he just normally answers his own phone," Akinyele hissed. "He never mentioned having a rude sister..."

"Oh, really?" she asked in a mocking and patronizing tone. "That's probably because I have been out of the country for the better part of the year. I am here now and I am back to stay. Thank you for entertaining him for me while I was away. Now, your mission is completed."

Before Akinyele could reply, the heifer hung up on her. Sitting there on her couch, she looked at the mouthpiece with her mouth hanging open. She didn't, Akinyele said to herself. She hit redial faster than you could say whodoesthisbitchthinksheis.

"Let me speak to Nakalem now!" Akinyele roared with fire in her voice as soon as the line was picked up.

"Ummm..this is me. Is there something wrong with you?"

"Yes, there is something wrong, but not with me. There is definitely something wrong with the bitch that just answered your phone," Akinyele spewed out.

"I tried to take the phone from her but she closed the door," Nakalem explained as Akinyele let out a sigh of relief.

So she got loud on me without his permission, Akinyele thought logically. *Hold on. What was he doing with a woman in his house?*

"Who is *she?*" Akinyele questioned.

"Brigette is my ex," Nakalem said in a defeated way.

"You never told me that you were married," Akinyele accused.

"That's because I never was. She is my ex-fiancée," Nakalem said as Akinyele heard her make a snide comment in the background.

"Okay. Well what is she doing there now?"

"Her marriage went sour and she came back to the States. She was actually on her way out when you called the first time," Nakalem said.

"All right. What is she still doing there now then? And why the hell are the people at your job saying that you are out of town until Monday?"

"I had plans to fly to New Orleans and surprise you. Things happened and I missed the flight. I came back here and that's when Brigette showed up. She is about to leave now," he said to Akinyele and Brigette at the same time.

"Look, I need to cool down... call me in an hour," Akinyele said. Her head was spinning; her heart was thumping; and there was an ache at the bottom of her stomach.

She never bought into the theory that men were dogs, but now she was starting to think that maybe millions of women were right. She should have known better than falling in love with a man that she met over the Internet. She felt like a fool. She'd flown to fuckin' Georgia and given her body to a man who was still mooning over his ex. Now that was some shit! Akinyele was angry. Moreso than angry, she was hurt. Crushed. She didn't notice when the first tear fell. Nor did she notice when a thousand others joined it, sliding down her cheeks.

Waking up with the leather of the sofa sticking to her skin, Akinyele rolled over and answered the phone.

"Hello?"

"Are you all right?" Nakalem asked.

She had just spent the last hour crying and here he was, asking her if she was *all right.*

"No, I am not all right," Akinyele admitted easily. "I am hurt. You used me and the worst part about it all is that I allowed you to use me."

"I didn't use you, Akinyele. I care about you. We enjoyed each other. Give me a chance to explain the way that things really are and you'll know that I care for you," Nakalem pleaded.

"I thought that you told me the truth about things in the beginning. Now you're saying that you left things out?" There was no way that Akinyele would allow Nakalem to talk himself out of this one. She had survived being single for so many years and a few more certainly wouldn't kill her. She loved and respected herself far too much to allow blinders to be put over her eyes.

"Akinyele, talk to me," Nakalem said.

"I would if I knew what to say," Akinyele admitted dryly.

"Look, as I told you, I had plans to fly to New Orleans and surprise you. They were foiled. Now, I don't care who goes where but I can't let the weekend go by without seeing you and setting the record straight," he said frankly. "By any means necessary. I don't care what I have to do. Either you're coming here or I am coming there."

"It really isn't that serious," Akinyele began.

"Yes it is. When I met you, I knew that you were going to become a part of me. Now, I am just not willing to let that slip away," Nakalem said. "There isn't another flight to New Orleans until 9 p.m. Can you come here?" he asked.

"You mean you want me to jump in my car and drive twelve hours on such short notice?" Akinyele asked nastily.

"No, no, no, Akinyele. Listen to me. There are no flights leaving New Orleans until nine. If you aren't willing to come here, I can wait until nine and come there. However, there is a flight leaving New Orleans coming here in exactly forty-five minutes. Don't say maybe. Don't say no. Just tell me that you'll be on it," Nakalem begged. "Say yes, Baby."

"Okay," Akinyele said, already switching to the cordless phone and running upstairs to pack. "How much is this flight going to cost me?"

"Nothing. I am purchasing the ticket as we speak. It'll be waiting for you at the Delta counter," Nakalem said. Hearing him tap on his keyboard had to be the most wonderful sound. But she couldn't let it melt her heart just yet. Nakalem had some explaining to do.

Speeding her Acura along I-10 west, Akinyele took the Metarie exit and raced to the airport. For once in her life, she looked like hell. She was one of those people who never had a bad day. She always looked so done. Now, she actually looked did. Her eyes had huge rings around them from crying like the damned fool she felt like. Her auburn Afro was on a serious lean to the left. She would have to do some magic on that plane.

Leaving her car in the long-term parking lot and catching the shuttle, Akinyele was at the Delta counter in no time. *He lied. I bet he didn't buy that ticket, the skeptic in her said.*

"Here we go," the ticket agent said as she handed Akinyele's license back to her. "You'll get your return boarding pass when you check your baggage in Tuesday afternoon."

Akinyele really couldn't lie. Nakalem was a man of his word. But Tuesday? Akinyele worked. Very hard, she had to admit. She couldn't just miss two days of work to frolic with him. After asking the agent if she would be able to change the flight day and time if necessary, Akinyele walked over to the boarding gate.

Within minutes, Akinyele was eastbound and airborne. This was crazy. Sure, she was grown but she couldn't just go galloping to another coast simply because someone wanted to see her. Sure, she wanted to see Nakalem and have him explain things to her in her face, but they were still basically strangers. Well, maybe not strangers, but damn near. She was feeling him, but he could still be a serial killer. She did meet him on the net. *Would a serial killer cause your vagina to do figure eights every time you thought about him?* the stupid inner voice asked her.

"Well..." Akinyele mistakenly answered out loud.

"Well, what?" her elderly seat mate asked.

"Well, what is your destination?" Akinyele asked him, trying to play off the fact that she had spoken out loud to an inner voice.

"Well, my ticket said Savannah and we're on a Savannah-bound plane so I might be going to Savannah," he said as he rolled his rheumy old eyes at her. Turning his head, he made a comment to himself about young people and *that dope.*

Akinyele's nerves were much too stringy for her to get up and go to the lavatory so she pulled out her magic bag of tricks and performed a few minor miracles. If Miss Thang had popped up at Nakalem's house after ages of being away, then Akinyele knew that she popped up looking good. The voice of vanity told Akinyele that she had to look just as good or better.

Chapter Eight

Was It Really Just A Dream?

Where the hell is he? Akinyele had been standing next to the baggage claim pit (looking very fly, if she had to admit it) for over an hour. When she tried calling, Nakalem's voicemail picked up on the first ring. Akinyele was mad. No. Take that back. She was fucking pissed!

What if this was one big joke? What if he and ole girl are standing somewhere, hiding and laughing their asses off at you? Some couples get off on role-playing, you know! What if sleeping with you actually improved his sex life with his wife and his marriage in general?

Shaking the voice of doubt that nagged her, Akinyele walked over to the Hertz counter and slammed down her purse. She was no bumpkin. She knew how to rent herself a car and find her way to Nakalem's house. She had dropped everything (ok, ok...so she had a long and lonely weekend stretched out in front of her before Nakalem called) and flown to Savannah. He was going to see her if it killed him. And if a woman was the reason that he had stood her up at the airport, Akinyele was gonna hurt both of them!

It's really hard to play Destructive Diva when you're struggling with the power steering on a tiny, white, three-door Geo Metro hatchback. The Hertz agent gave Akinyele some long drawn-out song and dance about nothing else being available without reservations because of some damned Garden Society convention. What else could she do? Her arms hurt, her ass was sore, and her knees were killing her! She couldn't tell if the brothers on the freeway were looking at her saying, *Damn, she's fly or how that big ass girl gonna get out of that lil car?*

It took Akinyele awhile to find Nakalem's street but about fifteen minutes later, she was fighting with the wheel in the hand over hand motion to turn in his driveway. No truck. Extracting herself from the metal matchbox, she knocked. No Nakalem. Akinyele was mad. No, she was fucking pissed! When this Negro got his Black ass home, she was gonna put on the clown suit for his ass. Did he know who he was playing with? She was runner up for Miss Poison! She had men all over New Orleans salivating over her fine self and he stands her up?

If you have so many men salivating, why are you a zillion miles from home, knocking the damn door off the hinges?

"Oh, shut the fuck up," Akinyele said aloud, catching the attention of Nakalem's neighbor. She made a mental note to see if her health insurance covered psychotherapy. Either she was going to get rid of all the little voices or she was going to get shot after making some kind of statement to them.

With a giggle and an apologetic smile at the neighbor, Akinyele walked back to the car and began unloading her bags. She planned on sitting on top of her suitcase and waiting until he got home. *As Jennifer Holliday sang, I'm not going!* Akinyele thought to herself. Just as she was taking out her carry-on, she looked up to see Nakalem pulling into the driveway.

"So nice of you to show up!" Akinyele screamed at him.

"I just left the airport. I was a little late and by the time I got there, you were gone," Nakalem began.

"Bull-fucking-shit," Akinyele said, exercising the wonderful words that twelve years of Catholic school had taught her. The fucker seemed to be ignoring her!

"Is this your car?" Nakalem questioned as he stared at the Metro in awe. Just then, Akinyele noticed it had Louisiana plates.

"Indeed not! Do I look like the Geo type of woman?"

"Well, actually, nothing is wrong with it," Nakalem said as he walked up to the car and began shaking it with just one of his hands.

"Hertz has rentals all over the country. This one probably got stuck here," Akinyele said logically. She had totally forgotten that she was mad. "Anyway, what gave you the fucking right to leave me at the airport?"

Looking at Akinyele, Nakalem shook his head and walked toward the house. Unlocking the door, he turned to look at her.

"Are you coming in or what?" Nakalem asked as he scooped up her bag.

"Not until you explain and apologize," Akinyele said. She was playing the angry diva role to the hilt. Nakalem was going to learn not to play with this femme!

"Okay, have it your way," Nakalem said as he picked up Akinyele's remaining bags and brought them into the house. *The nerve of him!*

Huffing and puffing, Akinyele burst into the front door. Whoever she was that held him up, he had strewn roses all over the carpet for her! Akinyele had noticed that Nakalem was dressed up and smelling heavily of cologne. His natural hair was freshly edged and shiny. Phyllis Hyman was crooning on the surround sound and... wait a minute! Sniffing the air, Akinyele realized that Nakalem had cooked something scrumptious for the bitch, too! Hot on his heels, Akinyele walked into the kitchen just in time to see Nakalem wrap tinfoil around a cake that said, "Welcome Akinyele" in loopy pink letters.

"Nakalem..."

"Yes," Nakalem said in a tone that was a little too business-like.

"Nothing," Akinyele rasped. Okay, now she felt like the letter after Z. She had just cursed him to pieces and now she realized that he was late because he was here...doing things just for her.

"Great," Nakalem said, eyeing the low look in her eyes. "That's just how I felt when I busted my ass coming back here to find out what happened to you and you attacked me, calling me everything but Nakalem."

"I'm sorry," Akinyele explained. "Really."

"I don't know what kind of people that you've dealt with in your life so far, but I am not going to put up with verbal abuse. I am not the one," Nakalem said as he looked Akinyele squarely in the eye. "Now, I know that I was dead wrong for being late, but you didn't even give me a chance to explain things. You just attacked. People may have pacified you all your life, but that all stops here. Now if you choose to act like an adult, I'll meet you on that level but if you insist on being Drama Diva, we can both get off the train right here."

That's when Akinyele bent to pick up her face from the floor. It was in pieces. Yes, Akinyele, the original Dramatic Diva, had been broken down.

"You don't know how I felt when I got to the airport and you weren't there. The agent told me that you had been on the flight," Nakalem said with a softer voice. Moving up to Akinyele, he put an arm around her shoulder and fingered her hair. "I thought you had turned around and went home. I felt awful for being late."

"It's okay. I really didn't mind getting the car," Akinyele lied.

Placing a finger tenderly across Akinyele's lips, Nakalem smiled and looked at her in the eyes.

"Shhhh! I want this thing that we have to work out. I really do. But you have to be willing to work with me. To compromise. To listen to the whole story. Things happen and perfect picnics get interrupted," Nakalem said.

In the back of her mind, Akinyele knew that Nakalem was speaking of both his tardiness and Miss Queen Bitch popping up and going off on her over the phone. Speaking of which...nah...that could wait until later.

Inhaling the scent of magnolias, Akinyele smiled as the balmy night air hit up against her face. She could grow to love Savannah.

"I wish it was cold. I build awesome fires," Nakalem said as he handed her the glass of zinfandel and moved to close the window that she had opened to breathe in the evening air. "I spent a fortune on that fireplace and it hardly ever gets cold enough for me to use it."

Sitting down next to him, Akinyele discreetly unbuttoned her pants. Brutha had thrown down! If she accidentally cut herself right then and there, sautéed shrimp and scallions would have poured out instead of blood. The moment that Akinyele sat at the table, she understood why he was late. With each bite, she felt more and more like a fool for bawling him out. He'd really gone out of his way to show her a great evening and she had nearly ruined it!

"Okay. About Brigette," Nakalem said, sitting forward on the sofa.

Sighing, Akinyele set down her drink. She knew that the harmony had to come to an end.

"Akinyele, I was once like you," he began. "Just like you, in fact. Not meaning any harm or disrespect to you, but the world revolved around me. The only person that I looked out for was me. Which was good but which also became my downfall. I had other offers but I didn't want someone unless they were on my *level*. I had to have the best of everything. The smallest flaw would turn me off. A forgotten "s" at the end of a word, red lipstick worn with pink nail polish, anything. I looked for a fast excuse to dismiss people that I thought were not worthy of me. Then I made a mistake. I prayed for a woman and I learned God is ironic. You have to be careful what you wish for because you'll get it and live to regret it. I asked for a woman. Not just a woman, but a perfect woman. Enter Brigette. She was beautiful. Smart, savvy, educated, fine, smelled like heaven, voice like a siren, perfect. But everything that's good to you isn't good for you. When I met Brigette, I felt like my life was golden. Everything was complete. But just like I felt no one but her was good enough for me, she felt that I wasn't quite good enough for her. She strung me along until she met the legendary *one better*. Better car, better looking, better job. She jumped ship and I became Black history. It was the first time that I knew the true meaning of hurt. It was the first time that I cried since I became a grown man. My feelings weren't even considered. She was gone."

"And?"

"And now she realizes that better isn't always best. And she's back. To pick up where we left off," Nakalem said.

"And is that what you want to do?" Akinyele asked.

"No, what I want to do is concentrate on this special young lady who walked into my life. To show her that the best is sometimes overlooked in the quest for protection. To show her that the things we sometimes demand of others is much more than we would ever demand of ourselves. To show her true love and the real meaning of happiness. To make her forget Gucci and Godiva and instead become addicted to the feeling of a man that wants to be with her just because." Nakalem leaned down to kiss her. "If that's okay with her?"

"Yes, it's sublime in her book," Akinyele said, lost in his kiss.

As Akinyele slept in the curve of Nakalem's body, she felt safe. She felt home. You could've carted every pair of shoes and every purse away to Goodwill and Akinyele wouldn't have given a damn. She felt whole. She felt wanted. She felt needed. She felt...well...she felt *there*.

Chapter Nine

Forever and a Day

Walking down the stairs, Akinyele smiled with relish as she thought of last night. Nakalem had dicked her down! Her body sang out in agony as she discovered soreness and tender spots that she didn't know existed. She had been worked! Walking outside to the car to get the bag with her hair things, she hummed. Yes, indeed, it felt good to have...

Stopping short, her face crumpled when she saw the Metro. The smeared red lipstick streaks fought the cracked windshield and shattered side and back windows for attention. The antenna was bent backward and an unwrapped douche hung from it by a white string. Two of the tires were flat and airless while the other two were slashed to ribbons. The front bumper had "bitch" spray-painted all across it in red letters. The hood had a huge dent and if Akinyele wasn't mistaken, there was dog shit smeared along the door handles and fender.

Akinyele had no idea how long she stood there screaming before she felt Nakalem pulling her into the house. Rage engulfed her. She was going to kill that bitch! The Metro was a mere rental, but this was about principle. It was also about the fact that Akinyele could be held responsible for the damages. She had done some low-down things in her life, but she had never resorted to tire slashing. Every time she thought of the cruelty of the act, she broke down into fresh tears.

"Akinyele, it's just a car, Baby...she's ignorant." Nakalem embraced her. "It'll be fine."

Akinyele was just calming down when the doorbell rang.

"My Gosh! What the hell happened to the po' lil car?" Akinyele heard a female falsetto sing out when Nakalem opened the door.

Sitting up, Akinyele was treated to the sight of this high-yella, Veronica Webb-looking heifer who reeked of Youth Dew. Akinyele hated that fragrance. She hated her long, straight hair. She hated her butter-colored skin. She hated her perfect bow lips and her snowy white teeth. She hated her slim hips and perky boobs and inverted heart-shaped behind. She *hated* her.

As if that wasn't bad enough, she brushed past Nakalem, almost knocking him down, and extended her hand toward Akinyele.

"Hi, I'm Brigette," escaped from her lips before Akinyele drew back and gave her the hardest slap in the history of the world.

Slinking away from Akinyele, Brigette let out a yelp.

"Why'd you hit me? You don't even know me! I don't even know what happened to that car!"

"Who said anything about the car? Guilty?" Akinyele inquired as she reached out to strike her again.

"Akinyele!" Nakalem shouted as he ran toward Akinyele and grabbed her hand. "You don't want to do that. The car can be fixed, but my heart can't."

"What kind of stupid shit are you talking about now?" Brigette asked as she rubbed her cheek, compliments of Akinyele.

"I am talking about how you had enough idle time on your hands to come here and destroy a car that you assumed belonged to Akinyele. That's a rental. An insured rental, I might add. You might have trashed it but it'll be fixed. But my heart? Nah, it'll never change. You'll always be the silly, conniving slut that left me three years ago. Now, get gone before I have to call someone to help you find your way the hell away from here," Nakalem growled. Never had Akinyele thought such angry words could come from such a gentle man.

"Oh, so you're throwing me out on account of this fat bitch?" Brigette asked as she stared Akinyele up and down. "This ugly, fat bitch?"

"Brigette, go!" Nakalem shouted.

It was too late. Brigette's words stabbed Akinyele. Hurt and heartache leaked through the wound that Brigette had just inflicted in her soul. No one ever said those things to her face. She knew they weren't true, but why did hearing them hurt so much? Wait. Hold on. Stop tape. Was this the same Akinyele that told the world "fuck you" every time she advanced in life? Was this the same Akinyele that spent forever learning to love and respect herself so that she could stand tall when others attempted to crush her? Was this the same Akinyele that got off her comfortable couch to fly two fucking hours on an uncomfortable and bumpy plane to see a man that she knew she was in love with? Was this Akinyele giving up? *Oh, hell no!*

"Tell her! Tell her how this is an act and how much you enjoyed fucking me the night before last!" Brigette shouted.

"I never touched your filthy body," Nakalem affirmed. "Akinyele," he said, turning to her. "Would I have flown you here if I slept with her last night? Would I have you here for days simply because I was bored? Do you think all the work I did last night was some kind of joke? No. I did it because I know that I am in love with you. I did it because I want you to be what she can never be. I did it because I want you as my woman."

"This is some bullshit! You just imported this fat bitch from the fucking swamp to make me suffer, to make me beg! Well you better do better than this because this trick is pitiful," Brigette screeched like a banshee.

Akinyele lifted her hand to hit Brigette. Then she put it down as she watched her cower away from her. Brigette just wasn't worth it. Nakalem's words softened her. Made her feel all warm and fuzzy inside. He said he was falling in love with her! Brigette was beautiful and she once had one of the sweetest and most together men that Akinyele had ever known eating out of the palm of her hand. And now, here she was. Cursing like a Hussein soldier and talking about Akinyele's weight. Akinyele had stooped to Brigette's level when she hit her. That wasn't like her. She refused to stoop anymore.

Turning to look at Nakalem, Akinyele gave him a sheepish smile. "Well, my rental is no good. I guess we'll have to take your car wherever we go." Turning back to Brigette, Akinyele shook her head slowly from side-to-side.

"You know, Brigette, I don't know you, but I feel sorry for you. The same woman who puts herself above this fat bitch had to sneak here in the middle of the night and destroy a vehicle. Simply to prove a point. How immature she is and how dissatisfied she is with her life. I don't care about the past that you had with Nakalem because when he invited me back here, it indicated that you were just that...the past. You can cut my tires. You can call me fat. Hell, you can even call me a fat bitch again. But that won't keep me away. I have nothing but time and effort to put toward getting to know and love Nakalem. And that is exactly what I am going to do. So go ahead. Cut some more tires. Smash some more windshields. But this fat bitch has something that you don't and will never have. Oops. Make that two things. Class and now it looks like I'll have your man too. You don't know me but you helped me in a way that I can never thank you enough for. You kicked him. You taught him about human nature. And you put him out there. I found him. Now, I've claimed him. I call him mine."

Giving Brigette a genuine smile, Akinyele stepped past her and walked into Nakalem's waiting arms. They were both grinning like idiots. They were not sure when, but Brigette stormed out of the house. They didn't miss her. They just stood there, wrapped in each other's arms. Akinyele had found him. The one. It was such a short time but she just knew it. Nakalem was hers. Time and distance would be a challenge but she was determined to make this work. They both were. If this was love, who needed Godiva?

Delusions

By Zane

Chapter One

At five ten, a little over six feet in heels, Tasha Armstrong was towering over most of the men as she pushed her way through the crowded Silver Spring Metro Station toward the exit. Her honey-almond skin was reddened from the heat. Tasha's day had started out lousy. She'd barely managed two hours of sleep the night before, dealing with stomach pains caused by spicy Jamaican bean pies she'd gobbled down for lunch. Spicy foods always messed with her stomach. She risked the effects anyway because she loved anything that beckoned a glass of water before she even swallowed the first bite. She was just elated it was the Fourth of July weekend so she could take something to thoroughly clean out her system. Like most children, she used to frown up whenever her mother mentioned taking castor oil to get all the "yucky stuff" out of her insides, but as an adult, she kept at least two bottles in her medicine cabinet at any given time.

Two young teenage girls bumped into Tasha, practically knocking her down. That only intensified the attitude she had brewing inside of her. She hated catching the Metro and was grateful a three-day ordeal was about to end. Her car was in the shop so she'd been forced to catch the subway downtown to work.

When she finally made it out into the unrelenting sun, she made a beeline for a bus shelter when she didn't spot her roommate Roz's car. Tasha knew Roz would be late. She was always late for everything and would probably be one of those sisters that showed up an hour late for her own wedding–if there ever were a wedding.

Tasha couldn't fault Roz's lack of marital bliss. At least Roz had steady boyfriends. Not even steady boyfriends exactly, but steady lovers she could call up and have come over at the drop of a hat. All Tasha had was a contender; a man she'd never actually laid eyes on.

Tasha was scanning the heavy traffic at the corner turning left into the station, hoping Roz's cherry red Legend would materialize at any second. Her feet were killing her because she'd neglected to put the medicated pads on her corns the night before. She was too busy christening the toilet.

A brother in a navy suit walked underneath the shelter and placed his briefcase on the bench since Tasha wasn't utilizing it. Tasha shook her head when she spotted a sister, not a day over twenty-five, stepping down off a bus with a toddler in her arms and three other kids in tow. She wondered what kind of shiftless man would allow his woman to endure such difficulty just to get around. Then again, maybe she was like Tasha–manless.

Women have a sixth sense and Tasha was no exception. She could tell the brother behind her was staring at her ass. Tasha had a small waist, but was hauling a lot of junk in her trunk. Not too much. Not too little. Just right like the baby bear's chair, porridge, and bed in the Goldilocks story.

Tasha turned her head a little to her right, trying not to be too obvious. She figured she might as well take a closer look, even though she was certain she wouldn't be interested. He was definitely handsome, but her interests lied in one place and one place only. Unfortunately, that place was clear across country.

The brother inched his way closer to her and Tasha thought, *Uh-huh, here comes the pick-up line.*

"Don't look so sad," a deep voice stated into her ear. "It's the beginning of a three-day weekend."

Tasha held in a cackle. *Was that the best the man could do?* "I'm not sad. I'm just exhausted."

He stood right beside her. He had her by at least three inches, even in heels. That was a definite plus. The only one thus far.

"Long work week, huh?" he inquired, rubbing his goatee with his fingertips and trying to get her to make eye contact.

Tasha kept glaring at the stoplight. Still no Roz. "Isn't it always?"

"Some weeks are longer than others. At least it seems that way."

Tasha couldn't prevent herself from glancing at him and smiling. "You certainly have a valid point there."

He waved his index finger at her. "See, I knew you had it in you."

"Had what in me?"

"A smile. A beautiful one at that."

"Are you flirting with me?" Tasha inquired, blushing uncontrollably.

"I'm certainly trying. So what's your name?"

Tasha debated for a brief second and decided no harm could come out of giving up her name. "Tasha. And yours?"

"Joseph," he replied, offering his hand. "Joseph Montgomery."

Tasha shook his hand. "It's nice to meet you, Joseph Montgomery."

"So, are you waiting on a bus?"

"No, I'm waiting for someone to pick me up."

"Aw, your man?"

Tasha giggled, thinking that men always accuse women of being nosy when they are the real culprits. "My roommate."

"Does that mean you're not seeing anyone at present?"

Boy, he was past nosy!

"I'm sort of committed."

"What does sort of committed mean?"

Tasha sighed and stared at him, wondering if he was even worth the effort it would take to explain. She decided he wasn't. "It's hard to explain. Let's just say my heart is deeply involved with someone."

"I see," Joseph uttered with disappointment. "Too bad for me. It's not every day I run across someone so appealing."

Tasha inhaled his bullshit and commented, "Oh, come off it. This is the D.C. area. All these gorgeous sisters around here."

"True, but I don't often feel an immediate connection to someone. In fact, I never have before. There's just something special about you."

Was he for real? Tasha seriously doubted it.

"You're good!" she exclaimed, giving him props for effort. "*Real* good!"

Joseph threw his palms in the air and chuckled. "I'm serious. I'm not the type of man that strikes up conversations out of the blue."

"If you say so."

Tasha resumed her search for Roz yet again. *"Damn! Where was she?"*

Joseph, refusing to give up so easily, continued to pry. "You're not from around here, are you?"

Tasha kept her eyes on the light. She was ready to escape the rush hour madness. If not that, then at least the exhaust fumes the buses were leaving behind as they pulled off.

"I was born and raised in D.C. Right off 16th Street near Walter Reed Army Medical Hospital."

"Hmmmmmmm!"

"What does hmmmmmmm mean?" Tasha asked, on the brink of being insulted. Did he question the authenticity of her previous statement?

"It means you sound just a little bit country."

"Chile, please!" Tasha blurted out, before she could conjure up an alternative phrase.

"Chile, please?" Joseph raised an accusing brow and smirked at her.

Tasha fell out laughing. "Okay, you got me. I went to college in North Carolina."

Joseph's curiosity was peaked. "Oh, yeah, where about?"

"NCCU."

"Really? My baby brother's at North Carolina Central now. He's a senior."

"Cool. I came out in ninety-seven."

"I came out of Howard in ninety-seven."

Tasha began to relax a little. The brother was rather friendly, even though she wasn't presently in the market for a man.

"We probably know a lot of the same people then, Joseph. I have a ton of friends that went to Howard around that time. You know Michael Jones?"

Joseph got so slap-happy that he looked like he was about to breakdance. "Yeah, I know him well. We lived in the same dorm sophomore year. I just saw Mike at a party last weekend."

"Wow, small world," Tasha commented. "Six degrees of separation and all of that."

Tasha heard a car horn and turned to see Roz pulling into a passenger pick-up/drop-off space. *She would come now when things are becoming interesting,* Tasha thought to herself.

"Well, Joseph, there's my roommate. I have to run. It was nice meeting you."

Tasha didn't bother to shake his hand again. It was pointless. She started for Roz's car.

"Any chance I might see you again?" Joseph called after her.

Tasha glanced back over her shoulder. "You never know. After all, it's a small, small world."

Chapter Two

Roz almost broke her neck trying to get a look at the man Tasha was talking to under the bus shelter. Her microbraids and acrylic nails were both freshly-done, and the cream pantsuit she was rocking was nothing short of slamming. Roz was serious about looking good whenever she stepped foot out of the crib, and it showed. Besides, she couldn't drive a Legend and look like Broomhilda.

"Dang, who was that?" Roz asked while Tasha was still getting into the car.

"Who was who?"

Roz rolled her hazel eyes. Tasha knew good and damn well whom she was talking about. "The brother you were rapping hard to at the bus stop? Don't play dumb!"

"Just somebody." Tasha shut the door and reached underneath the seat, using the pull-up handle to push the seat back farther to accommodate her legs. "I wasn't rapping hard either. I was just being friendly."

"Please tell me you at least got his phone number or gave him yours."

"No, you know better. I don't get down like that. Besides, I have a man Roz."

Roz smacked her lips in disgust and put the compact car into drive.

"We're not even going to go there, Tasha."

Tasha ignored the comment and buckled her seat belt as Roz

pulled out of the space and entered the row of traffic exiting the Metro station.

Roz decided trying to convince Tasha that she had an imaginary man was a worthless cause so she changed the subject. "How was your day?"

"Same drama, different day. I didn't get much sleep last night."

"I heard you moving around half the night. What was up with that?"

"Jamaican bean pies." Tasha giggled.

Roz shook her head. "You'll never learn."

Tasha changed Roz's radio from the hip-hop station to jazz. She didn't feel like hearing a bunch of rap songs with masked curse words. If it said *thang* on the radio, that more than likely meant it said *dick, ass,* or even *pussy* on the actual compact disc. Tasha couldn't understand how music had gone from quality to shit, with rappers outselling people that could actually sing their asses off.

"Thanks for picking me up from the Metro, Roz."

"No big deal. When's your car going to be ready?"

"Tomorrow morning. They had to wait for a part to come in."

That was the one thing Tasha hated about owning a Saab. The parts were hard as hell to come by and when her car did experience problems, it was never an easy task to get it fixed. She couldn't complain too much though. Three days was a whole lot better than the customary two to three weeks.

Roz started bobbing in and out of traffic on Colesville Road, headed to the townhouse they shared in Briggs Chaney.

"Peeps at your job still going at each other's throats?" Roz asked rhetorically. She already knew the answer.

Tasha laughed. "Like the Hatfields and the McCoys."

Roz swung her braids from side to side, switching her eyes between the rearview mirror and sideview mirror. Tasha was always tickled by Roz's driving. If there were ever a poster child for aggressive driving, Roz would win hands down.

"I don't see how you stand it, Tasha. If people at my office were fighting every day, I'd be ready to jack somebody up."

"It's simple. I drown them out completely. I don't get mixed

Blackgentlemen.com

up in other people's problems. They're the ones with issues. Not me."

"Yeah, but still."

"I actually find it halfway amusing," Tasha confessed. "They're engaged in psychological warfare and don't even realize it. I'm almost ready to start a betting pool with a few sisters at the office. We can place bets on what order the people involved in the feud drop out of the company."

"I don't see why they haven't left already. Don't they all have degrees?"

"Yes, Roz, but a degree doesn't mean that much these days. Besides, it's not about getting a new job. It's the principle of the matter. No one wants to give their enemies the satisfaction of knowing they caused them to leave, or even worse, to lose their job."

"Sounds like they're seriously immature."

"Speaking of immaturity, are you and Juicy still going to that cookout tonight?"

Roz glared at Tasha like she had some loose marbles. "Hell, yeah, we're going! I had my nails done today and *everything*. You're coming, right? Dantè said his pool is open so you'll need to take a bathing suit."

"I think I'll pass on this one. I still haven't recovered from Dantè's *thrilling* cookout last Fourth of July weekend."

"Oh, please," Roz stated incredulously. "It was the bomb last year!"

"Roz, get real. Nothing but a bunch of horny, drunk brothers running around slapping sisters on the ass with wet towels."

"It wasn't that bad, Tasha. Your ass is exaggerating, as usual."

"Roz, I went in the kitchen and they were getting his pitbull high with a bong. They had a towel over the poor thing's head and all that."

"Okay, okay." Roz smacked her upper teeth on her tongue. "Point taken, but what else do you have to do tonight? Anything's better than sitting at home. It's the holiday weekend. You need to get out and do something."

"I will tomorrow. Tonight, I just want to wash my hair. It's itching like crazy. That gel you told me to use was not the move."

"After you wash your hair, then what?"

"I'll finish watching those DVDs from Blockbuster that are already three days overdue."

"Damn, three days?"

"Well, I haven't had my car and you're always hanging out."

"While you're watching the movies, I suppose you're going to get on the computer," Roz said sarcastically.

Tasha knew the computer comments would start sooner or later. "Only to check my email."

"What email can't possibly wait until tomorrow?" Roz asked as she turned off Colesville Road.

"Don't trip," Tasha responded defensively. "Stop trying to make me sound like an Internet junkie."

"If the shoe fits."

Roz pulled into their driveway. The automatic lights were on in the living room and the sprinkler was getting busy on their front lawn. It was also on a timer. Tasha and Roz took pride in their home. That meant taking care of the outside as well as the inside.

Tasha continued as they got out of the car and walked to the front door. "An Internet junkie surfs the web or hangs out in chat rooms twenty-four seven. I work every day."

"And stay glued to your computer monitor all night," Roz quickly added.

Tasha had heard enough. "Whatever, heifer."

Roz leered at Tasha's back while she navigated her key into the deadbolt. "Don't get defensive, calling me names and such."

Tasha got the door unlocked and walked in. "Sorry for the name-calling. That was immature and I need to practice what I preach."

Roz giggled. Tasha was always reading motivational and spiritual books encouraging her to treat everyone with respect. After much convincing on Tasha's part, Roz attempted to do the same.

"By the way, Tasha, I've been trying to stick to those spiritual guidelines you taught me. I try not to make assumptions, I don't take things personally, I try to stay true to my word, and I always do my best."

"Great!" Tasha kicked off her heels and plopped down on the plum-colored leather sofa. Her poor, poor feet. "Do you ever slip? I know I do from time-to-time."

"*Girlllllll*, I'm glad to hear you admit that." Roz plopped down across from Tasha on the matching loveseat. "The ones about assuming and not taking things personally are exceptionally hard for me. You know I think everyone should see the world through my eyes."

Tasha nodded her head. Being Roz's roommate, she knew that better than anybody. "Yes, but they don't. People see the world through their own eyes. The way they view people and situations is based on the way they were reared and the morals and value system they were taught."

"Maybe that's why I'm so materialistic. Because my mother taught me to be."

Tasha laughed so hard, her stomach started hurting. Roz's mother was the most materialistic person Tasha had ever met. Some people are compulsive shoppers and some people just feel like they have to own one of everything. Roz's mother was the latter.

"Did you ever doubt that for one second?"

Roz kicked off her black mules and reached for the television remote on the coffee table.

"You spend so much money on clothing and jewelry, I'm surprised you can even make rent."

Roz turned on the television and found the *Wayans* on the WB.

"I survive. I might skip a few lunches in the pursuit of spandex, but it's all good. Skipping the meals ensures I can fit into the dresses."

Typical, Tasha thought. Roz always found a way to justify her actions. Tasha picked up her shoes, got up, and headed for the steps. "I'm going upstairs to check my messages."

"Voice mail or email?" Roz chided.

"Very funny." Tasha paused on the bottom step. "Give me a shout out before you leave so I can lock up."

"Okay, but you can still change your mind."

"Not a chance."

"Suit yourself."

Chapter Three

Tasha entered her bedroom and tossed her shoes in the walk-in closet. She sat down on her bed and hit the button on her speakerphone. The dial tone was ragged, letting her know she had messages waiting. She dialed into her voice mail service. She had three new messages.

"Hey, Tasha. It's Mom. Your Aunt Mavis is having a cookout tomorrow. She says two o'clock but you know that means more like four. She and Rufus had that new deck put on the back of the house so they're anxious to show it off. Give me a call if you want your Daddy and I to pick you up on the way. She'll be heartbroken if you don't come. I'm definitely not showing up before four. She's not tricking me into doing half the cooking. If I wanted to do a bunch of cooking, I would've planned a cookout here at the house. Talk to you later, sweetie."

Tasha deleted the message, already trying to think of an excuse to get out of the cookout. She loved her family, but didn't want to spend every holiday listening to her mother and aunt argue about this and that while her father and uncle traded war stories over a bottle of Jack Daniels.

"Ms. Armstrong, this is Candace Bryant from Nubian Queen for a Day Spa. You recently signed up for a complimentary pampering session at the Sister My Sister Convention. I was calling to arrange an appointment time for you. Please return my call at your earliest convenience. The number here is 202-4-NUBIAN. Remember our motto: We treat you like a Nubian queen even if your man doesn't. Talk to you soon, my sister."

Tasha scribbled the number down on a pad on her nightstand. She could sure use a day of relaxation at a spa. She saved the message for thirty days in case she misplaced the piece of paper. There was a beep, but Tasha didn't flash over to the other line. She figured she might as well listen to the last message. The person calling could just leave one.

"Tasha, girl, this Angie. Have I got some shit to tell you. I did go out with that dude from BlackGentlemen.com. We hooked up last night. Girl, he rocked my world. Screwed me six ways from Sunday. I know, I know. I said I was gonna stop giving up the drawers so fast, but I just couldn't help myself. He was just too fine. Anyway, I just wanted to give you props for turning me onto that website. It's the bomb! I'm 'bout to go navigate through that bad boy some more and see what I can see. When you gonna hook up with the brotha you've been talking to off there? You should've picked someone closer to home, some convenient dick. Know what I'm saying? Imma jet but call me later, aiight?"

Tasha was relieved Angie had found someone. If there was one sister waiting to exhale, Angie was the one. She felt completely useless without a man hitting it from the back at least every other night. Still, Tasha planned to talk to her about going overboard. Especially on BlackGentlemen.com. It was a great site, the bachelor site of all bachelor sites featuring African-American males, but just like anything else in life, proceeding with caution was a must.

She deleted Angie's message and pushed off the speakerphone. Two seconds later, the phone rang. Tasha willed it not to be her mother.

"Hello."

"Hello, Tasha."

"Hey, Rinaldo," Tasha said excitedly. Her night had just perked up big time. "I was just thinking about you."

Rinaldo was the man Tasha felt committed to, even though she'd never actually seen him. She'd met him through BlackGentlemen.com six months previously, traded pictures, and fell head over heels in lust at first, and then love. She realized how crazy it seemed, but she truly loved the man. If someone had told her, even a year earlier, that she'd get hooked up with someone over the Internet, she would've laughed in their face. Not anymore. She understood how it could happen and never poked fun at others who'd met their men in cyberspace. After all, so did she.

The reason Tasha ventured onto BlackGentlemen.com in the first place was because she grew sick and tired of seeing her friends show up at this party or that party with fine ass men they'd located on the site. She figured her chances of meeting Mr. Right on BlackGentlemen.com was just as good as any, so she went for it. She was overwhelmed with joy that she did.

"Word? Were you really just thinking about me?" Rinaldo asked.

"Yes."

"I tried to get you a few minutes ago, but your voice mail picked up. I figured you'd be home by now."

"I heard the beep, but I was checking messages."

"Right, right. All your men calling you up to see what you're doing for the weekend."

Tasha giggled. "All what men?"

"Baby, I've seen your pic. I'm no fool. I know you've got homies falling at your feet."

"Not hardly!"

"Listen up, baby, the reason I was calling is cause I wanna see you."

"We're still hooking up in Hotlanta for Labor Day, right?"

"Of course. My word is my bond. I wanna see you this weekend though. Tomorrow."

Tasha was shocked. "Are you serious?"

"I'm past serious. What if I fly out there tomorrow?"

"But, but, how is that possible?" Tasha grew nervous. This was the last thing she expected to have dropped on her suddenly. "I thought you had to save up some money?"

"My dog, Sammie, set me straight. I got the money for the ticket. I got my reservation. All you gotta do is tell me to bring it."

It's too soon, Tasha thought. She was planning on dropping at least ten pounds before Labor Day and getting a complete makeover before she boarded the plane to Atlanta.

"Tasha?" Rinaldo blared into the other end of the phone. "You there?"

"Yeah, I'm here," Tasha replied, squirming on the bed.

"Aw, come on, baby. You not frontin' on me now, are you?" Rinaldo asked accusingly. "All these long distance calls I've been making. All the nights I stayed home sexing you on the phone when I coulda been hanging out with my dogs."

"No, I'm not frontin'. I'd love to see you."

Tasha did crave to see him, but couldn't shake the fear that things wouldn't turn out the way they both envisioned it. The way they had been talking about their first encounter transpiring.

"That's more like it. My plane lands at eleven. US Air Flight 236."

"Which airport?"

"Hell if I know, baby. The one in D.C."

"Oh, okay, Reagan International."

"So you'll be there, right?"

"I have to pick my car up early in the morning, but I'll be there."

Tasha heard the front door opening and slamming downstairs, followed by Juicy and Roz squealing at each other about their tight ass outfits.

"You look good, girl!" she heard Roz exclaim.

"I always look good," Juicy concurred. A victim of low self-esteem she wasn't. "You look awesome, too, Roz."

Tasha turned her attention back to Rinaldo, who was still flirting with her ear. "I can't wait to see your sexy ass when I get off the plane. Wear something seductive and revealing."

"I'll try."

"I want you to jump into my arms and give me a big, fat kiss the second you see me."

Tasha was about to respond when Juicy and Roz came barging into her room without even knocking.

Juicy didn't care if Tasha was on the phone. She needed attention and, as always, was prepared to demand it. "Tasha, you not going with us, *fa realllllll?*"

Tasha shook her head no. Juicy rolled her eyes, walked over to Tasha's vanity table, sat down, and started messing with her hair and makeup.

Roz sat down on the bed beside Tasha, staring at Juicy while she primped in the mirror. Roz was wearing a bikini with a sarong tied around her hips and a pair of white three-inch sandals.

"Promise me you'll give me a fat old juicy kiss when you see me."

Tasha was reluctant to continue the conversation. She knew how nosy Roz could be. "I promise."

Roz flung her head in Tasha's direction, almost slapping her in the face with her braids. "Who you talking to?"

Tasha mouthed Rinaldo's name. Roz rolled her eyes to the ceiling and crossed her arms in front of her in disgust.

"Good," Rinaldo said. "Well, I got a bunch of shit to do tonight. I'll see you tomorrow."

"Okay, see you then."

"See him when?" Roz asked, pushing Tasha roughly on the arm.

"By the way, do I need to get a hotel or sumptin?" Rinaldo asked. "If so, can you call around for me?"

Tasha knew Roz would talk shit about the words about to leave her lips, but she left them flow freely anyway. "Don't be silly. You're already coming out of pocket for the plane ticket. You can stay here."

Roz jumped up from the bed, threw her hands on her hips, and got loud. "Oh, hell naw! He's coming here?"

Juicy sensed some drama about to set off. "Who is she talking about?"

Tasha waved Roz and Juicy off so she could hear Rinaldo.

"Can I sleep in your bed?"

"I guess so."

"Mmmm, I'm rock-hard just thinking about it. We gonna do all the freaky shit we talked about?"

Roz responded to Juicy, still talking in an elevated tone. "Tasha met some brother on the Internet and now he's coming here from Cali."

Juicy exclaimed, "Damn!"

Meanwhile, Rinaldo was still waiting on a reply. "*Well,* are we gonna get freaky or what?"

"I guess so," Tasha said hesitantly. She wasn't so sure she was actually capable of bedding down a stranger, even though they'd talk for months by phone and through emails.

"Stop saying you guess so," Rinaldo said with an edge of sarcasm. "I hope you don't just lay there and make me do all the work like the others."

Tasha sat up on the edge of the bed. "What others?"

Rinaldo started laughing, trying to play off his slip of the tongue. "Just a figure of speech. I'm saying though, I'm coming all the way from Cali to see your ass. Now, you actin' all timid and shit."

"No, I'm straight."

"I hope the hell you are cause I plan to knock the bottom out that thang."

Tasha winced at his reference to her womanhood as a *thang*. She was anxious to get off the phone because Roz and Juicy were hanging on every word.

"I'll see you in the morning, Rinaldo. Okay?"

"Okay."

Roz started pacing the floor, realizing Tasha was serious about letting Rinaldo visit. She muttered expletives and made disparaging comments about Rinaldo to Juicy.

Tasha stomped her foot and held up her fist in a threatening manner, urging Roz to stop. Roz ignored her and went right on ranting.

"Goodnight, Rinaldo." Tasha tried to speed the goodbye along. She was afraid Rinaldo would hear Roz.

"Hey, hold up!"

"Yes?"

"Say that thing to me."

Tasha remained silent.

"Say that thing to me," Rinaldo repeated, "or I'm not coming."

Tasha looked at Roz and Juicy, turned her head away from them, and then whispered, "Kisses all over your body." That was her typical closing line to their phone conversations and her signature line on emails to him.

Juicy and Roz both gawked at Tasha, shaking their heads in unison.

"That's my baby!" Rinaldo was happy as a lark. "Later!"

Tasha hung up the phone and scooted back on her bed, hugging a pillow.

It took Roz less than five seconds to start in on her. "Have you completely lost it? Please tell me that I didn't hear what I just thought I heard."

Tasha, already angry about Roz's comments while she was on the phone, lashed back at her. "Rinaldo's flying in tomorrow. What's it to you?"

"What's it to me? What's it to me? I live here. You don't know that man from Adam. I've read all the news articles about women meeting men on the Internet. Who's to say he's not some serial killer or something?"

Tasha knew Roz had a lot of damn nerve. "Who's to say the men you bring home from this club or that club aren't serial killers?"

Roz was totally offended. "Oh, no, you didn't go there!"

"What's the difference?" Tasha shrugged her shoulders. "I can't count the number of times I've woken up to find some half-naked man in our kitchen raiding the fridge. Eating food I purchased, at that."

"She does have a point, Roz," Juicy said, agreeing with Tasha.

Roz glared at Juicy. "How the hell do you know? Your ass don't live here!"

"I may not live here," Juicy quickly retorted, "but I'm over here enough to know what's up. Besides, I know how you are, Roz, when it comes to getting your freak on."

"So what are you heifers trying to say? That I'm a whore?"

"Not exactly, but you're damn sure knocking on whoredom's door."

Tasha fought to suppress a laugh. She knew Juicy's comment had cut deeply.

Roz looked like she could spit fire. "Juicy, Tasha met this fool on the computer. She's never even seen him."

Tasha corrected Roz. "But I've seen his picture and we've been talking on the phone for months. That's longer than most people talk before they knock boots."

"Yet another valid point," Juicy agreed. "Most people hop in the bed after knowing each other a week or two."

Roz's head moved from side-to-side, braids just a swinging, while she sized up Tasha's and Juicy's facial expressions. She could see they were pulling a tag-team operation on her. "All I have to say is you're jeopardizing yourself and me by bringing a complete stranger up in here."

"No more than you do when you bring them," Tasha came back at her. "Besides, at least I confine my sexual activities to my bedroom."

"What the hell is that supposed to mean?"

"Don't play Ms. Innocent. You've screwed men all over the house. Even on the dining room table and that was just downright skank. I had to sanitize it. I almost called the Salvation Army to come pick it up."

Juicy was shocked. "Damn, Roz, you got busy on the dining room table? Remind me to eat in the living room from now on."

Roz waved her index finger in Tasha's face. "You're making a big mistake. Mark my words."

Juicy got up from Tasha's vanity table and came closer to the bed. "Excuse me. I have one comment."

"What's that?" Tasha asked.

"Aren't you the two sisters always talking about living by certain rules? Seems to me you're both breaking them right and left just about now."

Tasha instantly felt ashamed. "She's right, Roz. We're

making this shit way too personal and attacking each other. Plus, you're making assumptions about Rinaldo. He's not your man. He's mine."

"How can he be your man when you've never met?" Roz asked crassly.

Tasha placed her hand over her heart. "He's my man in here."

Juicy and Roz glared at each other, finding it hard to believe that Tasha had fallen for a man clear across country.

"Tasha, you really need to get out more," Juicy stated. She tugged at Roz's arm. "Maybe we should just go."

Roz decided to give up. "You driving?"

"Sure."

Juicy headed for the door with Roz in tow.

Roz paused in the doorway. "Don't forget to lock up."

"I won't."

Once she heard the front door slam, Tasha retrieved Rinaldo's framed picture from her nightstand drawer. She didn't keep it out in the open because she knew Roz would have a field day at her expense. Umph, he was just too fine. Dark-skinned, clean-shaven, chiseled features, bright vibrant smile, hypnotic brown eyes. She couldn't wait to see him in person.

Tasha got up and went into her private bathroom so she could do her ritual. She had a routine she performed whenever she made advance plans to sex a man down. She'd strip down to her underwear, position herself in the middle of the bathroom floor between the full-length mirror on the back of the door and the one on the wall over sink, and practice seductively removing her bra and panties. After years of practice, Tasha had the shit down to a science. Once she was completely nude, she inspected her body to make sure there weren't any cellulite bubbles or dark spots on her honey-almond skin. Everything was everything.

Tasha took a quick shower, washed her hair, trimmed her coochie hair, and shaved under her arms. She got out, set her hair, and did her fingernails and toenails while she sat under the dryer. By that time, she was starving and decided to borrow Roz's Legend to run to

Cameron Seafood in Briggs Chaney Shopping Center to get a half-pound of spiced shrimp and a cup of cream of crab soup.

She couldn't resist running into Ross for Less ten minutes before they closed to buy some sexy lingerie for Rinaldo. She selected two teddies, one white lace and one black satin, and fell in love with a toe ring on her way to the front counter.

Tasha went home, ate her dinner, and then passed out on the sofa watching the Friday night "Never Seen Before Anywhere" movie on HBO.

Chapter Four

Tasha got to the airport about ten-fifty and made a mad dash for the gate. She was pissed because Roz had purposely tried to prevent her from coming to pick up Rinaldo. First, Roz took her sweet time getting dressed so she could take Tasha to the auto shop to pick up her car, and then she stopped by the drive-thru at McDonald's. It took a good fifteen minutes for Roz to even make it to the pay window, during which time she tried to convince Tasha to pull a no-show.

"You know, Tasha, it's not too late to tell that fool to fuck off."

"Why would I do something like that?"

"*Cause* he might be some maniac or a bisexual or some shit like that."

"Or he might be the man of my dreams."

Roz turned the radio down and fished through her dashboard for her sunglasses. The sun was out in full force early. "Tasha, you met him on the Internet."

"So?"

"So, do you realize how asinine that is?"

"No. I also didn't realize you knew any big words."

"See, now you're getting all offended and stuff again. About to break your spiritual practices, huh?"

"Well, look at the way you're coming at me, Roz. What am I supposed to do? Just sit here and let you dole out a verbal beatdown and remain silent like I'm your child or something?"

Roz rubbed Tasha on the knee. "I'm sorry if I'm coming off

foul. I just don't feel right about this. I know I bring home some stranger dick from time to time, but I can't imagine having a strange man fly in from another state with the intention of staying with me for a couple of days."

"Rinaldo's not a stranger," Tasha said defensively. "I know everything about him."

"*Everything?*"

"Yes, I do."

"Okay, I guess we'll see about all that."

Tasha glanced at the clock on the dash, reached over, and tooted the horn. The woman in front of them glanced back angrily. "Damn, what are they doing? Killing cows or pigs up in there. This is taking way too long."

"Tasha, we have plenty of time."

Tasha broke out into a sweat as she dashed through the airport terminal toward the correct gate for Rinaldo's flight. She was in such a hurry that she flew right past him on his way to the baggage claim.

"Tasha!" she heard a deep voice yell out behind her.

Tasha froze in place, almost afraid to turn around. *What if he was jacked up or something?*

"Tasha," Rinaldo repeated, his voice getting closer to her back. "Hey, baby."

Tasha still didn't turn around. Not even when she felt a pair of strong hands begin to caress her upper arms and felt a presence looming over her.

"Turn around."

Tasha took a deep breath and went for it. When she spun around, she had to look up into his face, but he was everything she'd thought he'd be: perfect.

"Hey, Rinaldo," Tasha managed to blurt out.

"Don't you owe me something?"

Tasha was confused. "Owe you what?"

Rinaldo glared at her with disdain. "A hug and a big ass kiss."

Tasha looked around the terminal bashfully. Being a holiday weekend, people were everywhere. She'd never been one for putting on large public displays. "Right here, in the middle of the airport?"

"Yes, right here." Rinaldo chuckled.

Tasha bit her bottom lip and gave him a bear hug. He released her slightly and went for her mouth with his.

"Um, Rinaldo, can we just wait until we get into the car?"

"For what?"

"They're a lot of people in here. Kids even."

"And?"

"I don't think it's appropriate to slobber each other down in the middle of this chaos."

Rinaldo threw his head back in laughter. "Aiight. Aiight. I'll chill, but once we get out into your car, it's on."

Tasha had to admit to herself that she liked the sound of that. It had been months since she'd been sexed and she needed some of that sexual healing Marvin Gaye used to sing about.

While they waited at the baggage claim area for Rinaldo's garment bag, Tasha had a chance to really size him up. He was sporting a pair of black jeans, a skintight white body shirt accentuating all of his muscles, and a pair of black Nikes. As for his ass, Tasha couldn't wait to slap it. She prayed his skin was as soft as it looked.

Rinaldo flung his bag over one shoulder and used his free arm to place around Tasha while they walked to the parking lot.

"Boo, this car is phat!" Rinaldo exclaimed when Tasha hit the alarm button on her keychain and the rear lights blinked while they were still a few yards away.

"Thanks."

"You must be living large."

"Roz and I have a pretty nice townhouse, but I wouldn't call it living large."

"Do you have a sexy bedroom?" Rinaldo whispered in Tasha's ear while she unlocked the trunk.

"Sexy enough. I would think you'd be more interested in me than my bedroom."

"Oh, I am. I am. I was just wondering."

"Well. you'll see soon enough."

Rinaldo placed his bag in the trunk and closed it. Tasha was headed for the driver's side when Rinaldo pulled her back to him, lifted her up onto the trunk, and positioned himself in between her legs. She was wearing a navy sundress with spaghetti straps and a pair of navy sandals to show off her new toe ring.

He eased his tongue into Tasha's eagerly awaiting mouth and moved it around with expertise. Tasha could feel herself getting wet. She'd been without so long, even a man's tongue was making her cream in her drawers.

"You like that?" Rinaldo asked her, taking a breather to suck on her earlobe.

"Yes, I like that very much."

Rinaldo reached under Tasha's dress, moved her panties to the side, and started fingering her.

"You like that, too?"

"Um, I love that."

A plane took off directly above their heads, masking Rinaldo's next comment, but Tasha could read his lips. "I wanna fuck you."

And that's exactly what he did. He shimmied on a condom and took her for the first time right there on the hood of her Saab in the middle of the airport parking lot. So much for Tasha being against public displays of affection.

Chapter Five

On their way back to Tasha's townhouse, she took Rinaldo on a brief sightseeing tour. She drove through downtown and showed him all the things he'd read about in high school including the Lincoln Memorial, the Jefferson Memorial, the Washington Monument, and the Kennedy Center. Rinaldo was like a little kid that had left his hometown for the first time.

"This is awesome." He chuckled, straining his neck to look up at the top of the Washington Monument from Tasha's car.

"Yeah, this is good old D.C. Too bad you don't have much time here or we could actually tour the entire city. Today, my mother wants us to stop by Aunt Mavis' house for a cookout."

Rinaldo's entire demeanor changed. "What the hell do you mean, a cookout?" he blared.

"A cookout. Where they barbecue food on the grill, sit around and shoot the breeze, that sort of thing."

"I know what a damn cookout is, Tasha. I came here to see you. Not your entire fuckin' family."

Tasha couldn't believe he was coming off on her like that. "Rinaldo, don't talk to me like that. This isn't like you."

"Isn't like me? How do you know what I'm like when we just hooked up for the first time an hour ago?"

Tasha couldn't help but laugh. "You sound just like Roz."

"Your roommate's cool with me visiting and all, right?"

"Yes, of course," Tasha lied. "Even if she wasn't, that's too bad because I pay rent just like she does."

"Hmph, sounds like I caused some friction with my surprise visit."

"Look, I won't lie. Roz has some serious concerns about the way we met online."

"Does she go on the Internet?"

"No, never. She's the most computer illiterate person I know."

"Then how can she have *serious concerns* about you meeting me on there? She doesn't even know what's up."

"Roz thinks she knows everything. It's in her nature. Once she meets you, sees how nice you are, not to mention how fine, she'll realize the errors of her ways."

Rinaldo blushed. "You really think I'm fine?"

"I think you're more than fine."

Tasha pulled up to a red light and came to a stop. Rinaldo reached over, took her by the chin, and kissed her. "You're not too bad your damn self."

Tasha took her turn at blushing. "I'm glad you approve."

Rinaldo settled back in his seat when Tasha resumed driving. "I'm so relieved."

"About what?"

"That you look like I thought you looked. A lot of women online are frontin' big time with their pics."

Tasha wondered how Rinaldo knew that so she asked, "How many women have you met offline, Rinaldo?"

"Why the fuck do you care?"

Tasha was on the verge of cussing him out, but remembered her principles. *He must just be tired from the trip*, she told herself convincingly.

"I was just asking. I know your picture's been on BlackGentlemen.com for quite some time and, as good as you look, I'm sure you've had a lot of women email you."

"But where I am now? Who am I with?"

"Me."

"Exactly, so stop asking me a bunch of stupid ass questions." Rinaldo turned the air conditioning up and folded his arms across his chest militantly. "Fuckin' women!"

Tasha decided the best course of action was to remain silent until they got back to her place. She figured Rinaldo just needed to take a shower and relax. Maybe he'd let her join him and help him out. He'd flown thousand of miles to see her and blew her mind in the parking lot. She planned to hang in there for the long run.

The men in the D.C. area had never given her anything but heartache and strife. She was willing to go the extra mile with Rinaldo because men over in Cali couldn't possibly be as doggish as the locals.

Roz was outside washing her Legend when they pulled up. She lowered her sunglasses and dropped the sponge in the bucket, getting prepared to size Rinaldo up the second he stepped out of Tasha's car.

Tasha and Rinaldo walked over to Roz hand in hand.

"Roz, this is Rinaldo. Rinaldo, this is Roz."

Rinaldo flashed Roz a grin. "It's nice to finally meet you, Roz. I've heard a lot about you."

Roz smirked at him. "How long you staying?"

Tasha wanted to pinch Roz until she bled for being so rude. "Rinaldo's staying as long as he likes. That's how long he's staying."

Roz glared at Tasha. "Well, doesn't he have a return ticket so he can get back for his *J-O-B*?" She turned her attention to Rinaldo. "You do have a *J-O-B*, right, Rinaldo?"

"I work for a buddy of mine, so I'm cool. I can take time off whenever I like."

Tasha looked up at him. She'd been under the impression that Rinaldo worked in the telemarketing department of a large corporation. All of the numbers dialed out were random and the employees weren't allowed to receive calls in, which is why Tasha wasn't ever given his work number.

"Congrats on your lenient work habits, but do you have a return ticket? Yes or no?" Roz asked crassly.

"Rinaldo, why don't you go inside and make yourself comfortable." Tasha went over to her trunk and unlocked it. She took his bag out and handed it to him. "I'll be in shortly."

Rinaldo sucked his teeth, went up the walkway to the slightly-ajar front door, and disappeared inside.

"Roz, what the fuck is your problem?"

"What the fuck is yours?"

"Rinaldo is here as my guest and I won't tolerate you showing your ass in front of him!"

"Tasha, I know times are hard in D.C., but I'm still against this."

"Did you see him? Look at how fine he is."

"Yes, I saw him, and you know just as well as I do that fine don't mean shit when it comes to men. The finer they are, the louder their bark."

Tasha realized Roz had a point, but went on the defensive anyway. "Rinaldo's different. He's sweet. He's sensitive. He's..."

"So hard up for some punta that he'd fly across country to get some," Roz interrupted.

"I'm not just *punta* to him, Roz. I'm much more than that."

Roz squatted and picked the sponge back up out of the bucket. "If you say so."

Tasha lifted the bucket by the handle and tossed it across the driveway, the contents spilling out and tracing a path down to the street.

Roz leered at her. "See, now you're acting childish."

Tasha didn't respond. She walked inside while Roz headed down to the curb to get the bucket.

Tasha and Rinaldo spent the next couple of hours locked in her bedroom fucking like minks. She was finally able to do her ritual and seductively strip down to nothing. Roz kept walking past the door coughing, which Tasha found extremely ignorant. She turned on her boom box and let Kevon Edmonds' CD , highly regarded by Tasha as the best knocking-boots arrangement of the year, navigate her movements. She'd been dying to sex a man down off of the music.

After they fucked so hard that every shred of linen was on the floor and the mattress was halfway off the box spring, Tasha told

Rinaldo they needed to hit the shower so they could get to the cookout by five. She had two more messages from her mother on her voice mail asking if she was coming and, if so, to be there no later than five since her parents were going at four.

Rinaldo still didn't want to attend the family function.

"Why we gotta go over to your fam's house, anyway? I like chillin' right here, knocking the bottom out that pussy."

While not the most romantic thing ever said to her, Tasha still basked in his compliment. "Well, you can resume the bottom-knocking later. We don't have to stay long. I just know that if I don't show, my mother will be talking trash about me and my family values for the next six months."

"Your parents know about me?"

"Umm..."

"Well, do they?"

"Not exactly. In fact, do me a favor. When we get over there, don't mention how we met."

"What if they ask?"

"Tell them you met me at church."

"Church?" Rinaldo fell out laughing. "You know the last time my ass has been in a church?"

"I haven't a clue."

"Let's put it this way. I was still wearing Stride Rite shoes."

Tasha got up off the bed and headed over to her dresser so she could pick out something to wear. Rinaldo got off by watching Tasha's ass and breasts jiggle while she pulled out drawer after drawer. When she bent over to pull out the bottom drawer, he had to prevent himself from going over there and slamming her from the back one last time for good measure.

"Just tell them we met through a mutual friend then," Tasha said. "That doesn't require any elaborate explanation because they only know a handful of my friends anyway."

"Okay, cool," Rinaldo replied, licking his lips when Tasha turned around to face him, holding an armful of clothing. "What if they ask where I'm from?"

"Tell them you're from California. That you were living in

D.C. for graduate school, but moved back to California last year to accept a job offer."

"Graduate school?" Rinaldo couldn't believe she was trying to front on her parents like that. "Tasha, you're a trip. Do I sound or act like I've been to anybody's college, rather less graduate school?"

"Rinaldo, my parents aren't going to drill you with questions." Tasha was hoping like all hell they wouldn't. "It's just a cookout. It's not like I'm announcing our engagement or anything."

"So why lie then? Why we gotta pretend like I'm something I'm not?"

"It's not that."

"Sounds like *that.*"

"There's no need for us to go over there and be the center of attention. My Aunt Mavis always throws big ass cookouts. I know she is today since she wants to show off her new deck. Make sure you make a big deal over her deck. That's important."

"Whatever, Tasha."

Chapter Six

As soon as they pulled up to the cul-de-sac belonging to Tasha's Aunt Mavis and Uncle Rufus, Tasha realized she had made a mistake by bringing Rinaldo. She assumed there would be a lot of people there, but there were cars lined up and down both sides of the street for blocks. Tasha prayed that someone else on the street was also entertaining, but knew better. There was a back-up of people waiting to get through the gate.

"Dang, your family sure knows how to party!" Rinaldo exclaimed, having second thoughts about being there. "I thought this would be some dull ass thing, but look at all these fly ass honies. That redbone over there is fine as shit."

That hit a nerve. Like most women, Tasha found it extremely disrespectful for a man to talk about other women in front of her.

"Well, maybe you can just go home with her ass at the end of the night then," she lashed out at Rinaldo.

He started giggling like a bitch. "You're funny. You know that?"

"I don't see a damn thing funny about me or your hoochie comment."

"Look, I'm sorry. Shit. Just take a chill pill and park the car."

"What does it look like I'm trying to do?"

Rinaldo started beating on the dash like he was the drummer for a rock band. Tasha continued down the street to find a space.

Rinaldo fit right in with the family, joining Uncle Rufus, Tasha's father Douglas, and other men's men for a shot of Jack Daniels.

Tasha was relieved her father didn't ask any questions about Rinaldo when she introduced him. She doubted she would fare so well with her mother and she was right.

"Who's that?" her mother Allison demanded to know before she even bothered to say hello to Tasha.

"His name's Rinaldo, Mom."

"Rinaldo? What kind of stupid name is that?"

Tasha sat down on a stool beside the breakfast bar in the kitchen while her mother and aunt stared out the bay window over the sink into the backyard. They were scoping Rinaldo so hard that Tasha was surprised they didn't both break out binoculars so they could see what length his eyelashes were.

"Rinaldo is not a stupid name, Mom. It's just different. I happen to love his name."

Aunt Mavis decided she'd seen enough and went back to stirring relish into her potato salad. "He's a cutie, Tasha."

"Thank you, Aunt Mavis."

"How long you been seeing him?" Allison asked, still leering out the window.

"Long enough to know he's a keeper."

"A keeper? Hmph!"

"Mom, please don't start in on me today. I showed up. Doesn't that count for anything?"

"Yes, it does," Aunt Mavis said. "I'm glad you came, even if your mother is acting foul."

Allison switched her leer over to her baby sister. "Mavis, I'm trying to be cool, but don't make me show my ass in your home."

Tasha rolled her eyes, picked up a cracker from the tray sitting on the bar, and slapped a chunk of cheddar cheese on it. Her mother and aunt had a history of going at each other's throats. *Literally* in one instance. Tasha had heard the story about them beating each other on a school bus in high school no less than a hundred times. They were only two years apart in age, but eons apart in personality.

"Allison, you need to leave Tasha alone. That's a fine young man she brought to the cookout with her. Look at how well he's getting along with Rufus and Douglas."

"So where did you meet this *Rinaldo*?" Allison asked sarcastically. "At a club?"

"No, I met him through a friend."

"What friend?"

"Someone you don't know," Tasha replied crassly.

"Where does he live?"

"Right now, he lives in California. I met him when he was going to grad school at Howard. He's just here for the weekend."

"At least he's educated. Good job?"

"Yes."

"Doing what?"

"Minding his business," Tasha said angrily. "I'm going back out to the cookout if you don't need me to do anything, Aunt Mavis."

Aunt Mavis giggled and made circles around her temple while staring at Allison's back. "No thanks, sweetie. Your mother and I have everything covered."

Tasha laughed at her aunt's antics. Her mother did tend to act like a loony bird at times.

Tasha searched the large backyard for Rinaldo. He was no longer sitting with the other men's men. She went back in the house to see if he'd gone to the bathroom, but the one on the first floor was empty. She was on her way back outside when she heard laughter as she passed the basement door.

Tasha was ready to go into bitch mode when she descended the steps only to find Rinaldo curled up on the sofa in the family room with the "redbone" he'd spotted earlier from the car.

Rinaldo sensed her presence and looked up. "Oh, hey, Tasha. This is Maddie."

Tasha just glared at the hoochie in the skintight shorts riding up her ass and skimpy top made out of a bandana. "Who invited you here?"

"Damn, who are you? The cookout police? Security guard or some shit like that?" the woman lashed out at her.

Rinaldo started laughing, but clamped his mouth shut when he saw the expression on Tasha's face. He stood up and walked over to her. "Look, Maddie and I were just talking. It's hot as hell outside and I just wanted to chill for a few."

"What could you and *Maddie* possibly have to talk about? Other than how to dress like a skank ass hoe."

"Bitch, I will stuff my foot up your ass!" Maddie shouted, jumping up from the sofa and balling up her fists.

"Hold up! Ladies, no need to fight over me. I have lots of love to give." Rinaldo chuckled. "If you want, you can share. I don't mind being used."

Is this fool serious? Tasha asked herself, finding it hard to fathom that the words had even left his mouth.

Maddie walked over to Rinaldo and started rubbing his chest. "I'm not much for sharing but, as fine as you are, I might make an exception."

Tasha knocked Maddie's hand off of Rinaldo. "Touch him again and it's on."

Maddie smacked her lips and brushed in between them, rubbing her breasts up against Rinaldo. "If the little girl grows up, you know where to find me."

She disappeared up the steps.

"You bastard!"

"Aw, chill the fuck out already, Tasha. I was just kidding."

For the first time, Tasha noticed Rinaldo's slurred speech and got a whiff of the alcohol on his breath.

"You're drunk, aren't you? That's why you're acting stupid. How much of that Jack Daniels did you have?"

Rinaldo grabbed Tasha by the arms and jerked her. "Don't ever call me stupid! Not ever!"

Tasha pulled away from him. "Maybe we should just go. It was a bad idea to come."

"I'm not going anywhere but back outside to get my eat and drink on. You want to leave, go for it. I'll get Maddie to drop me off later."

"After you fuck her?"

Rinaldo grabbed Tasha by the arms again. "Don't make me angry, girl!"

He released her and stomped up the steps. Tasha fell down on the bottom steps and cried.

Tasha composed herself and joined the cookout again about ten minutes later, after splashing cold water on her face in the basement bathroom. Everyone was eating while seated at picnic tables or on lawn chairs, and there was a ton of food left on the long table when Tasha went to fix herself a plate.

She sat down next to Rinaldo, who was seated next to Uncle Rufus and Aunt Mavis and across from her parents.

"Tasha, where you been, baby?" Rinaldo asked cheerfully, like no drama ever went down in the basement.

Tasha leered at him and then faked a smile. "I was freshening up."

"You look flushed, sweetie," Aunt Mavis commented. "Are you too hot?"

"No, I'm fine. Really. By the way, Aunt Mavis and Uncle Rufus, I love this deck. The contractor did an amazing job."

Tasha elbowed Rinaldo. He took the cue.

"Yeah, this deck is all that and a bag of chips."

Allison just stared at her daughter as she ate her own ribs with a fork and knife. Tasha was always tickled by her mother's ways. She was the only person Tasha knew who ate hot dogs, hamburgers, and ribs with a fork and knife instead of just picking them up and grubbing.

"Rinaldo, Tasha tells me you're from California?" Allison asked snidely.

"Yeah, I am."

"What part? We have some friends in Bel Air."

"Bel Air?" Rinaldo chuckled. "Who? The Fresh Prince?"

Everyone at the table laughed except Allison. She had no idea who The Fresh Prince was.

"Actually, one of Douglas' college roommates is a paleontologist. He and his wife live in Bel Air."

"A paleon what?"

"Paleontologist. You don't know what that means?"

"Know what it means? I can't even spell it."

Tasha's father and uncle snickered, but Aunt Mavis knew things were about to heat up.

Allison repeated her previous question. "What part of California are you from?"

"Compton," Rinaldo announced proudly.

"Compton? Isn't that the center of a lot of gang activity?"

Rinaldo snickered. "Yeah, so, and?"

Allison looked like she was about to vomit. She darted her eyes back and forth from Tasha to Rinaldo and then settled back on Tasha. "How did you say you met this young man again?"

"Momma, if you don't stop this interrogation right now, we're leaving," Tasha replied angrily.

Tasha's father issued a warning. "Allison, enough! You're always complaining about not seeing Tasha enough. Let's just enjoy the rest of the evening. It'll be dark soon."

"This party's not ending when the sun goes down. Be for real. I have flood lights all over the back of the house and in the yard," Uncle Rufus bragged. He glared across the table at Allison with his bloodshot eyes. He'd had his fair share of Jack Daniels and then some. "Ally, you want some more ribs? You could sure use some more meat on those bones of yours."

Allison was so insulted by Rufus' comment about her body that she laid off of Tasha and Rinaldo while everyone finished eating.

Tasha was counting the minutes before she could make an escape with Rinaldo in tow. She figured if they stayed until nine, no one could accuse them of eating and running. Maddie AKA hoochie had finally left a few minutes before. It turned out she was the daughter of a man Uncle Rufus did janitorial work with. Her uncle was a janitor and, like most janitors, his own house stayed immaculate. Her mother had talked big junk when Aunt Mavis married him, but after all was said and done, they did have a fly ass home and were doing great for themselves.

Tasha was in the kitchen helping to do dishes while Rinaldo was outside on the deck, once again surrounded by all the men's men.

They were all drunk by that point. Tasha was determined not to drink anything alcoholic. Fourth of July weekend was infamous for drunk drivers and she didn't intend to be one of them.

"When is Rinaldo leaving?" her mother asked, sneaking up behind her.

"When he wants to," Tasha replied sarcastically.

"What field is his graduate degree in?"

"A good one."

"Tasha, you don't have to be so nasty."

Tasha swung around to face her. "And neither do you, Momma. No matter what man I bring around you, you always find something wrong with him. I'm not going to take it anymore. I'm an adult and, as an adult, I have the right to choose who I allow to become a part of my life. You better just learn to deal with that."

Allison was appalled. She took a few steps back and positioned herself on a stool. Aunt Mavis walked back in the patio door with more leftovers to wrap up and put away. She could sense the tension in the air so she just cleared her throat and went into the walk-in pantry to get some aluminum foil.

"Tasha, I never raised you to disrespect me."

"I know that, Momma. You raised me to be independent and strong, which is exactly what I am. I have a good job. I got my education. I never ask you and daddy for any money. Roz and I have a nice home. But, it's never good enough, is it? You always want and expect more."

"That's not true. I'm extremely proud of you."

"Then act like it!"

Tasha slammed a platter down in the dish drainer and flew out the back door.

Tasha was sitting in a lawn chair on the farthest end of the back yard when her mother sashayed over to her. She stood over Tasha and stared down her aquiline nose at her.

"I'm sorry, Tasha. I haven't behaved pleasantly today and I'm willing to admit it."

Tasha gripped the handles of the chair to release some of the anger she was feeling. Her mother always acted a fool and then said sorry, as if that made her actions disappear.

"It's okay, Momma. You're probably just tired from helping Aunt Mavis entertain and everything," Tasha said, trying her best to sound sincere.

Allison glanced back at the deck, where the men were still talking loudly. "Well, I guess I'll go back inside. I just didn't want you to feel like you had to lurk over here in a corner while everyone else is having a good time."

"Thanks."

"For what it's worth, I do think Rinaldo is nice. I just want you to make sure that you *choose* your gentlemen friends wisely. A lot of them are up to no good."

"I know that already, Momma. I've been hurt so many times by men that I've lost count."

"Exactly, and I see the aftermath every time one of them exits your life. Can you really blame me for showing concern? After all, you're my only child and like any mother, I feel protective of you."

"I understand, Momma."

"Your Aunt Mavis made some peach cobbler."

"She did?" Tasha's eyes lit up. She loved herself some Aunt Mavis' peach cobbler.

"Yes."

"I didn't see any on the table earlier."

"That's because she had it hidden in the oven. You know that cobbler wouldn't have last ten minutes with all those people that were here earlier."

They both laughed.

"I'll be in to get some in a few minutes."

"See you in the house."

"Okay."

Chapter Seven

Rinaldo and Tasha got back to her townhouse about ten. When she checked her voice mail, there was a message from her father.

"Tasha, baby, I wasn't even going to call but I felt like I had to. Your momma and I just got home. She's in the bathroom taking off all that makeup so I decided now was my chance. Normally, I try to stay out of your business. You know that. This time, I can't. Rinaldo let the alcohol guide him tonight and told your Uncle Rufus and I the truth about how you met. I'm sure you know I don't approve of you meeting a man over the computer. I've heard so many terrible, terrible things about young ladies meeting men that way. Please be careful. I don't know what I'd do without my baby. If you need anything, *anything at all*, you call me day or night. You hear? I'm not going to tell your momma. She'd have the Montgomery County Police banging down your door in less than five minutes if she knew you'd just actually met Rinaldo this morning and the circumstances. I just pray that you'll be safe. I love you, sugar."

Tasha felt like shit.

"Bad news?" Rinaldo asked, coming out of the bathroom after gargling some of that alcohol off his breath.

"Rinaldo, why'd you tell my father about the way we met?"

Rinaldo leered at her and sat down on her vanity seat to remove his sneakers. "Look, you might be used to lying to your parents, but I'm not. Pops was cool and so was your uncle. He asked me a few questions and I answered him honestly, unlike the bullshit you were over there trying to feed everybody."

Tasha felt like shit warmed over then. She was subjecting everyone to lies and having Rinaldo fly thousands of miles only to ask him to join her in the madness was unfair.

"You're right. We either should've stayed home or gone over there to be honest. I messed up. I'm sorry."

Rinaldo chuckled, pulling his shirt up over his head. "No problem. I'm going to give you the opportunity to make it up to me."

"How?"

"Get butt naked and give me some ass."

"Rinaldo, there's an appropriate way to ask for sex and that's not it."

"An appropriate way to ask for sex? Girl, you better drop them drawers and give me some ass."

"No, I will not drop my drawers and give you some ass. Not until you show me some respect."

"Respect? What the hell you think I've been doing for the last six months? I've spent a grip. No, make that two grips on phone calls to your ass."

"You didn't talk to me like this on the phone."

"So what, now you want to live in a fairy tale or something?"

"Sure. Why not?"

Rinaldo plopped down on the mattress beside of Tasha.

"This ain't no fuckin' fairy tale, I'm not a fuckin' prince, and I've never even seen a real horse in my entire fuckin' life. I came here for one thing. Sex on top of sex on top of mutha fuckin' sex. We've done enough talkin' for three lifetimes. I went to the bullshit cookout and..."

"Oh, so now it was a *bullshit* cookout? A minute ago you were talking about how cool my daddy and uncle were. Now, it was all *bullshit*."

There was a loud knock on the bedroom door. Tasha jumped because she hadn't heard Roz come in the house. She got up to answer it, but only opened the door wide enough for Roz to see her face.

"Trouble in paradise?" Roz asked snidely, letting them know she'd heard the arguing.

"Roz, I really don't need any shit from you!" Tasha rolled her eyes. "When did you get home anyway?"

"I just came in, but I'm leaving right back out. I just stopped through to get some board games to take over Juicy's house." Roz stood on her toes, attempting to see over Tasha's head. "You need me to stay?"

"No, I'll be fine."

"You know I've got your back."

"I'm fine, Roz. Really!"

"Why don't you come over to Juicy's with me?" Roz offered. "You can bring *him*."

"What's going on over Juicy's?"

"Just a bunch of peeps hanging out."

"You can go if you want, Tasha!" Rinaldo yelled out from behind her. "I'm not going another fuckin' place tonight!"

"Is that fool out of his damn mind?" Roz whispered. "He thinks we'd leave his ass here *alone?*"

Tasha came out into the hallway and closed the door behind her.

"Roz, you go ahead. Rinaldo and I are in for the night."

Roz started toward the steps and then turned around.

"I don't feel comfortable about this. Not at all."

"You don't have to feel comfortable. I do."

Tasha followed Roz downstairs, helped her locate the missing question cards from Scattergories, and then locked up after she left.

"So, what's up? We booty bouncin' tonight or what?" Rinaldo asked, as soon as she returned to the bedroom. He was sprawled out in her bed with nothing on but a pair of black briefs.

"No, we're not." Tasha laid down on the bed and stared Rinaldo in the eyes. "I don't like nor appreciate your sexual innuendoes."

"Innu what?" Rinaldo turned over on his side, away from her. "Fuckin' women! I shoulda done like my dogs and went elsewhere."

Tasha propped herself up on one elbow.

"What is that supposed to mean?"

"All of them got Latinas, white girls, or slant-eyed hoes so they can get a little sucky-sucky," Rinaldo replied over his shoulder. "Speakin' of which, you ain't even slobbed my knob yet."

"And I never will!" Tasha exclaimed angrily.

"This is bullshit!" Rinaldo climbed over Tasha so he could get up. "After all the time and effort I've spent on your ass, you're supposed to be giving up carte blanche pussy up in this mutha fucka."

"So you're saying that a woman of another race, any other race, would allow you to talk to her in such a nasty fashion?"

"That's exactly what I'm sayin'."

"I don't believe that. Not for one second."

"Believe it! I'll tell you what else. That fine ass Maddie woulda gave me some ass tonight and sucked me dry, too. For that matter, she probably woulda given you some ass while she was at it."

Tasha got up, went into her bathroom, and slammed the door.

"Why don't you just call Maddie, then?" she yelled through the wood.

"I ain't got her number. I wish the hell I did. Think you can get it for me?"

Tasha yanked the bathroom door back open and emerged holding Rinaldo's shaving kit.

"No, but I can get your shit for you!"

Tasha went to the closet, tossed Rinaldo's garment bag on the bed, and started throwing his clothes into it piece by piece.

"What are you doing?"

"What does it look like, stupid? I'm packing up all your shit so you can get the fuck out of my house!"

Rinaldo grabbed Tasha by the wrist, but she yanked free and kept packing.

"What'd I tell you about callin' me *stupid?*"

Tasha finished shoving everything she could find into the bag and zipped it up.

"And to think I actually cried over you at the cookout."

"Cried?"

"Yes, I cried, but it won't happen again. I've had enough. I thought you were different, Rinaldo. I thought you were special," she said, throwing the shirt and pants he'd worn to the cookout at him. "You're just like all the shitty ass men here in the D.C. area. If all I wanted was a man to treat me like a piece of meat, I didn't need to search a website for that. I could've just gone down the street to the Briggs Chaney Safeway, stuck a sticker on my tit, and climbed into the meat case between the ground turkey and porterhouse steaks."

Rinaldo tossed his clothes back on the floor. He had no intention of getting dressed.

"See, now you're being damn ridiculous."

"Then prove it! Prove me wrong!" Tasha pleaded, on the brink of tears but refusing to let a single one fall. "Act like the Rinaldo I fell in love with!"

"Fell in love with?"

Both of them went silent while the power of Tasha's last statement sunk in. She sat down on the bed and buried her head into a pillow for a few moments. When she looked up, Rinaldo was leaning against her dresser with a stunned expression on his face.

"I fell in love with you, Rinaldo. While you apparently viewed this as some sort of a big joke and took everything with a grain of salt, I took every lie you ever told me seriously."

"I never lied to you, Tasha," he said defensively.

"Yes, you did. You had to have lied because the Rinaldo that stepped off that plane this morning isn't the same Rinaldo I fell in love with."

Tasha went back into her closet and came out with an old shoebox. She sat on the bed, flipped the top off, and started rummaging through it.

"You want to know the kind of shit I've had to go through with men? Huh, do you?"

She pulled a tattered piece of yellow paper from the box and held it out to Rinaldo.

"I wrote this poem the night I lost my virginity. Read it!"

Rinaldo waved her off. "Naw, that's too personal."

"No, I want you to read it." She walked over to him and shoved it into his chest. "I insist."

Rinaldo unfolded the piece of paper and read it silently to himself while Tasha laid back down on the bed and stared at the ceiling.

How Dare You Do This To Me?
I didn't ask for this
I didn't want this
How dare you do this to me?
Take something I never gave
Take something I planned to save
How dare you do this to me?
They say women should trust men
That we can all get along and be friends
But then a man like you comes along
Treating us like animals, committing horrible wrongs
Men like you are such violators
No wonder so many sisters are man haters
How dare you do this to me?
I seriously thought you were the one
We hung out, had a little fun
But I never said you could come inside
Climb on board and take a little ride
Afterwards, your boy gave you a high five
While I struggled to breathe, grateful to even be alive
How dare you do this to me?
My life will go on, it has to
But no matter what you say or do
You could never make up for it
Might as well take your boy, get in your car, and floor it
Time will be my mender
And take care of you, my offender
How dare you do this to me?

Now it was time for Rinaldo to feel like shit. He had no idea that Tasha had been raped. Worse yet, that she'd lost her virginity that way.

He laid beside of her and draped his arm over her waist. She didn't look at him. She just continued to stare at the ceiling.

"Look, I'm sorry," he whispered sincerely into her ear. "I let the alcohol get the best of me and it was stupid."

Tasha glared at him. "Did you just use the word *stupid?*"

"Yes, I said *stupid.*" He gently rubbed his lips against her cheek. "Let's kiss and make up. Let's just rewind the clock and start all over."

"I'm not sure that we can."

"We can try," he said, slipping his tongue into her mouth.

Rinaldo was like a prince among men for the rest of the night, even though he'd never seen a horse. He gave Tasha a bubble bath by candlelight, used a bottle of scented massage oil she had to dig into the bottom of her bathroom cabinet to locate to give her a sensuous massage, licked chocolate sauce off her toes, spread honey all over her breasts systematically lapping up every drop, and made love to her slowly and tenderly.

They ended up downstairs on the sofa, covered up by a throw, about midnight.

"You have any breath mints?" Rinaldo asked.

"There are some in my purse."

Rinaldo got up, walked over to the dining room table, and rifled through Tasha's purse until he found a tin of Altoids.

He turned around and eyed her seductively. Tasha was taken aback by how beautiful his nude body was by the moonlight seeping in through the mini-blinds.

"Come here, baby."

"Over there?"

"Yes, over here."

Tasha got up and did as he instructed. He lifted her ass up on the table, sat down in a chair between her legs, popped an Altoid in his mouth, and went to town on her pussy.

Fifteen minutes later, she came all over his tongue. The heat from the Altoid brought about an earth-shattering orgasm.

"Did you like that?" Rinaldo asked, lifting his head and kissing her inner thighs while stroking her ass tenderly with his fingertips.

"I loved that," she replied. Then she started laughing.

"What's so funny?" Rinaldo chuckled.

"I was just thinking about something."

"What?"

Tasha recalled the conversation she'd had with Roz and Juicy about the dining room table. "I guess I'm a skank, too." She giggled.

"A skank?"

"Never mind. It's an inside joke."

"Well, I've got a joke for you."

"Really? Tell it to me."

"It's actually a riddle."

"Okay."

"How many times can Rinaldo fuck Tasha in one night without her passing out?"

Tasha giggled. "I don't know."

Rinaldo stood up slowly, licking a trail up her stomach to her breasts, palming them, and sucking them one at a time.

"I don't know," Tasha repeated, "but let's find out."

Chapter Eight

The next morning Rinaldo and Tasha were in her Saab on their way to the Chesapeake Bay Bridge before the sun came up. Tasha was amazed she had so much energy, considering she'd barely gotten an hour of sleep.

Rinaldo was anxious to go to the beach. He'd seen one coast and wanted to see the other one. They spent the morning shopping along a small, cozy boardwalk. Tasha was tempted to ask questions when she saw the roll of cash Rinaldo pulled out of his waist pack. He'd always made it seem like he was strapped for cash, which is why she was so shocked when he called with the news of his visit.

Rinaldo bought so many items in a men's clothing store, they had to make a special trip to the car to drop off the bags. Then he started in with buying her things. Tasha tried to decline his offer when he picked out a fly ass two-hundred dollar business suit for her, but he got offended. She decided to let him buy it, along with a few pair of jeans, and a pair of leather pumps. She didn't want any more arguments after the night before.

They put their name on a long ass waiting list at the Sea Barron Seafood Restaurant and then went for a long walk on the beach.

"Let me run in here and buy a phone card right quick," Rinaldo said, walking into a gift shop. "I need to make a phone call."

Tasha reached into her purse for her cell phone. "You can just use my phone."

"No, but thanks for the offer."

Tasha waited out front while he went in and purchased a card.
He came back out and headed toward a bank of pay phones.

"I'll be right back, Tasha. You wait here."

"Okay."

Tasha stood there for about ten minutes, watching Rinaldo
talk on a telephone several yards away. Then she began to get
suspicious. *Why did she need to wait over there? Who was he calling?
Was it another woman? Is that why he didn't want to use her phone? So
the number wouldn't show up on her bill?*

Tasha's curiosity finally got the best of her; especially when the
expression on Rinaldo's face transformed from casual to angry. He
turned his back to her and didn't see her coming, the sand masking
her footsteps.

"When do you think I can come back?"

"This is crazy, dog!"

Tasha listened intently, letting each sentence sink in every time
Rinaldo paused to allow the person on the other end of the line their say.

"You know this is all your fuckin' fault, right? I do your ass a
favor and this is what I get for it."

"I don't give a shit about the money! What about my fuckin'
life? My mom must be worried sick about me!"

Tasha had heard enough.

"Rinaldo?"

Rinaldo jumped, not realizing Tasha was within a stone's
throw of him. He turned around and forced a smile.

"Just a minute, baby."

He went back to his conversation.

"Is everything okay?" Tasha asked.

"Just a second, Tasha!" Rinaldo lashed out at her.

"I'll holla at you later." Rinaldo leered at Tasha, as if to imply
she was being intrusive. "I said I'll holla at you later!"

Rinaldo slammed the phone down.

"Who was that?"

Tasha noticed that Rinaldo was sweating profusely and
wondered what the deal was with that. It was only in the low
seventies.

"Don't worry about it, Tasha. Let's go. Our table's probably ready by now."

They started back to the Sea Barron. Rinaldo pulled a switchblade out of his waist pack, popped it open, and started digging dirt from underneath his nails.

"Where'd you get that?" Tasha asked, taken off guard by the sharpness of the blade.

"I bought it earlier in when you went to the bathroom. Is there a problem?"

"No, no problem."

Chapter Nine

Roz was sorting laundry in the basement early the next morning when Tasha came down ino the laundry room.

"Good morning," Roz said, smiling at Tasha.

"Good morning."

"You look well-rested."

"I am."

"So things are turning out good, then?" Roz asked, placing her dark clothing in the washing machine.

"Very, very good."

"You guys were up and out early yesterday. Where'd you go?"

Tasha helped Roz out by putting some washing powder in the machine. "Chesapeake Bay."

"Aw, how romantic." Roz was trying her best to practice the spiritual principles she and Tasha had agreed upon. She wanted Rinaldo gone, but figured she might as well be friendly since he had to be leaving soon. "From the looks of it, you also did some serious shopping."

"Not me. Rinaldo."

"He's going to have a hard time trying to carry all that back on the plane," Roz said jokingly.

Tasha sighed. "He's not going back."

"Excuse me?" Roz asked loudly. She was convinced she was hearing things.

"I said he's not going back to California." Tasha went over to the door and closed it, keeping her back to Roz. "I decided to come down here instead of waiting for you to come back upstairs. I have a feeling this is about to get ugly and I don't want Rinaldo subjected to it."

"You don't want him subjected to it," Roz said angrily. "Is he your son now or something?"

Tasha swung around to glare at her.

"Rinaldo's decided to relocate. He'll be staying here temporarily."

"Oh, no, the hell he won't be."

"Yes, he will. Rinaldo's going to get his own place, but he has to find a job first. That takes time."

Roz took a deep breath, trying to calm herself down.

"Tasha, I've known you to have problems dealing with men for quite some time, but this takes the cake. Don't you see how foolish this is? He set you up big time. He intended to come here and freeload off you the entire time."

"You don't know what the hell you're talking about. Rinaldo spent a ton of money on me yesterday and he didn't decide he wanted to stay until three o'clock this morning."

"Aw, I get it!" Roz slammed the lid of the washer closed and almost ripped the dial off setting it to heavy wash. "You think you pussy-whipped him so hard that he can't pull himself away. What'd you do? Deep throat his dick? Hum on his balls? Lick his ass? What?"

"I'm not going to even dignify that with an answer. I won't allow this to turn into a full blown altercation, no matter how tempting it is. The decision has already been made and it's final."

"So I have no say in the matter whatsoever?"

"No, not really."

"In that case, Rinaldo doesn't need to worry about getting his own place. He can just move in here permanently."

"What?"

"I'll pack my things, put them in storage, and go sleep on Juicy's pull-out sofa until I get another place."

Tasha rolled her eyes up to the ceiling.

"You're such a baby, Roz!"

"And you're such a fool!" Roz opened the door and walked out into the hall. "I'm not living in this house for one more day if that man's staying here! *Period!*"

"Fine!" Tasha screamed.

"Fine!"

Chapter Ten

"I thought the post office was closed?" Rinaldo asked.

Tasha parked her car in the empty post office parking lot. "It is. I just need to check my box. I haven't been here in a week and it's probably crammed. I ordered some new checks and they should be here by now."

"Okay, but hurry up," Rinaldo said while Tasha climbed out the driver's side and fumbled with her keys to find the one for her box.

Tasha went inside and checked her box, the sixth over from the top and the ninth one down. As suspected, it was overflowing with mail. Tasha realized she was bad about checking her box, but didn't appreciate the postal workers shoving too much in her box. They could rubber band it and put a notice in her box to retrieve it from the counter.

Tasha tossed the pile of mail on the service table where people filled out certified receipts and priority mail slips. Her box of checks had come and she was relieved about that. She was running extremely low.

In all the years Tasha had been coming into the Spencerville Post Office, never once had she glanced up on the wall in front of that table. Somewhere between the subscription renewal notice for Essence and her cable bill, her eyes were drawn upward. Tasha had to cover her mouth to hold in the scream.

Rinaldo cussed under his breath. Tasha was taking way too long in the post office and it was hot as hell outside. She had the keys so he couldn't turn on the air.

He got out of the car and stomped inside.

"What's taking you so long?" he demanded to know, spotting Tasha over at a table shoving mail into her purse.

"Sorry," she uttered, turning to face him. "I was just sorting out the junk mail so I can toss it."

"Anything interesting?"

"No, nothing."

"Well, let's go baby. We'll be late for the movie. Didn't you say there's always a line?"

"Yes."

"Then let's jet. I don't want it to sell out."

Tasha followed Rinaldo out to the car, trailing almost ten feet behind.

"You and Roz had it out this morning, huh?" Rinaldo asked, wondering why Tasha had been so quiet since they left the post office.

"Something like that," she replied despondently.

"She's upset about me staying?"

"She's moving out."

"Damn! I didn't mean for that to happen." Rinaldo turned the radio down until it was barely audible. "Maybe I should just go."

"Maybe you should," Tasha said eagerly. A little too eagerly for Rinaldo.

"Tasha, I can't figure your ass out for anything. You want me to stay. You want me to leave. You need to make up your damn mind."

Tasha didn't respond. She just kept her eyes straight ahead on the road, like she was doing some heavy thinking.

"You got any more of those Altoids?" Rinaldo asked, reaching over the back of Tasha's seat to retrieve her purse that she'd tossed in the rear. "My mouth's dry."

"No, I don't have any," Tasha replied, trying to grab the purse away from him before he could open it.

Rinaldo yanked it away from her.

"Please don't go in my purse!" Tasha pleaded.

"Why not? I went into it the other night," Rinaldo said suspiciously.

Tasha gripped the steering wheel, bracing herself for the madness that was about to start. It took Rinaldo less than five seconds to find it.

He unfolded the crumpled wanted poster with his picture on it along with his real name and a long list of felony charges.

"Now I get it. They had this hanging up in the post office, huh, Tasha?"

Tasha didn't utter a word. She was terrified.

"Fuckin' women! Fuckin', fuckin' women!" he yelled out, ripping up the wanted
poster and tossing the remains out the window.

"Rinaldo, I don't want any trouble."

"What were you planning to do? Turn me in the first chance you got?"

"No, I just want you to leave. I won't tell anyone about the poster. I swear."

Tasha prayed he believed her. She couldn't believe her eyes when she spotted the poster on the wall earlier. Rinaldo was wanted by the FBI for bank robbery and murder, among other things. She'd stayed in the post office as long as she could, trying to figure out a way to escape, but there wasn't one. The post office was closed, no one else came in to check their box, and her cell phone was in her glove compartment.

When he came in to get her, she shoved the poster in her purse along with her mail and decided she'd wait until they got to the movies to take action. The movie theater was always jam-packed and she would've told Rinaldo she had to go to the ladies room once they were seated and summoned the police.

"Oh, I know you won't tell anybody," Rinaldo lashed out at her.

"What does that mean?" Tasha asked, dreading the answer.

"Nothing. Just drive. I need to think."

"Think about what?"

Rinaldo reached over and slapped her on the side of the head.

"About what the hell to do with you, bitch!"

"Rinaldo, as far as I'm concerned, none of this ever happened." Tasha rubbed her head, feeling a migraine coming on. "You were never here."

"Cute. Real cute."

"I can just drop you off at the airport. You still have a ticket, right?" Tasha wasn't altogether sure Rinaldo had a return ticket. When she'd asked him about it the night before, that was when he'd brought up his interest in relocating. "Maybe you can exchange it to catch a flight out right away."

"I can't go back home."

"Then you can exchange it to go someplace else."

"I have a better idea. Get on the highway."

"The highway?"

"Yes, the highway. Head north toward New York."

"For what?"

"Because I fuckin' said so, that's why!"

"I don't want to go to New York."

Rinaldo took the switchblade out of his shirt pocket and popped it open. The blade glistened in the sunlight.

"And you think you have a choice?"

Chapter Eleven

Tasha reluctantly got on the highway and headed north. All the warnings Roz had doled out flashed through her head. She thought about her mother and how heartbroken she would be, even though they didn't get along most of the time. She thought about her father and how guilty he would feel because he didn't intervene when he found out how she'd really met Rinaldo. Mostly, she thought about dying and all the things she hadn't accomplished and all the places she hadn't seen.

"Rinaldo, can we please just talk this over?" she pleaded as they passed the exit for the Baltimore Harbor.

Rinaldo let the switchblade relax on his thigh but kept a tight grip on it. "Those bank robberies, they were never my idea."

"But you did them anyway."

"Sammie needed a fourth man and everyone else is either locked up, sporting wheelchairs, or six feet under. I had to be there for my dog."

Tasha thought about how stupid his comment was. *If someone asks you to do something because all of his normal partners are crippled or dead, why the hell would you do it?*

"Are you the only one they're looking for?"

"Yes. This bitch decided to be a hero and pulled off my ski mask," Rinaldo replied nastily. "I got caught on camera, just like in those stupid made-for-TV movies."

"Did you hurt her, Rinaldo? Is that the murder they're talking about on the poster?"

"Let's just say she won't be pulling any masks off again."

Tasha decided her fate was left totally on her shoulders. She had to fight to survive.

"I love you, Rinaldo. I really do," she stated convincingly since it was partly true. She had loved him until she saw his picture on the wall.

"Shut the fuck up! You're just sayin' that shit because you think I'll let you go!"

Rinaldo slapped Tasha upside the head again. Tasha started crying. *If he wouldn't even talk to her, what could she do?*

"Pull over. I need to take a leak."

Tasha had to force herself not to grin. That was the opening she'd been waiting for.

"I'll get off on the next exit and find a gas station."

"The hell you will! Pull over on the side of the road. I'll piss in the woods." Rinaldo lifted the switchblade and rubbed it up and down Tasha's arm. "Don't make me hurt you, Tasha. I'd hate to have to hurt you."

"Okay." Tasha put on her ticker and started to slow down. "I'll pull over. I won't make you hurt me."

Tasha pulled over onto the shoulder and put the car in park. Rinaldo turned off the ignition and took the keys. He opened the passenger side door and grabbed Tasha's wrist.

"Get out the car."

"For what? You have the keys. I can't go anywhere."

He slapped her again. This time, right across the mouth. She could immediately taste the blood.

"Get out the car!"

Tasha allowed him to pull her out of her Saab and down toward the dense woods lining the side of the highway. She looked at the traffic but cars were flying by at the speed of light. There was no way to signal someone for help and not get stabbed before they had the opportunity to stop or call for help.

"I promise if you let me go, I won't tell a soul."

Rinaldo tightened his grip on her wrist and jerked her. "Didn't I tell your ass to shut up?"

They got into the woods and Rinaldo selected a gigantic maple to do his dirty work. He made Tasha stand there and watch, never loosening his hold on her while he sighed in relief as he urinated.

While the mere thought disgusted her, Tasha came up with a plan.

"Ummmmmmm, don't put it away," she said seductively, staring down at Rinaldo's dick. "It looks so good to me."

"Stop playin' games, Tasha."

"I'm not. You know I never got to taste you." Tasha used her free hand to caress Rinaldo's shaft. It hardened with little effort on her part. "Isn't that what you wanted? Don't you want me to taste you?"

"Right here?" Rinaldo asked, starting to heat up.

"Why not? You already have it out."

Rinaldo pulled Tasha to him, pressed her back up against the tree, and shoved his tongue in her mouth. He pressed the head of his dick up against Tasha's bellybutton. She was still working the shaft with her hand.

He broke the kiss, sucked her bottom lip into his mouth and said, "Since you put it like that, go for it."

Tasha got down on her knees and went to work on his dick. She'd never imagined ending up like that. She could feel the switchblade teasing her hair as Rinaldo guided her head back and forth to catch a steady rhythm.

"Aw, that's it baby. Work it, boo."

Tasha started sucking him harder and harder until he freed up her hand. She reached underneath his shaft and rubbed his balls with her fingers. Rinaldo got caught up in the ecstasy, retracted the switchblade and put it in his shirt pocket. He wanted both hands free to aid Tasha with fucking his mouth.

That was the move Tasha had been waiting for. She slowly let his dick out of her mouth and started placing baby kisses all over it. She worked her way down the underside of his dick and then licked his balls. Then she bit them as hard as she possibly could.

Rinaldo shrieked in agony. Tasha jumped up and ran for the highway, flailing her arms and screaming, "Help!"

"You fuckin' bitch!" Rinaldo yelled after her, falling down on the ground in pain.

After it was all said and done, more than a dozen cars pulled over to see what was going on with Tasha after they spotted her and the blood covering her lips. One of them was a state trooper and Tasha had never been so happy to see a police cruiser in her entire life.

Chapter Twelve

Tasha broke down in tears when the police first brought her home. Roz was packing up her dishes in the kitchen when Tasha walked in and fell into her arms, weeping.

"What happened, Tasha?" Roz asked, staring over Tasha's shoulder at the uniformed officer in their doorway.

"Rinaldo! Rinaldo!" Tasha was hysterical.

"Rinaldo what? Did he hurt you?"

"Yes, but not just me. He's a bank robber and a murderer and the FBI was looking for him and he tried to make me go to New York with him and I just knew he was going to kill me!"

All Roz could say to that mouthful of information was, "Damn!"

People rallied around Tasha for the next week. Everyone from her parents to Roz to Juicy to Angie, who decided to take a break from giving up the drawers to men from BlackGentlemen.com.

Tasha was through with not only BlackGentlemen.com, but also the Internet period. She packed up her computer system and donated it to a shelter for abused women to use in their employment training courses.

Rinaldo was quickly extradited back to California, bandaged balls and all. They picked up Sammie on another charge and Rinaldo was considering trying to plea bargain by spilling all the beans on his friends.

Tasha's mother was the biggest shock of all. She was nice, *extremely* nice to Tasha. She stayed over for two nights and handled

Tasha with kid gloves. It became so emotional that Tasha finally came clean to her mother about the night she'd lost her virginity to a teenage rapist. A boy she'd thought she loved and the first in a long line of men who had eaten away at her heart until it became cold and hard.

Allison refused to allow her daughter to give up on the pursuit of happiness. "Tasha, love is never painless sweetie. If you never take a chance, you'll never be happy."

"I've taken chances, Momma. Haven't you heard all I've been saying?"

"Yes, I've heard every word. I don't think the problem is you. I think the problem is the men you've deemed worthy enough to become a part of your life. If you really take a long, hard look at the past, you'll see the similarities and learn to steer away from men like that in the future."

"You really think I can be happy, Momma?"

"I'm sure of it." Allison finished brushing Tasha's hair and got up off her bed. They'd been held up in her bedroom for more than five hours. "You just need to decide what you really want in a man and refuse to settle for anything less until you find him. Chances are you've already crossed paths with him and didn't even know it."

Chapter Thirteen

"Mr. Montgomery, can you step out here for a moment?"

"Cynda, I'm in a meeting."

"I realize that, but this is kind of urgent."

Joseph Montgomery stepped out into the receptionist area of his accounting firm, wondering if his secretary had lost her mind. She wasn't supposed to disrupt him during a meeting under any circumstances. He had one of his biggest clients in his office and couldn't risk them accusing him of being unprofessional.

"What is it, Cynda?" Joseph asked angrily.

He followed Cynda's eyes and spotted a chicken standing by the outer door holding a bouquet of roses, a box of candy, and a picnic basket.

"Hey, I remember you!" he exclaimed, his total demeanor changing.

"I remember you, too."

"Tasha, right?"

"Yes, Tasha."

"Interesting outfit."

Tasha couldn't believe she was actually standing there in a chicken costume. After the talk with her mother, she realized that Joseph was a man she'd like to get to know better. She hardly knew anything about him, but he had been friendly at the bus stop that day, despite her rudeness, and he was definitely sexy.

"I have a singing telegram for you, Mr. Montgomery." Tasha pointed to the sofa on the left-hand wall. "Could you please have a seat right there on the sofa?"

"A singing telegram?" Joseph took a seat, forgetting all about his client. He'd thought about Tasha often since he met her, but since she said she was committed, he didn't pursue her. "I can't imagine from whom."

"I can't reveal the sender until I deliver the telegram. That's like looking at the signature line on a greeting card before you read what it says."

"Okay, okay, I'm sitting." He smiled.

Tasha placed the flowers, candy, and basket on Cynda's desk, pulled a harmonica out of the chicken suit, and huffed out a scale before clearing her throat and flapping her wings.

> *If you want good lovin'*
> *Come and play in my coop*
> *If you want some honey*
> *Come and play in my coop*
> *If you want something sweet*
> *Come and play in my coop*
> *If you want a special treat*
> *Come and play in my coop*

> *Cluck Cluck for you*
> *Cluck Cluck about you*
> *I'm clucking a'iry day*
> *I'm clucking a'iry night*
> *Clucking for you*
> *Clucking about you*
> *Clucking in hopes you'll cluck tooooooooooo!*

> *Come on over and ruffle my feathers!*

Once Tasha was done, Cynda and Joseph stared at each other, willing themselves not to burst out in laughter. Tasha sounded like an ailing hyena. She waited in the middle of the floor for their reaction.

"That was outstanding!" Joseph lied, standing up and applauding. "Wasn't it, Cynda?"

"Oh, yeah, outstanding and then some." Cynda snickered.

Tasha blushed uncontrollably.

"So now will you tell me who sent it?"

"Your woman, perhaps?" Tasha giggled.

"I don't have a woman. I thought I made that clear when we met."

"When you met?" Cynda asked, being nosy. The fact that they already knew each other changed things. She went from slightly interested to enthralled.

"That was more than a month ago," Tasha replied. "Things can happen swiftly in the game of life."

"Well, not that swiftly. Since you shot me down, I've been shaking in my boots about approaching another woman. Not that any other woman has caught my eye."

Tasha couldn't prevent herself from blushing for anything. She was so turned on by him. His sexy smile. His bedroom eyes. His perfect skin. *How could she have let him get away in the first place?*

Tasha retrieved the items off Cynda's desk and handed them to Joseph.

"These flowers and candy are for you, along with this picnic lunch."

"Thank you, but who..."

"Me."

Joseph was stunned. "You?"

"Yes, they're from me." Tasha glanced down at Cynda, who didn't even pretend to be doing anything else but hanging on every single word. "Can we possibly go somewhere and talk privately for a moment?"

"Certainly. Cynda, could you please put these in some water?" Joseph asked, laying the bouquet on Cynda's desk.   "I've always wanted to say that. Never thought I'd get the opportunity."

Cynda smirked at him. "Hmmmmmmm!"

* * *

After they were in a vacant office with the door closed, Joseph asked, "So Tasha, to what do I owe such a surprise?"

"I got your contact information from Michael. I hope you don't mind me showing up out of the blue like this."

"Not at all. In fact, I'll have to send Mike a bottle of champagne."

"I don't really do singing telegrams."

Joseph chuckled. "I kind of got that impression."

"I borrowed this outfit from my friend, Angie. She delivers them part-time."

"Hopefully, she's got a better singing voice."

Tasha couldn't help but laugh. She knew she couldn't sing worth a damn. "I guess I deserved that one."

"Yes, you really put everyone in jeopardy."

"How so?"

"One octave higher and all the windows would have crashed in on us."

Tasha punched Joseph lightly on the arm. "Very funny!"

"So why all of this, Tasha? Don't get me wrong. I love the attention, but what did I ever do to deserve it?"

"I wanted to apologize for the crass behavior I displayed when we met at the Metro station. It was totally uncalled for."

"I wouldn't label it crass. You just didn't want to be bothered."

Tasha stared down at the gray plush carpeting.

"I made a mistake. Several of them. I was totally delusional."

"About what?"

"Men. One man in particular. I picked the wrong door." She looked back up into his eyes. "Now, if it's all right with you, I'd like to take a peek behind your door."

Joseph grinned from ear-to-ear. "Peek away."

"I was wondering if you'd like to get together sometime and do something."

"What did you have in mind?"

"Well, I bought you that picnic lunch. It would be a shame for it to go to waste."

Joseph frowned. "I'm in the middle of a meeting."

"Oh, I see."

Tasha headed for the door. Joseph wasn't about to let her pull a disappearing act on him twice.

"But, if you can wait about half an hour, we can go to the park across the street and have a long talk."

Tasha swung around, her eyes lit up like moonbeams.

"I'd like that. I'd like that a lot."

"Great! Why don't you have a seat back out in the waiting area and I'll wrap things up quickly."

"Do you have somewhere for me to change?" Tasha asked. She'd brought along a pantsuit, just in case he agreed to spend the afternoon with her.

"Change?" Joseph asked sarcastically. "I hope you wouldn't deprive me of a dining experience with a chicken. I'll be the talk of the town after this."

Tasha giggled. "Maybe we can be the talk of the town together."

"Maybe," Joseph said, taking her hand into his and intertwining their fingers. "After all, it's a small, small world."

About the Authors

Zane is the National Bestselling Author of Addicted, Shame on it All, The Sex Chronicles: Shattering the Myth and The Heat Seekers. She is the Principal/Publisher of Strebor Books International (www.streborbooks.com).

JD Mason is an accomplished novelist/playwright, and lives in Denver, Colorado with her two children. She has completed two novels which are scheduled for release in 2003, "And on the Eighth Day She Rested, and "One Day I Saw a Black King", and is currently working on her third.

Shonda Cheekes, a native of Miami, FL, currently lives in Pembroke Pines, FL with her husband and two children. She has completed her first novel titled, Another Man's Wife, developed a sitcom that she's shopping along with her writing partner Michelle Valentine, and is currently at work on her next novel.

Eileen Johnson is a graduate of the University of Southwestern Louisiana. Her obsession with fictional short stories began after reading "Pink Toes" by Chester B. Himes. She resides in Southwestern Louisiana where she is a full-time mommy and is working on a full-length novel.

Make sure you visit

www.blackgentlemen.com

ORDER FORM

Use this form to order additional copies of *Strebor Books International* Bestselling titles as they become available.

Name: _____

Company _____

Address: _____

_____

City: _____ State _____ Zip _____

Phone: _____ Fax: _____

E-mail: _____

Credit Card: ☐ Visa ☐ MC ☐ Amex ☐ Discover

Number _____

Exp. Date: _____ Signature: _____

ITEM	PRICE	QTY.
1. Shame On It All by Zane	$15.00	
2. Luvalways by Shonell Bacon & F. Daniels	$15.00	
3. Daughter by Spirit by V. Anthony Rivers	$15.00	
4. All That and A Bag of Chips by Darrien Lee	$15.00	
5. Blackgentlemen.com	$15.00	
6. Turkeystuffer by Mark Crockett	$15.00	
7. Nyagra's Falls by Michelle Valentine	$15.00	
8.		

SHIPPING INFORMATION		
GROUND ONE BOOK	$3.00	
EACH ADDITIONAL BOOK	$1.00	

Subtotal _____

shipping _____

5%tax (MD) _____

Total _____

**Make checks or money orders payable to
Strebor Books International LLC
Post Office Box 1370
Bowie, Maryland 20718**